W9-BHX-532

LORD OF THE
VAMPIRES

THE DIARIES OF THE
FAMILY DRACUL

JEANNE KALOGRIDIS

A DELL BOOK

Published by
Dell Publishing
a division of
Bantam Doubleday Dell Publishing Group, Inc.
1540 Broadway
New York, New York 10036

ISBN: 0-440-22442-X

Reprinted by arrangement with Delacorte Press

Printed in the United States of America

Published simultaneously in Canada

October 1997

10 9 8 7 6 5 4 3 2 1

OPM

For my mother, Geraldine Marie Pulver
August 8, 1923–July 27, 1995

And sister, Nancy Ellen Dillard
September 23, 1952–February 1, 1994

ACKNOWLEDGMENTS

Heartfelt thanks are due the following august personages:

First and foremost, to Dell editor Jacob Hoye for his exceptional patience and kindness. The book you now hold in your hands arrived on his desk terribly late, and he, as well as copy editors and publicists, worked at an insane pace to get it onto the shelves. On behalf of him and all the other brave souls at Dell, I offer up humblest apologies, plus the offer to inflict upon myself thirty lashes with a cat-o'-nine-tails at the time and place of their choosing.

To Elizabeth Miller, Ph.D., one of the world's premier Dracula experts and all-round nice person. Not only did she provide me with research materials and information about Mad Bad Vlad for the prologue, she also wrote the marvelous foreword included here.

To Sherry Gottlieb, fellow novelist, for her (and Bunny's) friendship and her wonderfully wicked suggestion concerning the ending of this book. (Go out and buy Sherry's fabulous police procedural with fangs, *Love Bite*, right now.)

To my brother, Kurt Rumler, for starting this whole damned vampire thing. You see, it was Kurt who, some twenty-eight years ago at the Mariner Hotel in St. Petersburg, shoved a paperback of *Dracula* into my hands and said: "Here, kid. Read *this*. . . ."

Absolutely to my agent, Russ Galen. My God, Russ, what would I *do* without you? (I mean, other than make a whole lot less money and have a lot more stress in my life. . . .)

And now, the best for last: To our beloved consort of eighteen years, with whom we are well pleased. George, I honestly could not have finished this book without your emotional and literary help. (Okay, so I steal your suggestions all the time—but, hey, I share the money, don't I?) I love you madly—for your Grecian good looks, your intelligence, your twisted wit, your warmth, your charm, your generosity and delightful desire to spoil me—but mostly because no one else has ever made me feel so thoroughly loved.

—*Jeanne Kalogridis*
e-mail: jkalo@opa.com
web page: http://www.opa.com/vampire

Author's note: Let me blow Dr. Elizabeth Miller's horn here, since she's too modest to do so herself. President of the Canadian chapter of the Transylvanian Society of Dracula, she is one of the most knowledgeable experts on Vlad Tepes and Dracula around, having written and presented numerous scholarly papers on the subject. At the 1995 World Dracula Congress, she was honored by the Romanian people with the title "Baroness of the House of Dracula"; and she is also one of the organizers of the Dracula Centennial, to be held in Los Angeles in August 1997.

DRACUL FAMILY TREE

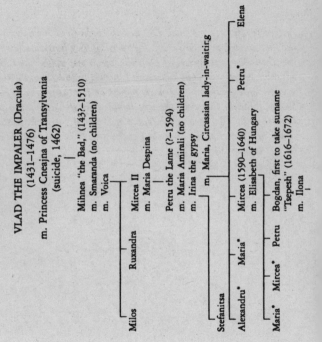

VLAD THE IMPALER (Dracula)
(1431–1476)
m. Princess Cneajna of Transylvania
(suicide, 1462)

Mihnea "the Bad," (143?–1510)
m. Smaranda (no children)
m. Voica

Milos   Ruxandra   Mircea II
m. Maria Despina

Petru the Lame (?–1594)
m. Maria Amirali (no children)
m. Irina the gypsy

m. Maria, Circassian lady-in-waiting

Stefanitsa

Mircea (1590–1640)
m. Elisabeth of Hungary

Alexandru*   Maria*   Petru   Petru*   Elena

Bogdan, first to take surname
"Tsepesh" (1616–1672)
m. Ilona

Maria*   Mircea*   Petru

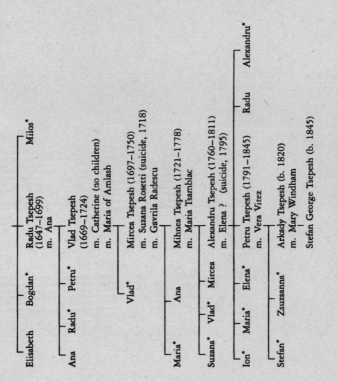

Elisabeth

Bogdan*

Milos*

Radu Tsepesh
(1647–1699)
m. Ana

Ana   Radu*   Petru*

Vlad Tsepesh
(1669–1724)
m. Catherine (no children)
m. Maria of Amlash

Vlad*

Mircea Tsepesh (1697–1750)
m. Suzana Rosetti (suicide, 1718)
m. Gavrila Radescu

Maria*

Ana

Mihnea Tsepesh (1721–1778)
m. Maria Tsamblac

Suzana*   Vlad*   Mircea

Alexandru Tsepesh (1760–1811)
m. Elena ?   (suicide, 1795)

Radu   Alexandru*

Ion   Maria*   Elena*

Petru Tsepesh (1791–1845)
m. Vera Vitez

Stefan*   Zsuzsanna*

Arkady Tsepesh (b. 1820)
m. Mary Windham

Stefan George Tsepesh (b. 1845)

* Died in childhood or born afflicted with physical or mental deformity

Loosely adapted from Radu R. Florescu & Raymond T. McNally, *Dracula: Prince of Many Faces*, (Boston: Little, Brown, 1989).

⊰ FOREWORD ⊱

The trilogy The Diaries of the Family Dracul, of which *Lord of the Vampires* is the third book, draws from history, legend, and fiction. But it is primarily a work that expands on the text of *Dracula*, by providing a "prequel" to Stoker's narrative, which overlaps with *Dracula* in this present book. The trilogy introduces innovative twists in the familiar plot that serve to fill in what some readers perceive as gaps in the original: Why was Abraham Van Helsing so obsessive about tracking down Dracula? What really happened to the good professor's wife and son? What were the origins of the female vampires in Dracula's Transylvanian castle? Who was the elusive Arminius? But most significantly, the trilogy creates a prehistory for Count Dracula himself, drawing on the connection between Stoker's vampire and the fifteenth-century Wallachian prince Vlad the Impaler (also known as Dracula). As this is not the first (and certainly will not be the last) time that the count and the *voivode* have been fused in fiction (and film), I thought it might be useful to delineate just what the nature of this intriguing connection actually is.

In spite of the attention paid to Vlad by historians both in Romania and the West, he is still to some extent an enigma. Even the name by which he is called is a matter of disagreement. While there is ample evidence that he himself used the sobriquet "Dracula" (or variations thereof) and was referred to as such in several fifteenth- and sixteenth-century sources, many Romanian historians still insist on using the name "Tepes" (meaning "Impaler"), a hardly flattering nickname first assigned to him by Turkish chroniclers. Historians attempting to reconstruct his life have had to sift through numerous printed accounts of his atrocities, many of which are clearly biased, as well as equally biased Romanian oral narratives and legends that paint him as a heroic patriot. There are also conflicting versions about key events, most notably how he was killed and where his remains are buried. But one fact does emerge from all of this material: Whatever Vlad might have been, nowhere is it stated that he was (or was believed to have been) a vampire. That association is clearly the result of the fact that Bram Stoker decided to appropriate the name "Dracula" for his villainous count—much to the chagrin of many Romanians, who see the novel as a denigration of one of their national heroes.

But this raises a key question. To what extent did Bram Stoker actually *base* his Count Dracula on Vlad the Impaler? Although for many people today the two have become almost synonymous, the nature of the connection is highly speculative. There is no longer any doubt where Stoker found the name "Dracula." We know from his working papers (housed at the Rosenbach Museum in Philadelphia) that by March 1890 he had already started work on the novel, and had even selected a name for his vampire—Count Wampyr. We also know that, in the summer of the same year while vacationing at Whitby, he came across the name "Dracula" in a book that he borrowed from the Whitby Public Library. William Wilkinson's *An*

Account of the Principalities of Wallachia and Moldavia (1820) contains a few brief references to a "Voivode Dracula" (never referred to as "Vlad") who crossed the Danube and attacked Turkish troops. But what seems to have attracted Stoker was a footnote in which Wilkinson states that "*Dracula* in the Wallachian language means 'Devil.'" Stoker supplemented this with scraps of Romanian history from other sources (which he carefully listed in his notes) and fleshed out a history for his Count Dracula. Wilkinson is Stoker's only *known* source for information on the historical namesake. Everything else is speculation.

And there is plenty, some of it rather far-fetched. For example, it has been suggested that Stoker drew the concept of the staking of a vampire from his knowledge of Vlad's penchant for impaling his enemies on stakes; that Renfield's fondness for insects and small animals is a reenactment of Vlad's habit of torturing small animals while he was held prisoner in Hungary; or that Count Dracula is repelled by holy symbols because Vlad betrayed the Orthodox Church by converting to Roman Catholicism. Such speculation has arisen from a basic assumption (yet to be proved conclusively) that Stoker knew much more about Vlad than what he read in Wilkinson; that his other major sources were the Hungarian professor Arminius Vámbéry, and his own readings in the British Museum (both of which are indirectly alluded to in the novel).

Much has been written of what Stoker may have learned from Vámbéry. Claims have been made that Vámbéry supplied Stoker with information on Transylvania, vampire lore, and Vlad himself; some suggest that Vámbéry may even have introduced Stoker to some of the fifteenth-century materials about Vlad. But all of this is speculation based on circumstantial evidence. We do know that the two met at least twice. While we do have a record of these meetings (Stoker refers to both in his 1906 book *Personal Reminiscences of Henry Irving*), there is nothing to indicate that the conversation included Vlad, vampires, or even Transylvania. Furthermore, there is no record of any other correspondence between Stoker and Vámbéry, nor is Vámbéry mentioned in Stoker's notes for *Dracula*. As for the theory that what Van Helsing in the novel learns from Arminius (the character is generally seen as a tribute to Vámbéry) parallels what Stoker himself gleaned from the Hungarian, just about every scrap of this material can readily be traced to Stoker's known sources.

While Stoker did conduct some research at the British Museum, there is no evidence to indicate that he discovered further material about the historical Dracula. Much speculation surrounds the possibility that he may have gained access to one of the fifteenth-century German pamphlets about Vlad the Impaler featuring a woodcut portrait accompanied by the caption "A wondrous and frightening story about a great bloodthirsty berserker called Dracula." This has led some to conclude that Stoker's physical description of Count Dracula is actually based on this portrait of Vlad. But again, the concrete evidence just is not there. It is much more likely that Stoker drew the description of Count Dracula from earlier villains in Gothic literature, or even from his own employer, Henry Irving.

Count Dracula, as Van Helsing tells us, "must have been that Voivode Dracula who won his name against the Turk." Indeed he was! But it is significant that nowhere in Stoker's novel is Dracula referred to as "Vlad," nor is there any reference to Vlad's famous atrocities, in particular his use of impalement as his favorite means of execution. Why would Stoker—a writer who meticulously included detail after detail (some very insignificant and obscure) from his known sources—ignore something that would have added so much to the delineation of his villain? Either he knew more and chose not to use it, or he used what he knew. Pending much more concrete evidence than has to date been unearthed, I would accept the latter. All we know for certain is that Stoker found the name "Dracula" in Wilkinson, obviously liked it, and decided to use it.

The fusing of fact and fiction, while of questionable merit in reconstructing history, is a superb tool in the hands of an imaginative writer. As we today know much more than Stoker about Vlad the Impaler (thanks primarily to the work of Radu Florescu and Raymond McNally), it is hardly surprising that the count and the *voivode* have merged. The most noted occurrence in film is in Francis Ford Coppola's 1992 rendition *Bram Stoker's Dracula*, though a connection between the vampire count and his historical namesake had been made almost twenty years earlier in the Dan Curtis production of *Dracula* with Jack Palance. Examples of the fusion in fiction are numerous, including such novels as *Anno Dracula* and *The Bloody Red Baron* (Kim Newman), *Children of the Night* (Dan Simmons), the trilogy Dracula Lives! (Peter Tremayne), *Drakulya* (Earl Lee), and this present trilogy. Fiction has made Vlad what he never was in life—a vampire—and has thus granted him, like his fictional counterpart, immortality.

Elizabeth Miller
Professor of English
Memorial University of Newfoundland

LORD OF THE
VAMPIRES

⇻ PROLOGUE ⇺

Memorandum of Vlad III, Prince of Wallachia

BUCHAREST, CURTEA DOMNEASCA, 28 DECEMBER 1476. Outside, the promise of snow; the weather has turned bitter and the sky leaden, cloaking the overhead sun. Yet the air tingles, as if with unhurled lightning. It dances upon my skin.

We wait.

He comes . . . Basarab is coming. . . .

I smile up from parchment, ink, and quill at my trusted aide Gregor's face, draped with shadows from the torchlight. Child of *boiers*, the Roumanian nobility, his features are mine—sharp, hawkish nose and chin, large heavy-lidded eyes, raven hair falling to his shoulders. No doubt we are related by blood, distant cousins at the least; he is at most half a thumb taller, so close are we in height.

The resemblance ends there, for the intelligence possessed by our forebears flows in my veins alone. Look at him: The fool cannot resist peering from time to time through the curtains, at the city spreading out below us, at the high, fortified walls built at my command. At what lies —what *will* lie soon—beyond those walls. He thinks I do not know.

Laiota Basarab with an army of four thousand Turks, come to murder me inside these stone walls and steal my throne, so recently reclaimed. And I with but half as many men, and my champions returned to their northern kingdoms.

The traitor comes. . . .

You know all that can be known of treachery, do you not, Gregor? Oh yes, you return my glance with the most fawning of courtesies, but I see your heart; I hear your very thoughts. You swear fealty to me, the *voivode,* but your loyalties lie with the inconstant *boier,* the nobles who will again deliver their country into the hands of Basarab, lover of Turks, for the sake of a mercenary peace.

All this did the Dark One reveal to me last night within the Circle. I doubt it not, for I have of late acquired further talents unknown to common mortals: the reading of the thoughts and hearts. As Gregor paces uneasily before the curtain, I see now his guilt as clearly as I see the words scrawled here before me.

I know treachery myself too well, having been often betrayed. Betrayed by my father, when he surrendered my brother and myself, both of tender age, to be the sultan's hostages. Betrayed by my fair brother, Radu, lover of women and men and the sultan Mehmed, on whose account Radu seized my throne from me.

(And you are dead now, are you not, my dear younger brother? Killed at last by the womanish acts that won you Mehmed's heart and army—and thus my kingdom. Those beautiful eyes the colour of blue-green sea are closed forever; those full red lips, which sought the breasts of women with the same fervour that they suckled at the sultan's lap, shall never kiss again. May your syphilitic Turkish lovers follow you soon!)

Betrayed even by my one trusted friend, Stefan cel

Mare, whose kingdom I helped him win. (You play the friend once more, my Stefan, now that it falls to your advantage. But I will not forget or forgive your maneuvers that put Basarab in my place. I take your help now that regret overtakes you; but the time for recompense will come.)

Still quiet. No cries from the watchtower, just the hiss of the fire, the scratch of the quill against parchment, the silence of imminent snow. And the scuffle of Gregor's boots against stone as he paces; I am far too entertained by his anxiety to give him leave to sit. An hour ago, I bade him: "Send to the stable for horses, one for each of us, and a day's provisions."

Ah, the look of ill-concealed terror in his eye, at the thought the *boiers*' scheme might go awry! "Where shall we go, my lord?"

Had I been in my usual humour, I would not have deigned to reply with more than a scowl (nor would Gregor have dared to ask, had his desperation not been so great). As it was, my amusement was such that I answered, "Riding."

And, as he backed away, bowing, towards the door, his expression one of comical dubiousness, I added—loudly so that those standing watch at the entry would hear: "And send in two guards. I am not of a mind to wait alone."

They heard and entered without waiting for Gregor's relay—two fine strong Moldavians, one dark and the other golden, both tall and armed with swords, both left behind as tokens of Stefan's guilt over past infidelities. This I did so that Gregor might not, should he arm himself in his absence, return and indulge his anxiousness to see me destroyed.

Later, when he returned, cheeks and nose reddened and glistening from the cold, to report that the horses should be ready within the hour, I sent him straightway on another errand: "Fetch clothing for me and yourself and bring it here, to my private chambers. We shall go disguised as Turks."

This gave him great alarm, which he barely stifled. Did I know of the *boier* plot to send Basarab and the Turks to slay me and my army? Did I suspect him?

In his veiled eyes I saw the machinations of a traitorous mind. I had given no clear sign of suspicion yet; certainly I could have easily ordered the bodyguards to dispatch him had I discovered the truth. Was this one of the fearsome *voivode*'s fatal games—was I delaying his execution in order to savour it—or was it chance that I had chosen this moment to leave my stronghold disguised, alongside the man who would play my Judas?

He left, and in moments returned with clothing: a peaked cap, tunic and wool cloak to shield against the cold. He assisted me with my dress under the attentive eye of the Moldavians, watched as I wound the turban round my head, and looked askance when I asked him:

"Ölmeye hazırmısın?" Are you prepared to die?, for I am as fluent in the speech of my enemies as I am my own tongue, having spent my youth as the sultan's prisoner. I know their dress, their mannerisms, and can pass for one of them. And I laughed, for though he is their minion—he who serves the *boier*s serves the Turks—he understood not one word I had uttered. He laughed also, yellowed teeth flashing beneath the drooping mustache so like mine, thinking my mirth sprang from my successful impersonation.

Then I went over to the wall and lifted down from its place of honour a great scimitar, gleaming in the firelight, and with it a curving sheath. This I fastened to my belt, then said:

"Dress."

He did so, and I looked on in silent approval at a body small in stature, but muscular, broad of chest and shoulder. His scars are fewer—he has not been tested in battle as often as I—and he lacks half a front tooth, but the similarities are enough.

After a time, a boy ran up to say the mounts were ready. But I would not be rushed. I had begun this entry and was obliged to finish it—for this will be my last remembrance as a mortal. I had learned from the Dark Lord in Circle the hour of Basarab's coming and knew I was still safe, and further, I was not inclined to end Gregor's anxiety. Let him wait! Let him suffer in uncertainty—which he does to this very moment, pacing in his Turkish robes, praying that I will change my mind and remain here, to be slaughtered.

Were the guards not here, he would risk killing me now. I know that the moment we are alone on horseback, he will seek the first opportunity; for that, I am ready.

I must not die now! Not so close to the touch of the Dark Lord, and Eternity. . . .

⊹ ⊹ ⊹

SNAGOV MONASTERY, 28 DECEMBER. To the north we rode upon black stallions, first along the banks of the Dimbovita, then across the frozen ground into the bare-limbed Vlasia Forest, tinged with evergreen. The air was grey with smoke and the approaching storm, and laden with a strange, fleeting smell: of lightning spent, of iron wielded; of blood and snow.

I galloped at full speed, wind stinging my eyes, keeping Gregor well behind me—a danger, perhaps, but I had seen him dress and knew he carried no weapon save the sword at his waist. If he wished to kill me at that moment (and he did), then he would have to overtake me, throw me from my horse, slay me before I could draw my own sword. Perhaps the singular intent in my eyes frightened him; if so, he was wise to fear. He might have turned and hastened away to the south, returned to his beloved Basarab, and warned them of my escape to the north—but that action would have alerted me at once to treachery and bettered my chance of survival.

So we continued apace over hard earth and rocks and dead crackling leaves until at last we reached the banks of a great lake, frozen solidly, its surface opaque grey-white dirtied by swirls of dark suspended flotsam. At its center stood the island fortress of Snagov, the spires of the Chapel of the Annunciation emerging from behind high walls at the water's very edge.

I dismounted and unsheathed my sword—with a smile to ease Gregor's growing trepidation—and led my horse onto the ice. "No need to draw your arms," I told my uncertain companion. "Mine are sufficient to protect us." I nodded for him to precede me across the river to the great iron gate.

In his eyes I saw once more the moment of decision: Should he smite me now, and return to Basarab's army a hero? Should he hope for an opportunity inside Snagov's walls, and venture forth upon the ice? (It was my right as sovereign to require that someone else test the ice's strength.) Why had I drawn my sword? Was this merely another of the prince's eccentricities, or had I deduced his deception?

A flicker of fear again crossed his features. I was, after all, Dracula, the son of the Devil, the passionate fighter whose madness and boldness knew no limits. I had ridden at night into Mehmed's very camp and slaughtered a hundred sleeping Turks with the sword I now grasped. If he drew his weapon now and openly challenged me, would he be the survivor?

With the softest of sighs he swung down from his horse and led the creature onto the frozen lake. So we made our way toward sanctuary, the horses' hooves ringing hollowly against the ice, displacing small clouds of mist. At last we arrived at the great stone wall I had built during my reign, which had transformed the island monastic village into a more suitable fortress for guarding the treasure of the Wallachian realm. Ringing that wall were trees, their naked limbs clawing at the stones as if pleading for entry.

A cry came from the watchtower as the sentinel spotted us; I cupped my hands round my mouth and called a reply which echoed off the stone. We moved toward the high wooden gate, studded with pales, and waited on the ice uneasily, I maneuvering myself so that I stood behind Gregor. The indecisiveness, the tension, the guilt, could easily be read from the cant of the man's shoulders. We stood without speaking and watched the first snowflakes sail silently down, stinging my cheeks like cold tears.

At last the great gate creaked open on its rusting hinges and we were received by two armed guards, who immediately bowed low when they confirmed that their guest was, indeed, the Prince of Wallachia. I ordered one to take our horses to the stable and have food brought; the other I bade accompany us, ostensibly to build a fire. The three of us walked together on the ice-and-mud road past the high watchtower, the beautiful chapel, the great monastery, up towards the beautiful palace I had erected in better days. The thought evoked a flare of anger: Gregor did not deserve to set foot in this place built by the blood of loyal subjects, a sanctuary dear to my heart and which I would never again see after this night.

But I held my temper and walked together with my

traitor into the palace's private chambers—which, being
long unused, were so cold that our breaths still hung in the
air as mist. I moved into my private dining-room, which
looked onto a small cell with an Orthodox shrine to the
Virgin Mary. The accompanying soldier, a strong young
man, set at once to the task of building a fire.

With a flourish, I removed my cape, belt, and sword,
setting them all down on the floor near the hearth—and
the soldier—and motioned for Gregor to do the same. I
saw his swift secretive glance at my weapon, then at the
soldier, then back at me; in his eyes shone the reluctance of
the coward. Slay me he could, but at the cost of his own
life.

"Gregor, my friend." I motioned for the now-tired
man to sit across from me at the ancient dining table. I was
cordial, conciliatory. "It is only right that you know the
reason for our swift journey. I have need of . . . funds,
and so I came here to avail myself of some of my treasure.
There are few I can trust with such a task, even at the
castle . . . and so I did not speak of it to you. We shall be
returning shortly to Bucharest, but in the meantime, rest,
and eat."

I saw the mercenary light in his eye which I had hoped
to evoke. He could wait until the treasure was in our
hands, and once he and I were alone in the Vlasia Forest . . .

After a time the fire grew, and the room began to
warm. I bade the soldier stay with us and stand guard. A
white-bearded monk with fewer teeth than I have fingers
entered with a tray of food—a cold roasted chicken, a flask
of wine, bread, cheese. He served us most capably, reaching out to refill our goblets with a hand so gnarled by age
—blue veins standing out in bas relief beneath a parch-
ment-thin layer of pale yellow skin—that I was astonished

it did not tremble. Even more laudably, he showed no fear,
no cringing, before the great prince, only silent dignity.
This I found agreeable, for I am usually tended by fawning
fools, but his singular self-possession may well have been
sparked by disdain for my heresy. (I had spent years under
house arrest in Hungary; the only way to gain King Matthias' trust—and regain my throne—was to convert to Catholicism. It was a political move, nothing more—in
Turkey I was forced to kneel upon prayer rugs facing
Mecca and pray to Allah—but an unfortunate one, for it
has earned me the contempt of my own people.)

Should I have chosen death instead?

No. There is nothing noble about death, even that of a
martyr.

Yet the old monk feels I have betrayed God, and therefore deserve His punishment, just as Gregor deserves mine.

Perhaps the monk would be surprised to know that I
indeed fear God. Fear Him because I know His heart is
like mine—blackened by power, thrilling at the ability to
dictate the hour and fashion of men's deaths; reveling in
their suffering.

Nay—His heart is more evil than mine, and more
pitiless. He strikes down young, old, man, woman, child,
without regard for their loyalty, their wit, their circum-
stance. I spare the innocent and kill only those who betray
me; I kill to instruct the survivors through spectacle.

God has no such qualms. He slays believer and infidel
alike, and the degree of suffering He inflicts bears no relation to the victim's piety. Nor does He concern Himself
with justice—He has permitted usurper after usurper to
steal my rightful kingdom, and now that I have reclaimed
it after years of arduous struggle, He will not help me
maintain it. Thus I could never ally myself with Him,

especially since He is too jealous to impart the immortality I seek.

Enough of God; I speak now of Gregor. He and I shared our Last Supper in silence, and when he had eaten to his satisfaction and pushed away from the table with a sigh, I told him:

"My friend. My heart is heavy of late, for I know that support for my reign is uncertain. The *boier*s have turned against me"—and when he began a supposedly innocent protest, I raised my hand. "Do not think I do not know it! And now that Stefan has withdrawn his forces, the situation is more precarious." This he could not disavow. After all, to spare them danger, I had not permitted my wife and sons to join me at my Bucharest court. I paused and, in a tone of utmost earnestness, asked, "Gregor. Will you pray for me? For your prince's safety and success? I know you are a man of faith, and I am deemed by some a heretic. . . ." And here I paused to steal a sidewise glance at the grizzled monk, who stood in readiness to serve (albeit closer to the fire, to warm his old bones). But the brother's gaze was hooded, his expression unreadable; perhaps he was deaf, I thought, and had not heard. Or perhaps he was simply too wise a man to make open his contempt, knowing that I would not forgive it. "Beseech God and the Virgin on my behalf."

Of course Gregor could do no else. He nodded, and with solemnity, I rose from the table and led him to the monastic little cell, whose door lay ajar so that its interior was entirely visible from our dinner table. I crossed myself (in good Orthodox fashion, which I had no doubt the old monk noticed) and, stopping at the doorway, gestured for my aide to enter and kneel on the small rug in front of the solitary shrine to the Mother of Christ.

He sank down with a groan and creaking knees; like

me, he is no longer young. "Pray for us," I said tenderly, and gestured to the young soldier by the fire to take up Gregor's own weapon and stand in my place. I could see my kneeling Judas' face in profile—how like my own it was! He might have been my brother; my own backstabbing brother. I watched that sun-weathered face, with its sharp but delicate nose and chin, its thin, trembling lips beneath the dark drooping mustache. I savoured the charming slow dawn of terror in those large eyes, black as mine were green, as the soldier lifted the sword. Then I returned to my place at the dinner table—the tableau was entirely visible from my seat, according to my own design (it was not the first time I had made use of the cell, though I suspect it will be the last)—and lifted my glass to drink deep of sweet, stinging wine ere I spoke again.

"Pray, my friend. Pray for my long life . . . and death to those who would betray me."

He let go a wrenching sob and pressed his palms together in earnest supplication, turning on his knees to face me. The little rug moved with him, rippling. "My lord, I swear that I have not deceived you!"

I let a long, tortured moment pass for him before I replied, my voice soft, curious. "Did I accuse you?"

His eyes widened; then he blinked, and pressed his quivering lips together. In truth, had he been able to think of a compelling reply, and had I trusted my magic any less, I might have spared him then. But I was certain of the vision that had come to me in Circle, and my own divinations. Even were I not, the look of stricken self-incrimination which descended at that instant upon Gregor's features would have convinced me. A single shining drop slid down his cheek.

"Oho!" I exulted. "Is this a tear?"

"My lord, I beg—"

"Turn!" I cried, gesturing for the soldier to brandish the sword. His cravenness so fuelled my rage that it would no longer be submerged. "Turn, and pray to the Virgin! Pray that she might grant you mercy, and me victory over Basarab!"

He knit his hands together fervently and once more faced Mary's shrine; beneath his knees, the small rug bunched up further to reveal a seam in the wooden floor. Yet my would-be deceiver never noticed; his attention had become sincerely fixed on the icon of the Virgin Mother, and he began to babble, knuckles pressed to the bridge of his nose, eyes squeezed shut.

"Have mercy! God and Holy Mother—have mercy! Grant my sovereign long life, and victory, and convince him that I have not betrayed him. . . ."

"Yes," I whispered. "Perhaps God will be merciful to you—but He has never been thus to me, and so I will not bargain with Him."

"My Lord," he cried, still facing the shrine with his eyes closed so that I was uncertain whether he addressed God or me. "My Lord, I am innocent of any crime against you! What can I say, what can I do, to prove my perfect loyalty?"

"Die with bravery," said I. "Your life is already forfeit, Gregor. Make your peace, and quickly. I shall not die outside Bucharest as my father did, struck down by an assassin."

He raised his face towards Heaven, then opened his praying hands as one might a book and pressed them to his eyes, weeping. I studied his reaction to the revelation that all hope was lost: noted the electric agony, the utter desperation, reflected in each aspect of his body, his voice (for his sobs grew resoundingly loud and shrill). I have been my whole life a student of the Death, staring into Its face in hopes that I might understand and be able to accept my own end. How many men have I killed in my life—a thousand? No, it must be more, many more. I *know* the face of Death; I watched more than a hundred Turks meet their slow deaths in the Forest of the Impaled alone. I have heard men's sobs and screams, and the slow sighing sound made by a body pulled down onto the stake by its own weight.

And in each instance I have looked into their eyes and tried to understand the Secret hidden there as they passed from life into the Abyss.

But as I contemplated Death—and came to see that God was not just, and that there *was* no meaning there, only indignity and suffering—I came to know that I could never accept it. I had been cheated of too much that was rightfully mine in this life; I had ruled my father's, my grandfather's, kingdom for only a handful of years before I was ousted unjustly. I am royalty by birthright; but I spent my whole youth as a Turkish prisoner, and eight of my middle years as a prisoner of the Hungarian king. My kingdom has been stolen from me twice, once by my own brother: if I relinquish it a third time, I shall have recompense—I who am shrewder, more cunning, more deserving of my people's adoration, than Matthias, than Mehmed, than Radu or Basarab.

Death is surely closer to me now than at any other time. Yet God and the angels would not grant me my desire: immortality. There is only One other capable.

❖❖ ❖❖ ❖❖

As Gregor wept and prayed in vain, the soldier in the doorway turned his hopeful young face (with its thin, patchy boy's beard on tender pink cheeks and chin) towards me and motioned with his sword, his gaze a question. He will make a fine assassin, that one, for his eyes were bright with eagerness and yearning, much as mine.

I gave a single small shake of my head; not yet. Instead, I rose and walked over to stand beside my cheerful young killer, taking care that my boots struck the floor solidly. As I'd planned, Gregor heard. His back tensed; I knew he expected Death to come up behind him, in the form of the sword gripped in the young soldier's hand. And though he dared not turn his head completely round to look straight at me—he had witnessed my sensitivity to the smallest presumption in these situations many times, and feared provoking a burst of rage—he inclined it slightly over its shoulder, and swiveled his eyes in an effort to look behind him.

Wild eyes those were, with more white in them than I had ever seen. I was reminded strongly of the bulging, frantic eyes of cattle at the slaughter.

"My lord, my lord, my lord, you kill an innocent man!"

"Indeed?" I asked, my voice once again calm. "Gregor . . ." And here I affected the utmost sincerity. "I am a hard man and cannot tolerate any degree of duplicity. I am cruel to those who betray me, but just to the loyal. Can you swear before God that you have acted with naught but total faithfulness towards me, your sovereign?"

"I swear it before God, my lord!"

I paused for a moment to watch his expression, and the wild swing there between hope and doom. After a time, I said, "Very well, my friend. These are dangerous times for me; I have no choice but to test the loyalty of those in my inner circle. I believe you."

Oh, the joy upon his face! And once again tears, but these were tinged with happy relief instead of fear.

"But," said I, for he had begun to struggle to his feet.

At that word, he sank at once back down. "You have passed only narrowly. Pray now for my victory over all enemies—and thank God for your deliverance."

He began to do so, and his exultant smile broadened when I motioned for the soldier—now bitterly disappointed—to retreat back to the fireplace, to stand beside the grimly silent old monk. But I remained within the doorway.

And when I deemed the time right—and could no longer restrain my fury at Gregor's betrayal and his cowardice—I reached for a wooden lever set within the wall just outside the cell. With vehement effort, I pulled.

The sliding sound of wood against wood. Arms flung into the air, a piteous cry of disappointment and fear. And upon his face animal terror again, a sight rapid yet indelible in the swift second before he disappeared down to Hell.

Then the sharper screams of pain as I ran forward towards the gaping trapdoor to observe my handiwork.

This is how God feels when He looks on the faces of the dead: a sense of power and accomplishment far, far sweeter and more intoxicating than love.

Gregor had fallen into the shallow pit upon his knees, and thus, kneeling, would he die. For the keenly sharp iron pales were fastened in the ground at regular intervals, to ensure death, and the pit so placed that he could not fall forward—only back, despite his flailing, onto the spikes. (This so I might better see his face.) One had caught his long dark hair and grazed the back of his skull, leaving his head tilted slightly forward; another emerged bloodied from his right breast. Yet others protruded from the crook of his right arm, from the center of his left palm (in Christlike fashion), while others sight unseen no doubt pierced his lower legs and held him fast.

His eyes were open wide, in blank astonishment which

was slowly fading. I think he was not quite dead, and so I squatted on my haunches and called softly down:

"May God send your faithless soul straight to Hell. You shall die, and Basarab shall die, but I shall live forever."

And I bent forward, turning so that the two living men behind me could not see, and lifted up Gregor's limp right hand. Upon this I put my own ring.

Then I rose and sent the young soldier just outside the room, to guard us, and took the old monk aside. Him I gave a mission: that he should take whatever strong young brothers he needed, and take the body across the lake into the Vlasia Forest, and there behead it. As for the head, they would cut a hole in the ice and throw it into the freezing waters.

Fear was in the old man, too, after what he had seen; he listened in silence and uttered no protest, even though I was asking him to do the unthinkable—to leave a body without proper burial for the carrion birds in the forest.

And when I had sent him away to do his work, I called my eager young assassin into my chambers and said, "The old monk will return with some brothers to fetch the body for burial outside Snagov. When they return from across the water, I want you to be waiting for them in the watchtower; do not let them back inside, but meet them at the gate and kill them."

This he agreed to eagerly. Then I bade him send another trustworthy soldier to stand outside the door and guard my private chambers throughout the night, so that no one should be permitted in.

But first, I helped him to remove Gregor's still bleeding, warm body (did he still breathe? I could not decide) from its bed of stakes and wrap it in the traitor's cloak and the now-tattered rug, to spare the floor from stain. Then the soldier dragged Gregor by the heels out into the hallway, and there they remained to await the brothers.

As for me, I bolted the door behind them, as I required privacy in order to properly cast a Circle. Now that I had made my escape from Basarab and my Judas, it was time to make my escape from Death. For it was clear to me that my success as an earthly prince was not to be, and that if I remained as I was, my death was assured. Thus I sought another realm, one that was deathless yet still allowed me power over mortals.

And so I turned, thinking to go back to the small shrine where so many have met death, and fetch from another hidden trapdoor my magical tools, that I might cast a Circle and summon again the Dark Lord for the consummation of our bargain.

Yet as I turned, I espied before the fireplace a ragged servant child stirring the fire with a poker. The sight so startled me that I cried out: "You! Boy! How and when did you come in here?" For I wanted to know whether the child had had opportunity to overhear my plan to leave Gregor's decapitated body in the forest, then have the monks killed. From the child's size, he surely was no more than in his sixth year, and most likely had understood little of what he had heard; but children are parrots, and I would not risk even the frailest chance of failure.

At my shout, the tiny creature did not so much as quiver, but continued tending the fire with preternatural calm. Infuriated, I strode up behind it, snatched up my sword, and drew it from its sheath, thinking to cleave that small body in two.

But in the instant ere I struck, the child turned to me and smiled.

Boy? Girl? I could not have said. I only knew in that instant that I gazed upon the most exquisitely beautiful creature I had ever seen. Its long, curling hair shone like gold in sunlight, its skin gleamed like polished nacre, its lips bloomed like the tenderest pink rose around the perfect pearls of its teeth. The wool cape round its frail shoulders was tattered almost to shreds, frayed, worn, and so smudged with grime that the fabric's original colour was impossible to guess. Yet the filth did not dim the wearer's glory, but served to enhance it by the contrast.

Surely there was nothing in this world lovelier or more delicate than this small creature. Yet it was not until I gazed into its eyes—eyes bluer than sea or sky or sapphire, framed by fine golden lashes and pale downy brows—that I saw the infinite intelligence there, the wisdom and knowledge greater than any man could ever possess . . . and at the same time, an innocence deeper and more genuine than any human infant could possess. I thought, *These are the eyes of the Christ.*

My weapon clattered to the floor. Despite myself, I shuddered, but through sheer strength of will did not fall to my knees; pride would not permit me so soon to echo Gregor. But—how difficult to be honest—I was filled with awe and fear.

For I knew I looked upon the Dark Lord, come to me for the first time without my summoning Him in Circle. Always He had come at my urging; *I* had been the one in control of my fate, of my contract with Him. The Circle gave me power over Him, made me *His* lord, made Him subject to my command—so long as I was willing to make the appropriate sacrifice.

Now, it seemed, He was no longer mine to control. The thought provoked bitter horror.

"You are the Dark One," I told Him, though in truth I had never seen anything so bright and shining as this smiling little pauper. He had come to me many times in the form of darkness, as the featureless shadow of a man blacker than midnight; twice, he had come to me as a bearded man more ancient and wizened than the old monk, with eyes as innocent and wise as these.

Innocent as a dove, yet wise as a serpent. . . .

"I am He," said the little beauty pleasantly. "I have read your intent and have saved you the need for a formal summons. What do you offer in exchange for my gift, O Prince?" He spoke with a soft, lisping child's voice, yet his words and demeanour were those of a sage.

"If you have read my intent, then you already know."

He laughed, sweet and high. "Let us affirm the contract by your stating it."

I paused. I had never had great regard for any of my family, because of my betrayal at the hands of my own father and brother. And I had no love for my second wife, the Hungarian noblewoman Ilona; she had been like my conversion to Catholicism, or the raid on Srebrenica, one part of a long-term plan to win King Matthias' favor and thus my freedom and kingdom. She had given me two sons: my namesake Vlad, for the moment heir to the Wallachian throne (though unfortunately not to my intelligence), and Mircea, who even in his youth clearly resembles my treacherous brother, Radu, in both appearance and feminine affectation.

But of all my family, I possessed—still possess—some paternal interest in my eldest son, Mihnea, given me by my beloved dead Ana. He alone shares my shrewdness and ambition; were I to choose one person on earth I should least wish to sacrifice, it would be he.

Yet I was a keen and ambitious child, eager to learn from my father and fulfill my duties as his heir, and he betrayed me without hesitation to the Turks.

So it was I answered, "In return for immortality, I offer up the soul of my eldest son."

"Not enough," replied He sternly, to my astonishment. "Not enough; for immortality lasts forever, but my pleasure at receiving Mihnea's soul is temporary. We must have a *continuing* bargain. The soul of the eldest son of each generation. And you shall bear the responsibility for delivering it to me."

I paused only a heartbeat at the thought of such a responsibility's cost. "Very well. Each generation, I shall deliver into your power the eldest son. But at what moment shall I become immortal?"

"The change shall begin this night, once the sun has set, and be accomplished by the dawn. One warning: In the morning you must closet yourself away to rest undisturbed. You will no longer be a man, but an altogether different creature."

"How shall I be changed?"

The child smiled, but there was no contempt, no condescension, in His eyes. "That depends upon your own heart and mind. For each one it is different. You shall become more powerful, but there will be conditions upon that power. There are always conditions. I leave you to discover them yourself."

"Conditions?" I savoured this new information, and experienced a sudden revelation which restored a shred of my former confidence that I should be able to control this entity, and thus my ultimate fate. "And have *you* no conditions upon your own power?"

Another laugh, sweet and tinkling, then silence. The child regarded me with abrupt solemnity. "There remains only one thing to be done to complete our exchange."

As he spoke, the flesh upon my arms and nape prickled. This was the moment I had long awaited, the moment which had sustained me during these last bitter days of knowing my earthly kingdom and my life would soon be forfeit: the moment I stepped over the threshold into immortality.

"A kiss," the Dark One said. "Only a kiss." And He stepped from the hearth and rose on tiptoe, arms at His sides, the pink petals of His lips pursed in anticipation.

I moved towards Him, at last understanding as I sank down why He had appeared as a child: that I should have to bow to Him to accept His gift. The thought rankled, as I have bowed to no one but my father and Matthias, and then only with reluctance. It also filled me with foreboding, for it underscored the fact that the Dark Lord was no longer mine to control, and summon when I wished; I was now under His control.

But I could not accept death, and so I bowed and kissed Him. And at the moment my lips touched that infinitely tender and immortal flesh, I felt a surge of power, of exhilaration, move from Him into me.

I stared into His eyes and saw them deepen from sky-blue to indigo, the colour of night. Dark and shining they were, and magnificent, eyes that made a man want to do nothing but stare into them for eternity. I could not resist. As I looked deep into those eyes, I saw in them the gaze of the Beloved, the gaze of the dead. The gaze of the only female I had permitted myself to love, my dead Ana; the seductive, beautiful, treacherous gaze of Radu; the shrewd, calculating gaze of my father, Vlad, and behind it, infinite Darkness. . . .

So deep did I fall into that Darkness that when I came to myself some moments—or was it hours?—later, I opened my eyes to find myself kneeling before the hearth. The child had vanished, and the fire had gone out, leaving only ash and glowing embers. Yet I felt no chill; my limbs, my head, my chest, were atingle with strange sensation. Not the tingle of limbs gone numb, but rather an odd sense of internal movement, as though my body had been emptied of its contents, then refilled with humming bees. I felt strangely light. And when I rose to my feet, I did so easily, without the pains of age and creaking bones that have afflicted me these past years.

Even my vision was enhanced; the glow from the ashes in the fireplace seemed impossibly bright and kissed by rainbow colours. Indeed, as I gazed around the room, I saw each object more sharply and in more detail than I ever had as a youth; each was imbued with a startling depth of colour and texture. I turned slowly, taking in each sight with a child's sense of wonder and laughing aloud at the sheer pleasure of it. I could see every sparkling grain of sand that comprised each stone in the hearth, every hair-fine crack in the mortar.

Yet the light from the tapers (which were still burning, though half consumed and standing in pools of wax) dazzled my eyes so painfully that I blew out each but one. That meagre light proved more than sufficient, for the colour and detail faded not at all, even though a swift glance through the window showed darkness and swirling snow. The sun had set, and the storm come at last.

I hurried to the mirror, eager to inspect my face for changes—but alas! When I peered into the polished metal surface, my visage was paler and indistinct, fading away as one might imagine a ghost dissolves into night. I had feared such might happen, for I had heard tales from my nursemaid and other servants about the faces of the dead not reflecting in mirrors. Was the undisclosed cost of my bargain invisibility?

A discreet knock at the door: I called out and heard in reply the polite voice of my young assassin. The monks had returned from the forest and had been killed according to my instructions.

As a test to see whether I remained visible to mortals, I opened the door and peered out at the scraggly-bearded soldier. "Excellent," said I, expecting him to scream at my disembodied voice, or instead to walk past me and peer beyond me, searching for me inside the room.

At the very least, I expected him to see what I saw: a disappearing man. Yet he gazed directly at my face, and bowed, giving no sign of distress or amazement. "Very good, my lord," said he, and I told him to ready my horse and bring it to the palace, for I would be leaving the monastery shortly.

"But the snow has come, my lord. It is not safe for travel."

I laughed in disdain, then repeated my request and gave him leave to go. I no longer possess any fear of cold or snow or Basarab. I fear but one thing: the Dark Lord.

The horse stands ready now, but I am obliged to write the story of my transformation down first, for surely over the coming centuries I shall forget the circumstances and the wonder of it. One day soon the announcement shall be made that the Wallachian prince is dead, for it is only a matter of time before Gregor's headless body is discovered in the forest. I have no doubt that Basarab has laid waste to my army and my castle at Bucharest, but I have my victory. In a generation, he shall be dead, whilst I shall live forever. I have sent a courier with a message for Ilona and my sons to meet me at our new estate in the Carpathians.

And now I ride north, to become Legend.

❧1❧

Letter from Vlad Dracula, Bistritsa, to E. Bathory, Vienna:

15 *April 1893*

Dearest Cousin:

   It seems like centuries since last we corresponded, and longer still since you and I met in the flesh. Much has happened since that time; I have encountered difficulties of a grave nature—so grave, in fact, that I know not whom to call upon for aid save you, my shrewd and talented cousin.

   Will you come, Elisabeth? Unfortunately, I find myself too compromised to travel at present, or I would have gone to Vienna to make my request in person, to spare you the journey here. I promise you sweet reward, and the delight of meeting my charming niece Zsuzsanna and her maidservant Dunya, who have both become my eternal companions. I promise also that I shall be as beholden to you as I was to your ancestor Stefan of Bathory, who so long ago fought by the side of a certain Prince Vlad Dracula to help him reclaim his throne. Once again, I rely on your family's loyalty and kindness.

   Come quickly, for time is of the essence. Any guest you might bring would be truly welcomed.

Your grateful servant,
V.

❧ 2 ❧

The Diary of
Abraham Van Helsing

(Translated from the Dutch)

2 MAY 1893. EVENING. So quiet here at home, and so sad. The student nurse, Katya, was still here when I arrived home from my lecture at the hospital, and so I took my dinner and went in to sit with Gerda for a time. As usual, no change, though I told her the simple details of my day and the neighbors' news in as cheerful a tone as I could command. It is becoming increasingly difficult, for she is becoming a skeleton. I fear she will die before Zsuzsanna is destroyed.

Now I sit watching Mama as she sleeps. I am glad again to stand the night watch over her, and always restless when I must be away after sunset. (Gerda I am not so concerned about; the mark on her throat means that little further harm can be done her.) Katya stays the night when I must be away, and was able to come this evening during my lecture. She is young but responsible and levelheaded and can handle any medical emergency—though it is not those I fear so much now that Mama nears the Abyss. I have sworn to my mother that I will see her safely to the other life—not that her poor diseased brain comprehended what I told her, though I know her spirit understands. I will let no vampire deprive her of an honest death.

But it is so hard to watch her die.

She looks a bit worse to-night, with her once-beautiful silver hair spread brittle and tangled upon the pillow, her face sallow and haggard and pinched from constant pain.

It is hard to see her thus—she who had been my one comfort and strength during all these difficult years. Since little Jan died so many years ago (can it truly be twenty-two now? The pain is so fresh), leaving my poor dear Gerda quite mad, Mama and I have depended so upon each other. We were all that remained of our little family. She was uncomplaining and brave, even all those many nights when I would travel and be gone for days—or rather, nights—at a time, ridding the world of Vlad's evil spawn. At times, I feel guilt at leaving her to accomplish my grisly work, but I know she would have it no other way. How else shall I avenge the death of her little grandson and of her first and truest love, my father, Arkady? How else shall I give them and all my victims peace?

What a blessing it would be to have my father here now, to have his knowledgeable help (yet how strange to write this of one who was a vampire). Remembering back to the first days after I had met him, and my unkindness to him, my repulsion and mistrust, I am ashamed. For—from what Mama has told me and what I learned from her diary and from my interaction with the man himself—he was clearly the noblest of souls, and died in an heroic effort to save us all from evil. Even the curse of vampirism could not sully his good heart.

Mama's cheeks and eyes seem more sunken to-night as well, no doubt because of dehydration; Katya said she vomited her supper and would take no more, not even water. She had also been moaning in agony—damnable tumours!—so I administered an injection of morphia and now she sleeps peacefully. (I would take the drug myself if I did not fear its addictive properties, or the fuzzy-headedness it causes; I must always remain as alert as possible. As for Mama, I cannot deny her. What does it matter if she dies addicted, so long as she is not in pain?)

I yearn for peaceful sleep myself; mine has been uneasy of late, and filled with dreams which disturb me. I am convinced they contain some cryptic message I might decipher, and so I have brought my journal into Mama's room to write as I sit in the old rocking-chair where she had so often comforted me in my childhood.

So here is the dream: I am running with boyish glee through a great evergreen forest. The air is fresh and cool, scented with pine and recent rain; the tall trees' limbs and needles sparkle with droplets of moisture. I run and run, gasping and laughing, keeping my arm up so that the lower boughs do not slap my face.

But soon my glee turns to panic, for I hear footsteps behind me. Someone pursues me; I glance over my shoulder and catch a glimpse through the glistening boughs of Gerda, my wife. But it is Gerda monstrously Changed: her dark, dark eyes slant like the vampiress Zsuzsanna's, and her teeth are just as long and sharp. Like a wolf she growls low in her throat as she gives chase, her long brown hair streaming.

I cry out and run faster, faster, for I know she means to destroy me.

Of a sudden, I stumble over a fallen tree trunk—slowly, ever so slowly, with the great detail one experiences only in dreams. My forward foot becomes trapped between the damp earth and the heavy limb; my arms go flying forward as they scribe an arc in the air on their descent. My other leg goes up in the air also, following its own arc as I go down, down, my palms finally sinking into a thick carpet of wet twigs and pine needles.

My face strikes the fragrant earth. When I lift it at last, pushing up with my arms against the yielding ground, I see . . .

(Why is this image so disturbing? Why does my pulse accelerate even now as I write?)

I see a great dark creature—dark in the sense of pitch blackness, of an absence of light so intense it seemed someone had taken scissors and cut away that small portion of the world. A wolf, I think in fear; but no, it is no wolf. A bear? No.

And, at a distance, my angelic mentor, Arminius, looks on dispassionately—as shining and white as the hideous creature is black. His face is pink and unlined as a child's beneath his snowy beard, and his pure unsullied raiment gleams blinding in the sun. Like Moses, he holds a tall wooden staff, and beside him stands his familiar, Archangel, the tame white wolf.

"Arminius, help me!" I scream, and continue screaming until I am hoarse. But he gives no sign of recognition or acknowledgment, nor does Archangel; and he and the wolf remain detached onlookers.

Hopeless, horrified, I watch as the black silhouette metamorphoses from animal predator into human, shrinking first to a child, then ballooning swiftly to the shape of a man.

"Who are you?" I demand, trembling; despite my bravado, my cheeks are wet with tears.

No answer. An interminable length of time follows, during which the creature's outline gradually enlarges. I know it means to surround and absorb me—to devour me utterly—and I am afraid.

"Who are you?" I demand again, and after a heart-stopping pause, I hear the answer whispered in my own mind, in my Gerda's voice:

The Dark Lord. . . .

I am engulfed, and swoon from pure nocturnal terror. Abruptly I wake, heart pounding against my ribs like a captive demanding freedom.

My occult research has proven to me beyond doubt that such dreams are omens. Yet, try as I might, I cannot ascertain its meaning. Does the Devil Himself approach me? I do not even believe strictly in the concept, though I know there are a plentitude of entities in this world and elsewhere which are not human, yet are possessed of equal or greater intelligence.

I yearn for the comfort and help of Arkady's presence, though I know he is dead and cannot help me. But there is one who can.

Arminius! Arminius, my friend and teacher, you who guided me in the most difficult times during my past, you who trained me as the slayer of the undead. So many years ago you abandoned me, and I do not even know how to summon you. You who are immortal are surely still alive.

Arminius, help me. . . .

✠ ✠ ✠

Zsuzsanna Dracul's Diary

2 MAY 1893. For an interminable succession of years I have been trapped inside this castle watching the disinte-

gration of my benefactor, Vlad, from strong, handsome immortal to the most piteously gruesome husk of a selfish monster. Worse, I know the same horrible change has overtaken me; when I braid my hair, I am forced to acknowledge a preponderance of silver where once there was only jet. And my hands! I see them now as I dip my pen. They are such poor, frail, withered things, pale parchment over bone. If they are this hideous, what has become of my once-beautiful face?

It has been more than I can bear, in part because of my helplessness, and Vlad's. We have both come to hate each other because of our misery—and it is all the fault of that bastard Stefan! (Bastard I shall call him, though he is the legitimate heir of my dead brother, Arkady. He deserves to be called by fouler terms than that!) Or shall I call him by his alias, Van Helsing? He has discovered somehow that the covenant works both ways: that each time he destroys Vlad's spawn—those few we failed to properly dispose of ourselves (we dislike creating competitors) and all *their* many offspring—we are weakened. Our doom seemed inevitable, for we had no choice over these two long decades but to languish here, especially now that we are too weak even to hunt nourishment.

Last evening Vlad came to me—his skin grey as a corpse's, his eyes sunken and red, his hair and eyebrows stark, brittle white. And yet his pale lips were curved in a smile, and his voice oddly animated with excitement as he said: "Zsuzsanna. If we take no action, we shall soon be so weak that Van Helsing will come and easily destroy us. But no—do not weep on our account, for I have good news!"

For I had broken into sobs, so perfect was my misery; and now to think that I who had been filled with such power, such happiness, such hope, could only wait helplessly for final, eternal oblivion. . . .

But he waved me silent, and said vehemently, "Do not cry because of *him*. He thinks he is powerful enough to defeat us, but he will soon see his error. He will not escape me; I shall soon see him delivered into my hands. But here is the news: A mortal visitor will soon arrive at the castle, a healthy young man. . . . Do not sigh, for that is not the extent of it. I have received a letter, child, from my cousin Elisabeth."

"Elisabeth?" I had never before heard him utter the name, and in any case did not understand why this should be such a glorious thing, for his voice rose exultantly, as if he had announced our deliverance.

"An immortal like us. She is powerful and canny, shrewd enough to defeat your brother's son. And she *will* do so. But first, she will come to us from Vienna, and restore us to strength."

"How is this possible?" I asked, and at once realised my question was a foolish one. Of course this Elisabeth would be able to bring us an even larger amount of fresh, vital blood than one lone man could supply. That would at least ease the weakness that came from hunger, but certainly we could not recapture our full vigour until Van Helsing's rampage was ended.

The instant my question was stated, Vlad drew back, and his eyes grew wider, redder, with a rage I did not understand. "That is not your concern!" he snapped, and in an instant was gone again from my room.

Clearly this Elisabeth is a *most* powerful woman—more powerful than Vlad himself, else I would not have detected the clear note of jealousy in his voice. Yes, he brought me into this existence, and for that I must be always grateful. At the same time, I have come to despise him—despise him for his cruelty, his arrogance, his lies. To him, I am nothing more than chattel, at best an occasional companion, to be treated however he desires and dismissed without concern for my feelings when he tires of me. He gave me the dark kiss all those fifty years ago because in life I was timid, grateful, grovelling, smitten with love for him. And now that I am transformed into the strong, confident creature I was meant to be, he grows bored, even annoyed. When last he went out of the castle to hunt many months ago (for all of us are too weak for the long ride through the pass to Bistritsa, to post mail and thus invite guests to our castle, as we did in the old days—or so I had thought), I voiced a protest: Why was I required to remain behind like a prisoner of this castle, waiting for whatever small gift he chose to bring back, after he had supped to his content? For his custom was to bring me only an infant or a pale, anaemic child—to keep me weaker than he, I realise now, so that he should always be the one in control.

Had I possessed any physical strength, I should have defied him; but the first time he offered to hunt for us all, I honestly thought it was out of kindness, and so I accepted gratefully. And when he returned with only a tiny new-born for me to share with Dunya, he was full of profuse apologies and excuses. So it was that the second time he went out, I foolishly believed he would bring us something grand: a strapping youth or strong peasant woman.

But no; he returned with a single sickly infant. And I drank from it out of pure necessity, as I was faint with hunger, and shared what I could bear with Dunya. Afterwards, I was as he had hoped—far too weak even to protest when he went to hunt again.

Just as I am weak to-night; after Vlad left, I lay down. Night used to bring such sweet exhilaration; now it only brings consciousness and misery. There have been times (like to-night) when exhaustion has made me refuse to rise from my coffin—which used to lie beside his, but now is confined to Dunya's servant's quarters because he grew annoyed at my proximity. I lie here and weep and consider that I should close my eyes and greet true death here, that this might indeed become my final resting place.

Poor Dunya! I look over at her, lying motionless in her coffin. I fear she will greet the Absolute before me, for she is the weakest of us all; she rarely emerges from her slumber, but lies with pale, pale lids drawn down over dark eyes. Years ago, when I was strong and beautiful, I took pity upon her, thinking, *Why must she remain an anguished mortal, under our control, neither alive nor dead?* And so I led her gently through death into the dark life. Vlad was furious, of course—"How shall we accomplish those things which can only be done during the light of day if we have no mortal servant?" he roared, and for weeks would speak to neither of us.

I did not care; Dunya has been as sweet and constant a companion as she ever was. Her suffering was replaced by a marvellous delight, and we two have shared all joys as sisters might. It was Dunya who suggested I commission a portrait of myself, which I could use in place of the looking-glass, that I might not have to rely on her descriptions. So it was done—by a mortal artist whose trembling hands happily did not impede his skill—and out of gratitude, I commissioned a separate, smaller portrait of Dunya.

Now my dear companion is only a pitiful, aged shadow of the beauty that hangs upon the wall (as I must be also). In her coffin she lies with arms crossed over her breast like a corpse, and looks for all the world like a dead crone, her face worn and withered and waxen, her thin lips drawn back tightly over sharp yellowed teeth. How I miss all those nights when we would hold hands and whisper our dreams into each other's ear! I cannot bear to see her so. . . .

But the promise of Elisabeth has brought hope, and thus for the first time in many years I have risen and written in my journal. Can I truly reclaim my beauty and exuberance?

⊷ ⊷ ⊷

The Diary of
Abraham Van Helsing

3 MAY 1893. How strange life is. We make our plans and expect everything to go according to them—and then, in a single instant, everything is changed.

It had been a long, tiring night. News had come from The Hague of strange nocturnal attacks on the citizens by a sharp-toothed predator, possibly a wolf. And so after investigating, I travelled there and spent the darkness waiting outside a grand mausoleum for the return of a wealthy, well-respected businessman who had died of apoplexy after a Hungarian holiday. More grisly work, but I am happy to state that he is now at peace.

I returned home as quickly as possible from the task, as Gerda had begun to worsen terribly over the past two days. Early this morning I went to see her, as is my custom before retiring. Usually I make a vain attempt to hypnotise her, to see what news I can learn of Zsuzsanna and thus Vlad. But this morning when I went in, she was not staring at the ceiling as she always does. No, her eyes were closed, and her breathing laboured. I sat with her a long time, checking her breath and pulse and aura and trying to ascertain the cause of her decline.

There is no physical reason for it, other than her

psychic connexion with Zsuzsanna. Of that I am certain. If she was weakening and near death, it meant Zsuzsanna was the same.

The day I had so diligently been working towards for a quarter-century was now here. As Arminius had said so long ago, the covenant works both ways: by destroying Vlad's evil children, I weaken him—and strengthen myself. And at last the moment had come when I was the stronger, and could deliver Vlad his long-overdue fate.

So after I left her I did not go to bed; instead, I began to pack my trunk and checked the timetables to see which trains were headed east, and when. My hope was that, if I could arrive in Transylvania and dispatch both Vlad and Zsuzsanna in time, Gerda might be spared both death and a dark resurrection.

But I also knew that if I failed, it would not be safe for her to remain in this house with Mama and Katya, nor for the mortician who kept her body for burial. She could not stay here without the keen scrutiny of one who can perceive the symptoms of encroaching vampirism, and knows how to keep the undead at bay. As I packed, I puzzled upon this for some time, since there is no one in Amsterdam I can trust with such a task.

But there is such an one in London: my friend John, with his lunatic asylum. He does not know about the details of my wife's illness, but he is much interested in occultism and possesses an open mind. If I instruct him as to Gerda's confinement and care, he will follow my orders to the letter.

I was composing a telegram to him in my own mind when the bell rang. I answered it to find a stout German lady somewhat past middle age, with iron-streaked brown hair, broad jaw, and a ruddy complexion laced with spidery broken veins. (And, I admit, a vast, intimidating bosom; when she leaned from the waist to bow, I quite expected her to topple forward.)

"Herr Van Helsing?" She smiled most pleasantly, and I knew at once that she would make a suitable day nurse for Mama, for she projected both dependability and kindness. I had no need for psychic protection around her—she even wore a crucifix, hidden beneath her black widow's weeds—and so I relaxed and smiled as I motioned her inside.

"And you must be Frau Koehler," I answered in German, and at the sound of her native tongue, she positively beamed.

As I led her upstairs to Mama's room, we made pleasant small talk about the ease with which she had located my house, and about how I had been referred to her by a colleague.

Once we'd entered Mama's bedroom, she fell silent and gazed with reverence upon her prospective patient, then crossed herself at the sight of the crucifix hanging over the bed.

"Ah," she said with forthright sympathy. "She is dying, yes?"

"Yes."

"How sad for you!" Her tone was that of one who had been through the same terrible experience closehand. "And are you alone? I see no wife, no children. . . ."

I sensed a glimmer of marital hope in the widow Koehler's eyes and aspect. "I have a wife," I said at once, suddenly overwhelmed by bitterness at the recollection of how she had been taken from me in spirit; and by the recollection of my little Jan, taken in body by the vampires—by Zsuzsanna, the vile demoness for whom I can find no forgiveness in my heart. "But Gerda, too, is ill—"

"How doubly sad! God has given you a heavy bur-

den." She tilted her wide, strong-jawed face towards me
and studied me with at least as much pity as she had
directed towards Mama. "Then there shall be two patients?"

"No. I am taking my wife with me to London, to
consult a specialist. My mother has an excellent nurse who
relieves me during the night; but now that I must be gone,
I need someone to care for her by day."

"Ah. And what is your wife's difficulty?"

"Shock," said I. At the horror of being bitten, and
finding that the attacker had stolen her firstborn son.

"And our patient?" she asked gently, turning her kind
gaze once again upon Mama.

"Tumours of the breast and now, I think, the brain
and elsewhere. She is not altogether lucid; usually she
sleeps because of the morphia. There is pain."

She clicked her tongue softly. "And what is her name,
sir, if I might ask?"

Van Helsing, the same as mine, I almost replied. But her
demeanour was so much that of a trusted family friend
that I answered, "Mary."

"Mary." She savoured the word with loving approval.
"The Mother of God. Such a good name. . . ." And she
went over to sit in the rocking-chair beside the bed. "And I
am Helga," she said, lifting Mama's hand from beneath
the sheets and pressing it gently between her own, as if she
were introducing herself and exchanging information. I
doubt the woman was aware of what she was doing, but it
was clear to me that she was a natural psychic.

After a time, she confirmed this by looking over her
shoulder at me and saying: "You are a good man, sir, and
very brave. I also know in my heart that your mother is a
good woman. I shall be happy to give her excellent care.

And if God wills that she should die while you are gone, do not think that she died alone or with a stranger, for I shall care and pray for her as if she were my own sister."

I turned away, clumsily pretending to gaze out the window at that moment, for her compassion quite touched me. And when I am moved, suppressed grief wells within me and shatters my defenses like floodwaters breaking a dam; I could not prevent tears from spilling, but I moved quickly to wipe them away and recover myself.

"Weep, sir," she said behind me, and I heard the soft sound of her patting Mama's hand—as if Mama were fully conscious and aware of my tears, and Frau Koehler wished to comfort her. "You have a right to."

I feigned a cough so that I could withdraw my kerchief and wipe nose and eyes, then turned apologetically towards the two women and nodded at Mama, whose eyelids had begun to flicker. "Not so much right as she. *She* is the one who is suffering, not I."

"Untrue, sir. Because you love her, all her suffering has become yours. And because you are more able to keenly observe it, you are even more aware of its extent than she. Is it not more painful to see someone you love suffer than to endure that suffering yourself?"

I wanted to protest, for a part of me was incensed to think that *I* suffered more than Mama. Yet I could not deny that because I was conscious, lucid, and still graced with adequate eyesight, I could look upon my mother's face and see the wasting there, see the lines traced by years of grief, see the sunken cheeks and slightly jaundiced skin. See, also, the raw bleeding bedsores devour her flesh while she screamed in anguish in a futile effort to void. Her whole life has been pain: the loss of two husbands, a son, a grandson, terror of a fate truly worse than death. All this she has borne cheerfully, courageously—and for what purpose? To die in agony after an unhappy existence? To lose all her dignity and beauty—

I must not continue, or I shall break down weeping again. Enough, enough!

It took me some time to compose myself sufficiently to answer Frau Koehler: "It is difficult, indeed. But I am some judge of character myself, and I perceive that you will give my mother such wonderful and compassionate care that I need have no worry." And I shook off all grief and tried to change my tone to that of the brisk businessman. "Is it true that you can start this morning? For my trip cannot wait; the sooner I and my wife leave, the better. I should like to have you stay now, if you can, while I pack and make arrangements."

"I would be pleased to stay," she said, rising, and gently replacing Mama's hand upon the covers.

"Excellent!"

I showed her where all the medical necessities were kept in the bedroom: the syringe, the morphia, the bedpan and paregoric, the salve and bandages for the bedsores. She was well trained and quite intelligent, and we soon swiftly dispensed with the details of the patient's care. The time then came to escort her down to my office so that I might pay her an advance portion of her salary.

But as I led her back towards the staircase, a sudden cry—muted, so that I could not judge whether it was joyous or agonised—pricked the small hairs at the nape of my neck. For an instant, I feared it was Mama, calling out in pain; but then realisation dawned, so forcefully, so fearfully, that the gooseflesh on my neck branched downward to my spine and arms.

Twenty-two years had passed since I had last heard my wife's voice; thus I had not recognised it at once.

With neither explanation nor apology to Frau Koehler, I turned and ran at once down the hallway and into Gerda's room.

And there she sat in the bed—eyes open, shining, all signs of weakness vanished. My heart felt as though it had flipped over in my chest, and for a fleeting instant I dared hope that she was returned to me, that Zsuzsanna and Vlad had both been destroyed and that my darling was now freed.

Alas! Her eyes, though open, remained fixed upon a distant and invisible vision. But she was strong, radiant, her skin no longer pale but slightly flushed, as though she had recently taken sun, and her hair—her hair! Still dishevelled above the long, neat braid Katya faithfully tended each night . . . but *every streak of silver had departed from her sable-brown locks*.

I peered again at her face, unable to believe what my own eyes perceived, but there it was: she had grown younger since the early morning. Every grey hair, every wrinkle and fold of sagging flesh, had *disappeared*.

"Gerda!" I breathed, then louder: "Gerda, my darling, can you hear me?"

She gave no sign of either hearing or seeing me, but something she regarded in the invisible distance made her face brighten with pure joy. "She has come!" she said, and laughed aloud. "She has come. . . ."

"Who?" I urged, as Frau Koehler came and stood in the doorway, watching in silent amazement. "Who has come, darling?"

She replied not a word, but began gradually to calm as I watched her in silence. After a time, her lips curved upward in a brilliant smile, revealing slightly elongated eyeteeth.

"Amazing," the nurse whispered behind me. "What shall I do, sir? Do you still intend to take your wife to London?"

"I—I do not know." I stared at Gerda, stricken. Her joyous cry had made me dare hope, but now I saw that all was lost. For Gerda's moods and health had, for the last twenty-two years, been tied to those of Zsuzsanna. If Gerda was now young and strong and healthy, it meant that Zsuzsanna was too—and Vlad.

And Gerda was beginning to Change.

What had the vampire done to strengthen himself and his consort?

I promised the good Frau Koehler that I should be in touch with her directly once a decision had been made, and quickly dismissed her so that I could return to Gerda's bedside.

Efforts to rouse my wife from trance failed, as did all attempts at hypnosis (which I knew would probably be futile, given the time of day). Yet I was determined to sit with her and learn what I could; so I locked the windows and rose, thinking to lock the door behind me—from the outside, so that Gerda could not escape. There was little chance she would, since I had fastened crucifixes and the Host over the lintel of door and window, but the extra safeguard reassured me.

Yet before I had passed over the threshold, she whispered a single phrase: "The Dark Lord. . . ."

It seemed at once a question and an admission of fear, voiced in an apprehensive yet curious tremolo.

I froze in the doorway, overtaken by terror at the abrupt mental image of the dark, devouring creature in my dream.

Who is this creature, and why are even the undead afraid of his name?

Arminius! Arminius, my rescuer of times past, do not remain silent any longer. Help me!

❧ 3 ❧

Zsuzsanna Dracul's Diary

3 MAY 1893. She has come!

I was lying in my casket, having awakened hours before but too overwhelmed with exhaustion to rouse myself; there seemed no purpose in doing so, at any rate. I felt like a dying woman who, at God's insistence, was forced to live beyond my time. I desired nothing more than to be released from my suffering.

And as I lay, I detected voices within the castle. At first they were only barely audible murmurs, and in my self-pitying weakness, I paid no heed. (Once I would have heard them distinctly, but my ability had faded to the degree that I could distinguish only the voice and the cadence, but not the words.) They continued for some time, and then they neared, so that I could recognise one of them: Vlad spoke with the tone of a cordial host, which thus far I have only heard him use to welcome victims.

And then I heard another voice—one that, for a moment, I mistook for a man's, for it was deep and throaty and so utterly, confidently sensual that I thought, *I am in love.* . . . Thus I naturally assumed that the visitor he had been expecting had arrived, but the thought evoked only pale joy. I knew that Vlad would tend first to his own hunger, leaving only the dregs for me and Dunya. If, in hopes of getting more, I dared interrupt him as he fed, his rage might very well prompt him to deny me so much as a single drop.

Then came silence; or so I think, for I drowsed a time.

But I came to myself at once when suddenly this other laughed, an utterly joyous sound which for an instant rose so high that I realised I was hearing instead the voice of a woman.

Elisabeth. . . .

Why did the knowledge of her arrival fill me with excitement? I cannot say, for certainly I found in her far, far more than I could have anticipated; and I am damned, therefore I dare not trust in the kindly interventions of God or fate. I only know that I rose from my resting place at once and hurried down the corridor and up the stairs to Vlad's private chambers, from whence the laughter had originated.

And when I arrived, I flung open the door without so much as a knock.

There before a burning fireplace stood Vlad, still ancient and white-haired, but clearly more vigorous than he had been of late. His lips had taken on a rosy hue, his shoulders were no longer stooped but straight and square, and for the first time in years, he was in an excellent humour. But his smile faded instantly at the sight of me, and his eyes flared red. I knew at once that I would bear the brunt of his wrath again for my interruption.

But I cared not, for my gaze had fallen upon Elisabeth.

To say that she was comely is to slight her. *I* am lovely beyond any mortal—this I know from looking at Dunya, and from the portrait that hangs upon my wall (though Dunya says oils cannot do justice to the shimmering phosphorescence of my skin, or the molten golden gleam in my eyes).

But Elisabeth! She was beyond beauty: regal as a queen in a modern plumed cap and fitted satin gown of pewter-blue, with sapphire eyes to match, and skin as fine and white as an infant child's, save where the tenderest pink bloomed upon her cheeks and lips. Her hair was tied at the nape of her neck—a delicate porcelain swan's neck, with the most bewitching hollow at the collarbone—and the curls brought forward onto one shoulder, where in the fire's glow they shone pale golden as the sun.

She was as fair as I am dark, and at that instant, had she been a man, I would have fallen utterly in love. Even so, I believe I cried out weakly in awe; and when she turned her brilliant, omniscient gaze on me, I feared I would faint.

"Vlad, Vlad," said she, in a voice deep as Lake Hermannstadt and soft as smoke. "Will you not grant me the pleasure of introducing me to this lovely lady?"

The question brought tears to my eyes, for I knew that I looked a walking corpse and far from lovely. Her kindness touched me, and I managed a wavering smile as Vlad—without protest, to my surprise—at once bowed and said:

"Countess Elisabeth Bathory of Csejthe. May I have the honour of presenting to you my niece, Zsuzsanna Dracul."

Elisabeth held out a hand, gloved in powder-blue and marvellously perfumed—and, to my utter astonishment, warm. I took it and made with difficulty a small courtesy as she said to Vlad, "And not Tsepesh? Have you discarded the name entirely, then?"

He gave a solemn nod. His anger seemed to have entirely evaporated, as if he was actually hesitant to berate me in front of this woman, seeing as my presence pleased her. "While living, I was famed as the Impaler, the *tsepesh*. But now that I am immortal, I have other interests, and am more pleased to be known as Dracula—the son of the Devil."

"So the Dragon is indeed a Devil?" she asked cockily, then laughed—a sound as sweet as her perfume. But she fell silent and turned her attention to me the instant I murmured: "Your hand. It is warm—are you vampire or living? But you are far too beautiful to be mortal. . . ."

At that, her pink lips curved slyly, and she peered sidewise at Vlad from beneath a fringe of golden lashes, with an expression that said, *Shall I tell her?* But he lowered his gaze with a grave expression—and I felt she withheld something from me as she laughed ruefully and replied, "I am neither young nor mortal, my dear, but I suppose that, compared to Vlad, I am still a girl; I died a mere two hundred and eighty years ago."

As she spoke, the sensation of swooning overtook me again, and I would have fallen backward had she not caught my arms.

"Why, my dear Zsuzsanna, you are so weak! And how thoughtless we are to insist you remain on your feet." And she favoured Vlad with another enigmatic glance, saying, "I should like to be alone with her for a time."

Reluctance flitted over his features, but it was soon replaced by a look of maliciously smug understanding, as if some wicked revelation had just come to him. "Ah. Of course. . . . She can lead you to her chambers. There is another one there too—the serving-girl. . . ."

"Even better," answered she, and coiled a satiny arm round my waist. "Lead on, Zsuzsanna." Her aspect was one of helpfulness, as I was still unsteady on my feet; and so I permitted myself to lean my cheek against her shoulder that I might study that magnificent porcelain neck and breathe in her perfume. It had been so long since I'd laid eyes upon immortal beauty that her striking appearance quite overwhelmed me.

We made our way down the winding stairs while I listened to the music of Elisabeth's cello voice. She chattered on about her home in Vienna, of how wonderful that city was, and I whispered in reply that I had travelled to that city once and fallen in love with it.

"Well, then! You *will* come to my house there, and enjoy all that I have at your leisure. You are exhausted now for lack of power, but I can see beneath this premature aging. You are far too beautiful a creature to languish here in this desolate ruin of a castle." She glanced over her shoulder as if in recognition of Vlad's keener hearing—but I said:

"Do not worry. He can no longer hear so well as—"

"I know precisely how well he can hear, and he cannot detect us at this distance. Perhaps you were too weak to notice, but I did restore a modicum of his former strength to him to-night." She paused and turned her delicate features towards me, the long gold-gleaming curls falling forward from her shoulder onto an ample mother-of-pearl bosom. "We can speak in confidence now. My dear—did you know that he directed me not to restore your power to you?"

My lips drew back in an angry grimace; I managed to press them together, but still they quivered with rage. "He has been so cruel and heartless—you cannot imagine! I have only been good to him, and obedient—"

"*Obedient.*" She spat it out like the most onerous curse.

"—but he has tricked me, starved me until I was too weak even to hunt. For half a century I have trusted him, thinking that he had honest concern, even love, for me. He is my own uncle, whom I adored without reserve during my life, and he has preyed upon my affection in order to deceive me."

As I spoke, she came to a stop and listened intently to my words, her full lips compressing gradually into a thin line. I told her of his "generous" offer to hunt for us all, and of his cruelty to me and to poor Dunya. And when I had ended, she said slowly, "It is as I thought. The stupid mediaeval bastard!" And she took off again at full speed, dragging me along.

I broke into explosive laughter despite my weakness, and though I gasped, I could not catch my breath—or stop my giggles—to reply. I had never heard anyone refer to him without awe or fear, and to hear him so bluntly described startled and pleased me without end.

"Ah, the term amuses you," she said, her perfect forehead marred by the crease of a frown. "But think: Is my term for him so inaccurate? The year is 1893, but Vlad thinks it is still 1476. He treats women like chattel; I would not be surprised to hear that he has kept his serfs."

Still grinning, I confided, "No, they fled fifty years ago, out of fear when he broke the covenant. . . ."

She drew her head sharply up and back, her gaze keen and searching. "The covenant? His agreement with the Dark Lord? Is *this* why I was called?"

"This has nothing to do with the Devil," I said, and paused to gesture at my chamber door, for we had arrived at our destination. "He had broken his vow not to share immortality with one of his family, and the villagers all feared that he might begin to feed on them. Why do you laugh?"

For she had pressed a hand to her white bosom, spreading the blue-gloved fingers there, and begun to laugh without reserve. Indeed, she flung back her head, causing the cascade of golden curls to fall behind her shoulder and spill down her back. I drew my face close to hers and peered, mildly insulted that she should find mirth in such a serious thing.

But injury soon changed to amazement, for at that proximity my weakened vision could clearly detect her teeth: small, blindingly white, and even. And precisely like a mortal's, without the sharp, elongated eyeteeth.

"You are not a vampire," I marvelled.

She sobered then, though her lips still curved in a half-moon crescent; and keeping one arm round my waist, with her other hand she clasped mine, infusing me with her warmth. "Zsuzsanna darling, I am what I wish to be. As for my laughter—it is directed not at you but at Vlad, who obviously has infected you with his mediaeval idiocy. My dear, there is no Devil."

"Then what of the Dark Lord?" I had never encountered Him myself—in truth, I would be afraid to do so—but I had overheard many of His encounters with Vlad.

Her lips twitched with faint amusement, but she restrained her merriment out of consideration for me. "He is called the Dark Lord because that is what He prefers to be called. And He is not necessarily a he."

I stared at her, confounded, as she pushed open my chamber door and drew me across the threshhold. "Come, my darling. You have much to learn."

❖❘❖   ❖❘❖   ❖❘❖

3 MAY 1893, CONTINUED. Returned, returned—all my strength, all my power, all my joy and beauty, returned!

Elisabeth led me inside my own chamber (which, appropriately, were now the old servants' quarters), where my polished black casket lay open beside Dunya's. Again she worked to repress a grin at the sight of the coffins, and was not entirely successful. At my questioning glance, she murmured, "How very dramatic . . . and how like Vlad. He has always been more obsessed with death than life." She turned to me. "Zsuzsanna—are you able to keep a stunning secret from Vlad?"

"I am. My thoughts are my own; he is not privy to them."

"I did not mean that, my darling. I could protect your thoughts from him—though this is indeed better, for it will not provoke his suspicion. I meant: Can you keep patiently silent, even in the face of the most thrilling revelation?"

The diamond brilliant gleam of anticipation in her eyes quickened my own excitement. "Yes, of course—if silence is to my benefit."

"Oh, it shall be. I have returned only a portion of Vlad's power to him—I lied and told him I could only accomplish it in increments, for I wished to know his true intent before I restored him completely. I do not trust him. But I can see that you, Zsuzsanna, are possessed of a good, honest nature; therefore, I shall restore you to full vigour this very hour."

I clapped my hands together in eagerness, though the act took a great deal of effort. "And Dunya too?"

"As you wish. I have no doubt that she, too, must be deserving, if she has won the affection and loyalty of one so worthy as you. But here is the condition: You both shall perceive your restored beauty, and your strength—though to Vlad you will both appear as you are now. But you are neither to speak of your restoration, nor indulge your reclaimed powers in front of him. Do you swear to this?"

"I do," I answered, smiling for pure joy. I knew it

would be difficult to keep from striking Vlad a mighty blow, or flaunting my greater abilities before him; but I was desperate to regain the life I had known. I would have sworn to anything.

"Excellent," she breathed, then glanced round the vast, cold room. "Darling, lie down."

I moved obediently towards the casket, but she shook her head. "No, not there. That is too gruesome a place, and we want no reminders of death! On the bed, Zsuzsanna."

Together we moved to the room's far end, where a narrow, long-unused bed stood near a window. I drew back the heavy curtain surrounding the bed, and lay down upon the grey homespun blanket covering an ancient, lumpy mattress of straw.

Elisabeth followed and knelt beside me, then patted the unyielding mattress with a groan of pure indignation. "Zsuzsanna, this is a servant's bed!" She looked round the chamber with dawning realisation. "He has put you in the servant's quarters!"

I sighed. "I know. . . ."

"No more for you, my darling! When you come with me, you shall sleep on pure down, in silks and satins and grandeur befitting a queen!"

When you come with me . . .

Had I a heart, it would have begun to beat faster then, for the notion that I should live with one who truly cared for me—and was so exquisite to behold—evoked a thrill of anticipation. Had I understood her aright? Was she truly suggesting that I break away from Vlad, and go to live with her?

Was such a thing possible? I had always believed that Vlad's fate and his power were inextricably bound to mine; that if he perished, I should too. At least, that is what Vlad himself had told me—and I had always believed him. Had I suffered here needlessly in this desolate castle because he had lied?

Any anger I felt at Vlad was eclipsed by hope: perhaps he *had* lied to me, but that fact was actually more comforting than the thought that he had not. If I could break away from him, abandon this grim castle without fear and go with this amazing immortal woman to enjoy all that the grand cities of Europe have to offer . . .

"Do you mean," I whispered, "that I am not obliged to remain with him? He has told me that my existence depends upon his; is it—"

Before I could utter the word *true,* Elisabeth countered angrily, "Believe nothing he has told you! There is no Devil—but the Prince of Lies lives, and his name is Vlad. My dear, I have known him almost three centuries, and I know his selfish mind: he made you as you are not because he was lonely or because he loved you, but because you flattered him, appealed to his masculine pride. And if he has told you that his destruction will bring about your own, it was only because he wishes to keep you enslaved by loyalty."

At this notion, I began to weep, for the truth was that I *had* worshipped him slavishly when I was alive, and there were still remnants of girlish adoration in my heart. To think that his motive in Changing me had not been love—

"Ah, sweet child, don't waste your tears over the likes of *him.*" Still kneeling, she pulled off the powder-blue gloves and carelessly cast them onto the floor; then she reached forward and took my hands into hers. Her flesh—softer than a child's, and finer—possessed a febrile warmth, as though she had just held her palms over the fire for an hour to capture the heat. At the touch of it, I sighed. "You shall be returned to your former glory—perhaps more—and will have no further need of him." She leaned forward until the entire world consisted of nothing but her glittering diamond-and-sapphire gaze.

Brilliant as diamonds and just as cold, I thought, and shivered, abruptly seized by strange and irrational fear. "What shall you do to me?"

"A kiss," she whispered, bringing her face so close to mine that her sweet breath warmed my cheeks. "Only a kiss . . ." And she bent down until at last those soft, soft lips pressed against mine.

How shall I describe it? How does one describe infinity or bliss to those who have not experienced them?

I remember the night of my Change, after Vlad had left me to die—the sweet sensuality of it, the euphoria, the intriguing sharpening of all faculties: sight, sound, touch. The memory of those moments has stayed with me these five decades of undeath. Nothing, I thought, could supplant them; ah, but that was before Elisabeth's kiss!

So intense was that pleasure, so consuming, that for an unknown period I lost myself—lost all sense of my surroundings, of Elisabeth, of time, of anything at all in the world, save darkness and bliss. There was no I, no thing separate from this union with eternity.

Given a choice, I would never have left it, for beside it even the attraction of immortality dimmed. But all too soon, I discovered that I had returned to my body, and that I lay upon the uncomfortable straw mattress and rough blanket staring up into Elisabeth's delighted eyes.

"Oh," she breathed, putting a hand to her heart in amazement. "My Zsuzsanna . . . How beautiful you are!"

And with the other hand, she drew me up to my feet. I rose easily, gracefully, and laughed aloud at the infinite strength that suddenly flowed into my limbs. Still holding my hand, she stepped back a pace to study me, then abruptly grasped a lock of my long hair and said gleefully:

"Look, my darling, look!"

I looked—and saw that the silver was once again coal-black, and imbued with a sparkling indigo sheen.

"A mirror!" she cried, pacing about the spartan chamber, scanning its grey stone walls. "Where is the mirror? You must see!"

"There are no mirrors," I told her sadly. "Vlad destroyed them all long ago. Even if there were, I could not see my own reflection."

"Bah!" And she pulled my hand and dragged me out into the hall. "To my chambers at once!"

And together we ran up and down staircases; this time, I had no difficulty remaining by her side. When we had at last come to her room—on the eastern side of the castle, where we house guests—she flung the door open, revealing countless suitcases and trunks, and a stout, surly-faced young woman, as plain as Elisabeth was fair.

She gestured at the woman. "This is my attendant, Dorka; she is utterly discreet. Dorka, this is Vlad's niece, the Princess Zsuzsanna. You must treat her with the utmost respect."

Dorka gave a half-hearted, unsmiling curtsy.

"Fetch my mirror at once," Elisabeth ordered, her admiring gaze on me as she held out an impatient hand to her servant. When Dorka had moved from the sitting-room where we stood to the bedchamber, her mistress said, "So, Zsuzsanna, have you never seen yourself as an immortal?"

"Never."

"Well, you shall," she replied, just as Dorka came running and huffing back into the room with a lovely handheld mirror encased in fine gold and inlaid with pearls and diamonds. The servant placed it in Elisabeth's waiting hand, then withdrew to give us our privacy. "Look, Zsuzsanna. Look at what you have become."

I took the glass. And cried out in pleased amazement at the woman I saw there. Nay, *woman* is too unflattering a word. *Angel, vision*—these are words that better describe what I saw. Dunya had been right that my portrait did not give proper tribute to my beauty.

For fifty years I had not seen the woman in the mirror: a raven-haired young beauty, black tresses agleam with electric indigo, sharp teeth of pearl, lips of ruby, brown eyes asparkle with molten gold. My skin was as delicate and porcelain as Elisabeth's, and shimmering with mother-of-pearl glints of colour: rose, turquoise, seafoam-green. Even the sharp features I had inherited from Vlad—the thin hawkish nose, the pointed chin, the thick black brows —were softened now to delicate perfection.

I gazed up from this wonderment to see Elisabeth grinning broadly in approval, like an artist greatly pleased with her creation. She reached for the mirror, but I would not let it go; at that, she laughed softly.

"I was tempted to change the teeth," said she. "But I left it to your discretion, in case you found them aesthetically pleasing."

"But I *must* have them! How else shall I feed?"

Her voice lowered as though she were indulging a dark secret, and feared that someone might overhear. "My dear. There are as many different ways of 'feeding,' as you call it, as there are those brave enough to attain immortality."

"But Vlad created me," I protested. "And a vampire's bite begets another vampire. How else can it be?"

"It can be however you desire it, Zsuzsanna."

"But how?"

"Vlad's pact with the Dark Lord need not control you."

The thought of that mysterious creature, Devil or no, terrified me; I lowered the looking-glass and recoiled, whispering, "The Dark Lord . . ."

To distract me, she took my free hand and pressed the palm to my own cheek. "Tell me what you feel, my darling. Tell me what you feel."

For a full minute I was too overwhelmed to speak. At last, I sighed, "Warmth." My eyes had filled with tears; one at last spilled onto my cheek, my fingers. A hot tear.

"Is that not more pleasant than being cold as a corpse? Vlad is so obsessed with the ghoulish."

"You must revive Dunya!" I cried, grasping her arm and pulling her towards the closed casket. I returned her mirror to her and flung open the lid to reveal the sleeping occupant—so withered and frail.

Elisabeth approached and peered inside. "Ah . . . A sweet young peasant girl." She gazed up at me. "You must be patient. I have restored you in full and Vlad in part; my reserves of strength are diminished. I shall have to rest now, but I promise you I will deal with her to-morrow."

"But dawn is only a few hours away," I protested, eager to remain in her company. "And then you can rest all day. . . ."

"No, I shall be up in time to enjoy the sunrise. I only require two hours' rest as a rule, more when I have exerted myself as I have to-night. Dear me, child, Vlad's silly notion that you are restricted to the night hours has taken quite a toll on your enjoyment."

"But it is true—the sun pains me horribly. Yes, I can venture out if I must, but it weakens me and is dreadfully unpleasant."

"It need not be. Why should you not be able to enjoy both night and day?"

The question gave me pause. I remembered my one journey to Vienna a quarter-century before, and the disappointment I felt at not being able to ever go into the *Konditorei* and sample the buttery pastries, or enter the dress shops, with their glorious new fashions. The one dress I purchased in Vienna—from a trembling old tailor, near blind, the only one who would venture out at midnight to a hotel to fit me—is now two decades outdated. I looked at Elisabeth's gown, with its more modest *décolletage*, fitted hips, and narrower skirt—and a flounce of gathered fabric at the *derrière*, which I had never before seen.

"But how—" I began.

She shook her head. "We have much to talk about. Don't worry, darling"—for my disappointment was no doubt visible—"we will meet again to-morrow night. Until then . . ."

And she took my hand, bent down, and kissed it as a man might; a disturbing and undeniable thrill passed through me as she did so.

Dear God, I am in love!

✦✦ ✦✦ ✦✦

4 MAY 1893. I woke at sunset to find Elisabeth sitting in a chair beside my open casket—a sight that quickened my hope and excitement. To my further delight (and surprise), a smiling and beautiful young Dunya stood beside her.

"Dunya!" I sprang from my slumbering place with a single graceful leap. We embraced like sisters, laughing and weeping, and I kissed her cheek—warm like mine now, like her strong, strong arms. "My sweet! How beautiful you look!"

"Not so beautiful as you, *doamna!*" she cried. In truth, she looked faintly like me—with the thin chiselled nose and long dark hair (though hers was kissed with Russian red), and the soulful dark Roumanian eyes beneath arching brows.

"How do you know?" I teased her.

Smiling, Elisabeth held up the golden mirror.

I slid an arm round Dunya's tiny waist and turned to proffer my other hand to our benefactor, who rose and clasped it at once. "Elisabeth. You have been so kind to us, so good! Surely there must be some gift we can bestow upon you, some kindness which can serve as a pitiful attempt at repayment."

"Your happiness is sufficient joy for me." And she turned over my hand to reveal my palm, and kissed it.

Such an electric thrill coursed through my renewed body that I released Dunya and pressed a hand to my heart, lest I gasp aloud.

At that moment, the chamber door flew open; in the doorway stood Vlad. For a fleeting moment, I expected him to scream in fury to see Dunya and me fully restored. I tried to pull my hand from Elisabeth's grasp, recoiling as if ready to flee—but she held it fast, and gave me a reassuring glance that said, *He does not know.*

To my amazement, Vlad remained at the threshold, his expression one of benevolent courtesy.

"Ah, Cousin! I see you have taken pity upon our frail ladies. Please: I have prepared a banquet for your pleasure. It awaits you in the great dining hall, where I shall join you in but a few moments. Go there now. I need to consult with Zsuzsanna briefly in private."

I felt a fresh surge of dismay as Elisabeth gave a half-curtsy and left the room; even more dismay when I heard her footsteps echo down the hall, then the staircase.

He remained in the doorway peering after her, his eyes squinting with the strain. (Clearly, neither his vision nor his hearing could match mine.) And when she was what he believed a safe distance removed from us, he stepped inside and shut the heavy door behind him. I studied his expression, trying to judge from it whether he saw me as crone or beauty, and could find no astonishment, no rage, there— only cunning.

Such an old, ugly husk of a man. I had been mad all these decades: what use had I for him?

Abruptly he demanded, "Zsuzsanna, do you love me?"

I hesitated but an instant. In that brief time, he understood my silence too well; his expression darkened as he continued:

"It is Elisabeth. She has told you lies, put you under her spell, to make you fall in love with her. She has promised to restore you, has she not? I warn you—conspire with her, and you will embark on a dangerous path which can only end in your destruction."

I protested, my cheeks flaming hotly (such a long-forgotten sensation!). "Do you threaten me?"

But he thundered on, oblivious to my beauty or my words. "Do you know who she is? Surely she hasn't told you. She is the Tigress of Csejthe, the slaughterer of virgins. . . . During her lifetime, she tortured six hundred and fifty maidens to their deaths, and bathed in their blood; no doubt the figure has increased tenfold since her movement into undeath. You can trust nothing she says!"

"You are a liar," I said—then marvelled in silence at my own boldness. Never have I dared speak to him thus; I knew it would have meant my ruin, for I had always believed that he alone controlled my life and death. But I knew that, at last, I was stronger than he. Had he struck me at that moment, I would have killed him.

Such freedom! I laughed, drunk with the power of fearlessness.

He did in fact swing his arm to strike—but halted abruptly in midair in front of my face, prevented by an invisible force (ah, Elisabeth, my powerful saviour!). His eyes reddened with rage, and he parted his lips and released a low lupine growl, his face contorted into a Medusan mask.

"Stay away from her, Zsuzsanna. Stay away, or I shall be forced to retaliate!"

I said nothing, only watched him spin on his heel and storm out, slamming the door behind him with such force that it rattled for several seconds.

Dunya stepped up to stand beside me; I think she had been cowering behind me all this time. She put a soft hand upon my shoulder and whispered, "*Doamna*. Do you think he can really hurt us if we see Elisabeth again? She is so kindly. . . ."

Again I slipped an arm round her waist, but stared ahead at the trembling wooden door.

"To hell with him," I said slowly. "To hell with him."

⇥4⇤

The Diary of Zsuzsanna Dracul

5 MAY 1893. I woke from a sweet dream to the sound of my dear dead mother's voice calling softly:

Wake up, Zsuzsanna. Wake up, child, it's almost mid-day. . . .

I opened my eyes, not to my mother's worn face, but to the exquisite and youthful countenance of Elisabeth. This time she wore a fetching gown of cream-coloured moire, with a narrow standup collar of stiff lace that fringed a more daring *décolletage*.

I smiled at the sight of her; but then my expression turned to wide-eyed awe at the realisation that beyond her, a yellow shaft of sunlight was streaming in through the unshuttered window.

And it did not pain me. Nor did I feel in any way weakened by it.

Those revelations widened my eyes even further, and I emerged once more from my grim resting-place with a bound and hurried over to the window to gaze unblinking out at the beautiful day. Above, in a blue, blue sky, the sun blazed.

"It *is* mid-day!" I cried, and whirled round, slack-jawed yet smiling, to stare in tearful gratefulness at Elisabeth. "How is this possible?"

She returned my gaping grin and, rather than reply to the posed question, said instead: "Will you accompany me for some fresh air?" At my hesitance, she added, "Vlad is sleeping, as you know. I have made sure he will hear nothing. We can meet now during the day—every day, if you wish—and he shall never know."

I believed her gladly, for I remembered that yesterday night, he had not perceived my beauty. In answer, I grabbed her arm and together we ran giggling down the winding staircase through the grand hall and out the great spiked door into the blessed outdoors.

Elisabeth slowed upon the steps and let go my hand. I scrambled down them onto the grounds and pulled off my slippers. The instant my bare feet touched the soft, cool grass, I could no longer resist: I spread my arms like wings and spun round in circles like a frenzied child who has been closeted for a long bleak winter.

Such an intoxicating spring! The plum trees were fragrant with blossom, and the open lawn was scattered with wildflowers: bluebells, crimson poppies, daisies, snowy alyssum. The air echoed with the cheerful calls of birds—larks and robins, not the melancholy song of the nightingale nor the mournful cry of the owl, the only birdsong I have heard for half a century.

And as I spun in joyful delirium, I closed my eyes and lifted my face to the sky—to the sun, whose warm, soothing light upon my face seemed at that moment more delicious, more precious, than anything I had experienced as an immortal.

When at last I fell, dizzy and laughing, onto the cool ground beside a patch of intricately delicate Jack-in-the-pulpit, I rolled over onto my back to stare at the clouds in the turquoise sky, and called out to my benefactress:

"Elisabeth! You have been so good to me! You have returned my beauty, my strength—and now you have returned to me the whole world!" For that is how I felt: that I had been confined to the night, living only half an existence. And now the other half of life had been restored to me. "Can I do nothing for you in return?"

"You can share with me the young gentleman guest."

"A guest?" I sat suddenly, pressing my fingers behind me into the grass, into the damp soil, and stared at her. She had sat upon a step, as heedless of propriety as a young boy—knees spread wide, an elbow resting atop one of them, chin supported by a palm. Caressed by the warm breeze, the shining cream skirt billowed out onto the dirty stone, its wearer apparently fearless of its being soiled. Her expression signalled that she did not share my wild enthusiasm for the scenery; to her, it was something commonplace. What entertained her was my joy, for her gaze was fixed solely on me, and she wore the slight, delighted smile of an owner watching her puppy gambol unawares.

All this I perceived in an instant before I demanded, "When did a guest arrive?" The thought provoked a thrill of desire, and the realisation that I was indeed hungry, very hungry.

"Last evening."

"And how did we fail to hear them?"

Elisabeth sighed. "My fault, I'm afraid. Vlad must have put a glamour upon us so that we heard nothing when he arrived with his visitor; I confess I was so intoxicated by your beauty yesterday night that my vigilance lapsed, else I would have detected his pitiful attempt at sorcery and neutralised it at once. But there is indeed a guest, my darling: he lies snoring within his chambers now. I heard the noise and went to investigate. He is rather handsome, and quite healthy and strong. Shall we visit him?" Her tone turned coy and teasing. "I see appetite in your eyes, Zsuzsanna."

My desire warred with fear. "Vlad would never forgive it! He would destroy me if he found my mark upon his guest's neck!"

"Then he shall not find it. Regardless, I would not permit him to harm you."

"How is either possible?"

She gestured smugly at me amidst the springtime glory. "How can *this* be possible? All things are, my darling, if you trust me."

I drew in a long, yearning breath as I rose to my feet. "Then let us go greet our young guest at once!"

I picked up my slippers and hurried barefoot up the steps, where she, too, had risen and awaited me. We linked arms and once again ran laughing like mischievous schoolgirls through the great hallway, up a different set of winding stairs until at last we arrived in front of the carved wooden door that led to one of the guest chambers.

Elisabeth was right: from within emerged the sound of stertorous snoring, so loud that I was surprised the heavy door did not rattle. I clapped a hand over my mouth to suppress a giggle and, when I could manage to speak, whispered to my companion: "His poor wife!"

"You need not be so quiet," she replied, in a normal voice. "As you can hear, he is sleeping soundly." And at that, we both laughed softly as she swung open the door. "He is yours, my darling; take him as you wish. I shall watch, and indulge myself a bit afterwards. One caveat only: that you leave him alive and strong enough so neither he nor Vlad will be able to detect a change. I will take care that he has no wound; you must take care that he is not pale enough to arouse suspicion."

Had I been thinking clearly, I would have asked her why she could not deal with the problem of his colour, if she could cause the wound to instantly heal. At that moment, I was too intrigued by what her "indulgence" might be—and then, instantly, all thought was blotted out when my nose caught the gentleman's scent.

I smelled warm blood and skin, overlaid by the cloying smell of two or three days' sweat. Elisabeth must have detected it, too, for she whispered to me: "He has obviously been travelling for some time," and held her nose.

Smelly or not, the young man lying on his back, arms and legs spread wide in imitation of da Vinci's naked man, was a handsome sight—if one ignored his gaping, drooling mouth and the way it sputtered each time he released a window-pane-rattling snore.

But snoring or not, he had neatly hung a wool suit and hat upon a nearby chair; their quality indicated the owner was an up-and-coming, if drab, young gentleman. And he himself was of sufficient quality to suit me, for his uncovered arms (flung out atop the blankets at a ninety-degree angle to his torso) and upper chest were strong and muscular enough, neither too fat nor too thin. His brown curls were a perfect match for his face, which had slightly plump pink cheeks and a short turned-up nose; overall, the impression was that of a man whose boyish features would always make him appear five years younger than his actual age.

"He needs a bath," whispered Elisabeth; but in truth I did not care. So great was my hunger and eagerness to press my lips to the man's throat—but first, to take advantage of other attributes, so that his blood might taste all the sweeter—that I would not have cared had he been wal lowing in fresh manure. Indeed, I scarcely noticed when Elisabeth crept away, and felt no concern over it. My attention was riveted on the man; and slowly, delicately, that I might not rouse him, I lifted sheet and blankets from his chest. He wore a plain white nightshirt, but had left the top three buttons undone so that it gaped open to reveal more of his chest and its thick pelt of more brown curls. Carefully, I drew the bedclothes downward to his feet, to disclose further delights—for the nightshirt had ridden up and become twisted, entirely exposing him and another cluster of chestnut hair . . . from whence emerged an undeniably erect member.

Now, I have long believed myself damned; and early in my immortalhood, I vowed that I would deny myself no pleasure now, in case I should ever be destroyed and have to endure the eternal agonies of Hell. For I had lived life as a crippled, homely spinster, doomed never to experience the attentions of a lover. Very soon after my Change, I discovered the most wonderful of secrets: that the blood of a man in the throes of passionate release tastes more heavenly than any nectar, and that my pleasuring him increases my own ecstasy (from the act and from drinking his affected blood) tenfold.

And so I crawled beside him on the bed, using my ability to hypnotise to keep him from waking. I intended to take him at once, swiftly, before Elisabeth returned, for the truth was that I felt oddly shy at doing so in front of her. It had never slowed me before—I had never been shy in front of Vlad or Dunya or my poor dead brother—and I had taken two and three men at a time, upon occasion. But in Elisabeth's case, I felt oddly guilty . . . as though I were being somehow unfaithful.

But before I could lift my skirts and roll onto my beloved victim, Elisabeth hurried back into the room.

"Come, bring him," she whispered, gesturing, her sapphire eyes aglitter with anticipation. "Dorka is preparing a bath."

"You need not whisper," I told her. "He is entranced." I opened my mouth to tell her that I did not believe myself patient enough to wait for him to bathe; I was resolved at that point to simply drink his blood. But ere I could speak, she interrupted:

"A pity." Her features suddenly resolved themselves into an impish grin. "Let us have a bit of fun with him first, shall we?"

She simply stared at the sleeping man, and inclined her chin towards him. He groaned and at once stirred; immediately, I leapt up from the bed.

He opened his eyes—kindly, light brown eyes they were—and for a moment, clearly could not remember where he was. But then memory dawned, and he emerged more fully from slumber; at that point, his gaze fell upon us two women, and he pushed himself up to a sitting position with a start. At first those kindly brown eyes registered wild surprise at the sight of strangers in his room; and then he looked down at his exposed privates, and that surprise metamorphosed into such intense and pitiful dismay that I thought I should explode with contained laughter.

"*Dear God!*" he swore in a cultured English baritone and, moving swift as the undead, pulled the blankets up to his chin and held them there, eyes bulging, face and ears flushed impossibly scarlet. "Ladies, you have me at a *dreadful* disadvantage!"

I could bear no more; I clapped my hand over my mouth and shuddered with soft laughter. Before I could recover enough to reply, Elisabeth said, in excellent English (which should not have surprised me any more than her

facility with Roumanian, for the mortal Hungarians routinely master ten or twenty languages before they are
grown):

"Our apologies, good sir, for the intrusion!" And she
gave a sweeping curtsy, her expression as solemn as mine
was gleeful. "But we tried to rouse you by knocking, and
could not. The master"—and here I shot her a gaze both
astounded and merry, which she utterly ignored—"gave us
strict orders yesterday that we were to draw you a bath no
later than one o'clock this afternoon, and see that you
enjoyed it. I have come to tell you that it is ready. The
water will not remain hot for long. Will you kindly come
with us, sir?"

He hesitated, glancing from me to Elisabeth, unlikely
servants, either of us: me with my dark hair flowing un-
bound to my waist, in my grey Viennese gown of watered
silk, twenty years outdated and worn nearly to tatters, and
Elisabeth in the beautiful cream gown.

And both of us unworldly beautiful.

I saw that he was on the verge of refusing, but Elisabeth detected his reluctance and said at once: "Please, good
sir! Our master is stern, and given to outbursts of temper;
if he finds that you have refused, he will surely beat us both
until we bleed!"

That caused him to blink rapidly and stammer, desperately searching for an appropriate excuse; but all he
could think to say was "How barbaric!"

Elisabeth grew bolder now, and gave a gentle tug upon
his wool-sleeved arm, her voice distraught with feigned
terror (whilst I bit both my lips and struggled to maintain
a sober expression; this was becoming easier, as my glee
was quickly being overwhelmed by hunger). "Please, sir.
Come with me!"

His discomfort was complete, but the kindness reflected in his eyes won out. "Very well, miss," said he. "But please wait outside the door until I fetch my smoking-jacket."

To this she acquiesced, and we both withdrew to give the man his privacy; but behind the closed door, we grabbed each other's arms and rested our head each upon the other's shoulder, and shook hard with silent laughter.

Presently, we heard the stranger approach the door; by the time he opened it, we were once again poker-faced servants. He was dressed discreetly now, in long pants, leather slippers, and the smoking-jacket of plum wool with a black velvet collar and velvet belt at the waist. The brown curls were damp and neatly combed, but his cheeks were still flushed bright as he told Elisabeth and me, "Very well, ladies. Lead on to the bath."

We did so, walking towards Elisabeth's quarters in silence until at last our mortal companion spoke.

"I must confess, ladies—you are hardly dressed like serving-girls."

At that, I smiled, but Elisabeth said quite seriously, "Well, sir, our master can be quite cruel at times; but he can also be quite generous." Again, I had to swallow my laughter.

The gentleman accepted this with a nod, and we continued on without further conversation until we arrived at Elisabeth's room.

Dorka waited within with several large towels draped over her arm, and told her mistress in Hungarian: "I have prepared the bath."

Elisabeth nodded as she took the towels, then turned to gesture at the guest. "In here, if you would, sir."

He followed, his expression one of increasing awkwardness, and when we arrived inside the bedchamber—in whose center awaited a round, claw-footed iron tub filled with steaming water—he called us to a stop. "Ladies, I thank you for your help. That will be all, please." He nodded in dismissal.

Elisabeth gazed at him, stricken. "But, sir—if I do not follow my master's orders exactly . . . He told us that we should make sure of your enjoyment."

With wicked glee, I picked up her cue, and moved over to him; with a single pull, I loosed the belt of his smoking jacket, which opened to reveal the long nightshirt, tucked into his pants.

Are all men of this era such prudes? He scrambled to pull the jacket closed and said huffily, "See here! This is quite improper, and I am engaged to be married!"

Then Elisabeth moved in and, over his indignant protests, pulled off the jacket the instant I pried it open again. The jacketless Englishman struggled to free himself, but we were stronger and held him fast.

"Do not be so modest, sir!" Elisabeth told him, with such sincerity that I was almost convinced she was a servant, acting on Vlad's orders. "It is the custom in our country for women to assist men in bathing."

And as she pinned his arms behind him, he yelping softly in dismay, I knelt, unbuttoned his trousers, and pulled them off. Beneath was a knee-length pair of men's silk under-trousers. These I pulled off swiftly while the Englishman shrieked in horror; then off came the leather slippers, one at a time.

But a final challenge remained: the long nightshirt. Elisabeth released first one arm, then the next, as I quickly pulled the nightshirt up over his now-aubergine face to reveal at last his nakedness. At once he doubled over with embarrassment and dismay in a pathetic attempt to hide his body from our view; had his hands been free, he would undoubtedly have shielded his privates.

Elisabeth clicked her tongue in disapproval and addressed me in Roumanian. "These Victorians. Too many clothes. It's unhealthy." To the guest, she said in English, "Into the tub with you, sir!"

He made no move to comply. And so, still grasping his arms behind him, she lifted him straight up off his feet and deposited him into the steaming water.

He entered it with a small cry at the scalding heat, and at first remained standing tiptoe in water up to his thighs. But propriety soon overcame fear, and he let go a gasp as he squatted low in the tub. Soon water covered all but his head and neck; these were veiled by rising steam. He moved close to the side near us, which effectively hid the rest of him from our view.

From the tub's rim, Elisabeth lifted a cake of soap—fine, French-milled soap redolent with her perfume—and pointedly handed it to him. "Wash yourself, sir."

Still squatting, he extended a dripping arm and took it. A comical moment of indecision followed, one in which his expression telegraphed every thought: How should he accomplish the task in front of these feminine guards? Common sense dictated that he should rise in order to make best use of the soap—but once again, modesty prevailed. He remained squatting in water up to his neck, and thus ran the soap over his entirety.

"I am finished," he announced. "I should like a towel."

"You are not quite done," I told him, as I began to unfasten my bodice. The pewter silk parted to reveal my white breasts—unfettered by Victorian undergarments.

He gasped and averted his eyes in dutiful and gentlemanly fashion, his expression warring between horror and furtive desire. As the silk rustled to a heap on the stone and I stepped forward from it in my naked glory, lovelier than any vision of Venus emerging from the sea, he peered sly and sidewise at me.

I climbed into the great iron tub and knelt beside him, the liquid catching my waist-length indigo hair and setting it afloat like lazily drifting seaweed. Beneath the wavering water, my skin shimmered, phosphorescent white beside his darker, drabber skin. The warmth was delightful.

Behind me, I heard Elisabeth's voice, edged now with unmistakable excitement; and I knew then that I would be capable of doing what I wished in her presence without shame. "Do not be alarmed, sir," she said. "It is simply our custom to let the women bathe after the men. It is considered quite proper. . . ."

But the Englishman hovered near the tub's edge, knees and shins pressed against the hot iron, fingers gripping the rim. "Please, miss—a towel! I am rather uncomfortable, for in my country, the custom is decidedly different."

I moved closer until our legs touched; he recoiled at once, splashing water everywhere in his desperation. I knew then that his decision to be faithful to his betrothed was unfortunately a sincere one and backed by great determination, so I reached out with a dripping hand and turned his stubbled chin towards me.

His will was strong, but not unduly so; the instant his gaze met mine, he fell under my glamour and sighed, content to be relieved of all troubling inhibitions.

"You are the most exquisitely beautiful creature I have ever seen," he whispered, and reached for me.

We kissed, pressing our lips together feverishly—he with passion enough to meet mine, as though he, too, had been denied the experience of love for two decades. I thought I should go mad, so great was my yearning for his body and blood; my hungry kisses turned quickly to tiny, rapid nips upon his neck and shoulders. He rose, groaning, and lifted me with him so that his kisses might travel downward from my face to neck to breasts.

I moved backward then, to his dismay (for he reached after me in desperation), and leaned against the tub's side, beckoning him to come to me. This he did and, even under trance, experienced a temporary confusion at what precisely should transpire next: my Englishman, it seemed, was a virgin. But when he pressed next to me, I hopped up to sit upon the tub's rim, and wound my knees round his hips.

Intent on showing him how it was done, I had quite forgotten about Elisabeth's presence until she appeared beside us—now incandescently naked, and more gloriously so than I. I found myself gazing deep into her electric-blue eyes, simply astonished by her beauty. As taken as I was with our houseguest, I was even more taken by her bare flesh, aglitter like fresh snow in the sunlight. And, I confess, by her breasts—large and full, yet firm as a young maiden's, their milky whiteness crowned by nipples as delicately pink as cameo. I yearned to reach out and touch them, but was so startled to find myself lusting after a woman that I held back, and instead watched as she assisted the Englishman in his efforts to explore new territory.

As, her fingers tightly encircling him, she guided him towards me, I tilted my hips to permit him entry; at the instant it occurred, he gasped in astonished joy, the purely grateful sound of one who at last knows: *Ah, so this is what I have so long been denied!*

He began to thrust—wildly, urgently, filled with such unbearable desire that he could hold back not at all; I, too, could not restrain myself, but clung to him in desperation, crying out with each movement. In my delirium, I was but faintly aware of Elisabeth's arm between us, her thumb and forefinger a tight ring grasping his member at its base, that its increased firmness might grant my lover and me more pleasure.

But too soon, too soon, he arched against me, crying out as I was flooded with internal warmth. At that instant, my urgent desire gave way to an even more urgent hunger: I bit savagely into the warm, wet skin at the juncture of his neck and shoulder and drank blood sweeter, more ambrosial, than any I have ever drunk, for the taste was enhanced by the Englishman's intense virginal ecstasy and by my own hungry longing.

He moaned, arching now with a victim's delight, for to receive the dark kiss is an infinitely sensual pleasure.

"Tear him!" Elisabeth cried beside me. "Tear him, make him bleed—Vlad will not know!"

I tore with teeth sunk tight into his flesh (taking care to stay clear of the neck, lest I inadvertently kill him), shaking my head as a dog does when it has caught a rat. My lover groaned again, for pain was joy to him now. Strong dark blood spattered upon my cheeks, my eyelids, my chest and hands; I drank. Drank until I was drunk, until I was blind, until I forgot myself and my surroundings utterly, deaf to all save the slow throb of the Englishman's heart.

I would have continued mindlessly until its beating stopped—but strong arms pulled me away. I looked up, blinking like an owl in the lantern's glare, and saw Elisabeth, catching the young man as he fell, lifting him from the water, laying him upon a linen towel spread on the floor.

Beautiful Elisabeth, her face spattered with English blood.

No angel, no goddess, could dare aspire to such loveliness. And then she put those strong hands round my shoulders, beneath my knees, and lifted me from the red-tinged water. I clasped her neck, Psyche rescued by Eros.

And when she had set me down beside my lover with infinite gentleness and proffered me a towel, she knelt between me and my fainted victim and with relish rubbed cheeks and tongue, breasts and belly, against his wound, covering herself in his blood. Then she dipped her fingers into his wounds and reached, dripping, to paint my smiling lips, my belly, my breasts. The latter she approached with great delicacy and a feathery touch, spiralling slowly inward from the outside of one breast until she reached its centre. There she lingered, tracing ever smaller and more inward circles until I could bear it no longer and shuddered in delicious anticipation, my legs writhing against the cold stone as if they yearned to escape.

But my heart would not let me.

It was already a contented captive, even before Elisabeth bent down to embrace me. I was sated with blood, dreamy and dazed by the thrill of feeding. But when she pressed her mouth against mine and I felt her tongue work hard against my lips, savouring the blood there, I realised that my hunger had been appeased—but not my physical desire.

Was it the forbiddenness of our love that filled me with a hotter fire than I have ever known? I reached up to press a palm against her back, another against the nape of her neck, and pulled her down upon me. It was then I experienced another revelation: that to-day, for the first time in my eighty years of existence, I had experienced love as it was meant—warm flesh against warm flesh.

She kissed my face, my breasts, my belly, using her tongue to clean each area with sensual, deliberate grace. Then she rose and reached for the Englishman's wound again; once more, she dipped her fingers in his blood.

I cried out softly as she (my hands tremble so at the memory, I can scarce write) put those bloodied fingers betwixt my legs, and wiped the blood at the place where the Englishman had so recently been. Then with those fingers she entered me, and bent low again to lick away the blood.

I remember little else except for the instant I fell out of the world into that great and glorious abyss of pleasure, so distantly aware of my own screams it seemed as though someone else had made them.

Yet as I lay, eyes closed, undone by delight, I *did* hear the sensuous cries of another: Elisabeth, my darling Elisabeth, who lay beside me. I smoothed damp curls back from her forehead until she recovered and opened blue, blue eyes to smile at me.

I leaned down and kissed her tenderly. Then we two entwined our arms and held each other for a long silence.

At last, I have what Vlad long ago promised me but never gave: an eternal lover.

When finally we rose, I looked down at the sleeping Englishman, and saw that the wounds inflicted upon his shoulder had entirely healed.

Elisabeth took me out into the sitting-room, where a half-dozen large trunks sat beside another half-dozen suitcases, and opened one. For herself, she took out a stunning silk dressing-gown of pale yellow edged with broad eggshell lace; for me, a dressing-gown of electric-blue satin trimmed with black velvet. Together we returned to my chambers. At the open door, I stopped, and exclaimed in dismay:

"But Dunya! We have forgotten about poor Dunya!"

Elisabeth patted my shoulder reassuringly. "She will have many more chances; as long as I am here, she cannot starve into oblivion, regardless of what Vlad might do. But for now, my darling, it is best that no one else know about our secret meetings."

I sighed in reluctant acquiescence, though in fact I felt it utterly selfish to deny my trustworthy little servant a chance to feed.

At the unhappiness in my downcast eyes, Elisabeth put a finger beneath my chin and tenderly lifted it until our gazes met.

"Go and rest now," she said soothingly, "and when night comes, you will rise again so that Vlad does not suspect. I doubt he will let us meet then, but I promise you that I shall do everything possible to convince him that you and Dunya *must* feed. And if he agrees, then you can give your supper entirely to her." Pausing, she brushed my lips with the lightest of kisses.

"As for you, my darling . . . To-morrow, if it pleases you, we can watch the sun rise together."

The thought so gladdened me that I cried out, "Oh, Elisabeth! I shall love you forever!"

And at that, she smiled.

❖❖ ❖❖ ❖❖

9 MAY 1893. Once more, I woke to the sound of Elisabeth's voice, and to the sight of her glorious face.

Last night I can scarcely remember, save that I was happy to see that, as Elisabeth had said, Dunya was still looking and feeling strong. This was a comfort to me, as I still felt guilt over not having invited her to yesterday's feeding.

Ah, but yesterday noon I remembered then and remember now, and each time I do, I blush. Last night I did not see Elisabeth; I suspect Vlad felt obliged to keep her in his presence for lack of trust, and for my sake, she would not disobey his order to eschew my company.

It is just as well I did not see her then; for even in Vlad's presence, I would not have been able to restrain my joy at the sight of her.

"My darling," Elisabeth said softly, and reached down into my casket to smoothe a hand across my forehead and cheek, as tenderly as a mother would caress her child. "It pains me so to see you sleeping in this—this contraption. Vlad's limitations are *not* yours, though he might wish you to believe so. Will you not stay in my bed?"

"I will do whatever pleases you." I took her hand from my cheek and kissed it.

"It will please me to have you with me."

Her statement pleased me, but in truth I listened to it with but half my attention—for I was gazing beyond her at the unfettered window, and seeing there the first rosy rays of dawn streaming through pearl-grey clouds.

Eager as a child, I turned to her. "Can we go outside? Now? I want to see it!"

"It's drizzling, I fear, and at any moment will begin to rain harder." She touched a hand to her carefully arranged golden curls as if the mere mention of the weather might ruin them.

"I don't care! You can stay here—I just want to be out in it."

At the first three words, she tossed back her head and laughed indulgently, and remained smiling as I finished. "I'll go with you, my dear. I had no inkling you felt so strongly. But if you wish it, then it shall be done!"

And so I took her hand and climbed from my ghoulish resting-place, and together we walked the same path we had taken the day before. Her yellow silk dressing-gown and the dark blue satin dressing-gown she had given me rustled softly against the floor. As we walked, she turned to me, her expression one of unmistakable appreciation of my body, and said:

"That looks quite beautiful on you, darling. You may keep it, and I want you to pick out some of my dresses for you to wear; Dorka can do any needed alterations."

"You are so kind, Elisabeth!" I felt literally aglow with love, as though my heart were a great furnace, kindled at last.

"And you are so beautiful, my Zsuzsanna. . . ."

At last we arrived at the great wood-and-iron door and pushed it open. I drew in a breath at once of the damp fresh air, and marvelled at the fine misting drizzle. Beyond lay a grey landscape, and a grey, clouded sky.

True, I was disappointed—how beautiful the drizzle would have looked, asparkle like diamonds in the sunshine. Even so, I was so glad just to be out-of-doors in the day that I stepped forward, wanting only to stand in it, to feel the cool water against my face, my skin.

But when I tried to run over the threshold and skip down the stairs, I cried out in even deeper disappointment; for, try as I might, I could not move farther than the doorway, held back by an invisible force.

I could not go outside. In bewildered desperation, I looked to Elisabeth for help.

What I saw quite surprised me.

She, too, stood in the doorway and, with a vehement Hungarian curse, stomped her small slippered foot. As I watched, the whites of her eyes reddened to scarlet, ruby against sapphire, the contrast eerily pronounced against the paleness of her skin. It was the only time I have seen her look unlovely, and it quite startled me.

Indignant, she wheeled to face me. "He fears us! And so he has taken to *this* pitiful magic. . . ." She waved in disgust at the doorway.

But I had utter faith in her abilities; had she commanded me to walk upon water, I should have. I waited
for her to stride past me, to step boldly outside, then permit me to do the same.

She did not; she lingered beside me upon the threshold, her expression indignant. She could go outside no
more than I. My disappointment was complete, for I had
honestly believed her omnipotent.

Because of the doorway's angle, I could not see the
sun rising in the rosy clouds, nor the snow on the distant
mountains; with these, I should have to content myself by
gazing through the window. But I leaned forward as far as
I could, extended my arm through the doorway, and
turned my palm to the sky.

There I felt sweet, soft rain, cool and gentle upon my
upturned palm; the drops splashed upon black velvet—
upon which they beaded—and deep blue satin, which they
darkened. There is something soothing about rain during
the day, and something mournful about it in the dead of
night.

At last, I slowly lowered my arm and turned sadly to
Elisabeth. "We are trapped."

Her expression was one of poorly repressed outrage,
though the red in her eyes had faded somewhat. "Indeed
not!"

"Then why can we not go outside?"

She frowned, as if my question had been highly impertinent, and with exasperation explained: "Because Vlad has
pulled an unexpected trick. Don't worry, Zsuzsanna. I
shall soon set it right. But for now, come. Let us amuse
ourselves in other ways."

She led me back to the Englishman's room, from
whence, once again, the sound of snoring emerged. Elisabeth turned towards me, a cream goddess in sunny silk,

and reached forward to lightly trace the outline of my collar with her fingertip. I shuddered slightly at her feathery touch against the skin of my collarbone, my breast, and was at once on fire.

"He is not so strong to-day," she said, with a coquettish tilt to her head, and the shine of pure desire in her eyes. "But perhaps you could enjoy a small drink. . . ."

I wanted her more than him, and was about to say, *No, let us go to your chambers, and spend the day in your bed.* But she had already pushed open the door and entered.

I followed with only partial reluctance; the thought of dining again was not altogether disagreeable, as yesterday I had not been able to drink my fill. Even so, I was by no means overwhelmed by hunger. Thus I entered without haste, but with mild curiosity: who was this Englishman, and how had he come to be here? Obviously, on the nights Vlad went to hunt for us, he had gone instead to Bistritz to post letters to this man. . . .

Rather than go at once to the bed to claim my sleeping victim, I instead passed by the armoire, where a number of papers were neatly arranged in stacks. I glanced at the top letter, which was apparently a legal document of some type, prepared by a certain Peter Hawkins, Esquire— and signed by "Count" V. Dracula. "So!" I said, with a glance at the man snoring beneath the canopy—once again, with the bed curtains left open. I took no care to keep my voice low, for Elisabeth had shown me how to prevent others (including Vlad) from hearing me. "Our young Englishman is a solicitor employed by a man named Hawkins. And he has been transacting legal business on behalf of a certain V. Dracula."

Elisabeth's eyes narrowed with intrigue; she at once moved away from the bed to stand beside me. Whilst I riffled through one stack of papers, she examined another, then picked up a small leather-bound diary and began to read.

"What language or code he writes in, I cannot say," she said after a time. "But he has written his name here; Harker. Jonathan Harker, Esquire."

I scarce heard her, for I had more carefully examined the legal document and scanned the stack of correspondence. I was stricken like Saul on the road to Damascus with a blinding revelation; and now, I felt my eyes blaze with the same red fury I had earlier seen in Elisabeth's.

For I suddenly understood that this man was not here simply as a houseguest, to quench Vlad's thirst. No, he was here for a far more sinister purpose: to assist Vlad in moving to England.

A half century ago, Vlad had sworn to me that he would take me from this dreary country to an exciting life in London. Only our difficulties with my brother, Arkady, and his son, the accursed Van Helsing, have prevented us from escape.

Now he was going at last—whilst I would remain behind to starve. Why else had he prevented me from leaving the castle?

I turned to her, waving a paper in my hand. "This!" I hissed. "*This* is a title deed—to property Vlad has purchased in secrecy!"

She stopped reading the paper in her hand, and faced me, one golden brow arched in an extreme inverted V as she peered at the document I clutched. "London, it seems," she said, thoughtful, remaining calm despite my rage. "Purfleet is outside London." And she held up to my gaze another signed paper, this a bill of sale for another estate. "Piccadilly. In London proper."

Overwhelmed by rage, I sat abruptly in a faded brocade chair.

"Has he spoken to you of this?" Elisabeth stepped behind me and put a comforting hand upon my shoulder.

I shook my head, and she sighed. "My darling Zsuz-sanna . . . I think he means to abandon you here."

"The bastard!" I swore, seething. "He means to leave us here to starve! He means to *destroy* us—we who have only helped him!"

She knelt beside me, her expression one of utter sympathy, and wound an arm about my knees, as if to comfort me. "Zsuzsanna, I swear to you that he will not succeed! I have expected this all along, and made plans for it."

"Then why did you come here, if you knew he would betray you?"

"He told me of you in his letter. I did not come to help him. I came to free you."

At that, I leaned down and embraced her, pressing her face to my shoulder, and felt hot tears sting my eyes. "My sweet Elisabeth, you have been so good to me!"

She held me so tightly, and I her, that when we let go, we both gasped. "I shall be even better," she said, with a look of infinite resolve. "I only ask that you trust me."

"There is no question of that. But what shall we do? We cannot leave the castle."

"Wait, my sweet. Only wait. When the time is right, we shall leave."

"I cannot wait!" I cried, and struck my heel against the floor like an angry child. "Why can we not kill him *now*? You are so powerful, Elisabeth. Why haven't you yet destroyed him, and freed us from this castle?"

At that she sighed and remained quiet a time, staring beyond me at some distant, invisible sight. Finally, she met my gaze again. "When another century, perhaps two, have passed, Zsuzsanna, then you will understand. Immortality carries with it one unavoidable burden, that of *ennui*. It pleases me to have a new sport—to avenge your suffering by destroying Vlad.

"But it would be far too simple to destroy him here; and, I confess, it would be difficult, because his power is greater here than anywhere. And it would be far too swift —for he has inflicted far too much suffering in both life and undeath to die quickly, without anguish." She straightened, suddenly infused with excitement. "Let us give chase! Let us pursue him to London and torment him there, unravel his plans. And when he is utterly confounded, only then we will reveal that *we* are the source of his suffering."

She clasped my waist and drew me closer to her, then planted upon my lips a fervent kiss. "Let me take you to London, Zsuzsanna! Let us conquer both Vlad and the city. I will dress you in the finest satins and silks, and adorn you with jewels; you will be so beautiful that the entire country will fall at your feet and worship you." And she stroked my cheek with her hand and gazed so lovingly at me that I was mollified.

In silence, she rose and drew me to my feet, then led me over to the young man. It pleased me to let him sleep this time. I ever so delicately pierced the unblemished skin of his throat, and just as delicately drank.

And when, lips smeared with Mr. Harker's dark blood, I lifted my face, there was Elisabeth beside me— gasping with lust, her eyes as desirous as those of any man who has gazed upon my beauty. At once she lunged against me, tore open my robe, and licked clean my lips. And again she dipped her fingers in his wound—small this time and not so bloody—and smeared the blood upon my bared breasts.

I yielded, giggling as I fell backward on the bed, against Harker's legs (who, because of my doing, never woke nor even stirred). There I let her take me as she had before, licking away the blood and applying more to the most tender area until I again fell screaming into the blissful void. . . .

I did the same for her, although I confess it was not entirely to my taste. Nor did she seem to enjoy it as much as I; she clearly preferred to be the one giving rather than receiving, and once the Englishman's small wound ceased bleeding, her desire appeared to ebb. Yet I managed to bring her into the void, and afterwards, we lay flushed and warm in each other's arms atop the snoring solicitor.

"Now," she said softly, "come with me to my room. I will have Dorka tailor some of my dresses for you, so that you can wear them when we go to London. And when we are there, you shall buy all the new frocks and jewelry you desire, and then you shall buy more."

I went with her to her chambers, and tried on frock after frock, peering into a larger mirror which Dorka held. Such delight! The gowns were all brand-new, the latest fashion with a "bustle" in the back, and all exquisite (although they were slightly too long, and too generous in the bosom and waist). Dorka is taking them all in now.

And then Elisabeth took me into her bedchambers, where I slipped naked between the most marvellously fine cotton sheets, and pulled the great down comforter, covered in satin, up to my neck. (Now I see the reason for all the trunks: There are no such elegant bedclothes in all of Roumania! She has brought her own linens.)

She lay down beside me, and I quickly fell into a marvellous cosy sleep.

When I woke, it was sunset again, and Elisabeth was gone, no doubt in Vlad's company. I had slept most of the day, but was not disappointed, as I felt greatly refreshed. So I returned to the chambers I share with Dunya—*had* shared with Dunya—and gathered my diary and portrait and brought them back here, to Elisabeth's room. I shall never sleep in that casket again.

And now, as I write this, nestled again in Elisabeth's sumptuous, comfortable bed, my thoughts return to Vlad's betrayal and Elisabeth's insistence that we should not harm him now, but follow him to England.

In truth, the thought of going with her to London— to London at last!—thrilled me beyond words, and to take revenge upon Vlad with her by my side seemed sweet. But how long must I wait? How long?

❧ 5 ❧

The Diary of
Abraham Van Helsing

9 MAY. Gerda has become more animated during both day and night. I have shifted my routine to accommodate her, rising shortly after noon rather than the hour before sunset. To my surprise, she is hypnotisable most often during the late afternoon—but at times, the hour of her vulnerability shifts. Some days, she will not enter trance at all.

To-day when I rose and unlocked the door to her room (poor thing, I am forced now to keep her under lock and chain, lest Zsuzsanna at a distance bid her to harm herself or, God forbid, Mama), she was amazingly animated. She sat cross-legged on her bed, long white nightgown carelessly bunched about her upper thighs as she gestured smiling at an invisible visitor and chattered away like a little girl at an imaginary tea party. I could not decipher what she was saying, though the lilting cadence and whistling sibilants clearly marked the language as Roumanian—a language which she does not speak, and with which I have some limited facility. But the words were not completely formed, so that the effect was rather like listening to a young parrot who has captured the rhythm and intonation of his master's speech, but is yet unable to enunciate clearly.

For the space of a minute, perhaps two, I stood in silence observing this odd babbling pantomime. Gerda gave me no notice—until, abruptly, she turned to cast me a sidelong glance, snorting to her invisible companion: *"Him!"* This time she enunciated the word in clear, precise Roumanian.

But as she peered at me from beneath half-lowered lids, her eyes widened slowly, and both smile and derisiveness faded from her face. For the most fleeting of seconds, she knew me and I her. For I beheld the face of my tortured beloved, my wife, a prisoner held not by locks and bars but by that infinitely crueler jailor, madness. This was Gerda as she had appeared almost a quarter century ago, with the pale, dainty face of a gentlewoman and the dark suffering eyes of a lunatic—eyes so troubled and despairing that, when they looked out at me from behind a dishevelled curtain of long sable hair (Katya had washed and brushed it out), tears of compassion filled my own.

"Gerda," I whispered longingly, and reached to touch her hand. But she turned away, slack-faced, all animation and expression just as swiftly gone, replaced by the blankness that I have come to despise so.

Nothing I said could rouse her, so I surrendered and tended to Mama a few hours before checking on Gerda again.

This time, my efforts came to fruition. Gerda quite easily and naturally slipped into hypnotic trance, though at some points she fell stubbornly silent (most notably at the questions "How is Vlad? Is he strong or weak?" and "Are you and he still trapped within the castle?").

Yet while she would not divulge information about Vlad, at the query "And how are you? Are you strong?," she cried out with girlish enthusiasm: "Ever so strong, and happier than I have ever been in my life!" At this, my heart sank; yet my dismay was quickly submerged by curiosity when she added, "It is all because of Elisabeth. . . ."

"Elisabeth? Who is she?" No doubt, *she* of *she who has come,* but I waited for a more specific description.

She grew silent and pressed her lips together, as if resolved not to answer; I feared our session had come to a premature halt. But then she replied softly, "My dearest friend. . . ." And would say no more on the subject, not even whether Elisabeth was mortal or no. (She cannot be, of course, if she is capable of so easily restoring Zsuzsanna's strength. In all frankness, this terrifies me. What manner of immortal is this, who is more powerful than even the Impaler? And how could I ever hope to defeat such a creature?)

I pressed further. "And are you able now to leave the castle?"

At once—to my relief—her expression darkened. "No," she said, with clear anger. "But I shall soon, when we go to London."

London! My heart began to pound against my breastbone as if fervently demanding escape. My father, Arkady, had told me that Vlad had expressed a desire to go to England as long as fifty years ago—to London, where he is unknown and unfeared, and has vastly greater numbers of potential victims.

I asked a few other questions, but in truth, I do not remember the answers she gave, for I was too shaken by the knowledge that Vlad and Zsuzsanna—and whoever this Elisabeth might be—would soon make their escape.

Thus to-night I performed a formal ritual for guidance and aid and, for the first time, attempted to evoke Arminius as one might a god or demon. To my disappointment, he failed to appear, and so I performed in Circle a divination to guide me.

Clearly, I am intended to leave for London—but not at once. I shall wait and watch alertly for the signal to go.

But two cards from the reading trouble me still: the Devil and the High Priestess. Meditation instructs me that they speak somehow of this mysterious Elisabeth.

My anxious mind was focussed on these symbols as I dozed at Mama's bedside, where the dream of the Dark Creature in the woods betook me. Once again, there stood my teacher, Arminius, gleaming and white in his purity and kindness, attended by his familiar, Archangel the wolf. Again I screamed, and again, no reply, no comfort, from him who had so helped me in the past.

Then came the time when the Great Darkness loomed nearer, and began to change shape. . . .

But no more did it shift from wolf to child to man. No, this time it transformed directly from animal to woman. And the darkness brightened slowly until the black silhouette had become instead filled with colour.

Speechless, I stared at the vision before me—that of an impossibly beautiful woman, her long waving hair catching the daylight like spun gold, her eyes the deep, deep blue of the sea. Her skin was alabaster kissed with the delicate pink of eternal youth—the preternatural glow so often seen upon the countenances of vampires eager to lure prey. Yes, hers was a loveliness to make the beholder weep in admiration at such glory, yet I felt no such joy, only the purest dread.

At my terror, she laughed, throwing her head back and tossing the golden waves so that they sparkled in the sun— sparkled like her small, unnaturally white teeth. The canines were not sharp, as I had expected, but of perfectly ordinary size; that realisation served only to heighten my fear until, overwhelmed, I cried out.

I woke perspiring to the sight of Mama watching me, and feebly picking at the covers as if in a confused effort to reach out and comfort me.

"Bram?" Her voice, frail and broken, seemed a parody of what it had been before her illness, but I was touched to see the look of recognition and worry in her exhausted eyes. Such radiant, gentle, loving orbs they are, the colour of cornflowers—the absolute moral opposite of those belonging to the woman in my dream, for Mama's shine with pure goodness. But lately, it has grown difficult for me to gaze long into them, for they look at me and do not see me, as though they are looking beyond at Infinity.

"Child, are you all right?" She spoke in her native English, for in recent months she seems to find it difficult to recall her Dutch.

I took her cold, thin hand and pressed it between mine to warm it, answering also in English. "I'm fine, Mama. I was just dreaming."

Her face suddenly contorted with pain, and beneath the covers, her legs writhed; though she bit her lip in an effort to keep from crying out, a groan escaped her nonetheless. I realised then that it had been *her* cry, not my own, that had wakened me. Yet she was more concerned about my mental distress than her own physical anguish.

Another round of morphia would have been dangerous; I had dosed her only an hour before. So, with profuse apologies, I followed the wise old medical adage concerning the elderly and the dying: When in doubt, check bowels and bladder. I did so quickly, grateful for the fact that both illness and sedation eased any overt sense of embarrassment—for her (she was quite too exhausted to care), if not for me. Examining a patient is one thing; examining one's mother is quite another.

What I found made my heart sink, for I knew I should have to cause her further agony. "Mama," I said gently, "I'm afraid I will have to help you again. There is a great deal of stool lodged here against your bedsores; I shall have to extract it for you."

With almost lucid resignation, she released a disappointed breath, then made a pitiful effort to roll onto one hip. "Do what you must."

So I fetched bedpan and salve, and helped her to turn onto her side—that alone was excruciating for her. Then I performed what was necessary, praying the whole time that God or whoever had the power would see fit to make my thick fingers as thin and small as Katya's. Mama screamed in a way that broke my heart, and struggled feebly to push me away. Fighting tears, I said, "I am so sorry to inflict this indignity, Mama; but you will become terribly infected if I do not remove this stool."

At once she cried out, "No, no! Don't remove it, dear, or you shall certainly fall!"

For one moment, I was confused; the next, I struggled to contain sad laughter at her darkly comical and entirely unwitting remark. "Don't worry, I shan't fall," I soothed her. "It is quite steady."

She seemed to take some comfort from that, and cried out only twice afterwards. Soon I was done, and elected to give her a very small extra dose of morphia; now she sleeps soundly and well, her expression the lax, unfurrowed one of deep, painless sleep.

I checked on Gerda quickly—no change—then returned to Mama's bedside to watch that her breathing remained strong and steady.

And here I sit again in the rocking-chair at Mama's

bedside, listening to her soft snoring and knowing that the familiar sound is one I soon will never hear again. Yet I feel as though I have always sat here and always will, and that her suffering will never end.

Clearly, I must go to London soon and take Gerda with me, so that I will be waiting there when the vampires arrive. They cannot be permitted free rein in England— dear God, victims are so plentiful there that they would never be detected . . . not until the whole country was changed into vampires! My responsibility there outweighs all others, even that to my family. This I know in my brain; but my heart knows that it would be a crime to leave Mama alone in this house to die in the presence of strangers.

Golden Elisabeth, what are you?

And what chance do I have against one so powerful, without Arminius' intervention?

❖ ❖ ❖

Zsuzsanna Tsepesh's Diary

16 MAY. No entry for a time; things had settled into a pleasurable enough monotony—but a monotony all the same. Day after day, our routine has been to enjoy ourselves freely during the sun's heavenly reign, nibbling upon the Englishman at our leisure, then straightway enjoying a sensual interlude. Afterwards, Elisabeth takes me back to her chambers and picks clothing from her numerous trunks and suitcases, and Dorka alters it for me; or Dorka grooms my hair in a fashionable style (though my poor locks refuse to hold the slightest curl, despite her heroic

efforts); or Elisabeth educates me in the cosmetic arts. Lipstick, powder, kohl—I would never have thought these silly things could enhance even further my immortal glory, but they do indeed. I am not only more beautiful than ever, I look like what the British call the New Woman: sophisticated, modern, fashionable . . . and soon, I pray, independent.

In the afternoon, we sleep together beneath Elisabeth's sumptuous linens for a handful of hours, then rise again at sunset. Elisabeth dutifully repairs to Vlad's chambers to "visit," for apparently he wants to be sure that she spends little time with me (although he sometimes releases her a few hours before the dawn). No doubt he fears that she will tell me too much of the truth—little does he know that it is too late!

Nights are the hardest time, for without Elisabeth or our Englishman, little awaits me save boredom—and poor Dunya, who is not returned to full vigour. She sleeps all day still, and clearly needs to feed. But each time I broach the topic, Elisabeth tells me that it is better to simply let the poor girl rest until the time comes for us all to leave the castle. I suspect that restoring Dunya would tax Elisabeth's powers too greatly, though she will not admit to it. She likes to maintain an aura of omnipotence—and indeed, she very nearly is omnipotent.

And if she is, why can we not *leave*? It is anguish to remain here upon this ruined, deserted estate, thinking of the glories of London! Each dawn, I go to the open window and stretch my arm forth, yearning for the warm, delicious kiss of sunlight upon it.

How long must I wait?

I sigh, impatient, as I write this while Elisabeth and Dunya still lie sleeping in the great bed. I sigh, and write: Enough! I must maintain my sanity; dwelling upon my captivity will only serve to torment me. And so, now that restlessness has come upon me, I write. . . .

Yesterday I woke at morning's first blush (how strange to write these words again, after so many years) in Elisabeth's arms, and stared for a time out the unshuttered window as the grey light warmed to pale rose. (We had missed our afternoon nap, and so used the darkest morning hours for rest.) After a time my darling stirred and gazed up at me with a sleepy smile, her long sunny curls spilling with delightful haphazardness over her ivory shoulders, back, breasts. The warmth of her body was pleasant, the morning cool; I therefore remained beside her, and we indulged ourselves in languid conversation beneath the covers. I, as always, asked: *How long? How long?* And Elisabeth, as always, replied, *Soon, soon.* . . .

Presently our conversation turned to Vlad, and her demeanour became markedly curious. She sat up suddenly, letting the covers drop away (though the early morning air was cool)—and, knees bent with long, slender arms wrapped round them, she demanded:

"You have spoken before of the covenant Vlad had with your family, and with the villagers. But I have not heard yet of the covenant he surely has with the Dark Lord. What do you know of it?"

At the sound of that entity's name—and at the diamond-hard, diamond-brilliant intensity in her eyes, focussed keenly on mine—I shuddered. Yet I answered honestly and in full: that Vlad had offered up to the Dark One the eldest son of each generation of his family. That a sacrifice was required each generation in order to purchase Vlad's renewed immortality. That in 1842, my brother Arkady had (as both mortal and subsequent vampire) resisted being pressed into Vlad's evil service. Arkady's second death—as a vampire—should have brought Vlad's immediate destruction, but did not because my brother had left behind an heir, which his wife, Mary, took into hiding. So long as the heir lived and there remained a chance that Vlad could deliver his soul to the Dark Lord in place of Arkady's, Vlad survived.

But Vlad's weakness had come about because this heir —whose name had been deceitfully changed from Stefan Tsepesh to Abraham Van Helsing by his mother when she fled with him to Holland—was told by his father, Arkady, the truth of his heritage. And so Arkady instructed Van Helsing in the foul art of killing vampires.

Yet Van Helsing, a mere mortal, was no match for Vlad's strength, and his efforts to destroy the Prince of Wallachia met with utter failure . . . and my dear brother's death.

However, the wicked Van Helsing soon discovered another terrible truth—that by destroying other vampires (those of Vlad's victims who died, were not properly destroyed, and subsequently rose), Vlad's powers were gradually sapped. Thus, over the past two decades of Van Helsing's killing spree, Vlad and I had grown weaker and weaker, until we had become the pathetic remnants Elisabeth greeted upon her arrival.

She listened with fascination and care and, when I had finished, added, "Clearly Van Helsing was preparing to come here and dispatch you both. Vlad is too suspicious to trust anyone, least of all me; for him to beg for my aid means that he was in terror of death. . . . But here, my darling! Why this sudden unhappy shower?"

For I was quite overcome with grief at the memories that assailed me at the telling of this sad history; and I cried harder still when she lifted her hand and tenderly brushed away my tears. Sobbing, I said, "Because, those twenty years ago, I was lonely, dreadfully lonely, because

Vlad had emotionally forsaken me. And so I took Van Helsing's little boy, Jan, as my own immortal companion. Just a baby, he was, barely able to walk and talk, and so sweetly innocent—and Van Helsing murdered him!"

She held me, patting my back as if soothing a wailing infant, then withdrew and gently held my arms. "And did this beast also murder your poor brother?"

I shook my head. "No. Arkady died in an encounter with Vlad. . . . He is here in the castle. Would you like to see him?"

Her lips, pink and glowing as the dawn, parted abruptly in unmasked amazement. "His body has survived all this time? Zsuzsanna, that is impossible!"

"Possible or no, do you wish to see him?"

"At once!" she cried, springing gracefully from the bed and pulling on her dressing-gown with such alacrity that, before I could myself rise, she was already holding out my gown to me.

I led her down the stairs and through a rotting and rusted oaken trapdoor bound with iron, to the cellar—a subterranean cavern beneath the castle's stone foundation, a place I have come to think of as the first circle of Hell. Years ago, I wept as I carried my poor brother's body there —a dark, mildewed womb of earth laced with spiderwebs, sprinkled with dust and the faeces of rodents. Oh, yes, the bones of martyrs rest in the catacombs of that grotto; the bones of so many hundreds of unfortunates who served as Vlad's supper that the servants had no more room—and came to dispose of later victims in the forest.

And chief of those martyrs is my brother.

To spare myself the need to tread upon too much Death and suffering, I had laid Arkady's body in one of the first empty catacombs, those which were not enclosed by heavy rusted iron bars hung with chains and disintegrating padlocks. I had constructed for him a catafalque of stone, surrounded him with tapers, and draped a banner of black silk upon the rough earthen wall.

There we found him, lying just as I had left him on that terrible day: impaled through his bloodless heart by a stake so thick I cannot encircle it with one hand. And so handsome at rest, with his narrow but prominent nose, his severe black brows and hair, his long-lashed eyelids closed forever over the gentlest hazel eyes I ever knew.

At the sight of him, I wept openly. For though his last desire was to see me and Vlad destroyed—as he put it, to free our souls (as if we could ascend to Heaven instead of fall straight to Hell)—he still loved me, and I him. The bonds of mortal siblings are not easily broken, even by the afterlife or differing loyalties. So overwhelmed by grief was I when I first laid him to rest that, had I been capable, I would have offered up my own existence gladly if he could return. Given the chance, I might do so even now. . . .

My compliments concerning his physical appearance are not due to sisterly bias; even Elisabeth gasped at the sight of his perfect and beautiful corpse, and could not extinguish the gleam of lust in her eye quickly enough to hide it.

"Zsuzsanna!" she exclaimed softly. "How can this be? He should have crumbled to dust, or at the very least decomposed in some fashion. . . ."

I kept my gaze fastened upon my younger brother, my sweet little Kasha, as I replied, "The stake killed him, a vampire. But the regenerative powers of the undead are so great that, because his head was never separated from the body, he has maintained his form. I suspect the instant they are twain, the physical form will dissolve." Again, the burn of tears as the images returned to me. "Just as Van

Helsing no doubt accomplished with my baby, my poor little Jan!"

Elisabeth put her arms round me, and stroked my hair as I rested my cheek upon her shoulder. "What sort of bastard is capable of murdering his own child?" she fumed. "Don't cry, my darling. I shall see that he meets his long-deserved fate. You shall be doubly avenged, for should Van Helsing die, then Vlad himself shall do the same—or rather, descend into the arms of the Dark Lord—shall he not?"

"Yes," I murmured into her soft, silk-clad shoulder.

"Then that is what we will do, dear Zsuzsa. We need only kill Van Helsing to see Vlad destroyed."

❖❖   ❖❖   ❖❖

Reassured but sad, we walked together back up the stairs. I felt a small gnawing hunger and should have liked to visit our gentleman, but Elisabeth became very stern: I had been taxing poor Harker of late, and if we did not allow him another day's rest, Vlad would certainly notice and take action against us. (Him again! Sometimes I become annoyed with Elisabeth; she possesses such amazing powers, but tiptoes round Vlad as though secretly afraid. Oh, yes, she says she does it out of her own hunger for the chase to come, that without such games she would grow bored of existence—but I grow madder with boredom each hour I remain here!)

I yielded to her reluctantly, and together we returned to our chambers. Though she tried valiantly to cheer me with more of the usual gown fittings and hairstyles, I remained restless. At last she made to me the presentation of a small velvet box, a gift that she had meant to save for our first night in London.

I opened it with as much show of delight as I could

manage, and was truly moved and delighted to find nestled within a pair of striking earrings—large round diamonds from which hung suspended even larger sapphire tears—and to match, a gold necklace from which hung a great pendant of the same design, a diamond weeping sapphires.

I was enormously honoured and flattered to receive such an expensive token of Elisabeth's affection, even more so when I asked her when and how she had managed to purchase such a gift, and she replied:

"They were mine, given to me in marriage as a token of esteem. So I give them to you with the same meaning."

I rose and kissed her upon each cheek, and she solemnly returned the gesture. And so she began to speak of London again, and the different places she intended to take me shopping—to Piccadilly and Hyde Park, and Savile Row, but I could not feign interest for long. My frustration at being trapped inside these stone walls would not ease, so at last she tore off my clothes and carried me to the bed, where she attempted to relieve my anxiety in a more sensual fashion.

As I write this, it occurs to me that this was the first time we had made love without blood smeared upon our bodies, and without my having recently fed. Elisabeth was determined to better my mood, but her efforts were curiously lacking in passion. When even her pale enthusiasm began clearly to wane, I waved her away. Offended, she stormed off—where, I cannot say, for even with my preternatural hearing, I could detect not a sound anywhere in the castle. I did not see her again until after dusk.

By then the full moon had risen, large and yellow and ringed with a radiant halo of mist in a starry indigo sky. It was a warm, beautiful night—even more beautiful because I sensed that Vlad had departed the castle, leaving behind an atmosphere of ease—and unbearably romantic, especially now that my Elisabeth was gone. Before I met her, the full moonglow used to pain my eyes so that I avoided hunting then; but tonight, it seemed delicious, inviting, and the moon's incandescent whiteness, rippled through with pale gold, reminded me of my lover's skin and hair.

Fortunately, by that time, Dunya had risen from her coffin and I distracted myself from my loneliness by talking to her; she was too sweet-natured to show it, but I know she is becoming jealous of Elisabeth's obvious favouritism towards me. Here I sit in new gowns and jewels, marvellously coiffed, and Dunya still spends the day in the worn (but fetching) dress I bought her twenty years ago in Vienna, with her dark reddish hair braided and coiled in the same fashion Vlad's serfs wore four centuries ago. Since she joined us undead, I have tried consciously to treat her less as a servant and more as an equal, but there is a clear class distinction which cannot be violated. I think when she is reminded of it, it hurts her feelings. What Hell to know one is doomed to remain a serving-girl for all eternity! But there is nothing to be done.

At any rate, I did my best to reassure her. I had, I told her, demanded that Vlad bring us food, which was bound to arrive very soon. This heartened her a bit; for although she is slightly stronger than she was, hunger has again weakened her to the point where she cannot hunt for herself. (Even if she could, thanks to Vlad's foul magic she probably would find herself trapped inside the castle, same as I.)

But just as I finished my tale, Dunya sat up in her chair, and lifted her nose to savour the air.

"Warm blood!" She rose at once and hurried to the door of her bedchamber, following the scent. "*Doamna*, there is a mortal here!"

She projected herself with blurring speed out into the

sitting-room. I followed, and heard her release a small gasp as our gazes beheld, at the same time, the Englishman.

He was sitting at the desk, pen in hand, writing furiously in a pocket-sized diary in the glow of lamp and moon. We both had rushed into the room with such haste that his mortal eyes could not possibly have perceived our entry, but he is clearly a sensitive, for he glanced frowning in our direction.

"Sleep," I said. Straightway, he rose, pen and diary in one hand, and clumsily pulled the long couch into a bright pane of moonlight in front of the grand window—the one which looks down onto the great chasm and the forested valley far below, and the mountains far beyond. At once he lay down—on his side, fortunately, so that the snoring which immediately commenced was less stertorous than usual. (If he is indeed engaged, I pity his poor wife-to-be.)

Dunya clapped her hands and giggled, gleeful as a child introduced to a new present. "How handsome he is!"

"Vlad's visitor," I murmured, as I silently agreed with Dunya's comment. Awake and dressed and neatly groomed, he looked even more attractive and gentlemanly in vest and shirt and trousers, and brown curls sternly pomaded. He also had the beginnings of a dark beard, which gave his boyish features an agreeable severity, and made his jaw and cheeks appear thinner and more sculpted.

So deeply did he fall into trance that the diary and pen, which he heretofore had jealously clutched, dropped from his now-relaxed fingers onto the couch. Before I could react, the nib fell directly onto the centuries-old brocade and the ink was immediately absorbed, leaving a small black starburst that could never be washed out.

"Thoughtless guests!" I exclaimed. "Really, have they no concern for others' property?" And I slipped the pen into his vest pocket—nib down. The diary, however, I took into my hands, hoping to fool Dunya into believing I had never before met the genteel Mr. Harker.

"Hmph! What sort of chicken scratchings are these? Why does he not write in English?" I peered up from the small book to address the sleeping man. "Well, you shall, sir, from now on," I commanded, in the voice of a mesmerist. "You may *think* you are writing in this bizarre scrawl, but you shall in truth write everything down in proper English. How else shall I indulge my curiosity?" And I bent low and slipped the diary next to the pen.

When I rose, I glanced over to see poor Dunya transfixed—staring down at Harker with lips parted, sharp, shining teeth bared, and eyes filled with a wild hunger that was painful to see. And yet she was restrained by an invisible wall of fear.

"I must not!" she whispered—to neither me nor Harker, but to herself. "I must not! He would destroy me. . . ."

He meaning Vlad, of course, and I opened my mouth to say, *There is no more reason to fear Vlad anymore, dear companion. The man is yours. Take him!*

But ere I could speak, I sensed rather than heard the rustle of soft skirts against stone, and the click of hard, tiny heels. And there in the arched entryway stood Elisabeth. How had I failed to sense her approach . . . unless she had intentionally kept her movements silent?

To my relief, she was no longer angry; indeed, she was smiling and cheerful, and glanced at Harker with amusement as she entered briskly, skirts in her hands. "Ah! Our Englishman seems to have wandered astray."

I left Dunya slavering over our unexpected visitor and sidled up to Elisabeth, who put her hand upon my waist and kissed my cheek as though her furious departure had never occurred. Thus I dared ask her—in English, which to the uneducated Dunya might as well have been Chinese: "I cannot bear to see her suffer so any longer, or to fear Vlad's wrath needlessly. For my sake, let her drink safely, as you have let me. . . ."

I half expected more anger from her, or at least an annoyed repetition of how it would be better not to overtax her powers until the time came for us to leave.

But she was in as jolly a temper as I have seen her, and she merely sighed with affectionate annoyance and stroked my cheek with her hand. One corner of her red mouth quirked up to reveal a deep dimple beside it as she turned to face Harker and his desperate admirer.

"Dunya, my darling. Take the visitor; he is yours. Only mark that you do not drain him to death, else I will not be able to protect you from Vlad's anger."

Atremble with desire and terror, the little servant glanced up at Elisabeth with wide, confused dark eyes. "But, *doamna,* if I do, then the prince shall see the mark!"

I stepped forward. "He won't. Elisabeth can cause the marks to disappear."

On her face, darkness warred with light: darkness, as she wondered how I should know such a thing unless Elisabeth had done it for me—which meant that I had withheld from my loyal companion nourishing blood, this visitor's blood. Light, as she tried to repress doubt and anger and focus instead on this hope-restoring marvel, that she could drink deep at Harker's well without danger of retaliation.

As always, rage succumbed to hunger. She bent low over the Englishman, whose eyelids fluttered; clearly, he was watching her with the same delicious anticipation she directed towards him, for as she neared, his lips parted sensually to draw in and release air more quickly. His sighs caused a warm, rapid thrill to course down my spine, at whose termination I felt as though I had burst into flame.

Closer she drew to him, and closer, with the most erotic reverence I have ever witnessed, until her mouth opened wide and her teeth pressed ever so gently against his flesh—not piercing, merely touching. I do not think I had ever seen her appear quite so classically beautiful as she did at that moment: her eyelids half lowered with desire, her profile pale and fragile against Harker's more rounded ruddy one. A single lock of her hair had escaped the long braid and fell straight onto Harker's cheek, where it coiled, a red-black serpent.

In that pose she lingered, and slowly closed her eyes, savouring the ecstasy induced by waiting.

And I was hungry, hungry, hungrier than I had ever been, yet aware that my yearning could not be sated by blood alone. I pressed a hand to my heaving breast and looked at my beloved, my Elisabeth.

She, too, was drunk with anticipation, for her mouth had fallen open and, like Harker, she panted. Unlike Harker, her blue eyes were open wide and frankly ablaze with lust.

But not for me, not for me. And not for our Englishman.

Jealousy abruptly replaced my arousal: How could she look at Dunya as she looks at me? How dare anyone else be the object of her passion!

Yet that emotion was just as swiftly replaced by surprise. Bony spine arched in a delicate curve, Dunya lifted her shoulders in a gesture I have come to know well, for it is that of the vampire preparing to strike.

At the same time, there came a sound like the rushing of a great wind, and its slamming into the motionless air of the sitting-room.

"Leave him!" Vlad thundered, and Dunya cried out in horrified alarm as he flung down a large burlap sack and rushed towards her. Before either Elisabeth or I could intervene, Vlad caught her neck between his thumb and forefinger and lifted her from her knees, then hurled her backward with such great force that she struck the wall.

She was, of course, unhurt (though she remained cowering in the corner), but the cruel disrespect of the gesture filled me with fury. What if it had been I or Elisabeth instead of a serving-girl? Would he have dared lay a hand on *us*?

My anger rose as he turned his wrath upon us two, shouting: "How dare you touch him, any of you! How dare you cast eyes on him when I had forbidden it! This man belongs to me!"

Able to bear it no longer, I cried, "But *we* do not belong to you, and *we* are hungry! What sort of tyrant starves his own family, then strikes us when the opportunity to save ourselves appears? You say he belongs to you, but he wandered into our rooms—we did not bring him here. Fate has decreed that we shall be fed!"

His eyes reddened with fury at my impudence, as I knew they would; I do think if Elisabeth had not been there, he would have killed me if he could. He glanced from me to her; she said nothing at all, but merely gazed back at him with an enigmatic half-smile and eyes hard, cold, deadly fierce.

I think she frightened him, for he remained silent a moment before answering slowly, "Harker shall be yours after a time, when I am done with him. Until then"—he nodded at the brown bundle on the floor; a shrill animal cry, similar to that of a cat, emerged from within, but the smell was definitely that of warm human blood—"let that suffice."

And he lifted the swooning Englishman into his arms and departed as quickly as he had come. Immediately relieved, Dunya scrambled over to the bag and loosened the drawstring; wet burlap fell away in folds to reveal a filthy, naked male child of perhaps a year, its smudged cheeks wet with tears. It gazed up at Dunya and immediately calmed, though its little torso spasmed comically with hiccups.

Elisabeth sniffed the air, her porcelain features contorted with disgust, and raised a lace handkerchief to her mouth. "It smells."

"Ah, no." I wagged a finger at her. "Remember Alexander Pope: *You* smell. It stinks."

"I think it peed in the bag," Dunya said, and grinned at it, relieved to find that she had not only escaped punishment, but would have her dinner after all. (The sense of smell, apparently, is first to fade when hunger overwhelms.) The child returned the smile sweetly, and reached for her with chubby fingers. "A baby," she said, and scooped it up at once, whirling round and round and tickling its fat stomach until it crowed atonally with delight. She snapped her fingers beside its ear, then added, "I think it's deaf."

Another prize from our oh-so-generous Vlad: a dirty, piss-soaked deaf boy whose own parents had probably offered it up gladly. "And he is all yours," I told Dunya.

She neither questioned my abstinence nor protested the gift, but immediately pressed her lips to its neck in a hungry kiss; the child giggled, writhing as if tickled. But its laughter turned at once to a terrified scream as Dunya opened wide her mouth and struck. The cry soon faded; the boy grew glassy-eyed and still as the muscles in Dunya's jaw worked, and soon he was limp in her arms. She cradled him then, lifting high the elbow beneath his head so that she could drink comfortably without bending too far down—the mother suckling the child.

The tableau seemed both strangely tender and erotic; I found myself yearning to join her in that gently passionate embrace. A glance at Elisabeth confirmed that she felt the same, for she stared at the two with the same intent lust she had directed at Dunya and Harker.

Was I again jealous? Yes, as I am now, watching Dunya as she sleeps enfolded in Elisabeth's arms in the great bed. But that verdant emotion did not stay with me for long. For this time, Elisabeth felt my gaze upon her, and favoured me with a faint, seductive smile. Oddly, that small gesture caused all jealousy to lift, and filled me instead with fire. So I did not resist when Elisabeth took my hand and, laying it upon her breast and her own hand atop mine, drew me with her to Dunya's side.

What possessed me then I cannot say, nor can I remember clearly what transpired afterwards. I only know that we indulged ourselves in an orgy of blood and sexual excess, and that I violated each woman just as each one violated me. Only one image remains with me clearly— that of Elisabeth naked and kneeling upon the stone, crying out *More, more!* as Dunya and I each held one of the dying child's heels and shook him so that the dregs of his blood spattered down upon Elisabeth's breast and face. This she frenziedly rubbed into her skin, as if somehow she might absorb some good from it.

When it was over, Dunya was too sated to move, and all three of us were sticky with the remnants of the child's blood. Elisabeth carried her and I trailed behind as we three made our way to Elisabeth's chamber. There we piled into the big bed, where I slept until the dawn.

How strange this all is, and how confused I have become. I am jealous of Dunya and angry at Elisabeth—and yet I am not. I know but one thing for certain: that I shall convince her to wait no longer, but to take me to London at once.

❧6❧

Zsuzsanna Dracul's Diary

17 MAY. When I went alone to Harker's chambers this morning—Elisabeth had gone off again, without explanation—I found, to my delight, that my hypnotic suggestion to him had worked, after a fashion. He was still writing in shorthand in his diary, but he had taken to transcribing the whole thing into English on some parchment he had apparently brought with him in order to post letters. He had begun with the most recent entry, the sixteenth, and I was amused to see *his* perspective of what had happened the night of 15 May.

Clearly, he was quite fixated upon Elisabeth, for he spoke of nothing but the "fair girl" and her wavy masses of golden hair. She had taken the place of Dunya in his shoddy memory, and he spent an inordinate amount of time describing her and overstating the "count's" show of anger. Quite insulting, really, and where did he get this business about "you never love"? All fantasy.

But the worst insult came in the previous day's entry —the entry he must have been writing when Dunya and I caught him in our sitting-room. I was so infuriated that I committed it to memory: "Here I am, sitting at a little oak table where in old times possibly some fair lady sat to pen, with much thought and many blushes, her ill-spelt love-letter. . . ."

Ill-spelt? *Ill-spelt?* Sir, I have avoided insulting *your* pitiful attempts at poetic prose, nor have I chided you in *my* diary for your faulty spelling. I resent the implication that the Tsepesh (or Dracul, or Roumanian, for that matter) women were ill-educated, or that they wasted their time blushing over silly love-letters. My mother was a renowned poetess, sir, and I alone possess more literary skills than you and all your future heirs together dare ever hope to have. I have never misspelt a word in all my life.

Ill-spelt, indeed!

As for the misspoken Mr. Harker, I gave him a small nip, and took just enough blood to stave off hunger; this time, I skipped any sexual encounter, for I had little of that sort of appetite after the long, strange night with Elisabeth, Dunya, and the deaf child.

When I had drunk (much less than my fill), I left Harker and wandered out into the hallway. I was filled with restlessness, as I had wanted badly to tell Elisabeth that I could no longer wait to go to London. Yet I could find her nowhere in the castle—save for the one place I feared to look, Vlad's chambers.

And if she refused again to leave this prison, I had resolved to attempt what heretofore I had never dared even to think: kill Vlad with the stake. Yes, he had told me that vampires could not directly kill each other, but he had managed to kill my brother by hurling a stake at him.

Why should I not do the same to him? For with Elisabeth here, I had come to realise that I *was* strong enough to face even the Impaler. "If I am destroyed, you are destroyed," he has always told me, but I know now in my heart that is a lie.

Yet before I could enter his inner sanctum, I needed to render myself invisible, soundless—for even hard at rest, Vlad was capable of sensing danger, and retaliating. Thus I carefully performed the necessary mental machinations and chant, and when I felt confident that he could never detect me, I set off.

Up the stairs I went, moving so swift and light that my feet literally never touched the stone. Soon I arrived at the great oak-and-iron door to find it closed and bolted from the inside; from within came no sound. Rather than dramatically break the bolt and fling the door open—which I could manage easily now, but which would also alert Vlad to my increased strength—I instead opted for stealth, and narrowed my body in order to slip through the crack into the vast chamber, which was modelled upon the Prince of Wallachia's private throne room.

There to the west stood the Theatre of Death, where black manacles graced a bloodstained wall, and the wicked chains of the strappado (from whence a victim might struggle, suspended in midair) hung from the ceiling. Beneath them both lay a large wooden tub, of oaken exterior but an interior the colour of red mahogany, a legacy left by its former contents. And beyond them both stood a large butcher's table, its surface worn and scored by the bite of countless blades. This in turn was flanked by a rack of knives of different sizes and shapes, and a stand of sharpened wooden stakes—some broad as a strong man's arm and taller than I, others shorter and thinner, destined for more delicate uses. In the halcyon days before Van Helsing's birth, all these were used to dispose of dead guests in a manner which prevented them from becoming competition.

These devices had long lain unused; but I had no doubt they represented the fate intended for our Englishman, no matter what false claims of generosity Vlad had uttered.

I approached them, tempted to arm myself at once and enter the small door to my left wherein my uncle slept (this I sensed beyond doubt), in hopes of achieving the brazen deed before my resolve fled entirely. But a slight, barely perceptible movement at the chamber's opposite wall caught my notice.

Elisabeth, I was convinced, though when I stared intently in the direction of the movement I saw and heard nothing—nothing save the Impaler's throne, and the wooden platform on which it rested, and the three stairs inlaid in gold with the motto JUSTUS ET PIUS. Yet I knew she was there—as invisible and undetectable as I; but even the strongest magic is not so powerful as love.

And with loving eyes I looked as I slowly crossed the Impaler's great chamber, nearing inch by inch until I discovered the boundaries of her spell. One instant, I stood several arm's lengths from the platform, and saw nothing save what I have above described. But one step more—a single hesitant step—and the air began to shimmer and roil like clouds caught up in a fierce storm; then, like a veil, it lifted to reveal my Elisabeth.

In front of the great throne, she had erected a polished onyx double cube as an altar. Around this she had inscribed a circle, on whose boundaries I had encroached, thus opening this secret ritual to my eyes.

Dressed in the simple black robe of a priestess, golden hair streaming freely down her back, Elisabeth raised her arms in a V before the altar, on which rested the same implements I have seen on Vlad's: pantacle, dagger, cup, and candle.

And a dead, bloody boy child lying beside locks of indigo hair.

Locks of *my* hair, I realised with an abrupt thrill of horror. Locks of my hair—and Dunya's, for I recognised my jet colour, kissed with blue, and Dunya's, kissed with red. What manner of evil did she intend to work against us? And what had we to do with the dead child?

This I could not determine, for as she faced west— faced me—she intoned words in a bizarre language that sounded like no earthly tongue I knew; but regardless of the language, I can recognise my own name, and that of my serving-girl. And those I heard.

Had I not been frightened of her powers and her anger, I would have broken the circle and stepped forward to demand explanation at once; instead I lingered on the perimeter and watched, hoping that I could ascertain the purpose of this ritual and knowing that I could not. But something—perhaps someone—compelled me to remain.

And then I saw Him.

Elisabeth had completed her chanting and now waited, hands crossed upon her chest like a penitent, head bowed. Unbeknownst to her, standing behind her back, towering over her like a titan stood . . .

How shall I describe Him? He was entirely dark, like a huge shadow cast by a lamp, yet He seemed quite solid. I could not see His face or features, yet He *had* both, for I saw Him smile at me. Neither had He eyes, but I gazed into them just the same.

He knew me. He smiled at me, and knew me. And I —I knew at that moment that I had always known Him, and felt no fear, no fear at all, for looking into His eyes I saw acceptance and compassion, and indeed love.

Such love that I was swept away into it, pulled as if by the tide into the infinite blackness, the infinite light, in His eyes. For He and I were Nothing and All Things, existence and annihilation, thought and mindlessness, all together, and all things and no thing the same. This was an ecstasy far beyond any physical satisfaction and desire, and as I reflect upon it now, I can honestly say that if Death is such a state, I would gladly kill myself now.

Then all awareness passed away, and I fell into an unconscious state and woke a short time later to find Elisabeth and the altar and—could it have been the Dark Lord? No! An archangel, at the very least, capable of only the whitest magic, for when I have heard of the Dark Lord or heard Vlad in session with Him, it brings only fear. But this creature . . . this dark, good creature . . .

I can only speculate. I fled to my room and have written this all down, lest time cause my memory of that powerful encounter to fade. As for now, I have not seen Elisabeth yet, and am fearful; if she detected me after my swooning, then she will no doubt be furious again.

But *I* must know what she is about. If she means to betray me, then my death is assured anyway, and I might as well face it swiftly rather than linger in an agony of doubt.

⁘   ⁘   ⁘

19 MAY. She is dead, she is dead! How can this be? How can any immortal be murdered, save by the hand of the living?

My hand trembles so, I fear I shall drop the pen, for I realise that *I* am no longer safe myself.

I went to her coffin to-day, filled with concern because the morning after the deaf boy's death—the sixteenth— Dunya, still sated and sleepy, crawled from Elisabeth's bed to her little casket in the servant's quarters and closed the lid with a weary *thump*.

It is not uncommon for a vampire who has had her fill after a long deprivation to sleep a day, a night, and another day, then rise refreshed and invigourated; I have done it myself many times. So when Dunya did not rise at all on the night of the sixteenth, I was unconcerned. And when she did not emerge on the seventeeth, I told myself: *She is enjoying a long, deep rest, and when I see her to-morrow, she will appear younger and stronger than she has for decades.*

She did not arise on the eighteenth. "Have no fear," Elisabeth said, trying to comfort me. (She has never mentioned my appearance at her ritual; I can only surmise that my invisibility spell was successful, that I was not detected, for she has only been kind to me since.) "Dunya is immortal. Who can harm her?"

Who, indeed?

This morning I left Elisabeth sleeping and crept in the hour before sunrise to Dunya's quiet chambers. How dark it seemed there, and how melancholy; from outside came the sweet, high song of a solitary lark, but that morning it seemed peculiarly mournful.

I lingered for a moment in the sitting-room where we had encountered Jonathan Harker, Esquire; my fears held me back from proceeding directly into the bedchamber. The couch still stood where the Englishman had placed it —in front of the large window. There I stood, gazing out at forest and mountains and fierce ravine as they slowly emerged from darkness into the pale grey light of dawn.

Then I steeled myself and moved into the inner room where Dunya lay inside her closed casket. And in the instant I stepped across that threshold, a startling revelation seized me: Dunya was not here, not here at all! I had always been able to sense her gentle presence, as she was entirely ignorant of magic and the methods of self-protection (this at Vlad's insistence).

For a fleeting moment, I felt overcome by the wild hope that Elisabeth had at last empowered her, that she had somehow managed to escape the castle; this was accompanied by an equally wild but vague terror—vague because my mind would not permit the admission of what I feared I might find. Consumed by those two incompatible emotions together, I approached the little casket and flung open the lid.

Bone and dust!

Bone and dust: her small, delicate skull was palest ivory, cleaned of any remnant of eye or skin, though a long, liquefying strand of reddish dark hair stuck to the white satin beneath, from neck to waist. It was as though she had truly died as a mortal those twenty years before, and her corpse left to the elements under a pitiless sun. The skull had fallen off the bones of the neck and stood on the bones of the upper jaw (the lower had collapsed), somewhat perpendicular to the dry yellowed bones of the limbs and torso. Her arms were crossed over the breastbone and ribs as neatly as if she had been arranged for burial, but the leg bones had detached and lay scattered in disarray.

I suppose I screamed; I must have screamed, though how loud and long I cannot say, for all fear fled and I knew only hysterical grief. And as I cried out, my breath stirred the dust in the coffin—truly her final resting-place now—causing it to scatter upward into the air and float like the white-hot ash of burning parchment.

I breathed in that ash, choked on it, wept for it; indeed, I crawled into the coffin and clutched the bones, kissed them, baptised them with my tears.

Sweet servant and friend! Loyal and unquestioning companion! I remember with pain each thoughtless act I ever committed against you, and know that now, I have failed in my obligation to protect you. . . .

I did not mourn alone long; in the midst of my sobs, I

felt a warm hand touch my shoulder. Above me stood Elisabeth, her own eyes aglisten with tears, her expression one of horrified shock and pity. She was naked, her hair in streaming tangles; apparently she had heard my wailing and hurled herself from bed.

"Zsuzsanna, my darling!" Her voice was low, softer and more tender than ever I had heard it—oh, but I was too full of grief and fury to believe her. "My dear, what has *happened*? Oh, this cannot—is this poor Dunya?" At once she fell to her knees beside the coffin and swore: "Damn him! *Damn* him!"

I whirled round and sat up at once, filled with an anger pure enough, grand enough, to consume the entire world. I cared not whether I offended her, or Vlad, or the Dark Lord, even if He be the Devil Himself; I cared not if in the next instant I, too, was reduced to a heap of bones and dust. I lashed out, wanting only for her to suffer as I suffered at that moment.

"You know it is. *You* are the one who has killed her! I trusted you—*trusted* you, but now—"

A flash of rage on her face, but only a flash; she controlled herself immediately and replied, with an expression of infinite hurt and sadness, "Zsuzsa, sweet Zsuzsa, how can you say this to *me*? How can you think that I would ever want to harm your friend and cause you such suffering? You are first in my heart, and I would never betray you. . . . This is all Vlad's doing!"

I would have none of it; all an act, all an act, one I had been foolish to believe. "You killed her, as you intend to kill me! I saw you perform the ritual; I saw Dunya's hair, and mine, upon your altar. I saw the Dark Lord. . . ."

At those last two words, her eyebrows lifted sharply, and her gaze became intense, ferocious, diamond-bright; she had not known. Then slowly, the golden brows lowered; her forehead smoothed and her entire expression grew composed. When at last she spoke, her words were measured and deliberate.

"If you saw, then surely you understood the ritual's purpose: to protect you and Dunya from harm. My darling, there is much I have not revealed for fear of frightening you. Vlad intends to destroy us all, and it has taken all my reserves of strength and wit simply to protect you. I admit, I have failed you in terms of Dunya, your good servant, whose death has clearly broken your heart. For my mistake has been to put especial protection round her whom I love most"—and here she kissed my hand, leaning down so that her hot tears spilled onto my flesh—"and to leave only a modicum for myself and Dunya."

What could I say to such a confession? I struggled onto my knees, inadvertently cracking dry, brittle bones, and reached for her. Sobbing, we embraced.

"Ah, my Zsuzsanna, my Zsuzsa, I am sorry I misled you, but I did so out of concern that you should not be afraid. Vlad is weak, yes, and I am the more powerful—except that he has studied magic some two centuries longer than I. His father and grandfather both ascended the throne with the Dark Lord's aid, and I believe he has invoked that powerful entity yet again in hopes of defeating us. For he fears us and anything, anyone, stronger than he—and that which he fears, he is bound to destroy. This is how he repays me, who have come to offer him help . . . and you, who remained his loyal companion for fifty years, despite his despicable treatment of you."

So gentle was her gaze, so wounded yet full of compassionate sorrow, that my heart was pierced by a fresh grief, that of the realisation I had hurt her unjustly. "I am sorry, I am sorry," I murmured, with renewed weeping, and pressed harder against her warm ivory flesh, against the soft perfumed hair that cascaded like Godiva's over her shoulder, breast, and belly. "I understand . . . you had invoked the Dark Lord for protection for us all. But you *must* have the same protection I have, for if I rise and find you so destroyed"—here I gestured at the pitiful heap of bones beneath me—"I truly will die of unhappiness. What shall I do to save you? Teach me, and I will bargain with the Devil Himself!"

A hint of wryness crept into her expression, and she chided quickly beneath her breath, "Do not call Him the Devil, Zsuzsanna; that is so superstitious and mediaeval!" Immediately after, she straightened and said more loudly, "I will not have you bargaining with Him, dear one. It is too unsafe, even for those of us long practiced in the black arts. He is a treacherous negotiator, and He deals only in lives and afterlives; He would all too quickly possess your soul."

"My soul? What would He want with it, if He is not the Devil?"

She lowered her eyelids and, in an obvious effort to distract me, said, "Come away from those bones, darling —it is too gruesome!" And she lifted me up by the waist as easily as if I had been a babe, and set me down beside her to brush away dust and bits of crumbled bone from my dressing-gown. Shattered, frightened, I clung to her as she led me out into the hallway and back towards the chamber we had come to share.

But still I contemplated her odd statement about her Master; if He was not the Devil, was He then God? Surely God would not stoop to bargaining for souls! As sorrow had removed all my courteous restraint, I demanded again, "Why my soul?"

"A matter of speech," she said, but her gaze was focussed straight ahead, on her destination, rather than on me; I could not help feeling that she wished desperately to avoid the subject altogether, as if it were too unpleasant even to contemplate. "You would be absorbed. Annihilated. Devoured."

Is this what Vlad has done to Dunya? Has her soul been eaten by the Dark One with the loving eyes?

Yet if that is what I felt in His presence—that ecstatic sense of No Thing and All Things—then I cannot, as Elisabeth does, fear Him. If that is where Dunya is, then I shall dry my still-streaming tears. . . .

And yearn to join her.

Elisabeth will not teach me any of the needed knowledge to contact Him directly—to seek revenge on Vlad, and safe passage for us both from this castle. But I will find Him.

I will find Him. . . .

❖❖ ❖❖ ❖❖

29 JUNE. No entry in all this time; grief has caused my strength and inclination to wane. I think often of the dead: my good mother and father, my brothers Arkady and little Stefan, and dear Dunya. Sometimes I even think of all the poor souls whose bodies and bones lie corrupting in this castle and the vast encircling forest. So much death and suffering everywhere I turn! The magnitude of it overwhelms, permeates, my mind and heart. . . .

But so many things have happened that I must record them before the details fade from memory. To-night, for the first time in months, my mind is directed towards something other than mortality—towards a distant land I have always yearned to see, but came to think I never would.

A month or so ago, *tsigani* men drove their wagons into the castle courtyard and camped there. It was a warm

day, and hotter still for the gypsies, as they had decided to cook their noonday meal—a kid—and so built a large fire and spit and sat round it half-naked, their bare chests and backs exposed and glistening with sweat.

Their presence was resounding evidence (although I had never doubted) that Vlad did indeed mean to desert me here, for when Elisabeth and I tried to signal the group's apparent leader from the windows, the men laughed derisively and ignored us—just as they ignored Mr. Harker, who also cried out from his window. (Obviously, he is just as much a prisoner as we; though certainly ignorant of dealing with gypsies. The fool threw them money—which of course they pocketed before turning away.)

"Shut him up!" Elisabeth ordered, her eyes narrowed in frustration at the smirking ruffians beneath us; like an obedient slave, I hurried at once up to Harker's chambers and entranced him. When I returned, I found Elisabeth a feminine parody of the men; leaning seductively out the unfettered window, her gown and camisole both unfastened and pulled down to the waist, baring her breasts, she sang a patently bawdy song in Romany to the captivated onlookers below. My first reaction was to be slightly jealous at her brazen display in front of those vile, untrustworthy creatures; but the jealousy was swiftly replaced by humour at Elisabeth's audacity, and the comically smitten expressions on the gypsy men's faces. This was the first time since Dunya's death that I had been graced by laughter, and that made it all the more powerful: I shut my mouth and bit my tongue in an effort to quell the chuckling that bubbled up within me, but all for naught. The laughter came regardless; thus I stood somewhat back from the window so that I could not be seen, but I could see both Elisabeth and her adoring audience.

Her little performance achieved her intent; the *tsigani* chief immediately ran from his place in front of the camp-fire—shouting an order to the other men to remain—and arrived at the castle entrance. This was apparently bolted from the outside, for as we rushed to welcome him in, I heard the scrape of wood against metal, then the hollow clank of a wooden bolt striking stone.

Although we were forced to remain inside, he had no difficulty crossing that threshold; like a lovestruck bull, he flung aside the heavy door and rushed straight for Elisabeth and her bared bosom. He grasped her breasts, one with each hand, and, with alarming disregard for civility, pushed her backward to the cold floor.

To my astonishment, she did not resist (though she could easily have held her ground, causing *him* to fall back as though he had collided with a mountain). No, she fell back, laughing, and when he threw back her skirts and petticoats, she laughed harder still, as if it were all the most amusing sport, and let her bare legs sprawl wide.

He was not an unhandsome man—in fact, his shining coal-coloured hair and strong beak of a nose reminded me somewhat of my brother—but there was a crudeness to his broad face and plump, barrel-chested body, and to his oily olive skin and ridiculously long waxed mustache that I found supremely distasteful.

And when he quickly unfastened his trousers and fell atop her, piercing her, bellowing, still clutching her soft breasts with his thick, inelegant fingers, the whole scene struck me as nauseous, and I turned away, thinking to leave before I was called upon next.

But at that moment, Elisabeth framed the *tsigani*'s face with her hands (so white and delicate in contrast to his sun-darkened cheeks) and mightily pulled him down into a kiss. At first he resisted—such silly feminine desires

were clearly not to be indulged, not by a whore who had so blatantly lured him here for one thing, and one thing alone! But I saw, in profile, Elisabeth open her eyes as she pressed her lips passionately to his, and I saw his flutter open in surprise, then slowly grow dull and dreamy as all his volition fled.

Throughout, his desperate thrusting never ceased, for this transpired in the space of a few seconds.

"Zsuzsanna!" Elisabeth gasped, in the clear unyielding tone that signalled she would accept no refusal.

I stepped back towards her and looked down: her glorious hair had been swept up so that it spilled above her onto the stone, encircling her head like a halo—or the pale golden crescent of the half moon. The big *tsigani* still flailed wildly, his face now pressed into the sweetly scented pillow of hair half an arm's length above the top of her skull. All the while, she pressed her palms into his chest, easily holding him up. He would have crushed and suffocated a mortal woman.

"I can't, Elisabeth. I—I have no heart for this."

"I don't care if you fuck him or not, dearest. But bite him! For me, please!"

"I have no appetite. . . ."

"You needn't drink! Just bite him—don't kill him— and let the blood run down upon my face. . . ."

With a sigh I obeyed, moving behind her impaler's sweat-streaming back and bending down to strike the front of his shoulder. At this, he stiffened and emitted a strangled cry of terror and ecstatic release.

Sweet blood, but I was too grief-stricken, too troubled, too bored with life in this castle, to savour it. I withdrew, unhappily pleased to deny myself, unhappily pleased to suffer at the hands of hunger; and I sat back on my haunches and watched as Elisabeth licked the gypsy's small, streaming wound and rubbed her cheeks against it as a cat rubs its face against its mistress' legs.

"You are mine," Elisabeth whispered into his ear. "You shall obey Vlad's orders so long as they do not harm us, but you are mine. And so, after you have taken the prince from this castle, you shall return for us—and you will secretly tell your closest friend, and make him swear that if you should mysteriously die, he must come and rescue us poor, helpless women. All within a day. . . ."

Within a day. And now that the time is almost here, I think, *Will they really come?*

But there were further signs to convince me that Vlad would indeed be soon gone. For within a matter of days, he had stolen all of Harker's papers and clothes—this we learned when we paid our customary morning visit to the guest chambers. These forays have become most enlightening now that Harker carefully transcribes the bizarre scribblings of his diary into English on separate parchment. He has written the entire journal out for us, and I know it will serve us well in England, for it is laden with the consummate details befitting a lawyer's diary.

"He shall be our spy in London," Elisabeth told me that day, "and before Vlad rises, I shall do a private ritual to ensure that Mr. Harker survives long enough to be of service to us. But first, a more pragmatic bit of protection. . . ."

As she spoke, she moved to the night-stand and picked up a crucifix lying there, or rather the gold chain attached to it, and let it dangle in front of her face.

I confessed I gasped aloud, for I had been quite aware of its presence all along, and rendered ill-at-ease. She saw my discomfort (or rather, frankly, terror)—and laughed, tilting her face skyward whilst bringing the tiny impaled

Christ overhead until it rested just above her unmarred, porcelain features.

"Do not be cruel," I begged her in a trembling voice, for I was at once on the precipice of weeping. "Do not toy with me so, for I cannot bear it. . . . You will scar your precious skin!"

Still she ignored me, laughing, as though holding a red-hot poker above such a perfect and beautiful countenance was delightful sport. I surrendered to tears and covered my eyes.

And when I looked again, she had pressed the golden cross to her lips and kissed it.

I screamed, and began to faint; at once, she rushed over and caught me in her arms, saying:

"My dear, my dear, I did not mean to alarm you so! I merely meant to prove a point. Here. . . ." She immediately carried me to the sofa and sat beside me, gently patting my cheeks until I at last dared open my eyes.

She held a closed fist up to my face, then slowly opened it to reveal the crucifix upon her white palm. Again I recoiled and began to cover my face, but she commanded urgently: "Look at me, Zsuzsanna. *Look*. . . ."

I looked. And saw that the flesh beneath the shining golden object was perfect, untouched. Awed, I raised trembling fingers to her ruby mouth and found it entirely unblemished and beautiful.

But when she clasped my wrist and turned my hand palm-upward, intent on handing me the cross, I cried out again. "I can't! It will burn me. . . . I know, because it has happened."

"Zsuzsanna." Her tone grew stern. "It's like the sunlight. It can only hurt you if you are afraid of it. These are Vlad's fears, not your own; why have you carried them so long?" And, too swiftly for me to resist, she pushed the object into my outstretched palm and curled my fingers tight about it.

I was too startled to scream, to react—to do anything, really, except gape at the gleaming image in my hand. And a few seconds after, the revelation came: The cross was cold and sharp in my palm, but it did not burn my skin, nor did its presence evoke the expected agony.

"You see?" Elisabeth said, smiling again. "It is a bit of *metal,* nothing more. But Vlad does not believe that; and so, let us employ his superstitions against him. Go on, Zsuzsanna . . . put it round Mr. Harker's sleepy little head."

I did so, marvelling at my own imperviousness, my own power.

"And now, dear Jonathan," Elisabeth intoned softly at the snoring solicitor, "you are to wear this necklace wherever you go, and if the chain should break, you must always carry the cross upon your person. If Vlad—the count"—and here she glanced at me, grinning at her intentional repetition of Harker's misinformation—"should threaten, shove this pendant in his face."

Thus did Mr. Harker become our agent.

A fortnight later, the *tsigani* contingent returned with great wagons, and the pattern of Vlad's scheme more clearly emerged. There can be no question: He is indeed abandoning this place, if not forever, then for a very long time. At that time, Elisabeth's gypsy lover returned—but their second meeting was limited to travel arrangements, both ours and Vlad's. He is taking the safest way for him —boat—but we are not so constrained, and will be waiting for him when he finally arrives.

When I saw the big uncovered wagons, each large enough to hold several caskets of earth (another of Vlad's ridiculous superstitions, to believe that he cannot leave

Transylvania without taking a bit of it with him), my anger at being abandoned again flared, and I begged Elisabeth to do everything in her power to destroy him *now*. She insisted that such an effort would most likely fail at this time (what is she not telling me now in order to spare me worry?); nevertheless she would try, by recruiting our Englishman to attempt the deed.

And this she did, sending Mr. Harker on a diurnal mission to kill Vlad (which he very nearly did)—but the fool quailed.

And so I sit, equally overcome by excitement and fear. To-night, Vlad finally came to me—I have not seen him for almost a month, but was not surprised to find him further rejuvenated, with hair no longer white but pewter, and complexion faintly rosy. His expression was one of exultation mixed with condescending generosity.

"To-morrow night," said he, smiling. "He is yours to-morrow."

I feigned an expression of hopelessness and said sullenly, "You are abandoning me here to starve. Do not think I do not know."

His brows arched in mock innocence; he placed a spread palm upon his lifeless heart. "Me? Zsuzsanna, have you in your crush for Elisabeth come to realise that *I*, not she, have been your benefactor all these years? No, my dear, I must go and see to the details of some very special property . . . in England. At long last, I have found a way to free us both. And I do not do so without first thinking of you: I shall leave you the English guest for your very own! When all is ready, long before you are hungry again, I shall return for you."

I would not meet his gaze, but kept my own fixed upon the window . . . and the freedom beyond. In a low, hostile voice, I slowly proclaimed: "Arkady is gone."

So consummate was his deceit that his expression of abject surprise, limned with fear, was quite convincing; but I was not fooled. "What?"

"It is true."

Too terribly true. Knowing that the time would soon arrive when I would leave this castle for good—either through the vehicle of death, or the carriage that would bear me across the continent—I had gone down this morning to the subterranean vault, to bid my dear brother's body farewell.

Gone; vanished. (I am too heartsick even to weep about it now.) No trace of the corpse, though the bloodless stake lay atop the bare earthen catafalque where he had lain. At the discovery, I had fallen upon the damp mouldering ground and sobbed to think of my sweet Kasha's remains defiled in some evil attempt at magic by that monster. And like the Marys at the unsealed tomb, I demanded of Vlad now: "Where have you taken him?"

His grey brows knit together like rushing thunder-clouds, and his colour grew livid as he shouted: "This is some new treachery, is it not? Some new plot for mis-guided revenge! You have been listening to Elisabeth's lies —and I will give you no further warnings, since you have not believed the first. My only satisfaction comes from the knowledge that soon you will see your own stupidity in having trusted her and abandoned me. . . . And then all your pleas for help will be too late!"

He turned on his heel and stormed away, slamming the door behind him with such force that, with the ear-stunning sound of a pistol shot, the wood cracked in a lightning-bolt diagonal.

Through it all, I kept my silence. My revenge shall consist not of words or arguments, but of deeds which shall see him hurled down to Hell in agony.

So at last, we have parted—forever. I feel no sadness, no melancholy gratitude to him who gave me the immortal kiss. He has taken from me my mother, my father, my brother, my friend, my dignity; he has turned all my love to vengeful wrath.

Bastard! We shall meet again in England—England! It seems an unattainable dream, a mirage which beckons in the distance; and I worry that when I at last draw near, it will waver and dissolve into dust.

No. No fear, no doubt. I will find you in London. And there I *will* strike you down. . . .

❧ 7 ❧

Telegram, Abraham Van Helsing, M.D., D.Ph., D. Lit., Etc., Etc., Amsterdam, to John Seward, M.D., Purfleet, England

28 June

Dear and trusted friend,

    Apologies in advance for the imposition: Need your help and discretion, and unpardonably soon. Am bringing psychiatric patient to Purfleet afternoon of 1 July and require lodging for us both—but need for secrecy paramount. No one else must know we are in the city.

    My companion requires a barred and padlocked cell; I request same for myself.

    Destroy this document at once.

⊹   ⊹   ⊹

Dr. Seward's Diary

1 JULY. The professor has come.

    He arrived as expected in the afternoon, dressed in black with a broad-brimmed straw hat and looking for all the world like a village priest. I stood in the entryway and watched him step from the cab, then turn and reach out as the driver handed down a small, frail woman. She, too, wore all black, including a veil which obscured her features.

He carried her easily in his arms down the flower-lined path, as if he were long accustomed to doing so. When he spotted me on the porch, he grinned broadly, his blue eyes brightening at once. I strode forward and clapped his shoulder; the impulse to shake hands occurred to us both, but was rendered impossible because of the mysterious patient in his arms.

"Professor Van Helsing!" I called heartily, while behind him, the driver set two large suitcases upon the ground. I hurried over and took care of the tip at once; my mentor is not very well off financially, from what I can gather. I believe he routinely undercharges his patients or charges them not at all, and I would be a gentleman of leisure now were it not for my "hobby," the asylum.

At my greeting, the professor's grin faded and some of the light left his eyes. He pursed his lips as if to hush me into silence; had he not borne such a burden, he would have also raised a finger to them. I heeded the warning and immediately lowered my voice to a whisper.

"It is good to see you again."

The smile and brightness returned immediately. "And you, friend John. Though you are looking rather pale and underfed. We shall have to find a young lady to fatten you up and lure you out for walks in the sunshine!"

I averted my gaze briefly down at the riot of yellow and crimson zinnias edging our path, but maintained a pleasant expression. Anything that evoked thoughts of Lucy was still painful, so I did not reply.

At once his tone softened with compassion. "Ah . . .

I see I have blundered directly onto the problem's source. Forgive me, my friend; I am a blind and foolish old man."

I believe I blushed, which only increased my discomfort, as it is for me an uncommon reaction. Then I glanced shyly at the silent patient, wondering how lucid she might be, and whether she had registered the exchange. How could I manage a dignified introduction now?

Once again, Van Helsing seemed to have read my thoughts. "Have no worry, John. She suffers from catatonia; her mind is far from us. Even if it were not, she would be unable to divulge your troubles, for she does not speak."

"You are far from old, and most certainly not blind," I told him. "Frankly, you are the most perceptive person I know." Indeed, he has been this way since I first met him. Sometimes, his ability to guess what I—or another person —am thinking is astounding. It is not simply that he knows me well; I have seen him do the same with strangers. Over time, I have developed two theories: one, that he has honed his observation skills to preternatural perfection; or two, that he is psychic.

The latter is difficult to prove, though of late I have become keenly interested in occult phenomena and the teachings of a local organisation known as the Golden Dawn. (My readings have led me to conclude that the professor is privy to much, or all, of their knowledge. This is based on countless comments he has made during our close eight-year friendship. Esoteric phrases such as *As above, so below*—a quote from our mutual acquaintance Hermes Trismegistus. And dozens more such opaque—at the time, anyway—remarks.)

More than that, the professor radiates an aura of power—not so much the physical sort as the mental. Like me, he was a *wunderkind,* but I do not speak of intelligence here, which he has in abundance; I speak of the metaphysical. In public—except when he lectures—he takes on the *persona* of the good-natured bumbler, the clown. I have even heard him affect the most outrageously comical foreign accent, even though his English is quite excellent. It is as if he wants to prevent the world from seeing the true man: the scholar, the genius, the philosopher.

Yet when alone in my presence, he sometimes permits me glimpses of an immensely brilliant and knowledgeable occultist beneath the fool's mask. He has never labelled it as occultism, of course; this is what I have gleaned. But now I remember a long-ago holiday in Amsterdam, when I inadvertently wandered into his private library and discovered inside a closed cabinet a treasure-trove of treatises on magic—*The Greater Key of Solomon, The Goetia,* the *Sepher Yetzirah,* and *A True and Faithful Relation of What Passed for Many Years Between Doctor Dee and Some Spirits.*

This is the man I met again to-day, though he had successfully adopted the guise of a not-so-educated country priest. But I saw beneath the simple guilelessness that veiled the wide blue eyes, beneath the cheerful expression. He looks older than when I last saw him; more of the red-gold hairs have faded to white, and he, like me, has lost weight and looks drawn about the cheeks and jaw. Despite it all, he radiates even more of that impressive internal strength, that deep sense of wisdom and calm even the fiercest tempest cannot shake—paradoxically making him —the *real,* interior man beneath the costume of flesh— seem far *younger* than when we last met.

"But here," I continued, gesturing towards the entry. We both headed for the open door, I reaching as if to take the motionless woman in his arms. As expected, he refused any aid. "Let's go inside at once and relieve you of your burden. I will call the attendant to carry her—"

"No!" The sharpness of his reply made me jerk my head to stare at him at once. More mildly, he added, "No attendants yet. The time may come when she requires one, but to-day, let us maintain as much privacy as we can."

I agreed, and told him I would wait to ring Thomas to fetch the bags until both he and his patient were settled into their rooms, then have the bags left outside the cell doors to guarantee their anonymity. Once we had stepped over the threshold, I convinced him to let go of his jealously guarded prize and deposit her in a high-backed wheelchair. It is the newest model, specially equipped with restraints for the more violent patients. As he tucked her with tender solicitousness into the chair and paused to regard the straps, I commented softly, "I doubt she will need those."

"Not at the moment." The jovial mask slipped again for an instant, no more. This time I saw a darkly troubled man, one who bore the weight of all the world upon his soul. "But the time may come soon. We must remain alert."

He insisted upon pushing the chair himself. I led him directly to the lift (a necessity here; dragging a violent patient upstairs or down is dangerous work). In the absolute privacy of the lift, I awaited an explanation of his "secret mission," but none came. So I made small talk and inquired after his mother, a true English gentlewoman whom I have met and come to fondly admire.

"She is dying," he said, in his blunt, matter-of-fact Dutch manner. "Ulcerated tumour of the right breast. She has had it more than a year, but her time is short now; it affects her brain. My concern is that she might die while I am away."

I put a hand upon his shoulder. I have rarely touched him other than to shake his hand in greeting or parting, and he acknowledged the gesture with a grateful glance. (Does anyone like to shake hands more than his countrymen?) "I am sorrier than words can say. She was so very kind to me when you both came to visit; I came to think of her as my own grandmother, since I never knew either of mine."

At that last comment, he let out a soft gasp as if struck in the stomach, and looked away; I think emotion had finally overwhelmed him. After a moment of silence, he said, "I do not mean to burden you, friend John, with my own difficulties. You have borne more than your share in your brief life. You are too young to have experienced so much loss; too young. At my age, it is to be expected."

He referred, of course, to the death of my father some sixteen years ago, and my mother three years ago this fall. The family estate is too vast and lonely for a single heir to occupy, so now I share it with my patients.

At last we arrived at the two cells closest to my own bedchamber, which I prefer to keep unoccupied unless the asylum is filled to capacity. As we have only three resident patients at present, one of whom I expect to release shortly, the closest inmate was a good half-dozen cells away. Van Helsing will have his privacy.

"Here we are," I said, unlocking and then flinging open the doors to each room so that the professor could peer in. One cell was windowless and contained the standard furnishings: bed, night-stand, and a gas lamp mounted so high upon the wall that it could be turned on or off only by an attendant with a special contrivance attached to a long broom handle. The other I had personally prepared for the professor. The barred window looked directly down into the flower garden (which is particularly bright and lush this summer), and I had covered the bed with a quilt sewn by Mother. I had added, too, a writing-table and comfortable chair which faced the window, and beside the unreachable gas lamp had left a long pole so that the professor could control the light as he wished.

I removed two keys from the jailer's ring on my belt and handed them to him. "This is yours . . . and this is the key to the lady's chamber."

"Ah," he said, gazing down at them and then back up at the rooms. "This"—and he gestured at the sunnier, more cheerful room I had fixed for him—"I will let her have. The other is suitable for me." And before I could protest, he wheeled her past me into the cell, lifted her from the wheel-chair, and deposited her in the more comfortable seat looking out onto the garden. It was rather frustrating, for if the lady was indeed catatonic, the view would be quite wasted, and I was not at all happy leaving Mother's heirloom quilt in the safekeeping of a mad-woman.

I followed them inside, wondering whether it would be too rude to speak up, when the professor reached down and removed his patient's hat and veil.

I drew in a breath. The woman was absolute skin and bones, but at the same time young and unnaturally pretty, with huge dark eyes and full dark hair coiled at the nape of her neck. And yet . . .

I blinked, and for a heartbeat found myself looking at a woman Van Helsing's age, one with streaks of grey in her hair and crow's-feet framing her eyes.

Another blink, and the lady was again young and beautiful, her hair a rich brown-black without a trace of silver. It was as if her youth was a veil which had lifted for an instant, then quickly lowered, masking the real woman beneath. The dreadful soulless vacancy in those half-closed, downcast eyes could not be hidden; yet beneath it I sensed a fathomless grief.

I looked up at last to find the professor studying me, his gold-and-silver brows furrowed intently. When our gazes met—his knowing, mine questioning—he said, "You are a sensitive, John. You see beneath the façade, yes?"

I was too taken aback to do anything but gesture my assent. Did I understand him aright? Was this a metaphysical case he had brought me, this strange, sad woman with the aged yet ageless face? The notion in itself was compelling enough. Still, there was more that drew me to her, some odd sense of kinship—a feeling that perhaps we two shared some secret sorrow.

To my disappointment, he revealed no more, but said, "And now we leave her to rest. I shall require some time alone with her at sunset." At once he bent down onto one knee at her feet, like a gentleman proposing to a lady (the painful memory of Lucy again!). Gently, he lifted her limp gloved hand from her lap; this he pressed to his lips with such pure, loving devotion that I was honestly shocked. Their relationship was clearly more than doctor and patient.

So piqued was my curiosity that when we exited and the professor shut and locked the thick door behind us, I demanded outright: "Who is she?"

He looked ahead into the distance and sighed. "Gerda Van Helsing. My wife."

I could not have been more astonished. I had known the professor for more than seven years, since I first arrived at university at the tender age of fifteen. A difficult situation: my first time away from home, and I so much younger than the other lads that I was constantly the butt of jokes and taunting. (Nor did it help that I looked far younger than my actual age.) Only the professor looked beyond my immaturity, at my talents, and took me under his paternal and professional wing.

We were very close, perhaps because I had lost Papa early on, and I was grateful to find a father-substitute; of course, there was also the fact that we shared a passion for medicine, and that he saw much of himself in me. He, too, was a boy genius who had taken his medical degree at a very early age; thus he encouraged me greatly to pursue my medical studies, though I was surrounded by men almost ten years my senior. (The professor is also licensed to practice law in Holland, but he ruefully admits that was a mistake.)

Yet during our years of association—and during my brief one-day visit to his home—I have never heard him (or his mother, for that matter) speak of family or wife. In fact, I had always assumed he was a bachelor. I had never asked for a tour of his bedchamber.

"Professor," I said, in a low voice, although we were quite alone and beyond anyone's earshot, "what is going on? I get the perception that your wife's malady is more than mere catatonia. Something else is involved; am I wrong to think it is metaphysical? Mrs. Van Helsing seems so young . . . yet I believe that she is not, that it is all illusion."

He released a sigh of infinite weariness, and all his cheeriness fled for good. "We are both men of science, John, trained to rely on our eyes and our logic to explain how the world operates. But there are instances where modern science fails utterly. We must adapt and, like Democritus when he postulated the atom, must accept that there is more to this universe than eye can see or brain can fathom." He paused, and seemed to consider whether or not to tell me everything all at once. To my disappointment, he apparently opted for the latter. "In time, I will explain more. But sunset will come in less than two hours; before that time, I must tend to Gerda."

"First," I said, "you must have a proper tea." And so I led him off and we ate together. He seemed deeply preoccupied, and spoke no more of his wife or mother, so I did not press. Afterwards, he disappeared into the garden cell and did not emerge until supper. Again, he was uncharacteristically tight-lipped about his purpose in being here.

Cannot sleep to-night, and so I have risen to record this: My mind keeps returning to the image of Mrs. Van Helsing's face. Why does it haunt me so?

✠ ✠ ✠

The Diary of
Abraham Van Helsing

2 JULY. An uneventful journey, and both Gerda and I passed a quiet night. Unfortunately, I missed my opportunity yesterday for a successful hypnotic session with her— we were both travelling at the time she was most receptive, and when I returned to her later in the afternoon, she would not speak.

How strange to indulge in the luxury of sleeping at night! First, I carefully secured each cell—put a crucifix over each door, and one over Gerda's window, in addition to a small medallion of Saint George. And of course, there is the cross around her neck—on a thick chain like mine, that neither she nor an attacker can easily break.

For the first time in many nights, I slept soundly. The realisation that the worst had already happened—that Vlad and Zsuzsanna had grown suddenly stronger and escaped the castle—was oddly calming. I had nothing more to worry about.

Except for John; he has always been like his mother, a sensitive psychic. When he stared at her face-to-face for the first time yesterday, I feared that he had indeed surmised the truth—and that I had made a fatal mistake in bringing Gerda here.

For I have worked all my life to spare the boy pain, to protect him from the Impaler's attentions. I wanted him to have a normal life, the life I and all my ancestors could not have, the life our sweet little Jan was so cruelly denied.

(And how horrified and moved I was to hear that his adoptive parents bestowed on him the English version of his dead brother's name: John.)

No one knows but me—and Mama, who took the infant with her to London and gave it to the best and kindest people she knew, who had long been denied children. They were never told the truth of the child's origin. Even poor Gerda does not know of his existence, for during her pregnancy and delivery she was quite unaware of her body's condition, and I worked hard to keep this knowledge from Zsuzsanna and Vlad.

Have I succeeded? I do not know; the question will be answered soon. I agonised long over whether to come here and expose him to danger—but *not* to come and watch over him might be even more perilous. He is too close to London now that Vlad is headed here. My only link to the vampires is through my poor wife, who tells me little; how else can I be sure that John is safe, and that Vlad and Zsuzsanna have not learned somehow of his existence?

But yesterday, when I saw him peer profile-to-profile into his mother's face, I was horrified: How stupid I have been to think that John, psychically sensitive, would not know he was staring directly into a genetic mirror? The resemblance between them is that marked: same nose, same eyes and chin, same colouring. Yet in my desperate haste I had failed to consider this problem.

Any harm that comes to him is entirely my fault. I am contemplating departure—for his sake.

At dawn this morning, an ominous sign from Gerda. Under hypnosis, her mood was gay and chatty. To the question "Where are you now?" she replied, "Moving."

This confused me; the day before, she had radiated passionate fury and had sworn, "He has left! The bastard has left!" Of this she would say no more, except to describe the sight of large, sturdy wagons outside the castle. I took this to mean that Vlad had abandoned Zsuzsanna.

But to-day, the news is changed. "Moving," Gerda says. "I hear rattling and the snorts of horses." Zsuzsanna was riding in her coffin in one of the large wagons, I assumed. Yet, to my surprise, there followed: "A bright, sunny morning; I had forgotten how beautiful the countryside is in summer. I am sad to leave my home forever, but at the same time, I am overjoyed!"

Impossible, of course, for Zsuzsanna to be peeking out at the sunshine. I do not understand the report; has she realised that Gerda endures my questions each day, and is she intentionally attempting to confuse me with false information?

I have taken such precautions that I strongly doubt it. The vampires are indeed on their way. I can only surmise that Zsuzsanna thought she was being left behind—but that Vlad decided, perhaps at the last moment, to take her on the journey. The rapturous description of morning I cannot explain.

If they travel by land, they will arrive here within a week; if by sea (which poses fewer risks) I have a month to prepare. I will assume the former, in order to be ready.

Thus I must make my choice concerning John quickly. Do I leave him, and pray that he will remain safe without my interventions? Or do I remain?

╌╌ ╌╌ ╌╌

Dr. Seward's Diary

3 JULY. As sole proprietor of a lunatic asylum, I am accustomed to the strange; yet to-day, I believe, has featured the strangest events I have ever encountered, here or elsewhere.

It began in the wee hours of morning. I had lain awake for some hours, unable to return to sleep after another bout of what I've come to call my "disturbing dream." I have been reluctant to record it—until to-day—because I had credited it to a combination of anxiety and hero worship. And, frankly, to a submerged bit of mania within myself which glorified the professor and me as two brave occult knights fighting against a great Evil that wished to overwhelm the world. The dream is rather simple, consisting of an image of myself and the professor wielding silver swords against a vast encroaching Darkness. That part of it is rather pleasant (and, in full consciousness, embarrassing). But the "disturbing" part comes when the professor disappears abruptly from view, and I am left alone in the struggle. The Darkness quickly enlarges and engulfs me, devouring me in the same way an amoeba does its dinner. This I have dreamt several times since receiving Van Helsing's telegram.

Enough of that! Silly as it seems to say the words aloud, it still terrifies me—especially after my encounter with the professor this morning.

So I lay awake for some time in bed, reluctant to return to sleep (perchance to dream), reluctant to rise and accept fatigue as my lot. At last, when the darkness had lightened to grey, I rose, made my toilet and dressed, and went out into the corridor to see if the professor was awake. My intent was to invite him to a hearty breakfast, for he has missed supper and breakfast both days, leaving me concerned.

His cell door was closed and locked. I gave up hope and had just turned to head for the staircase when I caught a sidewise glimpse of his wife's door—slightly ajar. I moved to it, thinking to knock, but instead remained silent a moment, listening. From within came the professor's voice; its tone reassured me that the conversation taking place was not an intimate one.

And, in reply, there came a second voice—a woman's, no doubt that of his "catatonic" patient. My physician's curiosity got the better of me, I confess; I knocked lightly, swiftly, then pushed open the door with such care that it made no sound.

Van Helsing was far too intent to pay me notice. His gaze was fixed fast upon his wife, who sat up in the chair, which had been turned away from the window to face the professor.

She wore such an animated expression that for an instant, I thought I was looking upon a different woman. Her dark eyes were open wide and brimming with mirth and charm, her lips curved upward in a dimpling grin. She was dressed like a matron in a sedate black dress and shawl, with her hair pulled back into a severe, unflattering bun— but her demeanour was that of a giggling debutante. This morning, the illusion of youthful beauty was so strong that I caught no glimpse of the older woman beneath.

"Looking through the window," she said prettily, chin

resting atop her knuckles. And, indeed, she had turned her head and seemed to be looking out a window (whilst the real one was at her back), as if she were sitting on a train staring out at the scenery.

"Is Vlad with you?" the professor asked, with such intensity that I realised I had stumbled onto a hypnotic session. I remained absolutely still, lest I disturb either of them and cause Mrs. Van Helsing to emerge too swiftly from trance.

She tossed her head and gave a disparaging laugh. "Not *him*. I'm with my lover." She sighed. "The sunlight on the mountains is so beautiful. . . ."

At this, Van Helsing's thick blond brows rushed together in alarm. "Sunlight! Are you in your coffin? Sleeping?"

Again, a playful laugh; astoundingly, it was not directed at the preposterousness of the question. "No, no, I'm awake. The scenery is so delightful, I wouldn't want to—" A fresh burst of giggles. "Elisabeth, stop! Someone will see. . . ."

"Who is Elisabeth? Mortal or vampire? Is she someone you have bitten?"

At this, I could not repress a small gasp. Despite his earlier inattention, Van Helsing glanced up sharply; all animation left his wife with the terrible abruptness of a house of cards collapsing, leaving her once more the dull-eyed, slack-jawed creature.

As for the professor, he rose with the speed and mindless determination of a whirlwind. With startling brusqueness, he seized my arm and pulled me from the room. Still clutching me as if to prevent my escape, he closed and locked the cell door; then at last released me and whispered fiercely:

"Never do that again! Never! Do you realise how much harm you might come to, listening to such things?"

For a moment, I was too astonished to reply; I had never seen the professor so red-faced with rage. And what did he mean, I might come to harm? Was he threatening me? When at last I found my tongue, I managed, "I—I merely wanted to invite you to early breakfast, seeing that you were awake so early. I apologise for any inconvenience, but because the door was slightly ajar and I could hear you speaking, I took the liberty . . . I *did* knock, but you were too intent to hear me."

"Then it is my fault!" he thundered—I say *thundered* even though he still whispered, for the anger still shook his voice. "You have heard things which you should not have heard—"

"About mortals and vampires," I said, unable to entirely restrain my amused skepticism. I was interested, to be sure, in occult phenomena, and solid evidence might persuade me of the existence of vampires . . . of a psychic variety. But a vampire who bites with sharp teeth —*this* was a topic straight from the pages of a penny dreadful. I looked askance at him, inviting a rational explanation for such an irrational question, an explanation that would set me at ease and provoke from us both a smile. Indeed, I had in my own mind volunteered one for him: that he was indulging for some reason his wife's delusion, in order to learn enough about it to help her.

But the fierce intensity in his blue eyes did not abate, nor did he reply; he merely averted his gaze and folded his arms, still troubled. Or rather, troubled afresh by his inability to provide the answer I so yearned to hear. Had there been a chair in the corridor, I should have collapsed into it, for I was suddenly overwhelmed by the sickening and unmistakable realisation that the professor had posed the question *in all seriousness.*

I released a short, gasping laugh of disbelief; the grin on my face began to metamorphose into a frown. All these years, I had believed my mentor to be the possessor of the deepest occult secrets. Could the secret instead be that he was a deluded madman? "Surely, Dr. Van Helsing, you do not be—"

In reply, he again seized my arm with such force that I broke off, startled into silence, as he pulled me along into his own grim chamber.

Once there, he shut the door behind us, then turned to face me. "John. I have indeed done a great disservice to you by coming here. I will stay no longer, but make immediate arrangements for myself and my wife to depart."

His mood was somewhat calmer but no less determined, no less angry—though I could see now that his anger was becoming entirely turned towards himself. And for some reason, that annoyed me more than his abrupt and inexcusable behaviour towards me.

"See here," I protested, trying to match his vehemence with some of my own. Although what I had heard remained unbelievable, it was becoming increasingly clear— just as Mrs. Van Helsing's true visage had peeked out from behind the youthful veil—that the professor was acting out of grave concern, not lunacy. As odd and inexplicable as the situation seemed, I knew at that moment (with the most purely unscientific instinct) that I had not misjudged my most trusted mentor all these years; that I could still trust him. "Whatever misunderstanding or embarrassment has just occurred here, I will not see you rushing off. You are my guest and my dearest friend, Professor, and the fault is mine, not yours. I swear to you that I will never so intrude upon you again; it was an enormously thoughtless act, for which I apologise utterly."

He sighed, and the determined anger on his features softened to sorrow. "Ah, my good friend, if only apologies could negate any harm done."

"How have I harmed you? Tell me, and I shall right things at once!" Even as I spoke boldly, I shuddered with a sudden chill, for the image of the encroaching Darkness came upon me with swift, distressing force. *This is the meaning of the dream,* I thought involuntarily. *This is why I am called now, to help the professor defeat It.* . . .

All too similar to my madman's delusions, and even more disturbing to find myself persuaded by such a compelling mania. As I looked at the professor, my attention shifted to the lintel behind him. Just above it, he had hung a carved wooden crucifix, so large that I could see clearly the expression of agony upon Christ's face. From his many comments, I have always taken the professor to be an agnostic, or at the very most, a Deist. What was happening to us supposed men of science? I struggled, I fought to disengage myself from my delusion.

And yet, I could not disbelieve.

Van Helsing did not notice my swift internal dilemma; he had averted his gaze to shake his head. In the yellow lamplight, his expression once again composed itself into the calm, wise face of the professor I had always known. "It is not *you* who have harmed *me,* John, nor you who must make amends. I have no concern for myself, but you have heard too much. And in this case, too much knowledge can lead to danger. How can I right this, other than to be sure that you are never again exposed to such opportunities?"

"Professor," I said, with such determination that he looked at me with frank curiosity. But words fled me again as I flailed on the precipice of commitment. I could not help but believe what I was about to tell him; but if I did confess my most secret thoughts, would I be exposing myself to ridicule—or worse, to the diagnosis that I belong among those I profess to treat?

I drew a breath and continued in a rush, before my will left me. I told him of the troubling dream, of my overwhelming sense that he had come here rightly because I have always been fated to help him in some secret struggle.

I blushed as I spoke, for it is not easy to confess such private and irrational beliefs, especially to the one around whom those beliefs cluster. But he listened quietly, respectfully, and gave not the slightest sign of skepticism. I do think he accepted everything I presented.

I finished by saying, "I have always believed it all to be a silly, boyish notion that would leave me as I matured; but it has only grown stronger through the years. And as you noticed when I first met your wife, Professor: when I look at people, I know their hearts. Yours is the purest and most trustworthy I have found. If there is any way, no matter how dangerous, that I can help you, I would be honoured to do so."

I fell silent, and for a time, neither of us spoke; Van Helsing's expression revealed that he was both touched and deeply troubled. At last he said solemnly, "I must consider carefully all you have said, my friend. Rest assured, I shall not leave to-night, but will give you my decision in the morning." He paused then and went over to his suitcase, from which he retrieved a shining golden object. "In the meantime, would you do me the kindness of wearing this at all times?"

A necklace dangled from his fingers; I held out my

cupped hand, and flinched ever so slightly as it dropped, cold and hard, into my palm.

A crucifix, this one on a long chain. I studied it, then looked up at him, intending to question. But I feared the answer—and so I pulled the necklace over my head, and let the pendant slip down beneath my jacket, where no one could see it.

From his demeanour, I judged it time to take my leave —after first inviting him down to breakfast. As I walked to the door, though, curiosity overwhelmed me, and I spun about, demanding:

"Professor! Do you really believe in vampires, the sort that go round biting people's necks in the night?"

He studied me unhappily before replying with a question of his own. "Friend John. Do you believe in lunatics?"

"It is not a question of belief," I retorted thoughtlessly, without pausing to consider his meaning. "Lunatics exist."

"Just so." And he would say no more.

❧ 8 ❧

The Diary of
Abraham Van Helsing

4 JULY. He knows, poor John knows. Not details, perhaps, but he has been sent the same dream as I; it can only mean that Fate or God or whatever Power that works to protect the good is trying to warn both of us.

And such warnings must be heeded, for they indicate danger's approach. Despite all my efforts to spare him his heritage, he is drawn to it all the same. Perhaps the Buddhists are right after all; he is biologically and psychically linked to Vlad, and it is his "karma" to help his father free the family from its centuries-long curse.

So my original instinct in coming here was justified. I dare not leave him now; I dare not.

❧ ❧ ❧

Zsuzsanna Dracul's Diary

13 JULY. A week in London, and I have never felt so gloriously *alive*! Elisabeth is apparently infinitely wealthy, and she has indulged my whims like a parent indulging a dreadfully spoiled child. And that is what I feel like—a child on holiday—when I visit the pretty dress shops, the cobblers, and sample all the new fashions. In the course of my entire existence, living or undead, I have never owned so many dresses or hats or slippers or gloves as I have bought this week.

And in the process, I am tended to like a real lady, embraced into the social bosom of those who are my prey. Nay, not a real lady but the princess that I am, for Elisabeth and I go by our titles, the Countess Nadasdy and the Princess Dracul. How everyone fawns over us!

We have even bought a house, a great French *château* in the most affluent part of the city, which Elisabeth has filled with servants. I have a wonderfully handsome coachman, Antonio, offspring of a black African mother and Italian father. For sport, I engage with him in what he believes to be a most scandalous affair. . . . Little does he know *just* how strange it is for a lowly coachman to be dallying with *this* particular princess.

But the house, the house, the house is beautiful. There are cut crystal panes in the windows which refract sunlight into rainbows and fine Turkish carpets, and peacocks strutting on the grounds, and flowers and gushing fountains and statues of Bacchus and Pan and Aphrodite. . . .

We are the exotic new darlings of society, the Hungarian and Roumanian representatives of royalty. People call on us, and we serve (and eat!) the finest French pastries

—the tiny decorated ones, of the type I had seen in Vienna's *Konditorei* but could not savour.

I devour it all. And I suckle on the city's rich and powerful elite—mostly men, who contrive to get me alone. How cheerfully I let them . . . and then, how cheerfully I drink.

But a pall is cast upon this bliss when I contemplate Vlad's arrival. He will try to find someone to try to kill us, just as we have enlisted Mr. Harker's aid. We left our Englishman in Buda-Pesth, raving in delirium. It will make for a nice excuse, especially since he will remember nothing of us women but everything of Vlad. His people will think him sick all this time with madness or brain-fever, no doubt, so that when he does resurface in his Exeter, no one will be suspicious.

And we will find a way to bring him to London.

But I have waited so many years to enjoy my freedom in this fair (but dirty) city that I dread the interruption of my happiness. I feel like saying to Elisabeth: *You go, and wage your metaphysical war against Vlad; leave me here!*

She seems happy, but has been preoccupied the past two days. She has enjoyed our socialising and indulging in sexual peccadilloes with those upon whom I dine; but yesterday and to-day, she closeted herself away beyond my reach, using a magic so strong I cannot detect where she has gone. I assume she is preparing for the confrontation with Vlad, or enlisting the Dark Lord's aid. But when she emerged yesterday, she was grim-faced and silent, and sent me out to shop alone.

To-day she did so again. When I arrived home late, I found her down in the cellar, where she had unwrapped packages sent from her home. The contents?

Dear God, the contents. . . . A woman-sized Iron Maiden—naked, the nipples on its hard breasts painted

gaudy red, its wide leer filled with human teeth of various
sizes and shades of white, yellow, brown. From its head
flowed long golden hair; upon its pubes was coiled the
same.

Nearby stood another obscene creation: a narrow cy-
lindrical cage—again, just large enough to hold a woman's
body. From its iron bars emerged long, sharp spikes . . .
turned inward, so that any prisoner who struggled or tried
to flee would soon find herself impaled. I stood and
watched in silent horror as Elisabeth directed Dorka and a
manservant upon a ladder as they suspended it from the
ceiling, then threaded the rope through a pulley.

"What is this?" I asked, in a low voice that trembled. I
knew the answer already; the devices' purposes were patently clear. But I had to hear Elisabeth's explanation.

She whirled smiling to face me, her eyes bright with
predatory anticipation. "Zsuzsanna, darling! Welcome to
our little dungeon." Her sulkiness was entirely gone, replaced by great good cheer; she reached for my hand and
pulled me to her, then planted a fervent kiss upon my lips.

I stood stiff and unyielding, for I was quite distraught:
I could only think of how desperately I had always hated
Vlad's Theatre of Death, where it pleased him to torment
his poor prey without mercy. I have dined on the blood of
strangers too long to feel any remorse for it—but vampire
or no, I have never shared Vlad's predilection for torture.
Bad enough the poor fools should die, so I long ago vowed
that I would send them to Hades on clouds of ecstasy.

Most times, I have managed to do so. But when I saw
Elisabeth's horrific devices, I panicked. I had judged her to
be like me, a woman of generosity and kindness, capable of
sympathy towards her supper; had I run from the Impaler's
arms into the embrace of another as secretly cruel as he?

At my coldness, Elisabeth merely laughed, and jovially

pulled me to her side so that she could wind an arm round my waist. "Silly Zsuzsa! Don't be frightened of them! They're merely . . . tools. Means to an end." Then she pressed her lips to my ear and whispered, so that neither Dorka nor the manservant could hear: "In time, dearest. In time, you will understand. Do not judge before you see for yourself. . . ."

"I do not *want* to see," I said stubbornly, and pulled away.

That was the extent of it; neither she nor I have spoken of the secrets in the cellar since. Frankly, I do not wish even to think of them, for when I do it spoils the sublime happiness of being here in London with the one I love. Tonight we met a group at a restaurant—a baronet and his wife, and a lord and lady!—and dined on a fine British supper of champagne, oysters, beef Wellington, and trifle. Food is such a delight!

I will do my best not to judge Elisabeth until I see what she intends with these implements. I cannot imagine anything good, but I must trust her. . . .

✥ ✥ ✥

Dr. Seward's Diary

21 JULY. After speaking to Van Helsing about Renfield, a patient, I have granted his request to privately interview our life-eater in his cell. I suspect the professor believes— dare I say it?—vampires are involved. Since he decided to remain here, he has spoken to me of his "mission" here only twice, and then in the vaguest terms. My belief still wavers from time to time; I suppose I will never be con-

vinced until I have irrefutable physical evidence of the existence of such creatures.

Last night's musings about our zoophagous patient affected me more than I had realised. Upon retiring quite late, I fell at once asleep, into vivid, gruesomely detailed dreams of Renfield regurgitating the bloodied, half-digested corpses of sparrows, cats, large dogs—even a horse, which emerged from his gullet impossibly whole. And everywhere floated feathers, painted with blood in more delicate, intricate designs than could ever be wrought by the hand of Nature.

Abruptly, over this nauseous spectacle fell a great darkness—the all-consuming evil void from the recurring nightmare I had relayed to Professor Van Helsing. It spread like a shadow over the vomiting man until he was entirely eclipsed. That sight evoked again in me an intense terror, a terror that grew to unbearable proportions when, even in the midst of my dream, I understood its meaning:

The Darkness is like Renfield—an Eater of Souls, desperate to consume life after life after life after life. And it means to devour Van Helsing . . . and me.

-+- -+- -+-

The Diary of
Abraham Van Helsing

24 JULY. Dracula draws near. This instinct and evidence tell me; in fact, I took the liberty of hypnotising John's "zoophage," Renfield, and am convinced that his new-found obsession with consuming "life" is in some way a sinister influence of the vampire's approach.

In fact, Vlad should have arrived in London a fortnight ago. Thus far, however, Gerda will not corroborate
this. In Zsuzsanna's voice, she speaks only of one other—
the mysterious Elisabeth, who seems to be neither mortal
nor vampire. Of Vlad she says: "Hmph! Who cares about
him? We shall see him soon enough. . . ."

I can think of one possible explanation: that Vlad and
Zsuzsanna have had a falling-out, and took separate routes.
For a moment this notion caused me some terror, as it
could mean that Vlad is headed elsewhere in England, or
to another country altogether.

But no; Zsuzsanna says that she will "see him soon
enough." And I know that she is here in London. Where, I
do not know; but I must learn soon and find her, before
she finds *me*.

⊹⊱ ⊹⊱ ⊹⊱

8 AUGUST. At last, at last! Word from Gerda: "He is
come," she said this afternoon—and that is all I could coax
from her. Then, like a little girl, she drew up her knees and
hugged them to her chest; and turned her face from me
and pouted. I confess that despite the chill I felt knowing
that Vlad had arrived (and with him, great danger), I
smiled. Not at my poor wife, but at the perfect mental
image I had of the immature Zsuzsanna sulking. Everything Gerda has told me so far fits: all the condescending
references to Vlad and to her freedom, and now this unhappy reaction at the arrival of him whom she had once
adored. My guess is right; they *have* had a falling-out.

But will Vlad join Zsuzsanna here? His arrival took
more than a month, which means he must have come by
sea. I had pressed Gerda on this, asking, "Where is he
now? London?"

She would say nothing, merely shook her head.

I can only hope that he makes amends and returns to Zsuzsanna—else my task will prove much more difficult, indeed. Without Gerda as my compass, I am lost.

✛ ✛ ✛

24 AUGUST. From the small bits of information I have gleaned from Gerda, I believe I can triangulate the area where Zsuzsanna must be hiding: near the East End, or Piccadilly. I have scouted the area extensively both by cab and on foot and, so far, have failed to locate any properties suitable for vampires. The neighbourhoods there are havens for the wealthy upper-class; they contain no cemeteries, no crumbling chapels, nothing sufficiently gloomy to suit Vlad's taste.

I have no further word, however, regarding whether he will rendezvous with his consort. It may well be that I have a double task—to hunt down both him *and* Zsuzsanna separately. I pray that will not come to pass.

I think it will not; for last night, we had quite a scare at the asylum which has convinced me that he is indeed come to London. John's "zoophage," Renfield, became so grievously obsessed that he scaled the asylum wall and ran onto the neighbouring property. (Fortunately, he did not get so far as to alarm the residents.) The disturbance drew me from my room, and when John returned (huffing and puffing), he told me all that had transpired.

What caught my attention most was a comment the patient had made in his delirium, that the Master had come and he, Renfield, would do this Master's bidding. As John reports it: "I have worshipped You long and afar off. Now that You are near, I await Your commands. . . ."

Renfield is, as I have always suspected, exceptionally sensitive. (Madmen usually are—forgive me, dear Gerda, but it is true of you as well.) He feels the vampire's evil presence nearing, and has incorporated it into his madness. But we must take especial care with him, for he has offered himself up to Vlad's service. He is therefore of great potential danger to us.

Vlad is indeed in the area; my guess is London, with Zsuzsanna. To-morrow, when Gerda is able, I will see if that guess is right.

✢ ✢ ✢

30 AUGUST. Everything points to a separation between Vlad and Zsuzsanna. When I question Gerda, she still refuses to say much about him; clearly, Zsuzsanna lives somewhere in the city with this Elisabeth, and no one else. But if she despises Vlad as greatly as her speech and demeanour suggest, why did she also choose to come here? Why not some other great European city, rather than share London with one she so hates?

This makes my work doubly difficult, for I had meant to rely on Gerda's knowledge of Vlad's movements. It torments me to think that the vampire is nearby, feeding on innocent victims, while I am unable to find him, much less stop him.

I see only one choice: to utilise Renfield as much as possible, in hopes that he possesses, somewhere in his troubled brain, information which can help.

✢ ✢ ✢

The Diary of
Abraham Van Helsing

1 SEPTEMBER. A slight change in Gerda. Under hypnosis, she seems crestfallen. Apparently Zsuzsanna has had some sort of falling-out with her friend Elisabeth; any mention of same, or of Vlad, elicits the vilest curses. But where Zsuzsanna is now, Gerda will not say.

One interesting piece of information: At the same time she curses Vlad, she also speaks of a "manuscript" or "parchment." This she does not elaborate upon, but from her expression and tone of voice, I gather she wants badly to obtain it—if only for the purpose of getting it away from Vlad.

⁘ ⁘ ⁘

Dr. Seward's Diary

3 SEPTEMBER. Van Helsing and I paid Lucy Westenra a professional visit at Hillingham to-day (at his insistence, though I told Art Holmwood that I wanted to bring in an expert). Poor girl! It breaks my heart to see her in such a state. She has lost a good deal of weight and is now too thin, and her pallour suggests severe anaemia of the sort that often costs young people their lives. Still, she was as pretty as ever, sitting in her bedchamber near an open window through which streamed warm sunlight; it saddened me to see that she was too weak to properly enjoy one of the last days of summer. She wore a white frock embroidered with white satin thread, and her hair was tied

back with a great white bow like a schoolgirl's. In the sun, hints of gold in her dark ash hair gleamed becomingly.

But she was clearly exhausted, lying upon a chaise longue against a plethora of pillows. Despite the day's warmth, one wool blanket was tucked around her legs, and another draped about her shoulders. When the maid brought us to her, she did not lift her head, but with great effort raised her arm that we might take her hand. Weak or no, she managed to thoroughly charm Van Helsing . . . and me, of course.

And I do believe he charmed her, though he again took on the *persona* of the witless foreigner, the slayer of English grammar and syntax. I wish he would not do it— at least, not when I am around. It embarrasses me for his sake (it makes him, one of the world's most intelligent and educated men, seem a bumbling fool), and sometimes his more outrageous locutions make me grin at the most inappropriate times.

Nonetheless, as much as it troubled me, Lucy was clearly taken with him. And when the time came for him to examine her, I gratefully took the excuse to stroll about the grounds, that I might be spared further intentional barbarisms.

When he had made his examination and we took our leave and headed for the station in the fly, his jovial mood disintegrated at once. In his troubled blue eyes I saw confirmation of my worst fear: that Lucy was in mortal danger.

"It is serious, then?" I asked, as the driver steered the horse into the park. It was indeed a glorious summer's day, full of sun and kissed with a delightful, cooling breeze; above our heads, birds sang in the lush, swaying boughs of trees.

Yet to me, there was nothing of pleasure in that mo-

ment. I remember only the sense of horror that chilled me
to the bone, despite the warm golden pool of light that
bathed us both. For I had only imagined that the worst
would be that Lucy was ill with pernicious anaemia; but
the answer he gave was even more terrible to contemplate.

He glanced at the back of the driver's head an instant,
as if making a decision. Then he said, "It is. She has been
bitten."

"Bitten?" I was honestly confused, thinking along
strictly medical lines in terms of a diagnosis. "But how
could that—" I was going to say, *But how could that cause
such a great blood loss?* It would have been such a massive
wound that neither Lucy nor any of us could have missed
it. In my concern for her, I had not allowed the professor's
obsession with vampires to enter my mind. But ere I had
finished my question, I realised from his intense, unhappy
gaze that that was exactly what he meant: a fanged creature
had been suckling at Lucy's sweet neck.

Van Helsing no doubt detected my dismay, for a look
of compassion came over his face and he asked softly, "You
cannot yet believe, can you, John? Cannot believe with
your whole heart?"

The bright blue sky, the wind-rippled leaves, the sweet
birdsong—all of it took on a hideously sinister hue. Nothing was as it seemed; all the beauty surrounding us was
corrupt, a cheerful facade built to disguise evil.

How long ago had it been—a fortnight, a month—
since he had first spoken to me of vampires? I contemplated all that he had said, of course; contemplated it, yet
found it so horrid and impossible that I could not mentally
commit myself to it.

And still, the dream of Darkness and my very instinct
did not permit me to entirely *dis*believe. Should I flee from
my friend, reject his diagnosis, and direct him to other

lodgings? Or should I distance myself from my own fears and skepticism? If I were to tell any other of my medical colleagues that I sensed people's "auras," they would deem me mad; therefore, I determined at that moment not to do the same to the professor, who in all other matters has proven himself to be a reliable source of information.

But to accept his claim was to open the mind to indescribable horror.

"Yes, I have difficulty in believing. But I trust you, Doctor. And if what you say is true: what shall we do, then, to help her?" I finally said, with such desperation and anguish that I could not repress them.

He tapped the side of an index finger against his lips and shot a pointed look at the cabbie; we two rode back to the station in weighty silence.

The train was not overly crowded, and we managed to get a compartment all to ourselves, where we could speak more freely.

"I must closet myself away," the professor said the moment we were alone. "I need at least three days' time where I can be guaranteed no disturbance."

"I have such a place—a cottage out in the country which is quite remote. Not a soul would bother you."

He brightened at once. "Excellent!"

"But before I send you off with the key, you must answer a question for me first."

At that he grew silent and uncomfortable, but waited to hear it so that he could decide whether he could comply.

"Why?" I asked. "Why are you so sure Lucy has been bitten by a vampire, and why must you go off by yourself?" Impertinent questions, to be sure, but if in fact we were truly dealing with such legendary evil, courtesy was our least concern.

He sighed, looking like a man who knows that his answers will not, cannot, be entirely trusted or even comprehended. "To the first, I can only say that instinct tells me so. To the second—I must take some measures that will allow me to save Miss Westenra's life, if need be. And I must try again to recruit one who can help me track Vlad."

"Vlad . . . ?" I had overheard the name before, when he had queried Mrs. Van Helsing. "This is the vampire?"

"One of them. There is also Zsuzsanna, and possibly an Elisabeth." He frowned suddenly at the occurrence of a fresh idea. "Before I go—might I have your assistance with Mr. Renfield? I should like to hypnotise him again, and would prefer someone trustworthy nearby. Let me speak openly: I believe he is so strongly drawn by evil that he has established a psychic link with Vlad. Perhaps I can get from him the information I need, and my excursion to the country will be unnecessary."

To this I agreed. When we arrived in Purfleet and returned to the asylum, I checked at once on Renfield to gauge his mood. Unfortunately, he was in something of an agitated state, so we decided to postpone our session. The professor has asked me to call for him no later than fifteen minutes before sunset.

In the meantime, I have dispatched a letter to Art giving a mostly fictional account of what Dr. Van Helsing, the great specialist from Amsterdam, has to say after examining Lucy. I'm afraid I told him so little that he might be alarmed; and I certainly could not lie to him about her symptoms or the professor's reaction to them. So there was a kernel of truth in my epistle, enough that one looking for evidence of vampires might find it there. (When guilt rears its disparaging head, I remind myself that to have confessed the whole truth would have troubled Art even more —for he would think his old friend Jack and the great Dutch diagnostician had gone quite insane, and would not have known where next to turn.) As jealous as I may be of him, I cannot be so cruel to my old friend. For his sake, I would have withheld Van Helsing's opinion even if the professor had not insisted I tell Art nothing.

Of course, the professor insisted in looking over my letter, and seemed to take perverse pleasure in garbling all the quotes attributed to him. Our plan is to pretend slowly to discover the signs of vampirism in order to make the others come to the same conclusion on their own initiative. Perhaps even I—if I one day do encounter solid physical evidence—might be convinced.

All I can say is this: If ever I have felt an attraction for things psychical in nature, the events of to-day have cured it. I feel as though I am trapped in a strange and fantastical dream, one every bit as disturbing as the one about the great Darkness. . . .

·I· ·I· ·I·

The Diary of
Abraham Van Helsing

3 SEPTEMBER. Whitby! The lovely Miss Westenra reported that the beginning of her strange malaise began around mid-August, when she was on holiday at the seaside—at Whitby, during the time when a "ghost ship" appeared! From what she said briefly about it, I have no doubt: that is where he came ashore. Her responses indi-

cate he remained there a week before continuing on . . .
to London, where he was drawn again to his victim.

As for John's Miss Lucy (he thinks I do not know, but
it was plain on both their faces that this was the young
lady who had rebuffed him), I left her with what protections I could—a tiny silver crucifix which I had charged.
She is clearly not of a religious bent, so I gave up any hope
of convincing her to wear it; what logical reason could I
give? When the garlic blooms come from Amsterdam, I
will at least be able to cite the medicinal power of the herb.

So I did something rash, which strikes me now as
amusing, though at the time humour was the farthest
thing from my mind. With her permission, I put Miss
Lucy deep into hypnotic trance, for as I explained it, it
would permit her to give me far greater detail than she
could remember consciously.

After I had asked all the questions regarding Whitby
and the "large bird flapping at the window" and gotten
satisfactory replies, I let her remain in trance, with her eyes
closed. Meantime, I performed a mental exercise—a spell,
if you will—which permits me to move about unheard by
others. And with a little crucifix in hand, I climbed upon
the radiator; standing on tiptoe, I wedged the protective
amulet between the wooden window frame and the wall.
(For all her answers pointed plainly to the window as the
place he had entered.) In addition, I produced some small
cloves of garlic and carefully laid them atop the narrow
lintel.

Whilst I was in that ever-so-precarious position, it occurred to me that Lucy might suddenly emerge from
trance and open her eyes, or that the maid might fling
open the door—and *then* how would I explain why I was
standing tiptoe upon the radiator? I should have done a
spell for invisibility first, I thought, but too late. . . .

It makes me laugh now, but at the time I was quite frightened. At any rate, I managed to finish my simple efforts in privacy, and now I pray they will be sufficient for a time. As soon as possible, I will notify Vanderpool in Haarlem to coax some garlic into bloom; he is entirely trustworthy, and it will save me the trouble of explaining myself to an English farmer.

It is unfortunate that Miss Lucy is not completely accessible; knowing that the maid was just outside the door (no doubt ready to burst in at the first sign of impropriety), I dared not ask directly about Vlad and his whereabouts. But perhaps the time will come. . . . Until then, we will use John's Mr. Renfield.

+⦙+   +⦙+   +⦙+

Dr. Seward's Diary

4 SEPTEMBER. A terrible day all round. Dismissed the attendant just before sunrise so that I could take the professor in to see Renfield without anyone else knowing. Van Helsing thinks that our zoophagous patient is sensitive to the vampire's movements and may be of some help in tracking it.

The patient remained quite calm when I entered, so I signalled Van Helsing to come in. He did and, to my surprise, had Renfield in a hypnotic state in less than a minute.

"Where are you?" the professor asked him, with admirable authority.

"I do not know," Renfield replied, in a tone of surprising dignity; when he is calm, he looks quite the cultured gentleman—except for the unkempt hair and beard. (We dare not trust him with a razor or even a comb, and he hasn't the patience to let the attendant groom him.) But comb the silver hair and shave the salt-and-pepper beard, and beneath them is a man with strong aristocratic features and intelligent ice-blue eyes beneath severe black brows. According to his wife, he is fifty-nine years old, but extremely well-muscled and fit for his age. (The attendant— and now Van Helsing and I—can confirm that!) "I think I am in a closed box. There is only darkness, and quiet— except for birds singing."

As if on cue, a robin just outside the window burst into song; the professor and I both smiled at the coincidence.

"Are you in London?" Van Helsing asked.

The question seemed to confuse Renfield. Eyes still closed, he frowned deeply and hesitated. "No . . . yes . . . I don't know. What do you mean by London?"

It was the professor's turn to be confused. "The city. London, the largest city in England."

"Yes, yes," our madman replied irritably. "I know what London is! I simply don't know—"

A cock crowed in the distance; abruptly, Renfield sprang to his feet and rushed the professor with alarming speed. Before I could move, he had his broad hands around Van Helsing's neck and was throttling him, whilst the professor gripped his attacker's wrists and tried to break free.

But already the professor's face had turned bright apoplectic red; he could take in no air at all, could only emit the most dreadful strangled gasps. I rang for the attendant at once, then leapt into the fray, grasping Renfield's forearms just above Van Helsing's white-knuckled hands.

In a matter of seconds (I suppose, though it seemed

hours), the attendant raced in and threw the whole of his massive bulk against Renfield, smashing him back against the wall. Soon the patient was restrained in a strait-jacket, while I tended to Van Helsing, who gulped down air while gently massaging his violated neck. I was concerned that there had been real damage done, for beneath his fingers there were dark red marks upon the skin that would soon turn to bruises. But he waved me away, and soon recovered enough to speak.

He is headed to-day for the country cottage. I am concerned about him being alone there; if his theory that Renfield is controlled by the vampires is correct, he is in grave danger indeed.

❦ 9 ❧

Zsuzsanna Dracul's Diary

13 AUGUST. I write this on the boat, on my way back to London after a brief visit to Amsterdam. (The Dutch public transportation is so clean.) It was Elisabeth's idea at first for me to go. We had both been out of sorts for some time; I have felt my own strength slipping, despite the fact that I have had my fill of "blue" blood. Elisabeth, too, seems paler, weaker, and so irritable that I have started avoiding her. It frightens me; I worry that Vlad has cast some sort of spell on us. London is still full of myriad marvels, but I begin to lose interest in what previously delighted me. How many new frocks can one have? I have a closetful. They are all lovely and I enjoy wearing them—but my desire for them is now sated, and I grow restless. . . .

Vlad has no doubt arrived at the English coast, but still he has not appeared at any of his properties—Carfax, Mile End, Bermondsey, Piccadilly. We visit them every day, hoping to find him; and every day, our hopes are crushed.

Some evenings ago, Elisabeth approached me smiling for the first time in many days, with a look of determination on her face. "Vlad is delayed," she said, "and we are both growing terribly anxious waiting. But why must we? You say that you know where Van Helsing lives. Why not surprise him there during the daytime, and bring him here? For if Vlad knows we have Van Helsing, he will be forced to deal with us."

"Why not simply kill the doctor?" I countered, for I was eager to do so, and have my revenge upon little Jan's murderer.

She clicked her tongue in disapproval. "But why fun is that, Zsuzsanna? If Van Helsing dies, Vlad merely crumbles to dust. No, we must use Van Helsing to draw him to us. I, for one, intend to witness both their deaths, and to inflict as much suffering upon them as they have upon you!"

"Very well," I agreed—though I was secretly determined to kill him anyway. "When shall we leave?"

"Not both of us, my pet. You go; you alone know Van Helsing and his house. I know Vlad, and so I will wait here for him; someone must check his houses every day."

The idea of leaving her alone gnawed at me. From Dunya, I knew that she was capable of infidelity; even more distressing was the thought of the torture-chamber beneath the house. Was her irritation due to her eagerness to test it? She had sworn to me that she would not, that she merely "collected" such horrific devices for amusement; and certainly, I had yet to find them used.

Still, I did not trust her.

Trust or no, logic won out. Within a day, I found myself standing at Van Helsing's door. I did not disguise myself, merely wore a hat with a bit of a veil, so that if he peered out, he would not immediately recognise me. All I needed was for him to open the door a crack—no more—and I would easily strike a killing blow.

I rang, and a full minute later, the door swung open;

the woman who answered was steel-haired and square of jaw. *Mary?* I almost asked, but this could not be she; this woman was far too heavy and tall. For an instant, confusion reigned: Had I come to the wrong house? Or had the Van Helsings moved?

No; this was the house, and the brass nameplate on the door proclaimed A. VAN HELSING, M.D., with a phrase in Dutch I could not decipher.

"I am looking for Dr. Van Helsing," I said tentatively in English; the woman frowned sternly at me and shook her head. I then translated the phrase into French, without success; but my German evoked a warm smile.

"Ah," she said, with a native accent and obvious relish to hear her own tongue spoken, "your German is excellent! But I am afraid the doctor is not taking appointments at this time." And she pointed to the brass plate above the bell, then laughed at herself. "But of course, you do not speak Dutch!"

I smiled prettily and drew back my veil a bit to expose her to both my beauty and entrancing eyes. "I am not a patient, but a relative, here to visit."

She clicked her tongue. "Ah, poor dear! I hope you have not come a long way——"

"From Vienna." I knew before she told me that the professor was not here; my heart sank at the realisation.

"He has gone"—she paused, and seemed to catch herself. I tried my best to put her in a trance, but she kept glancing away uncooperatively. This was a very willful woman—"abroad."

I did not hide my bitter disappointment. "May I ask where?"

She averted her eyes—lying, of course. "Many places. I do not have an itinerary." And then when she glanced back at me, I detected a sudden spark of suspicion in her gaze. "You are a relative? How so?"

"His sister-in-law."

Her eyes narrowed. "I have lived in Amsterdam many years, and have known of the doctor for some time. He has no siblings."

I sighed in honest frustration, deciding that if she did not let me in within a matter of seconds, I would break her thick neck. "I know it sounds strange—but I am actually his mother's sister-in-law. You see, Mary's brother was much younger than she, and—"

The ice melted away, leaving her with a more welcoming but oddly tragic expression. "Ah, poor Mary. . . ."

I feigned alarmed interest. "Has she died? Bram is such a dreadful correspondent; he never tells me anything. I wrote him weeks ago telling him I was coming, but he never replied—"

"My poor dear! How dreadful for you to learn this way. No, poor Mrs. Van Helsing—Madam Mary, as I call her—is not dead. But I am afraid she is not far from it. She is mortally ill with a cancer."

I put my lacy-gloved hand to my mouth and gasped in horror. "So she is here?"

"Yes, yes, would you like to see her?"

I kept my lips covered an instant longer, lest she should see them curve slightly upward in a smile. "Very much. I am sad to miss Bram, but . . ."

But I could learn a great deal from his mother, who was no doubt privy to where he had gone. This nurse was clearly operating under basic orders, and probably had no idea of our beloved Bram's true vocation.

So she swung the door open and let me inside, where she squeezed my hand with Germanic force, and vigorously pumped it while introducing herself as Frau Koehler.

The shadowed foyer was lined with bookshelves, all filled beyond capacity, some tomes lying atop rows of other volumes. The good Frau led me back through another dusty, book-lined room to the staircase, where she hesitated.

"Let me go and tell Madam Mary you are here." She blinked at me for a moment before I realised she was awaiting a response from me.

"Tell her"—I paused, searching my memory for my sister-in-law's maiden name—"tell her Mrs. Windham has come to visit."

Frau Koehler nodded, then lifted her skirts and climbed heavily up the groaning stairs. I heard her move across the creaking wooden floor, then pause to murmur a soft question to her charge.

But I detected no reply. As I waited, I espied between all the shelves a closed door, and felt inexplicably drawn. I slipped through the crack and found myself in the good doctor's study, surrounded by more books—these all esoteric in nature. Our brave vampire-killer, it seemed, had made an extensive study of magic in order to better accomplish his work. There was also a large oaken desk, with a number of papers and telegrams in the cubicles; I longed to look through them all to gain some clue as to Van Helsing's whereabouts, but above my head came more creaks, and the frau's heavy footfall.

I immediately slipped through the door again and by the time she smiled down from the top of the stairs, I was in the exact spot she had left me.

"Madam Mary is awake and will see you." Whilst I dashed up the stairs to join her, she added: "I cannot promise you that she will entirely understand who you are. She speaks little, and when she does, she is generally confused; I gave her an injection of morphia for the pain not long ago, so she is sleepy as well. Be patient."

"I shall," I answered warmly, though at the moment I was thinking of Mary not at all, but rather how I might convince Frau Koehler to leave. I was quite sated from the night before, to the point that the thought of dining upon her stalwart German blood made me queasy. So I was not inclined to use supernatural force upon the Frau; one quick drink from Mary, that was all I could manage, and then I would be gone.

My cavalier attitude vanished once I stepped into the room and was greeted by the duelling smells of piss and foul shit. Frau Koehler had done what she could to minimise it: the window was open, a candle flickered in the slight breeze, and a bedpan soaked in a tub full of soapy water.

It was all I could do to keep from covering my nose with my kerchief; but Frau Koehler seemed to notice it not at all. She stepped over to the bed, smiled with genuine affection, and took her patient's thin, limp hand. "Mary. Here is your sister."

I moved forward to take the German nurse's place, and clasped the dying woman's cold, bony hand. Her eyes had been closed, but at the sound of Koehler's voice, they fluttered open and gazed upon me. I was prepared at once to put a glamour upon her, and make her see an entirely different woman, so that she would not cry out in fear and alert the nurse—

Oh, Mary! When last I saw you, you were strong and young and beautiful, with shining gold hair and smooth skin, and your little son Bram in your belly. I loved you then; loved you even after my Change, for you had been so good to me in my life. I have come to realise that you and Kasha and Papa were the only ones who truly ever loved *me*—me, the homely cripple, the spindly spinster who evoked from men nothing but pity.

Now you are struck down by cruel Time. I have killed many in my strange existence, and stared often into the eyes of Death Herself; but I had never before seen Her linger so long.

This would be me, I thought, *had I not received the gift of immortality. An unlovely old woman, dying.* I looked upon the crone in the bed and did not recognise her, she with her coarse white hair knitted into a long braid that lay from shoulder to waist; the hair on the scalp, however, was broken off in places and had come partially undone, giving her a wild, unkempt air. The image came to me of a delicate bird perishing from starvation. Her smooth skin was sallow, sunken skeletally at the cheeks, pinched at the nose, and lined with wrinkles, especially beneath the eyes—eyes still blue as the sea, though the whites were jaundiced.

Eyes dulled by pain and suffering, eyes that recognised me.

I intended to silence her before Frau Koehler was alerted, to put her under my spell so that she would forget that she knew me, so that she would see another woman altogether. But I was too stricken by the sight of her to react immediately, and too distracted as the nurse slid a rocking-chair bedside and bade me sit.

I sat, and cast my gaze again upon the old woman who had once been Mary, ready to do my supernatural work. But those blue eyes—they looked back at me not with fear, not with hatred or revulsion, but such honest warm affection that tears of gratitude stung my eyes. This was not the fleeting love evoked by sexual passion or mutual need or convenience; this was love for its own sake.

"Mary?" I asked softly, and to my utter surprise, tears fell hot onto my cheeks—I, a hundred, a thousand times a murderess, so callous that I thought I would never know untainted compassion again. "Do you really know me? It is I—"

"Zsuzsanna," she breathed, in a trembling, reedy voice that broke my heart; never for an instant did the sweetness in her gaze waver. "How beautiful you are. . . ."

I lowered my face into my lace-covered hands and wept. She was adrift in the past and remembered only the mortal Zsuzsanna, I realised, and had forgotten my Change; even so, I was touched by her welcome. But I had another reason for allowing myself the outburst. Pathos aside, I was compelled to achieve my objective: knowledge of Bram.

Frau Koehler stepped up behind me and laid a broad hand upon my shoulder. "My dear . . . I know how difficult this must be for you," she murmured. "May I bring you a glass of sherry?"

I lifted my head and wiped away the tears with my kerchief. "Thank you. But . . . may I have a cup of tea instead?" That would allow me the time I needed.

The Frau's swift acquiescence cheered me at once; she departed down the stairs for the kitchen, while I leaned closer to Mary and took her hand in both of mine.

"My darling," I whispered. "I cannot bear to see you suffer so. But I can take all your pain away—forever."

I moved forward and down, and pressed my lips against the soft, loose folds at her neck; the ammonia-sharp odour of urine was overwhelming there, as were the strong sensations of Mary's goodness, her fear of dying, her sincere love for those who had gone before her and those who would be left behind. Death's approach had stripped away all else, until only the essence of the woman remained.

But something held me back. Perhaps it was the knowledge of the woman she had been, or the powerful sense of goodness and tragic suffering emanating from her;

I knew that the true Mary would rather die than turn to evil.

Indeed, she drew her hand from mine and, with heart-rending weakness, put her palms against my shoulders and tried in vain to push me away. "Please, no . . . I have lost two sons and a husband. Is that not enough?" She said it dreamily, calmly, without a trace of fear.

I drew back. "Mary . . . do you *want* to suffer? Do you *want* to die?"

She held my gaze directly; at the same time, she seemed to look past me, at something far distant and glorious, and her wizened face took on a radiant, wasted beauty. "My suffering is nothing compared to yours," she whispered. "Mine will not last forever."

I fell back into the chair, stricken by a pain sharp as a needle piercing my melting heart. I tried to protest: How could she say that *I* suffered? I who enjoy the best life offers, I who endure no physical pain, I who inflict suffering and death upon others?

But I could not deny it. In a flash, I saw my current existence as she would see it: the prettiest clothes, the finest champagne, the handsomest men, the beautiful and cruel Elisabeth. The vanity, the hollowness. Century after century without meaning.

I rose and again took her hands, massaging them a bit to warm them. This time when I bent over her, I gently pressed my lips to hers. "God bless you, Mary."

"And may He bless you." She sighed, and closed her eyes.

I heard downstairs the rattling of china upon a tray, and muted steps; Frau Koehler was returning with the tea. I settled into the rocking chair and waited, trying to determine the best way to return to the study, when Mary herself provided the answer.

Abruptly, she emitted a howl of pain, with the unbearable abandon of a wounded animal; I admit, I jumped a bit in the chair (and it is not an easy thing to startle a vampire). Again and again she cried out, and I called to her to ask what was the matter, but she seemed quite unaware of my presence. I felt enormous helplessness—and embarrassment when she suddenly clutched the blanket between her legs.

"Frau Koehler!" I cried, as the nurse thundered and rattled up the stairs; she appeared red-faced and gasping, and at once thrust the tea-tray upon a low armoire and went to the bedside of her charge.

"Ah," she said, relieved. "It is merely time for the bedpan again. I shall help her, madam. If you like, you may take your cup of tea and sit downstairs, where the noise will not disturb you."

"The noise?"

"It is all painful for her now; she drinks so little that it burns like fire, especially with her open bedsores. But I will help her feel better. Off with you, madam."

So this is a lingering death: piss and shit and helpless pain, the cruelest indignity.

She moved towards the soapy bedpan in the basin, and I made good my escape before I saw anything more. Abandoning the tea, I sailed down the stairs and again slipped through the door to the doctor's study. With immortal speed, I riffled through the papers on his desk—to little avail, for almost all of them were in Dutch and quite incomprehensible.

But stored neatly inside a cubby-hole were three telegrams, sent from A. Van Helsing, Purfleet, England, to Frau Helga Koehler, Amsterdam. The first was dated 8 July, the second 16 July, the third 4 August.

And all of them from Purfleet. *Purfleet.* Where Elisabeth and I went every morning to check on Vlad's arrival!

I would have sat down on the floor and quietly laughed—here I had come all this way to find someone back in London!—had the chilling realisation not come: Dr. Van Helsing was mortal, but he still was a force to be reckoned with. For he had somehow discovered Vlad's new location.

How could I be sure he had not also discovered mine?

I skimmed through them all, for they were blessedly written in German, with which I have intimate acquaintance. They all thanked Frau Koehler for her reports on his mother's condition, and volunteered the information that "Mrs. Van Helsing is unfortunately still the same." The most recent one stated that he would have to remain in Purfleet awhile longer, but that the Frau should notify him at once should she judge Mary to be dying.

Mrs. Van Helsing; the phrase filled me with trepidation, though I did not immediately understand or remember. Had there been a Mrs. Van Helsing? I had come to this house twenty years before, to take sweet little Jan with me and to steal Bram's brother away. . . .

Of course, of course. There had been a woman; a timid, large-eyed mousy little thing. I had bitten but not killed her, as she had been an obstacle in my way. She had one of those forgettable Dutch names that began with a *G,* that strongly aspirated sound like the Hebrew *ch,* repeated twice in the name "van Gogh."

For some reason, it had not even occurred to me that she was still alive. But the revelation that she was—and that she was in England with Van Helsing—filled me with horror.

What if he were using his wife to get information about me? For vampire and victim are linked together so long as both survive; and so this wild-eyed woman was linked to me, even though her personality was so timid, so cringing, that over the years I had become blithely unaware of her. I, who had been such an idiot that I had not thought to turn the tables and get information about *him*.

I have corrected my oversight.

Through all this, I had been listening to footfalls and terrible screams overhead, and Frau Koehler's soft, comforting murmurs. The screams had ceased, followed by the sound of pouring water. I slipped out of the study, and waited at the bottom of the stairs again until the nurse appeared.

She did not invite me up, but came down the stairs to stand beside me; perspiration shone on her forehead and upper lip. She raised her apron to her face and wiped it.

"I think she will sleep now," she said in a low voice. "She is very tired; she has had a very difficult day so far. Will you be back soon, Mrs. Windham?"

I shook my head, eager to leave this sad house, and troubled by what Mary had told me. "No. It's time for me to leave. I have my own family to take care of; and I have already given her my good-bye."

Her broad, square face grew genuinely sad. "I am sorry you must leave after such a short visit, madam. I can see Mary loves you very much, and you her."

I turned away before she saw my tears, and she led me back to the front entrance. When she opened the door, I paused and faced her, then lightly touched my fingers to her cheek.

As I'd hoped, she met my gaze, and fell at once into trance. "You will remember none of this," I told her. "Not me, not my name, not my appearance, and if Mary speaks of it, you will take her to be delirious. Most important, you will not, so long as you live, mention this to Dr. Van Helsing."

"Of course not," she said, and I smiled, breaking the spell.

"Thank you, Frau Koehler." I kissed her on the cheek as I would a sister.

"Godspeed, Mrs. Windham."

⁜　⁜　⁜

Now I am on the boat home, where I've found myself a secluded spot down below (it is a beautiful day and everyone is taking sun up on the deck). Here, I let myself go deep into trance and found my connexion with Mrs. Van Helsing. The threads tying us are rather weak, though with practice they will strengthen. This is what I saw, only moments ago:

A small, plain room with white walls, a window with black iron bars marring the view of a flower garden below. Over the window, a small gold crucifix.

Behind me, the sound of a door opening; a man's soft, deep voice calling: "Gerda, dearest . . ."

Gerda, yes! That was her name.

The view swings one hundred eighty degrees; I now find myself looking at an older man with white speckling his golden hair and thick eyebrows, and a smile meant to mask the worry in his blue eyes. He has not recently shaved, and the sunlight pouring in through the window catches the silver hairs on his chin and ignites them. There is such an air of heaviness about him, as if he were like Atlas, bearing the world's weight upon his shoulders. At the same time, there is an air of goodness, too, reflected in his eyes and the simple, rounded features on his face.

There is something familiar here, something disturbing: I look at him and think of my dead brother, though they look nothing physically alike. I know this man, but for an instant, I am stymied, for he is almost a quarter-century older than the last time we met, and the years and tragedy have aged him.

Bram, Gerda thinks, but the deep sorrow within her holds her tongue so that she cannot speak—and I at once remember. This kindly older man is my nemesis, Van Helsing, the murderer of my little Jan, who would still be beside me to-day had Van Helsing not killed my immortal adopted child.

So. Van Helsing is with Gerda—in an asylum, I think; how else to explain the bars? And at that very moment, he begins to ask her questions:

What do you see now?

"I'm not sure. I see water, a great deal of green water —and disappearing behind me, a coastline with tiny windm—"

I pull her up short before she can utter the word *windmills,* although damage has already been done. He will know now that I have gone to Amsterdam—but damned if he will know when or if I have returned to London.

He asks other questions, but she remains steadfastly silent, until he surrenders and leaves.

When I emerged from the connexion, I wrote this all down at once, lest I forget any detail. I will tell Elisabeth about the fact that Van Helsing is in Purfleet, somewhere near Vlad. She will be angry enough at the wasted time— so I must never tell her about my terrible error in forgetting about Gerda; she will never forgive me.

And if we fail, I will never forgive myself.

At the same time, I am deeply troubled. Whenever I think of Mary, it is as though my icy heart is gently warmed by a small internal flame—a flame she has rekindled; and I remember what it is to feel human compassion, human love. Shall I kill her only son?

Enough! Enough! Such thoughts are too dangerous. I *will* have my revenge. . . .

❧ 10 ❧

Zsuzsanna Dracul's Diary

20 AUGUST. No further clues from Gerda about Bram Van Helsing; I suspect she said or did something which alerted him to my interference, and he in turn has performed some powerful magic to prevent my repeating it. We have been going through the city bit by bit, looking for an iron-barred window that looks down onto a flower garden, and we did find two possibilities, including a madhouse adjacent to Carfax—but no Van Helsing, no wife. Is it possible that he is adept enough to make them both invisible?

It is my own fault that I could be so disgracefully outdone by a mere mortal; Vlad taught me only the most cursory exercises in mesmerism, invisibility, and self-protection, but I never pressed him for more information. (I know now he would not have given it even if asked, but there were times when I could have got hold of some very enlightening ancient tomes, and did not.) I honestly had no interest in such "boring" things . . . now comes the time for regret.

Elisabeth's welcome was sweeter than I'd expected it would be when I returned from Amsterdam; I never confessed to her about Gerda, but lied and said I had bitten Mary and learned that the good doctor is actually somewhere near London. This surprised and pleased her, and we spent some agreeable hours together over the following days. Yet as generous as her mood was, she seemed to grow somewhat haggard and irritable. I thought it was out of frustration over our vain search for Van Helsing, and that she was struggling to hide it out of concern for me. Now I know better; she was dissembling for my sake, all right— not out of kindness, but out of a wish to deceive.

To-night I am beginning to see just how much she has kept from me. And what she *has* told me: are those, too, all lies?

It began mid-morning. We had been going mad awaiting Vlad's arrival, but to-day I had an overwhelming hunch that *this* was to be the day. So Elisabeth and I at once hurried to Carfax. (What a vision she was, dressed in palest pink and cream satin, her long curls pinned up beneath a matching cap; it was as if she had intentionally made herself more beautiful in an attempt to extinguish my anger and doubt.)

Safely cloaked in our invisibility, we stood a distance from the dismal old house, beneath a copse of large, gloomy oaks—Elisabeth would go no farther—and watched workmen deliver the same wooden boxes I had seen the *tsigani* load onto their wagons and carry away. Fifty boxes in all—and one unquestionably containing Vlad! I recognised it by the enveloping elliptical glow— midnight-blue speckled with gold, like a starlit sky, larger than any aura I had ever seen him cast (mind that my abilities in this regard have always been less than remarkable).

I know Elisabeth saw it, too, for she gasped aloud—

then caught my arm and hissed into my ear, "We must leave at once!"

Confused, I turned to frown at her—and my confusion increased at the poorly masked fear upon her face. "What do you mean, leave? He has arrived; it is day. . . . Now is the time. When the workmen are gone, we must go in and destroy him!"

"Then you will go alone. Can you not see how powerful he has become?" She gestured at the glowing box, her expression and posture—with one impatiently tapping cream slipper—revealing intense anxiety. She turned and began to move away, but I grasped her arm and held it.

"You're afraid of him," I marvelled. "You who claim to be unconquerable, you who swear that you avoided confronting him only because you wish to relish your little cat-and-mouse game . . . You are afraid. Can it be that *he* is now the cat, and *you* the mouse?"

"Let me *go*!" She surrendered all pretense then, and uttered a Hungarian epithet as she swung at me with a pink-and-cream-striped arm. I have never seen her features so grotesquely contorted with anger; in an instant, she was transformed from porcelain doll to Medusa. "Don't be a fool—if we argue, he will sense us. Zsuzsanna, you have no idea what danger you're putting us in!"

I would have said more, would have asked, *And are you afraid, too, of Van Helsing, whom you refuse to kill? Is he, too, the stronger?* She broke free from my grip, and transformed herself directly into a golden butterfly that sailed away upon the late summer breeze.

I controlled my anger and rode upon the sunbeams, but I did not follow her back in the direction of the house in London. Instead, I left Carfax estate and made my way into Purfleet proper, where, beneath the cloak of invisibility, I slipped into a silversmith's shop and made off with a shining dagger and long-handled sword.

Then it was back to Carfax, for my fury at Elisabeth's deceit made me ever the more determined to destroy Vlad, and to destroy him at once. Why else had we been waiting all these weeks? I would show *her* what true courage meant, and then, having destroyed him, would leave her to her vanity, her decadence, her vile dungeon waiting silently for its first victim. As for myself, I needed neither the protection of man or woman, nor their love; the two I had dared love had both betrayed me, and I would never again permit myself so to suffer. Perhaps I should go to Vienna, or Paris. . . .

When I arrived, the workmen were still hard at their task. The anger wavered only once as I waited beneath the dying oaks, when I reflected that perhaps I had been hasty in thinking that Vlad's belief that no vampire could ever destroy another in traditional fashion, with stake and knife, was simply another of his mediaeval superstitions. What if it was true?

Then I shall leave and bring a mortal to do the task, I told myself. I would not be swayed, nor would I permit myself to believe I was in as terrible a danger as Elisabeth insisted.

The workers (a small group of lower-class cockney "blokes," as they would call themselves) took the boxes in through the front entrance, at a maddeningly slow pace, one box at a time. This, with several pauses for bawdy jokes, conversation, and laughter, left me so impatient for the hour and a half it took them to finish that I was tempted to appear to them in my most ferocious fang-toothed guise and send the lot of them running.

The sun was straight overhead when finally they left—mid-day, which realisation cheered me, as this was the hour Vlad was weakest. Even so, I took care to strengthen the veil of invisibility around myself and my silver weapons before entering, and with them slipped through the crack in the weathered front door, which the "blokes" had relocked.

Inside, the floor was carpeted with a layer of dust inches thick (how like Vlad!), leaving the workmen's every step visible. Making no footprints myself, I followed the trail through the corridor, until it ended at an arching oaken door bound with iron.

There was a sizable gap between the door's base and the dust-padded floor, as well as between its arched top and the curving lintel. One might expect to see rays of sunshine streaming through, illuminating errant airborne dust; but in place of brightness shone that ominous and sparkling indigo aura, darkness which was not an absence of light, but an equal and opposite force that could displace it.

For a brief moment, I quailed—then summoned all my anger and courage and again reduced myself and my burden to a hair-thin sliver which slipped easily beneath the gap at the door's base, through the radiant darkness which seemed to permeate my being. I emerged on the other side full of trepidation, for though the room (once a chapel, as the far wall bore the marks of a large crucifix which had been recently removed, above the rotting remains of a wooden altar) was vast and high-ceilinged, it was filled with the sparkling deep blue radiance that marked Vlad's presence.

I steeled myself and with my weapons moved forward, towards the box from whence the indigo non-light emanated. And here I can only describe the sensation in mortal terms, for immortal experience fails me here: It was rather like attempting to walk into and through a swarm of very annoyed bees, or to swim against a raging current; I felt myself being buffeted backward by a hostile, buzzing force, whilst the skin on my entire body stung as if pricked.

Excelsior.

I moved onward, struggling to submerge my fear. No matter how powerful Vlad might have become, I trusted in my own invisibility, and my plan: to reach the box in which he lay, fling open the cover, and, in the instant of surprise, pierce both heart and neck with silver.

At last I arrived at my goal, and there paused to gather my nerve even as I reached for the wooden lid—nailed shut, though I could tear it free with but a modicum of effort.

My fingers curled round the edge; I pulled. The lid did not move, but remained steadfastly bound.

Again I pulled, harder, silently cursing. Again, no result at all. I paused, infuriated and perplexed, wondering what immortal skill I might use to pry open the impossibly stuck lid.

Or was this a trick of Vlad's?

The lid in front of me suddenly exploded into a mighty whirlwind, hurling me back against the door in a flurry of splintered wood and dust; had I been mortal, I would have certainly been killed at once. As it was, I listened with pure astonishment at the sound of the door and my own immortal bones cracking . . . and at the ear-splitting clang of my weapons driven into the stone wall an inch from my head.

And when the storm eased, causing the dust and bits of wood to drop to the filthy ground with the abruptness of a funnel cloud belching out a tree or a terrified sheep, I sat and looked through the glimmering darkness to see that the box was open—and within it lay Vlad.

Not asleep, yet utterly still as a corpse, with his arms

crossed upon his chest, his malachite eyes opened wide, and a sneer upon his lips. He was a young man now, no longer ghastly but handsome, with flowing coal-coloured hair and mustache. I looked upon him and was at once smitten and horrified.

And desperately curious about the piece of iridescent white parchment pressed between his hands and chest, as if it were a great treasure that must remain close to his heart.

The sensuous lips moved. "Zsuzsanna, my dear," he said, in a voice beautiful, strong, godlike. "Surely you are not so stupid or foolhardy as to want to do me harm. Perhaps you have merely returned after realising that you have sided with the loser."

I was too stunned to flee. Clearly, Elisabeth had been right to fear; I knew that he would destroy me now, despite any lie I might think to tell him. The keen understanding that I was utterly lost filled me with numbness and an odd calm. If I was to die, then I should at least learn the truth that had been kept from me.

"Loser?" I asked. "Do you mean Elisabeth?"

"The same," he replied, all but his lips still motionless. "You are her pawn, my dear. She is too cowardly to confront me herself, and so she uses you. Ask her, Zsuzsanna; I know you will believe nothing I say. Ask *her* about the terms of her own covenant with the Dark Lord. Ask her what they have to do with *you*."

A sickening surge of dread overwhelmed me, for he spoke with the calm confidence of truth. "Why are you so powerful now? And what is *that*?" I pointed at the shining paper in his hands, leaning forward just enough to see a few lines of text written in pure, gleaming gold.

He smiled, but ignored the question. "Ask *her* what it is; ask her what she would do to you in order to get it. You must destroy her, Zsuzsanna. Destroy her before she destroys you. If you do not, I shall have no choice but to inflict upon you both the same grievous end. Take heed: I will not warn you again. And remember that I could have destroyed you here and now, but chose instead to take pity."

Immediately, the door behind me swung open, and another mighty gale pushed me—furious and frightened and spitting dust—out into the corridor and out of the house altogether, as easily as if I had been a feather and not an angry immortal.

Outside, I dusted myself off and travelled upon sunbeams into the city, to the beautiful house where Elisabeth sat waiting upon the sofa, golden curls freed and swept all to one side so that they spilled down onto her bosom. She sat with uncharacteristic stiffness, spine straight and unsupported, hands folded primly upon her knees. To test myself—and her—I entered the house with aura still retracted, maintaining my invisibility.

She did not see me at all—or if she did, she belongs onstage with Ellen Terry, for she kept sighing and frowning and glancing out the window as a concerned lover ought; one cream satin slipper tapped relentlessly against a Turkish carpet the colour of blood. When I materialised hastily in front of her, she rose, clapping her hands, and cried out:

"Zsuzsanna! My sweet Zsuzsa! I have been so terribly worried! Did you go inside? Did you see him? How did you ever escape?"

She flung her arms about me and repeatedly kissed my cheeks and lips. But I did not return the embrace; I stood still as Vlad had lain in his coffin, and said, "You are right; he is powerful, fearsomely powerful. I cannot defeat him alone."

At this she drew back, confused by my physical coldness yet approving of my words, and clasped my hands, waiting for some sign which might explain this contradiction.

I kept my expression solemn, my hands limp, my gaze direct. "He says that I must ask you about your covenant. Your . . . contract with the Dark One, and what it has to do with me."

The judgement? Guilty. Conflicting emotions rippled subtly over her features like ocean waves spilling onto the shore, only to be pulled back and swiftly replaced by others: rage, hatred, fear, cunning—and the last, indignance.

"Zsuzsa! Can't you see what he is trying to do to you? To make you hate me, to make you return to him. And what do you think will happen to you then?"

"I have seen the manuscript," I said quickly; she recoiled as if she had been slapped. Indeed, she turned away, clearly overwhelmed and unable to respond to this new development, whilst I affected a knowing expression. The intimation was that I had read and understood its value to Vlad (and clearly, now, to her)—a lie embedded in a truthful statement.

With her back still to me, she wrapped an arm round her ribs—clutching herself, really, though she tried to make the gesture seem casual. Her other hand quickly massaged her forehead, then her neck, just above the sweet, sculpted bone beneath milky skin. With utter—and unbelievable—calmness, she asked: "What did he tell you about it?"

"Enough. Enough to know that you have lied to me." She whirled about, setting pink and cream satin skirts aswirl, and began to protest, but I raised my voice and would not hear her. "At the very, very least, you have constantly kept the truth from me."

At once the porcelain face crumpled, and diamond

tears spilled from her sapphire eyes. "Zsuzsanna—do you think I did so simply to torment you? Yes, he is stronger than both of us together at the moment, but I have not given up hope. We will find a way to defeat him, but until then, we must use all our wits and caution." She reached forward and took my hand once more, pressing it between her own and bending down to kiss it, baptising it with her tears. "Have I been cruel to you in any way, my darling? Have I hurt you? Tell me, and I shall make amends at once. I did not bring you to London to make you un-happy!"

I wavered. She sensed it, and pressed her case with increased vigour. "You know Vlad, Zsuzsa. In all the de-cades you were with him, did he ever treat you with respect or genuine affection? No! He treated you as his own slave, to do with as he would; he gave you immortality, but not out of concern for you—only for himself! You know you cannot trust him; you know that he is a liar. I beg you—do not let him drive a wedge between us! He is telling you these hideous prevarications in order to achieve just that! And if he succeeds, then we all are lost, indeed. We must work together, darling, to defeat him. And our best hope, I tell you, is Van Helsing. With him as our pawn, we can succeed."

In truth, I was swayed—by her beauty, her tears, her words. Still, Vlad's charges gnawed at me. "If I am to help you, then, in such a difficult task, you must explain every-thing to me. What *is* your covenant with the Dark Lord? And what is this manuscript that Vlad clearly prizes?"

She sighed. "As to my covenant—that is not the sort of thing one discusses; if you had your own, you would understand. As for the manuscript, I cannot say. Please trust me, dear Zsuzsa. I, too, am trying to solve all these mysteries; perhaps we two can discuss them to-day, and come up with a proper strategy."

Then she put her arms round me and kissed me, and cajoled me until I yielded, smiling. For the rest of the day and night, she was as kind to me as anyone has ever been.

But I cannot do as she has asked: I can trust her no longer. I remain with her now only because I have nowhere else to go. Bad enough that I have attracted Vlad's wrath; I do not want hers as well.

I must find a way to destroy them both.

❖   ❖   ❖

26 AUGUST. The delay grows maddening. No Van Helsing thus far; Elisabeth and I have agreed that he is our best hope in conquering Vlad. Kill the Dutch doctor and Vlad will be destroyed as well.

I am convinced now that the lone lunatic asylum in Purfleet contains the view I saw through Gerda's eyes, for the flower garden looks just the same. Yet there we can find no trace of either Van Helsing, and my fear is that they *were* there for a brief time, but have since left. Either that, or the doctor is as powerful a mortal man as I am a vampire, and knows how to render himself and his wife invisible for days at a time. The second possibility is indubitably worse.

So we check the asylum almost daily, and we keep searching the city. . . . And each day, I grow more restless.

Yesterday evening I could wait for action no longer; so, some hours after the sun had set, I went out into the foggy night alone whilst Elisabeth took her rest. She and I are getting along together well enough on the surface, but I still possess a great deal of wariness around her, as she does around me. She scrutinises me for signs of disbelief or disaffection (which I have in abundance, but try hard to mask); upon finding them, she reacts not with anger but with great concern and sweetness. It is as if she is courting me anew, for she showers me with presents. Yesterday, she indulged my penchant for dogs and birds (*she* cannot abide either) by presenting me with a full-grown white Afghan with a diamond collar, and a great white cockatoo with a diamond bracelet round its ankle (to elegantly chain it to its perch).

The dog and bird are sweet enough and I adore them, but my presence terrifies them; so I keep them closeted in the sitting-room, and let the young downstairs maid give them the affection they deserve. In the meantime, Elisabeth showers me with white roses, precious jewelry, outrageous and exquisite ball gowns, and promises of social engagements. More delightful *things,* and, oh, how they bore me!

So last night when I slipped out into damp darkness softened by fog, I felt a sense of relief to be free of Elisabeth and all my beautiful gifts, to at last be doing something of worth. I sailed upon moonbeams across the city some twenty miles to the east, where Purfleet lay upon the north bank of the Thames.

I returned straight to the cheerless gloom of Carfax. No light emanated from behind the filth-encrusted windows—only the ominous, glittering blue-black mist, darker than the night.

This disappointed me, as I had expected him to go out hunting the very instant the sun slipped beneath the horizon; why would he linger in that vile and dusty prison when there were thousands upon thousands of warm, red-cheeked souls awaiting him in the city; when, for the first time in centuries, he could feed to his heart's content?

Alas, my plan had been to search the premises during

his absence for the mysterious white parchment. Instinct said its discovery would lead to the truth that neither Elisabeth nor Vlad would reveal, and perhaps even to my own liberation.

Fuming, I retreated at once to the property's edge. Now that I was sensitised to it, I could see the deadly aura's faint glow even from that distance; and I was tempted to keep my distance, for I knew that this time, Vlad would have no mercy. I lingered quite a time near the black iron gate, with its tall spikes, every few minutes deciding in disgust that I could not wait an instant longer— and every time, remaining. All the while, I prayed that my frail efforts at invisibility would permit me to escape detection.

After no more than half an hour, the blue-black aura abruptly vanished, like someone extinguishing a lamp that shed darkness rather than light. I turned my gaze skyward and saw a large bat flapping silently through the air—a beautiful creature with vast wings of bone and sinew covered by gossamer grey skin, and the whole of it veiled in sheer, shimmering indigo.

I took to the air and followed at quite a distance, taking care not to be discovered. He sailed along the Thames' north bank over regal estates and green bits of farmland, until the landscape grew dotted with buildings closer and closer together; and then we were in the city.

He knew precisely where he was going, for never did he slow or swoop down to inspect the area or search for victims. Not until we were in the heart of London proper did he gradually ease the flapping of his wings. Lower and lower he sank through the undulating white mist, until at last he hovered just outside a respectable-sized house of brick, set behind a gated stone wall bearing the sign HILLINGHAM.

Again, I kept a respectable length between us, and strengthened my invisibility as best I could. What I now report I saw from beneath a great sycamore a whole rolling grassy lawn away. From there, I put my immortally keen vision to good use and witnessed the following:

The bat hovered at a dark second-story window, the sash raised to let in the cool, damp air and release the day's heat. There the handsome creature lingered but a moment before transforming itself into the handsome, dark-haired Vlad, who slipped easily through the gap without awaiting an invitation to enter. This was a house he had visited before.

Though the room was dark, I could see inside with ease. Upon a white, lacy (and no doubt virginal) bed lay a young lady with waving sand-coloured hair and a pretty enough face. Apparently her sleep had been unrelentingly restless, for she had kicked off her coverlet and lay so tangled in the twisted sheets that one could not judge where they ended and her frilly white night-gown began; from beneath them both a pale, curving thigh peeked scandalously.

As Vlad approached the bed, she wakened drowsily and, upon recognising him, sat up and opened her arms to him, as the biblical man must have welcomed his prodigal son. He stepped into the embrace and held her, golden-brown waves cascading over his arms—and drank. (Almost fifty years ago, he did the same for me—and how well I remember the sweetness of it still!)

At the moment his lips found her tender neck, I turned and fled back to Carfax at the highest possible speed. I had seen what I needed, and knew the way back to Hillingham; now I was obliged to conduct a swift search of Vlad's new and dreary home.

What did I find? Dust, dust, and dust, and scores of

inhospitable rats—but certainly no gleaming parchment with golden script. I looked inside the box where he had lain and found nothing within but mouldering earth that I suspected had been dug from the chapel floor in Transylvania. (Elisabeth is right on one account—his superstitions are strange indeed!) All fifty of the boxes had been recently pried open, and I looked into every one.

Dust and vile-smelling dirt. I searched a few places elsewhere—in a cabinet built into the wall, and the lone table that stood near the entryway—without success. Yet I dared not linger; thus I made a swift tour of the house and the grounds, and departed for home, fearful of being discovered.

Now I am home, and although Elisabeth is solicitous to an annoying degree, I have stolen a moment of privacy to sit with my beautiful hound and cockatoo (the poor things, how they tremble at my very nearness, and when I speak tenderly to them, they are undone by confusion). I must write this all down and think hard in terms of strategy. I am alone in this and can trust neither Elisabeth nor Vlad; Van Helsing I might believe, for though he means me harm, he is not given to deceit. If I could only find him, I would question him first and kill later.

As for to-morrow, I can see no way around it: I must take a deadly risk.

⁜   ⁜   ⁜

26 AUGUST. Elisabeth was very moody to-day, and though she tried to master herself, she snapped at me irritably. Then she pressed a wad of pound notes into my hand in lieu of apology, and bade me go shopping.

So I and my handsome coachman drove through the city, and at one point, I ordered him to wait for me outside a fine dress-shop. Once inside, I made myself invisible and rode the wind the short distance to Hillingham.

It being shortly after mid-day, I was altogether unsure that I would catch Vlad's victim alone; but I knew that she would be too weak to stray far from home. Daylight gave the estate at Hillingham a far cheerier air; the gabled stone house no longer seemed grim and sterile, but quite cheerful with its red door and eaves and white lace curtains. Upon the deep green lawn, black and tan terrier pups gambolled whilst their weary mother watched beneath the shade of a tall ash; nearby, a servant tended a perfumed garden of roses.

Gone, too, was the dark blue miasma that marked Vlad's presence, and that was perhaps the most cheerful sign of all.

I located at once the window where Vlad had entered, and peered inside. The sash was closed today, despite the glorious warm breeze, but the young lady was exactly where I had expected to find her—in bed, propped up upon pillows, reading, with the covers drawn up as far as possible, as if she feared a chill on this, one of the warmest days of the year. She was quite a pretty girl, really, with light green upward-slanting eyes, sculpted cheekbones, and a small, thin nose, all of which gave her a rather feline look; and she wore a lovely dressing-gown of embroidered linen eyelet, pale sea-green to enhance her eyes. Whilst she read, a chambermaid stood beside the bed, devotedly brushing out the lady's long, waving hair—which, in the dappled sunlight, looked the colour of sand gilded here and there with gold. Lying against the pale-green gown, it looked like a shimmering shore beside the great ocean.

As I watched, a kitchen maid entered with a tray bearing a modest luncheon and tea; her young mistress sighed and shook her head, but the servant pressed her case, and left the tray on the table beside the bed in case the young lady's appetite improved.

The instant the servants had gone, closing the door behind her, I drew nearer to the window and materialised just enough so that I could tap my fingernails against the glass. As I had hoped, the girl looked up from her reading, and tilted her head, curious; I drummed harder, harder, projecting my aura outward as a fisherman casts a net, luring her until she could resist no more. She pulled back the covers and rose languidly; slowly (pausing once to close her eyes and press a hand to her forehead as if dizzied) she made her way to the window, and with great effort pulled up the sash.

This was my invitation. I lunged forward, thinking to leap through the open window into the bedroom, as Vlad had done the night before.

But something held me back at the instant I ducked my head beneath the glass. A talisman, something fastened above or below the window which made my skin tingle, then sting, then burn fiercely, as if I were attempting to swim through water which had been infused with ever-increasing amounts of acid until it was pure vitriol. I cried out at the pain, recoiling; my invisibility should have prevented the girl from hearing any sound, but she must have sensed something, for she frowned in puzzlement and peered farther out before shutting the glass.

This was Vlad's doing, I decided, and silently swore to him that I would not be so easily discouraged. Thus I went round to other windows until I found one unencumbered by any spell—the dining room, where I found the same serving-girl setting a long table for only one. Again, I tapped upon the window and mesmerised her quite easily; she pulled open the window without an instant's hesitation.

I wasted no time with her, but made my way directly upstairs to her young mistress' room. There I knocked, and was obligingly admitted entry by her call: "Come in. . . ."

There is one moment when we vampires lose our ability to hide ourselves: at the moment of feeding, not because of any limitation imposed on us by the Dark Lord's bargain, but because the act of drinking blood overwhelms us as utterly as it does our victim. Thus our mental concentration, so necessary for manipulating the aura, fails, and we are visible to those who nourish us.

So it was that when I stepped over the threshold into her chamber, I saw no point in veiling my presence; she would see me soon enough in any case.

When I appeared all at once in the entryway, pulled the door shut behind me, and locked it, she sat straight up in the bed and lifted a pale hand to pale lips with a look of intense curiosity tempered by gentle fear. She might well have cried out for one of the maids, but she was a gentlewoman, schooled in civility, and so she asked, with as much courtesy as she could summon in the face of such a surprise:

"Who are you?"

I smiled, and within me felt immortal beauty rise up and flower; felt, too, my magnetism instinctively increase and surge out through my eyes to the young lady's, drawing her irrevocably to me. Deep, deep behind the green ocean of her gaze, I saw the faint glimmer of indigo. I would have to strike quickly; I would have to keep my own mind as blank as possible. Even so, the danger to me was still great. Who knew the limits of Vlad's power? How could I be sure that even during the day, he would not reach out through this lethargic young creature and smite me?

"A friend, come to help in time of need," I said, crossing over to stand beside the bed. At once I became keenly aware of diluted vitriol tingling upon my skin, and glanced up to find over the single window a tiny silver crucifix. Impossible that I should be affected by it anymore, now that Elisabeth had shown me the truth . . . unless, of course, it had been charged by a powerful and educated magician: Vlad.

The young lady distracted me then from that miserable thought; she sighed and pressed a hand to her heart—whether to protect it or bring it forth to offer up to me, I cannot say, but her startled gaze became one of ecstatic love, and her lips parted in sensual recognition of the event to come. "You are so beautiful," she whispered, tilting her face upward towards mine, revealing a long white neck partially covered by a velvet band.

My smile grew ironic. Mary had uttered the very same compliment, but hers had been sincere (if not altogether lucid), and had touched me to the core; the girl's came as a result of her being thoroughly mesmerised, and so held no pleasure for me.

I bent for the kiss, and pushed the band of velvet down until I found the marks. I put my lips to her neck there, and licked the skin, feeling the tiny punctures with my tongue so that I might place my eyeteeth exactly upon them. There I briefly hovered—not from a desire to savour the moment, but from trepidation.

Knowledge is ofttimes carried on the blood; to drink is also to learn of the victim. But at such moments, it is impossible for us to hold back; our auras surge forth to mingle with those of our prey. This is generally of no concern, for when the victim is thoroughly entranced, all she learns is forgotten upon waking, while the psychic tie to the vampire remains.

Thus Vlad can know her thoughts, her feelings, her images, to a limited degree (unless he more thoroughly ties her to him by an exchange of blood, at which point he can know almost anything he desires). And if I joined with her when she was mesmerised, and most open to his thoughts, I would know them.

But would he also know mine?

The reward outweighed the risk. I closed my eyes as my teeth sank slowly into the path already cleared for them, and tried to focus my mind solely on the sound of the girl's breathing and her beating heart.

The blood rose up to meet me, and I drank.

Image of a plump, buxom woman—all breasts and belly, with no neck, thin greying hair swept into a scanty pompadour. *Mother is looking ill these days, poor thing.*

Am I dying? Arthur . . .

A young man with a riot of golden curls and a long, distinctly equine face.

The lines are six, the keys are two. The damned key! It must be here. . . .

Image of the shining parchment, emblazoned with gold beneath Vlad's youthful hands; I could decipher the letters now.

To the east of the metropolis lies the crossroads. There lies buried treasure, the first key.

A burst of searing force—a force more blinding than lightning, more deafening than thunder, more powerful than the deadliest whirlwind, a force that apparently originated from Miss Lucy Westenra herself—smashed me backward into the wall. I reeled, impossibly dazed by the blow; only when I heard the maids crying out, "Miss Lucy! Miss Lucy!" and running up the stairs did I come to myself and gain control of my aura. By the time the maids arrived, discovered the door was locked, and began to bang frantically on it, I was invisible; by the time the aforesaid "Miss Lucy" opened aforesaid door, I had already slipped through it and was fleeing the way I came.

I returned to the prim dress shop, where Antonio still waited with the carriage. From there, we returned to the relative security of Elisabeth's house; I was grateful she did not see me enter, as I was too exhausted after the strange attack to shield myself a minute longer from the gaze of others. Nor was I in a mood to hide my dishevelment or my shaking hands. I went straightway to my private sitting-room (private because Elisabeth so despised animals she would not enter it), where my white, bejewelled prisoners cringed at the sight of me. The cockatoo raised its crest and recoiled as I approached, and the Afghan retracted its tail and tried to slink away—but I was in too great a need of honest comfort. I picked the poor dog up and set it beside me on the sofa, then buried my face in its soft fur and we two trembled together.

Vlad had become acutely aware of my interference with Lucy Westenra. Indeed, he had very nearly killed me —an impossible thing for one vampire to do to another, yet the shock that had surged through my supposedly impervious body had nearly torn me apart. Even now, as I write this, I am so shaken my hand can scarce hold the pen. What has made him so strong—and why is Elisabeth now so weak?

Speaking softly to the hound, I raised my face to his— *his*, I say now, not *it*, for despite his dreadful innate fear, he sensed my own, and looked back at me with dark eyes so full of compassion for my own suffering that I could not hold back tears. They coursed down my cheeks, and that blessed creature gently licked them away with his tongue— which only made me cry all the harder. God Himself cannot convince me that this animal has no soul; indeed, his is infinitely worthier than mine.

After a time, we both calmed and ceased our shivering, and I think he honestly came to enjoy my caresses. I leaned my head against his thin shoulder, listening to the rapid beating of his heart, and wound my arm round him where he sat; when at last I grew too engrossed in my own concerns and ceased stroking him with my free hand, he nuzzled it tenderly.

I had never even thought to give him a name, for I had seen him only as a pretty ornament instead of a living, feeling being; but now I call him Friend. Indeed, he is my truest. Through my entire existence as an immortal, I have never met with such unbiased and unconditional acceptance and love.

As I sat and petted him, my mind grew steady enough to return to all that I had learned from Lucy Westenra, and thus Vlad.

The manuscript; the manuscript. I had no logical reason to believe it, but my instinct was adamant: its very possession must confer power. Had Elisabeth once possessed it, only to lose it to Vlad when we were all still in Transylvania? He seems far stronger now, however, than she was then.

The lines are six; the keys are three. To the east of the metropolis lies the crossroads. There lies buried treasure, the first key. . . .

Lines and keys: of them and their number I could derive no sense, only the obvious deduction that treasure lay buried at a particular crossroads, perhaps east of London. It was clearly a riddle—but to what end?

The damned key! It must *be here. . . .*

Most assuredly not Lucy's thoughts, but Vlad's, who had been meditating upon the riddle at the moment of my intervention. So the treasure at the crossroads—the first key, whatever meaning that might have—had not yet been discovered. Yet Vlad was desperate to find it.

A horrible thought seized me: If the manuscript itself conferred astonishing power, then what would possession of the first key confer? And the second?

And Elisabeth had followed him in hopes of regaining the parchment.

By this time, Friend had grown bold enough to lie down with his chin upon my lap; I sat stroking him for a long time, thinking of how the world would be if Vlad retained his amazing strength—or if Elisabeth took it from him.

At the moment, I could remember only Vlad's cruelties and Elisabeth's kindnesses. Yes, she had kept the truth from me, but not for any malicious purpose; her worst crime appeared to have been a lack of faith in my trustworthiness, but she had not known me long enough to understand that I am interested not in power, but in peace and pleasure. So I rose and bade Friend remain, and went in search of Elisabeth, prepared to reveal all that I had learned that day.

She was not in any of her habitual places: the great drawing-room, the bedchamber we shared, her favourite sitting-room, the formal French garden. I went back to Antonio's quarters on the main floor to see if he was there; he was not, which made me think that perhaps he had taken her on some social errand.

But if she had seen Antonio, she would know that I had returned, and it was most unusual for her not to greet me and praise whatever I had bought, especially since she seemed so desperate to stay in my good graces.

So I continued my search of the house, until at last only one room was left: the cellar, which Elisabeth so affectionately referred to as the "dungeon." An odd sense of dread overcame me the moment I set foot upon the landing leading downward, and touched the handle upon the iron-bound door; my reaction was to veil myself from all detection, for I think now I instinctively knew what I should find.

So I walked in silence down the stairs, and when I arrived upon the bottom step, I saw what I had always seen: the dirt floor, the long-unused fireplace, the terrible blond Iron Maiden, and the great hanging iron cage, with long sharp spikes directed inward. And surrounding it all, vast, empty darkness.

Yet I thought I espied upon the Iron Maiden's lip a drop of blood, and so I moved over the cold ground, forward one deliberate step, then another, then another . . .

Until at last I caught a flash of feeble indigo, and a glimpse into the circle—Elisabeth's circle, from whence emanated screams so fierce, so hoarse, so hopeless in their abandoned agony, that I knew not whether they came from male or female, adult or child, human or animal throat.

And in the centre of the vast dungeon, the fireplace blazed brightly, while nearby, the iron cage swung suspended the height of two women from the ground. At the pulley stood Antonio, chest bared and glistening with perspiration from the fire's heat; at the sight of me, he grinned, baring teeth—the Devil's own inviting smile.

Nearby, between the fire and the swinging cage, Dorka stood heating a long poker in the flames, her sweat-shining face reflecting fireglow and transformed from its usual sour expression to one of pure ecstatic transcendence. And when the metal grew white-hot, she hoisted it by the attached broom handle and jabbed it up into the black cage.

Or rather, at the prisoner within: a young, naked girl whose spiralling auburn curls spilled to her thighs and mingled with the blood streaming there. She was a lovely creature, slender, tall, and long of limb, with small and beautiful breasts, but in her death-agony, she had been reduced to a graceless, shrieking thing. She was far too beside herself to notice my entrance; her only concern was the approaching poker. It found the tender skin of her leg, and her screams grew impossibly shriller as she flailed, recoiling. Alas, her efforts to avoid pain only increased it: she had already been gored by two long metal spikes inside the cage, and her movements only served to drive them deeper into her tender flesh, and enlarge her terrible wound. The spikes pierced the length of muscle between her right ribs and hip, and held her fast. In a pitiful effort to free herself and avoid further impalement, she had wedged herself sideways between the row that pierced her and the row in front of her; the latter's spikes she gripped with her hands and pushed against.

But before she could free herself, Dorka jabbed again; I winced at the hissing sound of searing flesh and the accompanying howl. The girl struck out valiantly at the poker with her hands until, inevitably, one of them became impaled; then she began to kick as if there were still a remote chance of survival. But there could be no hope; blood streamed from the mortal wound at her side, from the singed puncture upon her strong white thigh, from a cut upon her otherwise perfect forehead. At the sight of her, I felt bitter pity—and also a strange pride that she who was so clearly defeated would not yield to her enemies until the very moment of death. She could not be far from it, for she had lost an impossible amount of blood; it streamed down her thighs, her legs, her feet, onto the floor of the cage. Had she not been held fast by the spikes, she would certainly have slipped.

I had never before taken notice of the cage floor's special design; it was flat everywhere and rimmed—except for one place where it slanted downward into a spout, forcing the blood to spill in a narrow stream.

Beneath that stream sat my erstwhile lover, her face tilted upward to greet the gentle crimson rain. I have seen Elisabeth enflamed with passion; I have seen her in the moment of sexual release. But never had I seen her wear an expression of such infinite bliss, infinite satisfaction—indeed, she looked up at her unwilling benefactress with all the adoration and love I had long searched for in her eyes, yet never found. Upon her lap she reverently held her victim's clothing: a plain grey gown with white cotton apron, a servant's humble frock.

As for the blood that dripped down upon her face, her hair, her bosom—she rubbed it into her skin with abandoned relish, her excitement mounting so quickly that I expected her to cry out any moment in ecstasy.

All this I watched with such keen revulsion that for some time, I could not quite believe what I saw; and then, when I believed, I could not think, could not move, could not intervene. What should I have said? What should I have done? Should I have freed the poor dying girl and killed her to stop her pain? The only death I could offer brought no true rest.

She would die honestly soon enough, without the loveless torment that undeath brought; so I did nothing, nothing at all.

Nothing at all save let a single tear of horror and pity spill down my cheek, for both the dying girl and Elisabeth. And at the surge of emotion, my control flickered; too stricken to struggle, I simply let it go, and stood unprotected and unveiled before the actors in that hellish tableau.

The girl was too far gone to detect my presence. But at last, Elisabeth sensed a change in her surroundings, and looked down to see me. "Zsuzsanna! Darling!" Her voice was shocked, exasperated, annoyed—and finally, terrified; her blood-painted face was a ghoulish mask darkening rapidly to violet-brown. She held out scarlet-spattered arms to me, beseeching, beckoning. "Do not judge me harshly, dearest. What I have done, I do for you. Come to me, and let me teach you the truest sweetness; come to me, and trust that this is all for the good."

I said not a word. I merely stood motionless and returned her gaze without hatred, without anger; but the revulsion in my eyes was its own rebuke.

I lingered upon that vile, unconsecrated ground no longer than the span between two beats of a human heart. Then I went upstairs, gathered Friend into my arms, and left forever.

❧ 11 ❧

Dr. Seward's Diary

7 SEPTEMBER. For the past five days, I have sat up through the nights with Lucy; never have I performed a more bittersweet task. During the whole time, I heard nothing from the professor, but each day sent him the requested telegrams on Lucy's condition—to a "Mr. Windham" at the parents' old cottage in Shropshire. The covertness of it all makes me feel rather sheepish, even though I understand the necessity for it.

For four days and nights, Lucy got along quite well, and began to markedly improve; the professor's "magic" was working. But on the fifth night, exhaustion took its toll on me; and Lucy (who was feeling more her merry self) insisted that, rather than continue my vigil, I sleep in the adjacent room upon a comfortable old sofa. I refused, but as I could not altogether resist Morpheus' lure, and since Van Helsing's unnoticed silver crucifix was still safely in place above the window, I allowed myself a "brief nap" in the chair.

So it was that I fell into the sleep of the dead and did not wake until late morning, when I heard the anxious voices of the chambermaids:

"Oh, my poor Miss Lucy!"

"The doctor! Wake the doctor!"

I heard the words through the veil of a dream, but their content brought me to full alertness, just as an infant's shrill cry provokes an immediate response from the sleeping mother. I leapt to my feet at once and followed the horrified servants' gazes to the woman on the bed.

There lay my sweet Lucy, golden hair fanned behind her on the pillow, her skin and lips a dreadful ashen grey, her breath coming in gasps. The poor girl could barely speak. I rushed to her and took her hand, which was quite cool, then instructed one of the servants to bring a glass of port at once, but to say nothing to Mrs. Westenra should they encounter her *en route*. The other I sent off to the telegraph office, to send a message off to "Mr. Windham," asking him to return to Hillingham at once. Lucy herself I ordered to remain silent, in part because I could not bear to watch her struggle so.

The next thing I did was to glance surreptitiously at the lintel over the window, as I completely expected that the small crucifix had somehow come loose from its place, fallen, and been swept up by one of the maids.

But no; I saw the glint of silver in the same place it had been the night before, and panicked. How could this be? I had trusted Van Helsing's explanations utterly, but now one piece of the puzzle no longer fit. And if he was wrong about the security ensured by a talisman, might he be wrong about everything else?

There was nothing more to be done than sit by Lucy's side and await the port, and, when it came, to put the glass tenderly to her lips and help her drink—she looking up at me with an expression of such sweet apology that it pricked my broken heart. She did her best with the port which was not much; and then she sank wearily back upon the pillow, sighed, and slept.

The maid brought me a piece of stationery from Lucy's desk, and so I hastily penned a note to Art telling of his betrothed's setback, and had it sent out by mid-morning post.

The hours awaiting Van Helsing seemed to drag on forever, especially when night again fell and he had still not arrived. The worst of it was the fact that there simply was nothing more I could do for Lucy. In my desperation I considered attempting a very novel and experimental procedure, the blood transfusion—but since there was no one at Hillingham except myself, Mrs. Westenra, and three young housemaids, there seemed no one suitable to donate the blood except myself. Even if I had the equipment (which I did not), it would have been impossible to perform the procedure upon myself, as I might faint and thus lose both doctor and patient.

By early evening, we received a reply from "Mr. Windham" that he would be arriving on the early morning train. Even though my confidence regarding the crucifix talisman had been sorely shaken, I was nonetheless greatly relieved to hear the professor was well and was indeed on his way.

Thank God we passed an unremarkable night; this time, I allowed myself not a second's sleep. The guilt I felt over failing my patient—the very one whom I most loved —negated all fatigue.

So it was that the professor at last arrived. He was in a somber mood—so somber that, in spite of Lucy's terrible situation, I suspected that he had even greater sorrows on his mind. The first thing he whispered to me after Lucy's mother (who seemed grateful to be kept in the dark concerning her daughter's health) welcomed him into the house was:

"The crucifix. Did one of the maids remove it?"

"No," I replied, as we began to ascend the stairs. "You will see. It is precisely as you left it."

"Then someone else must have invited him in," he said gravely. "Not Mrs. Westenra—"

"No," I seconded, surprising myself. "Not she. . . ."

Despite the situation, Van Helsing gave a faint, grim smile. "You are quite the psychic talent, friend John. Most assuredly you do not take after me; what paltry abilities I possess came only after the greatest effort." The smile faded at once into a thin-lipped expression of unhappy determination. "You are right about Mrs. Westenra. She has not been touched by those we fight; such things invariably show first in the aura, if only to the tiniest degree. But we must interview each one who slept in this house last night, even those who visited here after sunset. There we will find our answer to the mystery."

He fell silent as we two approached Lucy's room, and the little chambermaid opened the door with a slight curtsy. We requested privacy for our examination, which the girl grudgingly yielded; a good thing, for when Van Helsing stepped inside and saw Lucy sleeping, he whispered:

"My God!"

For a time, neither of us spoke, and as we both stood studying Lucy in the early morning light, I saw that she looked even worse than she had the day before. Her cheeks had sunken so that her face appeared skeletal. She was that close to death, perhaps only minutes away—and the realisation struck so hard that I came close to weeping, and actually stumbled.

The professor put an amazingly strong hand on my

arm and steadied me. "She can be saved, John, but we must act swiftly; there is one thing I can do, but there is no time for explanation—"

"Yes, yes," I answered, eager to focus on something other than my own grief. "I thought the same! A transfusion—"

He sighed and shook his head. "No; such is too risky. I have seen the operation perform miracles—but I have more often seen it bring death. I do not know how to explain what it is I propose, except to say that it *is* a transfusion . . . of sorts. But it is not on a physical level."

I was far too overwhelmed with emotion and confused by his words to reply. I merely blinked at him, waiting.

"I must have complete privacy; tell Mrs. Westenra and the servants—no one is to come near. Tell them—tell them that we *are* performing a transfusion of blood, and that the delicacy of the surgery is such that any interruption would endanger Miss Lucy's life." He paused, apparently struggling to make a decision as I turned towards the door; his hesitation made me linger. "John . . . I hesitate to ask such a favour, but the 'operation' I wish to perform does, in fact, require a donor."

"Then I am he," I answered at once.

"You should be aware, then, that this will drain some of the aura's strength, and thus your ability to protect yourself, for some hours."

"Doctor, I care not whether the cost is my own soul."

He nodded, clearly relieved. "It is not impossible for me to use myself—but it will likely be far less effective for our patient. Very well; I will go into the other room to prepare myself. Could you also fetch my medical bag from downstairs? It will enhance the illusion that we are indeed performing the act we claim."

I nodded, and we moved away from each other—I

towards the hallway and stairs, he towards Lucy's sitting-room. But sounds coming from downstairs—the sound of knocking, and the maid's high-pitched reply—caught our attention. The professor shot me a look, and said, "I suspect Miss Lucy has a visitor."

So it was he followed me quickly down the stairs, and just as we arrived in the hall, we saw Art Holmwood stepping in. At the sight of me, Art rushed up and took my hand, professing that anxiety over my letter had brought him here. "Is not that gentleman Dr. Van Helsing?" he asked politely, for the professor stood by my side, rather guardedly studying this young intruder. "I am so thankful to you, Doctor, for coming."

I knew that Van Helsing had no reason to trust Art, and was examining him on a psychic level to see if he posed a threat to us or Lucy. But I was confident my friend would pass inspection, and so he did. I saw a flicker of relief on Van Helsing's face, followed quickly by an honest look of admiration and satisfied approval. At once he took Arthur's hand and, to my surprise, told him that we needed a donor for a blood transfusion—to which Art of course quickly volunteered.

Van Helsing sternly informed the servants then of our requirement for privacy, and found his black bag (which was larger and heavier than the typical physician's bag; I cannot imagine what was hidden in it).

We three proceeded up to Lucy's room. Art was, of course, stricken to see her so ghastly weak, and out of kindness, the professor permitted him a kiss before the "operation." I was rather curious how he intended to pull it off with an outsider present, and Lucy now awake (though too exhausted even to speak).

He went into the other room, telling them both that he must prepare for the operation. He was gone no more than a handful of minutes, and when he returned, he bore in his hand a glass. This he said was a sleeping-draught for Lucy, and slipped an arm beneath her shoulders, lifting her up that she might drink it.

Perhaps it was indeed what he claimed, but I saw his gaze catch hers for an instant—and swear now that a distinctly bluish glow surged forth from his eyes into hers. At the conclusion of this, she promptly fell asleep. He then moved over to Arthur (who sat beside the bed in the same chair where I had so often sat vigil), and, bringing forth a long bit of tubing from his bag, pretended to affix it to his patient's arm. First, though, he stared into Holmwood's eyes with the same intensity he had used with Lucy, and within a matter of seconds, Art, too, was soundly unconscious.

I watched in fascination, scarcely breathing, as abruptly an egg-shaped glow enveloped the entire body of each patient—Lucy's a feeble pale green, Arthur's a strong, virile orange. Van Helsing moved first to Holmwood, whose head had lolled back against the high-backed chair. I was still so amazed by the brightness of the patients' auras that I did not realise, until the professor approached Art and reached a hand out towards the deep tiger-lily glow, that Van Helsing himself was surrounded by a larger and even more intense, brilliant blue shimmer.

The professor reached forth into the sparkling orange and withdrew a large globe-shaped portion of it from over Holmwood's heart. I could see the dark vacancy it left, and how the psychic wound immediately rushed to close itself and fill the void with shimmering orange; but the effect was that the entire aura paled and dimmed, as if diluted.

This orange "globe" the professor held between his hands for a moment. It did not mingle with Van Helsing's bright blue, but instead seemed to grow ever stronger, ever deeper in hue, as he gazed calmly down upon it. And then, when he judged the moment to be right, he stepped over to where Lucy lay, and tenderly placed it upon her heart.

The reaction was fascinating to see: her feeble green aura at once surged forth like a hungry amoeba and "consumed" the orange glow, enveloping it until its distinctive colour disappeared completely. The union of the two did not yield a third hue; to the contrary, the pale green brightened to bold emerald, and its borders noticeably enlarged.

"We are done now," Van Helsing said, and I looked up at him to see the blue aura quite gone. A quick glance back at the sleeping patients showed no trace of orange or green—only Art's now wan-looking complexion, and Lucy's cheeks kissed with a subtle trace of pink. It was as if I had been abruptly wakened from a strange dream, indeed.

When Art revived, we sent him home with instructions to sleep and eat as much as possible (though how he could with such worries about his ailing father and his fiancée, I cannot fathom). Lucy wakened vastly improved, which relieved me almost to public tears, for if she had died, her blood would have been on my head.

The professor then took me aside, and we two agreed that the best course of action would be for me to sit with Lucy the next few nights. Van Helsing himself will during the day keep to his cell at the asylum, and continue the "research," as he calls it, that he began during his stay in the country cottage. By night, he will come in invisible guise to Hillingham, and remain here to see if he can unravel the mystery of how the vampire entered despite the protective talisman. He will also take steps to increase the "security" here, sealing off *all* windows and doors, and ordering blossoms of fresh garlic, which he says are more powerful repellents than the heads.

❖ ❖ ❖

10 SEPTEMBER. A terrible, terrible day. I had spent the entire night of 8 September keeping watch over Lucy; when morning came, I was quite done in. But there was work to be accomplished at the asylum, and a new patient to be admitted. By the time I had attended to it all, dusk was approaching, and once again, I hastened to Hillingham for another all-night vigil.

Happily, Lucy was up when I arrived, and in fine spirits. Her mother reported proudly that she had dressed for an early supper, come downstairs, and eaten heartily. This was the best news I had had in some several months, yet my cheerfulness could not entirely mask my exhaustion. Lucy noticed it, and insisted that I rest upon the couch in the room adjacent to hers, within earshot. In case of any trouble, she promised to call for me.

Such was my fatigue that I agreed, telling myself that my sweet charge's improvement was due to the added measures the professor had taken against the vampire, and that we were now completely safe. And at any rate, the professor himself would also be silently and invisibly patrolling the rest of the house.

So I crawled upon the couch, fell fast asleep, and did not wake until a palm pressed against the crown of my head. I sat up with a start, and saw Van Helsing staring down at me with a faint smile.

"You are well-rested, I trust," said he indulgently, then lifted a hand for silence as I began to make apology; I had certainly not intended to sleep through the night. "No, John, explanation is not needed. You were tired and had earned the right. At any rate, I remained on watch around the servants' quarters and Mrs. Westenra's room. No disturbance there last night, nor on the main floor below. Shall we go see how our patient is faring?"

I assented eagerly, and together we stole into Lucy's room.

I (and the professor, I am sure) was confident that this would be a cheerful visit, that we would find Lucy ever more restored and blooming with health. The room was quite dark, so I moved to the window and opened the blind, letting the morning sunlight stream into the room.

"God in Heaven," Van Helsing whispered. At the abject horror in his tone, a thrill of unutterable fear shot through me. I closed my eyes and remained facing the window, for I knew what I would see the instant I turned.

Alas, I could not remain so forever. So I faced at last the heartrending sight upon the bed: Lucy unconscious, grey as Hillingham's stone walls and just as lifeless. For a sickening instant, I honestly thought her dead.

And then, blessedly, her chest rose as she struggled for breath. Van Helsing addressed me at once. "Friend John, now is the time to make your sacrifice. Lock the door, then sit; I shall go into the other room but a moment, and then when I return, I will do it swiftly."

I replied not a word, but moved directly to the door and locked it fast whilst the professor went into the adjacent room. Then I sat and tried to breathe slowly, evenly, in hopes of slowing my furiously racing heart. A miserable sense of failure washed over me, along with the irrational conviction that if Lucy died, I alone was to blame.

Directly Van Helsing came out, encompassed once again by the egg-shaped brilliant blue shield of his powerful aura. I glanced beside me to see that Lucy herself was radiating the pitifully dim emerald glow; as for myself, I spread my hand before me, curious to see what colour I might find there—but found nothing. (Van Helsing later reported to me that I have a "very healthy" blue aura with areas of gold.)

Beyond that, I remember virtually nothing of the exchange, except that it seemed over almost instantly, and the professor was directing me to the couch in the next room. I slept a time, then had a hearty breakfast; even so, the experience left me noticeably weakened.

As for poor Lucy, she was improved, though not as much as she had been by the "operation" with Arthur. When I returned to the professor, who was himself resting in the sitting-room, he confessed that he had not taken so much "life-force," or *prana,* from me. "After all," he said, "Mr. Holmwood is not attempting to fight the vampire, and you are."

Then he sighed, and stared disconsolately into the cold fireplace which faced the sofa; in his blue eyes was a deep anguish that was painful to see. "I am wrong, I think, to involve you in this any further, John. I thought I knew the danger we faced—but now I realise I know nothing at all. Until now, Vlad has been limited in how and where he can work his evil; yet in Miss Lucy's case, the talismans which once repelled him now slow him not at all. And if he can come and go as he pleases, then Miss Lucy—and all else whom he wishes—have no hope. Nor you and I, John. You, the one person on earth whom I had wanted to protect from him. . . ."

An abrupt spasm of grief crossed his features; he carelessly tore off his spectacles and tossed them aside, then put his great square face into his hands and wept hoarsely.

The sight of his despair pulled at my heart as much as the sight of Lucy had, as did his profession of concern for my sake (though I wondered why he should feel more protective of me than of his own wife). I set a comforting hand upon his thick shoulder. "Professor," I said gently. "You are yourself exhausted, and the whole situation seems to you quite hopeless. But you have again saved Lucy to-day. Remember that, then sleep and eat well yourself, for neither one of us is any use if we do not tend ourselves."

At that, he looked up and said haggardly, "I will rest and eat to-day, John. And this evening I will come and sit with Miss Lucy myself during the night while you go home." When I began to protest, he raised a hand. "No— no objections. Remember, you have been weakened in a most dangerous manner; by to-morrow, though, you will be fit again for duty, and then I will rest."

"Very well," I agreed, and rose to go. But before I could take a step towards the door, he added softly:

"In the country and at the asylum, I have sent out urgent call after urgent call for help—this even before I knew how desperate was our case. Now I know that all the knowledge, all the power, I have acquired over the past quarter-century has been in vain. If that help does not come soon, my son, then you and I both are lost."

❖ ❖ ❖

The Diary of Abraham Van Helsing

18 SEPTEMBER. Miss Lucy will soon leave us. This I know from looking down at her sweet face, still pale and drawn after the "emergency transfusion" Jack and I performed with an American, Mr. Quincey Morris, as donor. It is not so much the physical signs of anaemia—her bloodless complexion, the terrible blue-grey of her lips and

gums, her weak, rapid breath—that convince me of her impending death. These alone are painful enough to see, but far worse are the signs of an imminent, insidious transformation: the elongated canines, the look of sinister voluptuousness which comes over her in sleep, and the subtle gleam of indigo I see behind her green gaze.

After last night's events, I am shaken to the core. I, who arrogantly believed myself powerful enough to take on the Impaler—I have learned that I am nothing, of no use to anyone. I, the vampire "expert," could not even save dear Miss Lucy after weeks of effort! What advice shall I offer them all now, except to flee their native land and live the rest of their lives in dread of discovery?

Here is the sad story: The garlic blossoms arrived on the eleventh, after which Miss Lucy seemed to rally. I dared to hope that, although my talismans had failed, the delicate white blossoms themselves possessed a natural and therefore stronger magic which would repel the Impaler. At any rate, our patient declared that they permitted her to sleep peacefully.

For the past week, I had again closeted myself in my asylum cell during the day to repeat the Abramelin ritual —praying for a response from my mentor or indeed *any* quarter. As always, no reply. Hopeless as it all seems now, I would sell my soul to the vampire's "Dark Lord" Himself if I could be guaranteed no deceit and a certain outcome of Vlad and Zsuzsanna destroyed and all mortals protected. And, of course, no transformation of myself into a vampire. . . .

Most evenings I went to Hillingham and sat watch over our patient; some nights, John would relieve me after midnight. Again, I do not know what we expected to accomplish, as Vlad had already entered Lucy's room without detection; but it is a difficult thing to give up all hope and surrender to inaction.

Last night's plan was for John to sit vigil; I would remain the entire day and night in my cell, trying both to elicit help and further charge a special Solomon's Seal, which talisman represented our last hope. As I would be indisposed, John had told the Westenra ladies the day before that I had returned to Amsterdam and would be back in approximately twenty-four hours.

But that afternoon, John suffered a rather serious cut on his wrist, courtesy of Mr. Renfield, who had escaped his cell. Vlad at work again! Clearly, the vampire was planning something nefarious at Hillingham that night and did not wish Seward's interference; the safest thing was for John to remain at the asylum. This deduction I kept to myself, and merely told John that he was too weak to sit vigil at all, that he should go to his bed and sleep the night. I would keep watch all night at Hillingham. He had lost quite a bit of blood from the cut, and so readily agreed.

Thus yesterday I went to the Westenra estate alone and invisible, and knocked upon the door some ten minutes before sunset. The downstairs maid (a timid brown mouse of a girl, with large, gentle eyes) opened the door a crack—then wider, wider, until she stood upon the porch hands on hips, frowning, looking all about for the prankster who had summoned her then fled. I slipped past her easily, made my examination of the windows to be sure all the little crosses were in place (instinct was at work here, not logic), and finally went upstairs to Miss Lucy's room.

Even before I entered, the pungent smell in the corridor told me that the blossoms were still in place. The door to the patient's room was half-ajar. I slipped through easily —though tentatively, as I did not wish to compromise her modesty; as luck had it, she was in her night-dress, sitting in bed frowning down at Plutarch's *Lives,* with a tray of half-eaten food upon the night-stand. She was still wan, but much improved after her most recent setback; there was a hint of colour in her cheeks and lips.

I sat in the cushioned chair beside Lucy's bed, and a terrible sense of familiarity overcame me, what the French call *déjà vu.* I was stricken with the same hopeless sadness I felt in the rocking-chair beside Mama's deathbed; and even to the same degree, for though a month ago this charming young woman was a stranger to me, I had grown paternally fond of her. Now I could not shake the sense that she was as doomed as poor Mama—even more so, because her ultimate fate would be far more hideous than the sweet repose of death.

With such grim thoughts circling my tired brain, I sat, fighting to maintain keen alertness for all those signs of Vlad's approach that, the last time, I had completely missed. And I took out the Solomon's Seal from my vest pocket and held it in my hand, contemplating its shining silver surface and the geometric designs and Hebrew letters inscribed thereon. The sight of it gave comfort and a faint hope that perhaps it and the fresh garlic blossoms, shipped daily from Haarlem, would be sufficient to repel Vlad.

Hours passed. Lucy reached for a pear from the supper tray, took a half-hearted bite, and tossed it back; then she closed the book and set it, too, aside. I was hopeful sleep would come soon for her, but she gave another restless sigh and rummaged through the night-stand drawer for a little diary and pen. With these in hand she sat back, opened the diary, and raised the pen, poised to write.

That inspiration, too, failed her, and with a small noise of disgust, she replaced them, extinguished the lamp, and fell back into the bed.

At last the shift in her breathing that signalled sleep

came. I rose and went to the window ledge, and there gently placed the Seal, the most powerful of magical protections I could offer up on her behalf.

Then I returned to my familiar post and sat in the chair watching her sleep. After a time, a soft flapping came at the window; I did not rise to peer out, for there was nothing to see—no aura, no animal disguise. But the hairs that rose, prickling, on my nape and arms told me that the vampire had indeed arrived. The flapping grew louder until it woke Lucy. Even in the dark, I could see her fearful expression, and wished that I had created a new lie saying that my Amsterdam "trip" had been cancelled, so that I might speak to her now and take her hand, and offer what paltry comfort I could. For some minutes, she clearly struggled to remain awake; at last, her anxiety grew so that she rose and opened the bedroom door, calling out:

"Is there anybody there?"

The hall remained dark and silent, and so she closed the door again. By this time, the sound of nearby howling accompanied the flapping, which sent her to the window. She lifted the edge of the blind and peeked out; I caught a glimpse of a black bat's wing in the instant before she screamed softly, then ran back to the bed.

There she huddled pitifully, eyes wide and terror-struck. My desire to comfort her grew so overwhelming that I decided to exit the room, become visible, then knock softly at her door, saying that I had returned early from Amsterdam and was overwhelmed by the sense that she needed my help.

Indeed, I rose to do just that—but at that instant, a knock came at the door, and Mrs. Westenra appeared in her dressing-gown; apparently *she* had been overwhelmed by maternal instinct for her child. I was grateful, for she climbed into bed with her daughter, and the two lay in each other's arms, and found a moment of peace.

Yet again, the flapping sound came again at the window, alarming Mrs. Westenra; she struggled to sit, crying: "What is that?" Now it was the daughter's turn to offer reassurance with pats and soft words. Soon the mother sighed and settled back against the pillow, and, for an all-too-fleeting moment, found rest.

A howl—this one nearer, as if the animal responsible now stood directly below the window. If confrontation were to come, it would be soon; I calmed my mind and focussed on the Solomon's Seal at the window, and its radiant golden "wall" of power which only god or devil could penetrate.

The next instant: the sweet, high crescendo of breaking glass, the screams of the ladies Westenra, a shower of razor-sharp diamonds spraying forth from Solomon's wall of gold, borne upon a gust so powerful that the blind snapped up, spinning. I squeezed my eyes tightly shut and felt the sting of tiny shards against my face and hands. Invisible or no, protected or no, I was slammed at once against the far wall.

Abruptly, the maelstrom ceased; I opened my eyes. An inky mist a hundred, a thousand, times blacker than the night streamed slowly over the remaining jagged panes, unaffected by the Solomon's Seal, whose golden gleam had been abruptly extinguished. I knew not then what horror Mrs. Westenra saw; she flailed in an hysterical effort to sit, pulling the wreath of blooming garlic from Lucy's neck in the process, then pointed in stark terror at the window.

And with a strangled gurgle, fell over dead.

Her head struck Lucy's full force; I struggled to rise, to help my patient, to place myself between the girl and the vampire, to offer myself up in her stead. But I could not move—could do nothing, in fact, save stare in helpless horror and fury at what transpired.

And as I watched, the mist completed its entry and formed a tall column just inside the broken window; a blink, and the column had transformed itself into Vlad. Vlad as I had never seen him: dressed like a virile and dapper young nobleman in a tailoured black silk suit, white skin and white teeth gleaming like pearl, onyx hair aglisten with sparks of indigo. So much *life* seemed to emanate from him that he no longer seemed undead— only gloriously, magnificently powerful.

Smiling, he stepped gracefully over to the night-stand, entirely ignoring the two women (one dead, one swooning), and bent down to pick up an object from the floor: the Solomon's Seal, now dull and lifeless. This he tossed at me, sneering: "I believe this is yours, Dr. Van Helsing?"

I could say nothing; the facility of speech had left me, and my legs and back seemed quite pinned to the glass-strewn carpet. But my hands and arms were now functional, so I caught the talisman and held it reverently. My greatest fear at that moment was not death, nor even his bite, but that I could no longer stop him from performing the blood ritual—the ritual by which he had linked my ancestors to him, the ritual by which he renewed his immortality, that he might not perish. If he performed it upon me now, he would know my every thought . . . and I would be his mortal slave, to accomplish the evil that he could not.

He must have seen my thoughts in my face, for his mocking grin widened. "How you flatter yourself, sir, to think that I might need you. I need no one anymore, do you understand? The world belongs to me, *not* to you silly mortals. I can go wherever, do whatever, I list!" And he spread his arms in a grandiose gesture, then lowered them and raised a warning finger at me. "But you would be wise, now, to come to me of your own accord. Why struggle, when it is clear you can do nothing to stop me?"

"Then kill me," I said. It was not merely a dare; my grief at being unable to save Lucy left me in an agony of hopelessness. "Kill me honestly, and deliver me to Death uncorrupted, if indeed I am of no worth to you."

A spasm of fury contorted his features. He swept the air with his arm as though dealing a back-handed blow; my head and upper torso smashed against the floor again so violently that the air was forced from my lungs, leaving me for an agonising minute unable to draw a breath.

In the midst of my struggle, the maids rushed in crying out as their bare feet found the scattered glass. When one of them managed to light the lamp, they began to shriek in earnest. Lucy miraculously revived and, once they had freed her from beneath her mother's weighty body and wrapped it in a sheet, tried to calm them. When that failed, she sent them all away to have a glass of wine once Mrs. Westenra's corpse was laid out on the bed, for they were weeping with hysterical abandon. All this took place without any of the women noticing either intruder in Miss Lucy's bedchamber; nor did they notice when Vlad abruptly disappeared.

Yet I know he remained nearby, I lay in anguished helplessness on the floor, unable to move, and though I could speak, my cries went unheard. Mental concentration? I had none, and therefore my own efforts to remain invisible had lapsed when Vlad appeared. Yet he had apparently power enough to spare in that regard, for poor Miss Lucy could neither see nor hear me. Weeping silently, she put on the slippers beside her bed, then gathered up all the garlic blossoms strewn upon the floor and window ledge, and even the crushed ones her mother had pulled from around her neck. These she laid with heartbreaking tenderness upon her dead mother's shrouded bosom.

I tried to cry out a warning to her then, but caught myself: there was no point in trying to pierce the veil Vlad had erected between us. Even if I could, what good would the blossoms do her? They had not held the vampire back any better than the Solomon's Seal.

This was all that was left to her now—this one moment of loving and dignified grief. Beyond that lay the grave, and even worse horrors, none of which I could help her escape.

She stood with head bowed before her mother's corpse for some time. Then she lifted her face and stared curiously out at the doorway, for it was clear that the maids were lingering overlong at their wine. Worse, the sound of their voices had faded away into total silence. I knew all too well what evil had befallen them, but Miss Lucy did not; even so, the look of fright in her wide eyes indicated that she had some instinctual sense of what had occurred —and was yet to come—that night.

She stepped to the open door and called for them, only to receive no response; thus she left the room and searched them down. I waited in the most horrid suspense, thinking that I might next hear her scream. But all without was silence until she crept back into the room, wearing a look of such helpless terror upon her pale face that I felt the sting of tears.

She went straight to her night-stand and took out the little diary and pen; this time she wrote, swiftly and in earnest. I expected Vlad to arrive any moment and interrupt her chronicle, but it was as though he were allowing her this time as a last gift. At length she finished, and tore this final testament page from her diary; then she folded it, and slipped it between her breasts.

Grief crushed me. For whose sake I struggled to hold back my tears, I cannot say; perhaps I did not want my enemy to gloat. I did not yield to them until I saw her final gesture of surrender: she lay down on the bed and carefully arranged her nightgown and hair, then folded her arms over her breast—as if she were already a corpse like her mother, who lay beside her.

Thus she was when Vlad came to her. By that time, I could bear no more, but closed my eyes, and would not open them, even when he mocked me and impugned Miss Lucy's honour in ways too vile to set down on paper. His verbal slings I could ignore, but when I heard the sounds of his suckling and poor Lucy's sharp little cries, I understood too well why Gerda had surrendered to madness.

⁘   ⁘   ⁘

In the early morning, Seward came—in quite a rush, as if he sensed that disaster had befallen us. By then, I was the only conscious soul at Hillingham; I had wakened moments before from a deep vampire-induced sleep to find Lucy near death, almost as cold and gaunt as her mother's corpse. I attempted an emergency transfer of psychic energy from myself to her, but the previous night's events had left me curiously drained; not only was I unable to complete the exercise, I became faint and nearly fell upon the poor child.

Soon I heard knocking upon the door, and John's voice calling out. I staggered downstairs and let him in; from my dishevelled appearance, he knew that the worst had indeed happened, and took immediate action. He found the four maids asleep in the dining-room; to my great relief, they had not been bitten or killed, but were merely drugged with laudanum. He managed to rouse three, and they in turn set to work, preparing a warm bath and fetching brandy to revive Miss Lucy.

Of course, such measures were of little use; we needed a transfusion of energy, but I could see that John was still weak from Renfield's attack, and so refused to let him risk himself. But one was sent to us, as if from the gods: a good friend of both John's and Arthur Holmwood's, Mr. Quincey Morris from America.

I had thought that Arthur was John's best friend, but clearly Mr. Morris is just as close to the two of them. When he arrived, I saw a flicker of honest joy for the first time in weeks upon John's haggard face, and the two men grabbed each other's arms, then happily thumped each other's shoulders almost to the point of injury. This Quincey is a very tall, thin fellow, mostly gangly arms and legs, with thinning red hair and ubiquitous freckles. And a beak for a nose! When he stands sideways, the effect is comical (I can write so cruelly here because he is jovial and would be first to laugh at himself): first there is the great white boat of a hat called the Stetson, then the great beak of a nose, then a huge lump of an Adam's apple, all set atop a body slumped in an effort to reduce the great height.

It is a sad story I must tell, and Quincey Morris was the only bright spot in it.

Once the violent thumping of the shoulders and greetings were done, John explained the need for a "transfusion." Mr. Morris agreed, with the same unhesitating vehemence John had, which made me think that he, too, shares an unrequited love for Lucy.

So it was done—in Mrs. Westenra's bedroom, as the dead woman still lay in Lucy's bed.

John and Mr. Morris now sit talking at the breakfast table, whilst I remain upstairs to watch Miss Lucy, and write this record. As robust a man as the American is, the transfusion of his energy to her has had little effect. Her breathing is a bit less rapid, and her pulse a bit stronger, but it is not enough.

I have not spoken aloud to John of our hopeless situation in terms of Miss Lucy or ourselves, nor explained in detail last night's events. But when he saw Lucy's room with the corpse and the shattered window, some of the grim helpless fury I had felt only hours before came over his face. He knows; he knows.

It will not be long now.

⊰ 12 ⊱

The Diary of
Abraham Van Helsing

20 SEPTEMBER. A day of the blackest sorrow and despair; yet in the midst of gloom shines a ray of love and valour. My heart vacillates so between the two extremes that I grow wearied and confused—but I must make sense of it all, as there are decisions to be made and lives in the balance. So I write, for writing ofttimes brings illumination.

For two days and two nights John and I sat with Miss Lucy, never leaving her an instant without one of us at her side—though I knew there was no hope of protecting her from her murderer, or from an unthinkable fate. The most we could provide her was the comfort of our presence. It was the hardest of tasks; but my own grief at failing this sweet child, who had so trusted me, was nothing compared to John's. Many times I went in to relieve him to find him with silent tears streaming down his cheeks as, tenderly, he clasped her hand whilst she lay sleeping. It is a bitter thing for him; he is still deeply in love with her, but cannot mourn her openly—cannot even profess his love a final time before she dies. That right is Arthur's, whom I have come to learn is one of his dearest and oldest friends.

And she was dying indeed. That final transfusion never restored to her any vigour, only prolonged the inevitable, which was clearly devastating to her donor, Quincey. (I cannot refer to him as "Mr. Morris," for he is, like most Americans, charmingly casual, and refreshingly forthright in stating his thoughts and feelings in his musical Texan accent.) But there is one feeling that he does try to hide—his own unrequited love for Miss Lucy. I have seen the flicker of pain in his dark eyes when he looks down at her; he cannot bear to linger in the sickroom lest his love should show, and cause John or Arthur any unhappiness. Thus he busies himself with various ways of helping: he has been our errand-boy, and when I said that Arthur should be notified at once, it was he who went to send the telegram. John tells me that Quincey would not sleep last night, but instead patrolled the grounds with pistol in hand. (John also ruefully confessed that Quincey has convinced himself the culprit is a large "vampire bat," of the sort found in South America. Apparently he once lost a beloved horse to such cause, and says he has seen a big grey bat flapping around the house. He is closer to the truth than I thought!)

As for Arthur: His father, Lord Godalming, had taken a turn for the worse on Sunday—the day after Lucy's final encounter with the vampire. So the poor boy had remained the whole day and night at the elder man's deathbed. His father died shortly before dawn Monday, leaving Arthur—or, I should say, the new Lord Godalming—with little time to grieve that loss before he received our telegram saying that Lucy was failing and had asked for him. Quincey picked him up at the station, and he arrived here so red-eyed, grim, and exhausted that it pained me to lead him into Lucy's sickroom and see his sorrow multiplied. (Quincey himself disappeared, I think because he feared breaking down in the sickroom and further upsetting Arthur.) As it happened, the new Lord Godalming arrived at precisely six o'clock, when I was coming to relieve John from his vigil; so Arthur sat with me the whole of my watch, until midnight.

As overwhelmed as the poor man must have been, he was cheerful with Lucy in a way that rallied her a bit—and she, too, affected such cheerfulness that I could not bear to watch them both be so brave for the other's sake. But weakness overcame her soon, and she went back to her pattern of lapsing into frequent periods of unconsciousness; other times, she gave up struggling to speak and just lay in silence. Through it all, Arthur sat beside her, holding her hand and gazing down at her with the same expression of despairing adoration I had seen John wear. Despite his privileged upbringing, Lord Godalming is a strong, strong man.

In thirty years of medical practice, I have visited many families who cared for a mortally ill member. All are different, of course—some loving, some not; but all share one constant, especially when death draws nigh. The experience causes formality and pretense to fall away, not only for the dying member, but for those who tend him, so that only the truest essence of all persons remains. In some cases, this is a sad thing, for anger, regret, or sorrow might be revealed, or inner weakness wherein the individual lapses into morbid despair from which he cannot recover.

In other cases, the experience melts away the more superficial aspects of the personality, revealing a golden core of strength and compassion. This is what I saw in John and his friends Quincey and Arthur, and in Miss

Lucy herself; and despite great sadness, I felt warmed and privileged to be among them.

At last the hour struck twelve, and John appeared in the doorway. I rose, patted Arthur's shoulder, and bade him come to rest, as he had not done so in almost two days. He resisted heartily until John vowed that, should Lucy's condition take a change for the worse, however slight, he would wake his friend immediately. At last he came, and we went into the drawing-room, where two comfortable sofas faced a blazing hearth.

There I rested, but did not sleep, as my thoughts were anxious and many; blessedly, Arthur fell almost at once into a doze. I listened to the clock chime hour after hour, until at last it was sunrise again—six o'clock. Arthur was still sleeping soundly, so I stole away, back into Lucy's sickroom, where John sat writing in the dimmed gaslight.

The blind was pulled, and the room shadowed. I could not see the patient's face, but above her heart and head hovered a fatal telltale sign: the glittering indigo aura that marked a vampire. At once, I ordered John to raise the blind. The pale dawn sunlight streamed in, illuminating Miss Lucy's face—which caused me to gasp, for at first I thought I was looking upon a corpse. But she still breathed, and so I hurriedly untied the black silk scarf I had fastened about the puncture wounds.

It was as I had feared; the vampire's mark had vanished, leaving the milky skin there smooth and flawless.

John saw, too, and, even before I told him, seemed to know that she was dying. He went and woke Arthur—for in truth, I could not bear to break the news to the lad myself. Instead, I busied myself with straightening Lucy's pillows, and quickly removing all signs of sickness from the night-stand—the laudanum bottle, the morphia, the chamber-pot. Then I brushed out her hair so that it lay in becoming waves upon the pillows, for I knew that Lucy should have liked to look her best for this last moment shared with her fiancé.

So the stricken lover came—or should I say, her *two* stricken lovers, for John, his expression and posture one of the utmost resolve, came in with his arm firmly wound about Arthur's shoulders in a gesture of unreserved support. Yet his eyes, as much as Arthur's, shone with unspilled tears; he felt the coming loss just as keenly, but Fate had not dealt him the right to show it.

As the two approached the deathbed, John let go his grip, and let his friend rush at once to Lucy's side. I do not mention my pity for my son in order to make light of Arthur's suffering—far from it, I think it shows how good a man Holmwood (that is, Lord Godalming) must be, to inspire such deep loyalty in a friend. And John, too, for many lesser men have broken off long friendships over their shared love for one woman.

As for Arthur, having come from the deathbed of his father to that of the woman he loved, he entered the room pale and trembling, with fresh tears upon his cheeks. But the closer he drew to Lucy, the more firmly he put aside his double grief, wiping his eyes and running his fingers through his dishevelled curls that he might present to her his best. He is a strong man, that one. I remembered how stricken I had been when my little son Jan died, and Gerda went mad; certainly I could never have put up as stolid a front as Arthur did.

It was then that he ran to her side, and bent low to kiss her—but I had seen the growing indigo aura surrounding her; were he to consummate his intent, she might well mesmerise him to the degree that after death, she could influence him for ill. Thus I moved between them, and gently warned, "Not yet. Take her hand; it will comfort her more."

He was perplexed, but sorrow had stripped him of any defiance, so he did as told. It was a difficult thing, to tell a man that he could not kiss his dying lover, but I knew no other way to protect him.

Miss Lucy took great comfort in his presence and his touch, and sank back into sleep with a sigh. But after a time, honest sleep turned to trance, and a veil of illusory beauty such as the vampire can produce enveloped her. John saw it, I know, for he gave me a sharp, knowing glance. Lucy then opened her eyes—or rather, a demoness' eyes—and begged him to kiss her, in a seductive, wicked parody of her own sweet voice.

So swiftly did Arthur bend down to oblige her that, abandoning all civility, I caught hold of his neck and flung him away, shouting, "Not for your life!"

Remembering it now causes fresh pain, for I know how unspeakably cruel—indeed, mad—my act must have seemed to him. In fact, a gleam of violence came into his eye. But almost immediately it passed, and he merely stood, awaiting explanation.

I did not give it, for very shortly thereafter, Lucy came to herself, and took my great coarse hand in her fine small one and kissed it. This in itself was sufficient to summon my tears; but then she gazed up at me with beseeching, loving eyes, and said in a breathless whisper: "My true friend, and his! Guard him, and give me peace!"

Atremble with emotion, I sank to my knees beside the bed. These were difficult, perhaps impossible, things she had asked of me—if Vlad was now so powerful, so impervious, how could I know that she, his offspring, would not also become so?

Yet for love's sake, I answered solemnly, "I swear!"

I *do* swear, Lucy. I swear it with every fibre of my being, with all my strength and soul. Impossible it may be, but I shall accomplish it, or die in the effort. . . .

Her breathing became more of a struggle, until I heard the faint rattle in her throat. I rose and turned to Arthur, who no longer fought to hold back the tears that streamed down his wan cheeks. The end had come, and so I bade him take her hand and kiss her only once, upon the forehead.

This he did, and then she slowly closed her eyes. The death-rattle grew louder then, and so I took Arthur's arm and drew him away. Yet before we reached the door, the sound stopped abruptly; our sweet Miss Lucy had died.

I returned to her side, and let John take his sobbing friend away. There I sat some time, gazing in grief and horror as Lucy's worn, wasted face began at once to bloom with life—or rather, undeath.

For more than twenty years, I have hunted vampires all over the European continent, and in every case, I prevailed: the vampire was destroyed, and his progenitor, Vlad, weakened. Again and again was the same scenario repeated—the hunt, the capture, the destruction, always according to the same rules. The vampire's abilities and limitations never varied, the cross and the garlic never failed. In time I grew more powerful, and my task easier; so strong was my aura that I could move in complete confidence of invisibility around the undead. They could neither mesmerise nor overpower me. But now . . .

As I bitterly contemplated my failure, John returned and stood beside me in silence, both of us contemplating the corpse. For a time, neither of us spoke; and then John asked:

"Professor. Does a dying man have the right to know he is dying?"

His tone was so calm and conversational that I believed he was trying to distract himself, perhaps by trying to decide whether Lucy herself had been so aware; thus, I answered in the same manner. "Of course. If he does not know, how can he properly prepare himself?"

He spoke again, and this time I noted a faint but growing anger behind his words. "And does a man engaged in battle—even a battle he cannot possibly win—have the right to know who it is he fights?"

A slight chill seized me, for I suddenly understood where his line of questioning led—yet I could not bring myself to reply. Instead, I gazed up at him, and saw that he was struggling terribly to hold in a powerful tide of emotion.

When he realised no answer would come, he said heatedly, "Professor, you cannot bear this terrible burden alone any longer. You have seen Arthur and Quincey and, I hope, come to know them as the brave, honourable men they are. They have—"

"What do you suggest, John? That I tell them the truth? Even if they believed it, what good would come of it? Only that they would be endangered—"

"Lucy was ignorant," he cried, with a sudden vehemence that flushed his cheeks scarlet. "What good came of *that*?"

For this I had no answer, so I stood mutely as he continued to release grief in the form of anger. He shook, he raged, he lifted his fist and shook it in my face.

"They have as much right as I to know the cause of Lucy's death so that they might avenge it—and wipe this terrible scourge from the earth! They are my dearest friends, and I will not stand by and see them die of ignorance! Good God, Quince could very well have been bitten himself, wandering around outside in the night, trying to make himself useful in some small way!"

And at that, the storm of tears finally came, with such fury that he sank to his knees beside Miss Lucy and buried his face in the bed, one fist helplessly pounding against the mattress.

I said nothing; I let him cry. But his words pricked me, and evoked within me a different sort of tempest.

After some moments, he raised his damp, flushed face and rose to leave. Before he reached the door he turned, and said with calm, quiet dignity so that I would know he'd meant every word, despite the accompanying emotional display:

"Dr. Van Helsing, you have long put your trust in secrecy and science, in magical protections and rituals. Now all those things have failed you. But there is one thing which will never fail, one thing which will always be stronger than any evil: the human heart. I offer you mine and those of my two closest friends in the coming battle, for their sake as well as your own."

❖ ❖ ❖

26 SEPTEMBER. Lucy was buried in a double service with her mother on the twenty-second; a bitter affair for all, especially those two who knew she had not gone to a peaceful end.

Intense contemplation has not permitted the truth of John's angry words to fade; indeed, the more I savour them, the more I come to believe that he is right. We have agreed that when Miss Lucy is truly set to rest, it shall be Arthur's hand which performs the deed, and John, Quincey, and I will all be in attendance. I have written Arthur and Quincey letters, asking them to accompany me to the gravesite. Beyond that, I offered no explanation; words cannot convince as thoroughly as physical evidence.

In the meantime, the last few days have been busy ones for several reasons. As there were no surviving kin, Mrs. Westenra left her estate to Arthur. He in turn asked John and me for assistance in sifting through papers and making burial arrangements, as he was already quite overwhelmed by similar obligations in connexion with his father's death. I asked him for leave to examine Lucy's personal papers and diary for more insight as to "the nature of her disease." This he granted, being too distracted even to question my request.

In going through those papers, I discovered a thick bundle of letters from a Wilhelmina Murray, whom Lucy also mentioned constantly in her diary as "Mina." It seems these two women were the best of friends; in fact, Lucy often summered with Madam—that is, Miss—Mina at the Westenra cottage at Whitby. Lucy did not keep a diary at the time (upon returning to London, however, she succumbed to Miss Mina's journalistic influence and began one), so we have no record of what precisely occurred. But I know it was there she was first bitten.

Mina's letters, some of which were sadly never opened, reflected a lady of great kindness and intelligence. Upon reading them, I felt at once as if I had already met and befriended her; so I was even more fearful to learn of her time at Whitby with Lucy. For if Lucy had been bitten, why not her friend?

Two days after the Westenra funeral, I wrote Miss Mina Murray (now Mrs. Mina Harker) asking if I might interview her, as I had been Lucy Westenra's physician and was investigating the cause of her death. She responded promptly and most warmly, inviting me to her home in Exeter the very next day.

With some trepidation, I went. My heart was still sore after the terrible defeat with Lucy, and I dreaded finding yet another kind gentlewoman stricken with the vampire's curse.

Fortunately, when I arrived in Exeter and stepped into Mrs. Harker's drawing-room, I saw a young lady blooming with health: the rosy cheeks and lips were a welcome and beautiful sight after poor Lucy's pallor. Even lovelier was the sight of her long neck rising pure and unmarked from a collarless gown. Yet Madam Mina (I could not resist calling her so at once, for it was clear that Lucy's death had already united us in friendship) looked nothing like what I had expected. Her letters indicated a woman of such great maturity and wisdom that I had imagined her as older than Lucy, taller, and more solidly built.

But she was a good head shorter than her late friend, a tiny, fragile-looking creature hardly larger than the schoolchildren she had taught before her recent marriage to Mr. Harker. Her face, too, was that of a child—heart-shaped beneath a dark brown pompadour, with great hazel eyes, small nose, and rosebud mouth—so innocent and ingenuous that she would go through life always looking far younger than her years. Ah, but those eyes . . . They reminded me of John's, for they were sensitive, intelligent, quick to absorb every detail—and blessedly free from any trace of treacherous glittering indigo. Indeed, even in the bright daylight streaming through the open shutters, a definite violet glow could be detected surrounding her: a strong aura for a strong woman.

She had apparently been hard at work when I arrived, for I heard clacking out in the hallway, which ceased the instant the maid knocked to announce my arrival. When the door swung open wide, I saw that one corner of the drawing-room had been converted into a study. Behind her stood a desk upon which rested stacked newspapers, a small black diary, white paper stacked in a wire basket, and a large typewriter with a sheet of paper inserted.

And in that second's pause when we two faced each other and I verified that she was indeed Mrs. Harker, *née* Mina Murray, those intelligent eyes scrutinised me most intently, yet swiftly enough that courtesy was not breached. Apparently I impressed her as favourably as she had me, for a look of subtle warmth came over her cherubic features.

She approached with a gracious smile, and held out a delicate, pale hand one third the size of my large, callused brown one. I took it, grateful to sense by touch that my visual appraisal of her had been accurate: she was uncursed, unmarked. Thus the smile I returned to her was the first genuine one in many days.

"Madam Mina," I said, instinctively using the less formal form of address, which seemed to please her. "It is on account of the dead that I come."

Her gaze was refreshingly intense and direct (as we Dutch prefer), without the averted glances and eyelash-fluttering so favoured by Englishwomen. And I saw in it love for her dead friend and honest gratitude towards me; and when she spoke, I knew she did so directly from the heart. "Sir," replied she, in a strong, mature voice that belied her juvenile appearance, "you have no better claim on me than that you were a friend and helper of Lucy Westenra."

The moment of introduction over, she asked as to precisely what information I desired from her, and I explained my need for certain information about Whitby—as much as she could remember.

"Why, I can tell you everything about it," she said,

gesturing for me to sit upon a nearby sofa. "I have written it all down. Would you like to see it?"

Of course. So she retrieved the black diary from the desk, and handed it to me with a sudden impish glint in her eye; Madam Mina, it seems, has a wry sense of humour.

I opened the diary, intending to begin reading at once —but upon the page were neat but totally incomprehensible squiggles and curls and lines. "Mr. Jonathan Harker is a lucky man," I said, handing it back to her, "to have such a talented wife. But alas; I do not know shorthand. Would you be so kind as to read it for me?"

The child blushed as she took the diary, and at once retrieved a stack of papers from the wire basket. "Forgive me. Here: when you told me you wished to inquire about Lucy, I went ahead and wrote all the Whitby entries out on the typewriter for you."

I thanked her most sincerely for her labour, and asked whether I might read it then; she agreed and excused herself, saying that she would check on lunch.

Enclosed in the privacy of the drawing-room, I read swiftly through the entries. They spoke of Whitby and Lucy and several sleepwalking incidents; in one place, it was clear that she had rescued Miss Lucy from the vampire's very grasp without knowing it. The diary had obviously been intended to be private, for it mentioned her extreme anxiety over her then-fiancé, Jonathan, who was apparently abroad and had not written in some time. I thought nothing of this at all, focusing all my attention on the events where Vlad was most clearly involved. Until, that is, I read the entry of 26 July, when Madam Mina had just received the long-awaited letter from Jonathan, forwarded by his employer. One sentence seemed to leap from the very page:

"It is only a line dated from Castle Dracula, and says that he is just starting for home."

I was glad then that she had left me alone, for I swore aloud and struck the sofa with my fist at the sight of the name. Jonathan at Castle Dracula! And here this sweet lady, by whom I was immediately smitten, was not safe at all—she was in the very heart of danger! The vampire's evil had touched her not just once, through the death of her dearest friend, but through her poor husband as well.

I read further, and learned that Jonathan had suffered from "brain fever," for he had raved wildly at the station-master in Klausenburgh for a "ticket home." Though he was penniless, his violent demeanour terrified the locals so that they gave him a ticket for the train's westernmost destination, Buda-Pesth. There he was of such a mental state that he was promptly taken to a sanitorium, and the good nuns there notified Madam Mina, who came and brought him home to England. (It was at the Buda-Pesth sanitorium that they were married.)

After I had read it all, I set the papers aside and began to think. The decision had already been made to bring Quincey and Arthur into our (that is, John's and my) confidence concerning the vampire, as it only seemed right that they take part in avenging the death of the woman they loved.

Did not Madam Mina, too, have the same right? Even were Jonathan not bitten, he had already suffered great mental torment. I remembered John's bitter statement: Lucy had been ignorant about the vampire, yet that had not protected her in the least. I suppose it is true, then— knowledge *is* power, even if, in this case, it is only the power to surrender . . . or flee.

In any event, it was too late; I had already opened my heart to this young woman, and cared about her welfare the same as I had cared about Lucy's. I could not simply go and leave her here to make the dreadful discovery about her husband alone, or become the victim of his or Dracula's attack.

Therefore, when Madam Mina returned, I thanked her roundly for her illuminating manuscript—though she would have been horrified to know what I had discovered in its light. As casually as I could, I remarked upon her husband's brain fever and asked whether he had recovered completely.

At once a shadow came over her expression, and a deep crease appeared between her dark, delicate brows; she paused, and said carefully, "He was *almost* recovered . . . but he has been greatly upset by his employer's death. Mr. Hawkins took Jonathan under his wing and has been like a father to him for many years."

I nodded and, with a few sympathetic comments, urged her to speak a bit more of it.

This increased her discomfort until the crease was joined by others on her brow, and the full rosebud lips thinned to a flat line. "He had a—a bit of a shock last Thursday, when we were in town, strolling in Piccadilly."

Again I coaxed her to reveal more and more, until I learned that the sight of a man (ha! No mortal man, I suspect!) had upset him, a man who clearly had had something to do with his brain disease.

Of a sudden, she was on her knees. Not in tears or hysteria, but so overwhelmed by fear and concern for her husband that she lifted her arms to me and beseeched me to help him, to make him well again. Though she did not say it, I knew she feared her Jonathan was going mad.

I gently took Madam Mina's imploring hands in mine and helped her to her feet. As I led her to the sofa and sat down beside her, I said—with the utmost sincerity:

"My dear Madam Mina, since I have come to London in answer to my friend John Seward's call, I have found a number of people—including Arthur (that is, Lord Godalming) and our Miss Lucy—whose strength in the face of despair and whose compassion have touched me deeply. I am honoured to call them friend, and to know that they would think of me as one. From your writings and your mere presence, I know that you are as good and deserving as they. Please think of me as your friend, Madam Mina, and know that I will help you and your husband in any way.

"But first—you must calm yourself, and when lunch is ready, you must eat. Afterwards, you can tell me the details about his troubles."

As I spoke, she had already grown calm, and the shadow had lifted from her face, leaving her subdued but hopeful. We went down to lunch, and afterwards, we re-tired to the drawing-room, and I urged her to speak of Jonathan.

She lowered her gaze—in fact, seemed to look within herself for the solution to some dilemma. "Dr. Van Helsing"—and here she looked up at me again with that frank, honest gaze—"what I have to tell you is so queer that even I am not sure whether I believe it. It all sounds like madness; so you must promise that you will not laugh at what I confide in you."

My pulse quickened; I knew we were about to speak of Dracula and his doings. Mrs. Harker was no madwoman, of that I was certain. And so I smiled ruefully as I con-fessed, "My dear, if you only knew how strange is the reason for which I am here—it would be *you* who would laugh. I have learned over time never to dismiss anyone's belief without investigation, regardless of how bizarre or impossible it may seem."

She watched me intently as she spoke, and I think it was the understanding in my gaze more than the meaning of my words that convinced her. She relaxed and nodded, reassured. "Thank you, Dr. Van Helsing." She rose, went to the desk, and took again from the basket another stack of paper, which she presented to me.

"This is the diary which my husband kept whilst in Transylvania. It is long, but I have typewritten it out; it will explain better than I can in a few words the extent of his trouble. To tell the truth, when I read it—only recently, and for the first time—the details were so intricate and consistent that I half-believed it. Even now, I am in a fever of doubt. I can say no more: Will you take it, read it, and judge? I will wait to hear from you."

"I shall read it to-night," I promised, for I was just as eager to read it as she was to hear my opinion concerning it. "I will stay in Exeter to-night so that I can let you know my thoughts at once. May I come again in the morning to see both you and your husband?"

The great relief upon her face was wonderful to behold; so our meeting was arranged. She of course assumed I desired it so as to make a subtle examination of Jonathan's mind, but in truth, I wanted to see for myself whether the vampire's mark was on him.

Thus I spent that night in a quiet hotel room, reading the private journal of a man who had lived through hell and emerged somewhat intact. He had been entrapped in the castle by Dracula for two months, poor devil. And if his impressions can be trusted, he was never bitten by Vlad, but was intended as food to be left behind for three vampiresses he christens the "three brides." I might have thought that, in his fear, he miscalculated the number—for Zsuszanna clearly features in that entry, as does Dunya, and when last I had been to the castle, those were the only two "women" there. But to hear one distinctly described as "golden-haired" and "sapphire-eyed"—this could be neither of them. My hypothesis: that this was Zsuzsanna's "Elisabeth"; if so, she must be here in London too.

Another disturbing thought came to me as I read the manuscript—might Jonathan have been bitten without his knowledge by Vlad or one of the women? At any rate, I was determined to find out during my next visit to the Harker home.

But along with my fear for both Madam Mina and her new husband came a growing sense of admiration for him. Here was a young and far-from-worldly young solicitor who found himself abruptly in the most harrowing of circumstances—in Dracula's castle, confronted by disappearing vampiresses and Vlad's sadistic hints at his eventual demise, the realisation that the prince (that is, the "count," for so it amused Dracula to present himself to his Exeter-based solicitors) cast no reflection in mirrors, commanded wolves, captured small children and gave them to the evil women for sustenance; and worst of all, the fact that he, Harker, was locked inside the castle with no means of escape.

Did he surrender? Did he yield to his immortal seductresses? No. Instead, knowing himself dead if he took no action, Jonathan crawled from his window some several hundred feet above the rocky ground, and through sheer will clung with feet and fingers to the stones and crevices on the castle wall. Thus he made his way down and escaped on foot—an almost impossible task.

And before he fled, he encountered Vlad asleep in his coffin—not once, but twice. Most men would have run in terror at the first sight; but Harker sensed that the "count" was a monster to be destroyed at all costs. Thus he returned *willingly* to Vlad's resting place, and attempted to murder the vampire with nothing more than a common shovel. A solicitor he might be, but a brave and true one, and if he had passed from the vampires' lair unbitten (though surely not unscathed), he deserved more than any to join in the battle that now faced our little group.

Upon finishing his amazing tale, I wrote to Madam Mina that her husband's diary was entirely true, as was his brain and heart, and that her concern about his sanity was warrantless. I sent a courier from the hotel, that she might receive this news (can we really call it good or bad? Nay, it was both) at once.

Within an hour I received a letter from the same messenger; Madam Mina had penned an immediate reply, asking me to come not for lunch the following day, but for breakfast.

⸎ ⸎ ⸎

At precisely twenty minutes to eight this morning, I answered the knock at my hotel-room door and found myself face-to-face with the courageous Mr. Jonathan Harker, who had come to pick me up. He was, like his wife, far younger-looking than his years, with light brown curling hair and a business-like demeanour; one would never have thought him capable of the amazing physical feats and courage professed in his journal. I at once invited him inside, under the pretext that it would take me a moment to fetch my coat; but my real motive was to have him to myself a few moments unobserved.

When he entered, closing the door after him, I at once approached and held his gaze. He was an easy subject and fell into trance almost instantly.

There was no immediate sign of the indigo aura, but I wasted not a moment; I unfastened his collar and pulled it away, then unbuttoned the top of his shirt in order to thoroughly examine the neck and collarbone.

No mark. I released a sigh so deep I scarce could stand, and with silent apology righted Jonathan's clothing as best I could. Then I went to waken him—but something subtle in his gaze and aura (scholarly orange, like Arthur's) troubled me. It was bright, vibrant, gleaming wherever I looked; yet in the periphery of my vision, I sensed a hint of encroaching indigo.

I did not know what it portended. In all my hunting years, I had seen traces of the dark aura only in those the vampire had bitten. And in such cases, it always showed up obviously, directly—first in the victim's gaze, then swirling throughout his own, brighter aura.

Never had I *sensed* it like this: hovering nearby, just out of sight. Perhaps, I thought, it was only the lingering psychological effects of his imprisonment in the tower; but I could not be sure. Therefore, I deemed it wisest not to reveal all that I knew to Mr. and Mrs. Harker, lest the Impaler be privy to our plans.

The decision made, I gently released Jonathan from his trance. He came to consciousness easily, without any notice of a change. Waking, he seemed entirely free of any trace of the vampire's hold. I at once took his shoulder and turned his face towards the light coming through the window, studying it carefully as I said, "But Madam Mina said you were ill, that you had had a shock."

To which he smiled, and replied that he *had* been ill and *had* had a shock, but that I had cured him of it by my letter. He was an honest, pleasant fellow—he must be, to have won a wife so good as Madam Mina—and we had a pleasant ride over to his home. On the way, he told me that he wanted to provide whatever help he could against the "count." In his eyes shone a burning desire (perhaps, even, as great as mine) to see the monster destroyed.

Masking my disquiet, I told him that I indeed needed his help, and immediately: my work would be greatly eased if he could provide information concerning all business transacted with "Count Dracula" before his, Jonathan's, trip to Transylvania.

This he promised to provide before I left Exeter later that morning—and in fact, after we two had returned to his house and breakfasted with Miss Mina, he handed me a bundle of papers so that I might read them on the train back to London.

He and his wife are good, kind people, and when I see what they have already suffered at Vlad's hands, I can only think of myself and Gerda when we were young—before our small family was destroyed by the vampire. Here in London, for the first time in many years, I have begun to feel myself surrounded by a family again, of brave and loving souls united by a common evil. I could not bear to think of Harker and sweet Madam Mina torn apart, or turned into vile undead parodies of themselves.

Yet how could I protect them, without possibly exposing John and the others to more danger if Jonathan was Vlad's unwitting spy?

I did not know. But as Jonathan drove me back to the station, I asked softly, "If, in the future, I were to call both you and Madam Mina to London, would you come?"

"Call us when you will," he said, "and we will come."

⊹ ⊹ ⊹

I have spoken with John frankly about the Harkers. He agrees that we must do what we can to help both Madam Mina and her husband, but, same as I, is perplexed about what Jonathan's oblique indigo taint might mean. Therefore we have decided that, when the Harkers come to London (and I have no doubt they shall), they will stay here at the asylum. They shall not know that *I* am here—I shall maintain invisibility for myself and Gerda in our respective cells—and this will assist me in keeping surreptitious watch over Jonathan until we establish whether he is Vlad's agent or no. Until then, we will assume that he is, and will secretly use such precautions as I already do with Gerda. This will be safest for Mrs. Harker.

John has agreed that he will reveal no information to the Harkers that will alert them to the full depth of our knowledge; rather, we are to seem as bumbling fools who know nothing of Vlad's new strength. Thus, if Vlad is privy to Jonathan's thoughts, he shall discover little of our plans. I have also warned John that Madam Mina has copied her and her husband's journals out, and offered them to me; the time may come when he will be called upon to surrender his. As for myself, I can easily say that I *have* no diary, for the Harkers will see no evidence of it—or me—on the asylum grounds. But John records upon his phonograph daily, sometimes several times a day, and his equipment is too difficult to hide. I have asked him not to record any details he does not wish everyone to hear—or at the very least, to record them secretly by pen, so that he might not be overheard and the diary might be hidden away. He has agreed; and will also go back and listen to what he has already recorded. Any cylinders containing entries which reveal too much will be hidden in my cell, and he shall re-record them to make them consistent with what we want the Harkers—and by default, Arthur and Quincey—to know. We have agreed that John shall play the sceptic, who knows nothing of the vampire and is slow to believe.

I have another reason for dissembling, one which perhaps is foolish: If Madam Mina, that brave and stalwart soul, were to learn the extent of Vlad's powers, she might lose hope. And that I could not bear to see.

❧13❧

Dr. Seward's Diary

29 SEPTEMBER. How strange to write this by pen, and in my bedroom rather than the office. It goes against the grain to agree to deceit, especially one that might affect my two finest friends, Art and Quince; but I understand the reason for it, and must take comfort in the fact that by doing so, I protect them.

So here is the truth—I must record it somehow, lest I forget all and begin to believe my own lies.

To-day, shortly after noon, the professor took me back to Lucy's tomb. Our plan for gaining entry to the cemetery was quite simple: We would wait for a funeral, which could be counted on to take place at mid-day, then hide ourselves when the mourners left. (There seems little point in arousing suspicion by climbing over the wall in broad daylight.) The sexton, thinking all had gone, would lock the iron gate behind him. Then we would be free to do as we wished, for Van Helsing confided to me that he has retained the key to the Westenra tomb, which the mortician had given him to give to Arthur.

I admit, I accompanied Van Helsing with a great deal of trepidation. My grief over Lucy's death, though no longer raw, was still fresh, and to finally witness the reality of vampirism with *her* as example seemed too painful. I think I agreed in something of a daze, for I could scarcely believe her dead, much less transformed into a monster. Part of me hoped that the professor was a deluded madman, and that all this talk of blood-sucking and Vlad Dracula was but a dream from which I soon would wake. So I went only half believing that I would see the proof of Van Helsing's claims.

Our plan proceeded like clockwork. We went to the churchyard and waited until the gate was unlocked and mourners had arrived. Then we, too, entered—dressed in black, to better fit in. The professor had brought his medical bag, which caused me some consternation, for I felt it would draw attention to us; luckily, he was right that no one would notice or think anything of it if they did.

It was a chill, grey day, bleak and damp with mist; an appropriate day for our task. Throughout the burial, we stood quietly at the fringes of the crowd. And when it was done, and the crowd began to scatter, we moved behind the farthest tomb and waited until we heard the clang of the sexton closing the gate.

Finally, when all was clear, Van Helsing led me back to the small, square stone building at whose entry was carved the legend:

WESTENRA

I had been too distracted during Lucy's funeral to remember where the tomb lay; my gaze had been focussed on her casket, draped in linen and strewn with white flowers, whilst I tried to picture how she would appear as undead. Would she still be beautiful, or even recognisable as the sweet girl she had been? Would she have long, slavering fangs and inhuman strength, bursting through the lead

lining intended to hold in the stench of putrefying remains?

The professor clearly sensed my growing reluctance,
for he briefly laid a warm hand upon my shoulder that
conveyed both comfort and encouragement. Then he set
upon the lock with the key. The former was ancient and
somewhat rusted, requiring him to play with it several seconds before, at last, the large metal door gave a mournful
screech and came open.

It took us both some effort to push it open—I all the
while wondering how Lucy would ever be able to manage
it. The professor motioned me to enter; a darkly chivalrous
gesture if ever there was one. I did, and started as a squeak-
ing black rat skittered over my foot. Inside, the air was cold
but stale, and heavy with the scent of mouldering flowers.
It was, I think, the most hopeless place I have ever stood,
for within a week's time, the spiderwebs had grown heavy,
and numerous shiny-coated beetles crawled before my feet.
The whole of it—high octagonal windows, bleak walls,
crawling shadows—was coated with a very fine layer of
dust that seemed to absorb all light. I suppose the grimness
distracted me, for the professor touched my shoulder to
bring me to myself.

Once more I started, to my embarrassment, then began to follow Van Helsing, who had moved past me with a
sense of purpose, out of the narrow entryway into a wider
room where a good twenty coffins lay upon marble cata-
falques. It was easy to guess which were Mrs. Westenra's
and Lucy's, as the others were all shrouded with such a
thick film of dust (which demonstrated how long it had
been since any had visited here) that neither the coffin's
colour nor the nameplate could be seen.

To the cleaner coffins the professor went at once, bag
in hand, and squinted down at the silver nameplates to

ascertain which was Lucy's. That decided, he set down the bag and retrieved from it a turnscrew and fretsaw, both of which he rather callously set upon Mrs. Westenra's nearby casket.

I must say here that I was altogether amazed by his incredible calm and matter-of-factness. Being a trained physician, I had long ago lost my squeamishness around the dead; but this was no ordinary corpse we were approaching now, nor ordinary circumstances. Yet Van Helsing behaved as if it were something he had done his whole life.

Without fanfare or even a hint of reverence, he raised the coffin lid, so swiftly that I barely managed to keep from drawing back. It was foolish of me to do so, for my brain knew well that we would only see the lead lining; but my heart had apparently caused me to forget for an instant. The dead flowers which had rested atop Lucy's casket—one of which I had laid there myself a week before—scattered with a rustling whisper to the ground, a cruel reminder that even grief itself was not everlasting.

The professor paid them no heed but, with the cool detachment I have seen him wear in surgery, picked up the turnscrew. With a sudden savage movement, he made a hammer of his fist and struck the turnscrew's handle so that its tip tore open the thin lead casing.

This time, I recoiled in earnest, and drew out my handkerchief, fully prepared to protect myself from the ensuing rush of noxious gas that would come from the week-old corpse. But no stench came. I permitted myself to draw a breath, and stood fascinated by what came next.

Van Helsing set down the turnscrew and picked up the tiny fretsaw. After working it into the gap left by the puncture, he sawed some few feet down one side of the coffin, then across the top, then down the other side. Both fretsaw and turnscrew he replaced in his bag. Then he grasped the tongue of metal at the top and pulled down to the foot, as a mother might pull back a too-warm blanket so as not to wake a sleeping child.

But there was nothing of tenderness in the professor's movements; when he drew back the lead casing to reveal the corpse beneath, his expression was colder and harder than I have ever seen it.

"Friend John," he called, with a voice so deep and stern none would have dared disobey it. "Look away from her! Look away!"

Actually, I had not yet steeled myself to gaze down at her, so his warning came in time. He stepped between me and the coffin and said urgently, "I have done you a disservice in not warning you first. No, look up at me, not at her —yes! And now listen: Sense your own aura, and withdraw it inward, towards your heart. Strengthen it there. This protects you from her pull, now and in the future. Yes, yes!" he cried in approval; apparently my features had changed as I put into practice his lesson. Indeed, I found the result was that I had "hardened my heart." The emotional strain of the painful encounter was abruptly eased, and I found myself possessed of some measure of the professor's calm concentration.

I let go a sigh as my equilibrium returned.

"Very good!" the professor said. "Very good. If you wish to look down at her now, you may; if I see that you have trouble, I shall help. I apologise that I had not schooled you in this technique earlier. I was foolish enough to hope that the talismans I had left with her would remain, and keep her in the tomb until we could send her to a more honourable rest. Before she was placed in her coffin, I had left them upon her lips and breast—but see? Someone has taken them." He sighed. "I had set them upon her at her wake, but someone in the house stole them then—two crucifixes of gold. So before her burial, I paid the mortician and set two more upon her before I watched them seal her fast beneath the lead. Now someone else has cheated us again—but no mortal, I fear, or the lead would already have been rolled away."

I listened to him with only half an ear, for at his permission I had at once looked down at Lucy. To say that she was beautiful would have been an insult; in undeath, she was beyond beauty, beyond radiance. Indeed, it was if the sun itself had been wrapped in white cerements, revealing only in places—head and hands—its full blazing glory. Her hair, which had been dark ash bleached to blond in places by the summer sun, was now a glorious and shimmering bronze streaked with molten gold. Her lips were the delicate, iridescent pink of mother-of-pearl, just as her eyes—her open eyes, which gazed sightlessly at a point beyond the ceiling—were the seafoam-green of polished nacre. And her face was that of the full moon, possessed of an internal radiance.

One thought—one small thought, *Dear God, she is beautiful!*—and one fleeting and subtle desire to give up on all that was moral and right, to join her in eternal ecstasy, and I felt my heart go out to her as the tide seeks the moon. I was lost, smitten.

Once more, a touch of the professor's hand brought me from my dangerous reverie. I looked up, and caught a gulp of air; staring into Van Helsing's dark blue eyes, I focussed myself and again took control of my heart and emotions.

"I am all right," I said. "I shall look at her no longer." And to show my determination, I stepped away from the corpse and faced the entry.

He was there only a few seconds longer in order to

leave more talismans and roll the lead lining back over her, then close the casket lid. "For Arthur's sake," he said grimly as we left, "and the fact that I was too arrogant to bring with me stake and knife, thinking that my pale magic would hold her here—I do not kill her now. But if we do not succeed in doing so to-night, when Arthur and Quincey come, there will be much blood upon my head; much blood."

It is evening now, and Arthur and Quince will arrive in a few hours in response to the professor's letters. Thoughts of what is to come leave me too restless to eat supper.

⊹⊹ ⊹⊹ ⊹⊹

The Diary of
Abraham Van Helsing

29 SEPTEMBER. Arthur and Quincey arrived last night at ten o'clock, both of them wearing expressions of confusion. As agreed, John herded the lot of us into his study and locked the door, which only added to the mysterious sense of secrecy.

Once the others had taken seats upon the long sofa, I stood before them to address them, and they all three looked up at me with curiosity and even faint hope—as if there might be something good in the midst of all this sorrow. Arthur himself looked dreadful; he had aged fifteen years in the course of a week. His formerly smooth forehead was creased with wrinkles, and his eyes were still dazed; in them, I saw thoughts of sadness enter and leave like passing clouds. He was at that terrible early stage of mourning where any sight, any sound, any memory, might touch him and reignite his grief.

Quincey, too, was suffering in his own quiet way. His already thin lips had grown noticeably thinner, and shadows had gathered beneath his tired eyes; beneath the freckles that so perfectly matched his dark red hair, his skin had grown pale. He sat with his big white Stetson in his bony fingers, and toyed with the rim so that the hat slowly revolved round and round. Yet despite his suffering, he maintained a forced brightness for his friends' sake.

It was for me a difficult moment, staring at these good but troubled souls; I had contemplated long about this meeting, and had come to the unhappy conclusion that there was simply no kind way to do it. So I began by saying that I had finally learned what had killed Lucy, and that she was now in such a state that we had one last task to perform, for her sake.

Arthur stiffened with horror. "Dr. Van Helsing, do you mean to tell me she was buried alive?"

I shook my head: no, no. "Dear Arthur, dear friend; do you trust me? Do you believe that I honestly cared for Miss Lucy, and that I wanted, and still want, only the best for her?"

"Yes, of course," he said, but his eyes remained tormented.

"Then let me take you to her tomb, for there lies the only physical evidence necessary to explain what we must do. If you will only trust, and come with me—"

The look of confusion and pain on Arthur's face pulled at me, but I remained cold and resolute. "First," Arthur replied, clearly struggling to contain his feelings, "I must know *why* we need to go to the tomb. What terrible mystery can it be, that you cannot tell me plainly as a friend?"

"I can only tell you that it is for Miss Lucy's sake that we go," I told him. "There is something that remains to be done for her, that she might rest peacefully in death."

Quincey Morris set his hat upon his lap and leaned forward to say, in a heated tone, "Now, see here, Professor! Going back to the tomb for mysterious reasons is a cruel thing to do to Arthur, don't you think? Can't you see how difficult this is for him?"

I held my tongue but thought: *Ah, poor Quincey, I know it is no easier for you!*

He continued, scowling, "If the poor girl's dead, she's dead; what more can be done for her?"

Quite calmly I answered, "We must cut off her head, put a stake through her heart, and fill her mouth with garlic."

John's eyes widened at once with pure dismay at this blunt and heartless outburst. Quincey, on the other hand, leaned even farther forward and rested fingers upon the pistol worn on his belt.

As for poor Arthur, he turned livid and rose in a burst of fury, bending his right arm at the elbow and pulling it back in preparation for the blow aimed squarely at my jaw.

And before John could rise to restrain him, he struck out with his fist. I was prepared for such a blow; before it could land, I had already taken a step backward and withdrawn my aura, rendering myself quite invisible.

Arthur swung at the air, then drew back in utter amazement and gaped down at his fist, as if expecting to find there some defect. Finding none, he stared open-mouthed at the room surrounding him.

Our friend Quincey slowly sank back into the cushions and quietly replaced his hands in his lap. I watched as the big freckled Adam's apple slowly bobbed down once, then rose back up. Beside him sat John, whose expression was a curious mixture of sorrow, wry disapproval and mounting hilarity.

For the space of several seconds, no one uttered a sound.

Duly satisfied that I had made an impression, I walked behind the sofa where the two men were sitting, materialised, and said quietly, "Gentlemen."

They all snapped their heads round to stare at me. Arthur was so utterly stymied that he began to sway on his feet; I quickly stepped around the sofa and back to him. He clutched my shoulders, wide-eyed and mute, and let himself be led to the sofa, where he sat between John and Quincey.

"Gentlemen," I continued, "what you have just seen could be the result of the three of you having simultaneously gone quite insane. Or there could be another explanation, one not acceptable according to our current understanding of science. I must swear you to silence concerning it; if you choose instead to speak of it, be aware that I will deny it and label you mad."

Again, not a word of reply.

"Miss Lucy has been bitten by a vampire—" I began. At this, Quincey grew excited and opened his mouth to speak, but I silenced him with a look. "Not the bat, as friend Quincey suggests, but an actual man who has been transformed into a creature neither dead nor alive; the undead, which the Roumanians call *nosferatu*. In English, a vampire; one who sucks the blood of the living, who in turn become vampires after their death."

"What are you saying?" asked Arthur slowly; there was no anger, only pain, in his voice. "That Lucy died from the bite of one of these?"

I nodded, hardening my heart at the sight of this terrible revelation's effect upon him.

Quincey tossed his hat aside and ran his hand over thinning hair. "Professor, I respect you," he said, clearly troubled. "Maybe even more so since your little demonstration here to-night." At that, we two gave a faint smile. "And even if I hadn't seen it, I would still believe you to be an honest man of the very best intentions. But . . . this isn't something that I—that Arthur—can readily accept. Because what you're saying is that Miss Lucy is—is . . ." His voice trailed into silence.

"I do not expect you to believe me without seeing the proof. So I have asked you to come with me to-night to the Kingstead churchyard." Here I addressed Arthur, who was still dazed. "And if you believe it, Lord Godalming, to permit me to destroy the creature so the true Miss Lucy can rest."

✢ ✢ ✢

We arrived in Kingstead shortly before midnight, and made short work of the low stone fence (Quincey, with his long, thin legs, could simply step over). It was a chill, windy night, and though the moon was still radiant, jagged fast-moving clouds at times obscured the light. I had brought my medical bag with the few necessary items, and an unlit lantern. John and Quincey flanked Arthur, forming a barrier between their friend and the terrible experience to come. John was grim but resolved; Quincey remained silent, but kept casting solicitous glances at Arthur as if determined to stop the proceedings the moment his friend registered distress.

As for Arthur himself, he bore up admirably well. His expression showed the strain of returning to this place of grief, but only subtly; and it did not change the nearer we drew to the tomb.

Once there, I quickly unlocked the door, then turned

to John and said: "You were with me yesterday; was Miss Lucy's body in her coffin?"

"It was," he affirmed solemnly.

I pushed the heavy iron door open, to the tune of metal scraping against stone; seeing that the other three men lingered, hesitant, I walked in first, then lit the lantern. The light it cast was dim; I wanted to draw as little attention to our entry as possible.

Once I was inside, the others entered, and I directed them over to Miss Lucy's coffin. Once more I set down my bag and retrieved the turnscrew, and with it unscrewed the lid, then removed it. The lead casing I had drawn back over the corpse; when Arthur saw how it had been rent, he blanched, but still remained silent, waiting.

I pulled down the leaden flange to reveal a dark, empty coffin. It was as I expected, for I had come before sundown that evening to remove the talismans. I knew Arthur's heart, and realised that to reveal her asleep and beautiful would do no good. To-night would have been their wedding-night; thus I had to show her as the monster she had become, without any trace of beauty or romance.

"Tell them," I commanded John.

So John spoke—most eloquently—of our earlier visit to the tomb. Man of medicine that he is, he explained—averting his own gaze when he saw the flicker of pain and disgust in Arthur's—the decay process, and what one could expect of a corpse in a week's time. Yet there had lain Lucy, unspoiled and perfect, more beautiful than ever she had been in life.

Quincey's eyes narrowed above his long waxed mustache; Arthur's strained expression never changed, though his pallour grew.

"And now outside," I said, and led them out into the sweet, cold air. My three companions remained silent—

Arthur clearly deep in thought in an effort to decipher the mystery of the disappeared corpse, John anxious at what he knew he would soon see. And Quincey—he is as pragmatic and open-minded a man as I have ever met. He had given up trying to make sense of the empty casket, and so now waited patiently to see what would come next before arriving at any conclusions. With remarkable casualness, he took a roll of tobacco from his jacket, cut a plug, then began to chew.

In the meantime, I had taken two more items from my bag: the sacred Host (charged with as much power as I could inject into an object) and a mass of putty. The Host I crumbled into the putty, kneaded it, and rolled the mixture into strips. These I used to to seal off the crevices around the door.

Then I directed the others to hide near the tomb where they would not be seen by one approaching. So we remained, silent, for an eternity: fifteen, perhaps twenty minutes.

Abruptly, I spotted a swift-moving white figure advancing through the yew trees—a white figure that clutched something dark to its breast. I signalled the others, and pointed.

At that instant, the white figure stopped, and bent down over the dark object; there came a child's sharp cry, then silence.

John, Quincey, and Arthur all three started at the sound; John made to move forward to rescue the child (as did Quincey instinctively, though he could not have known the depth of the danger the child was in). But I motioned them back, and they obeyed reluctantly.

Soon the mysterious figure grew closer, closer, and in an errant shaft of moonlight, Lucy Westenra's features became clearly visible.

Her features, I say, but all else was different. There were Lucy's eyes grown hard and seductive and cold; and Lucy's lips, no longer tender and sweetly smiling, but sensuous and mocking, pulled back to reveal long, sharp teeth. And from those lips dripped blood—fresh and crimson, dribbling in a thin line down her chin and onto the virginal linen of her burial clothes.

I moved out at once from behind the tomb, with my three companions close behind me. At the sight of us, she hissed like a threatened feline; and then, upon recognising Arthur, threw the poor child to the ground with infernal indifference.

"Arthur," she said, her voice soft and languid as a purring cat's. "My sweet husband, come!"

I glanced sidewise to see Arthur advance towards her, his arms outstretched, his formerly grief-dazed eyes now dulled by trance. He saw her, yes, but not as she truly was.

I leapt between the two lovers, taking a small golden crucifix from my coat pocket and lifting it high in front of her face. This I did with some anxiety, for I had no way of knowing whether she would be impervious to the talisman or not. Certainly, she was young and inexperienced, and therefore far, far weaker a foe than Vlad himself; but she was the first spawn of the new vampire, of Dracula the All-Powerful.

Through some inexplicable grace, the latter held true. She proved susceptible. At the sight of the cross, she snarled, then recoiled. I stepped sideways, forcing her into a narrow opportunity, which she took. With preternatural speed, she dashed towards the door of the tomb, intent on finding shelter there (indeed she was a neophyte, for any experienced vampire would have simply disappeared, then fled to another hiding-place, far from threatening mortals).

I signalled my companions to surround me, and th

four of us approached the tomb door in a half-circle, effectively capturing her between cross and Host. She hesitated,
a trapped animal trying to size up her options: should she
yield, fight, or flee?

Fury contorted her features. So she turned upon us,
eyes narrowed but ablaze with hell-fire, mouth pulled into
a square rictus lined with sharp triangular teeth. It was the
face of a she-demon from the Pit, and at the sight of it,
Arthur let go a horrified gasp.

Without turning my face away from the monster, I
called out: "Lord Godalming! Friend Arthur! Do you give
me permission now to proceed in my work?"

I did not need to see his expression to know it was
tortured; the pain in his voice was enough. "Do as you
will," he said with a groan. "Do as you will. There can be
no horror such as this ever again!"

I set my lantern down, and moved towards the hissing
vampiress; my intent was to dig away from the chinks
some of the sacred mixture, so that Lucy might enter, then
be resealed. But before I could accomplish this, there came
a sudden burst of wind—so strong that it knocked me
away from Miss Lucy onto my back in the cold, damp
grass.

The whirlwind grew so forceful that it pinned me to
the ground, so loud that I could hear nothing of my companions behind me. I struggled to lift my head and saw
before me Miss Lucy, grinning sultrily—locked in an embrace with Vlad.

It was the most horrid of sights, for she looked up at
him with violent adoration, whilst he stood behind her,
one arm wound tight around her waist, one hand upon her
breast. I could not imagine how Arthur bore such a sight; I
believe it would have shattered me, were I in his place. As
he looked down at her, such a passionate gaze passed be-

tween them that I was surprised they did not couple there and then.

Then he raised his face to me; it was livid, full of a madman's fury, a madman's hate. Yet young and vital beneath its full, wavy crown of blue-black hair, drooping mustache, and goatee—and so unnaturally handsome that even I felt its magnetic pull.

"How dare you think to harm her, our beloved!" he thundered, in a voice three times louder than the wind. "How dare you—!"

Abruptly the wind ceased. He cast Lucy aside as cruelly as she had dispensed with the child, and reached out with a sculpted alabaster hand for my neck.

And John—John, who of all of them knew what a deadly risk he was taking—dashed between us, and struck out at the Impaler with bare mortal hands.

The blows annoyed Vlad no more than a fly might a man. As John swung harder, harder, the vampire laughed, revealing dimples in the porcelain skin that framed his mustache; laughed, as he picked John up by leg and arm and held him overhead—then turned, facing the unyielding white marble of the tomb.

Arthur began to shout, and moved in closer, threatening; Quincey merely drew his pistol from his coat, and fired once, twice, thrice—each time striking Vlad directly in the chest. But the bullets merely exited his undead body without causing harm, and the perplexed Texan looked down at his gun, then back up at his target with wide, wide eyes.

Even with his former strength, the vampire could easily have dashed out the man's brains with such a move. As it was, I had no hope for John's survival, and with a father's desperate, unthinking love, I cried out:

"Stop! Stop! It is my *son* you hold in your arms! Kill him and you kill yourself!"

I had worked so many years to protect my only heir by hiding the truth; now the truth was my only hope of saving him. Vlad paused, then frowned up at John and said, "You lie! *He* does not think he is your son!" But an instant later, a subtle doubt came over his features—reflecting, perhaps, John's own mental wavering on the subject.

That instant was seized by us three mortals—Arthur, Quincey, myself. We hurled ourselves bodily at Vlad and John; the vampire, of course, was unmoved, but the attack evoked within him such fury that he loosened his grip on my son and instead caught hold of me, whilst the others pulled John to safety. Even in the midst of my relief, a horrifying thought occurred: Where was Lucy? And would all her lovers be able to resist her without my help?

Yet I could see nothing but the Impaler's face, for he had grabbed my throat with his cold, cold hands and stared so close into my eyes that I could smell his fetid breath—the stench of the rotting dead—ere he spoke.

Vlad's countenance gleamed so brilliant, so white-hot with fury, that I closed my eyes bedazzled, but the image still remained. "I am tired of you and your games, old man!" he roared. "For things have come full circle. Not so long ago, you were strong and sure and invincible, and I decrepit, aged, hopeless; I needed you for my very survival. But now *you* are the old, feeble man without a hope, and *I* am the one invincible! Bow down and worship me—for now it is you who need *me* to live."

I croaked, opened my eyes, and moved my head, indicating that I wished to answer. And when he eased his crushing grip upon my neck, I did not hesitate, did not waver. I said simply, "Kill me."

At that he let go a scream of frustration that left me near deaf. And when he recovered, he sneered:

"You are so arrogant, so self-assured! You think I cannot kill you, that I am afraid because of the covenant! But hear this: I need it no longer to survive. *I* am the *maker* of covenants! And you and your friends are dead."

The world swung suddenly sideways as he lifted me high above his head, hands still round my throat so tightly that I could scarce draw a breath, and was too dizzied to see what had become of my friends. I prayed that they had fled—not only for their own safety, but that they might be spared the horror of seeing their only "vampire expert" done in by the object of his hunt.

I blinked, and the world swung round again, and became a dim white wall of marble. This was to be my fate, then—to have my brains dashed out against the Westenra tomb. It was not so terrible a fate (considering the horrendous alternatives), but in the exceptional detachment brought about by mortal fear, I regretted leaving my friends, including Miss Lucy, in such a hopeless situation. And even, curiously, the terrible mess I would leave behind, which some poor working-class soul would be forced to clean up.

The hands holding me drew back, then propelled me like a slingshot at the marble. I must have been in flight no more than the merest fraction of a second, as we were no more than twenty feet away from the wall. Yet I remember it as clearly as if it had taken several minutes, for I was aware of many things: of the cold wind whistling past my stinging ears, of my regret at leaving Gerda (though I knew John would care properly for her), of my regret at not living to hold my mother's hand upon her deathbed, of my regret at not having freed Miss Lucy from the curse, of my regret that John should always wonder whether I had lied when I claimed him as son.

Of my regret, of my regret, of my regret.

And of the marble looming, and even in the dim light, my noting every swirl within the stone with morbid fascination. How should my blood look there? My brain?

Look, Bram, here is Death coming: close your eyes, and be grateful that you have died uncursed.

So I did and was, and tensed my body, waiting for impact—which, God willing, would be too swift to inflict unbearable pain.

Impact did not come.

Oh, I was still in midair and waiting, heart hammering like a prisoner bent on release. But I seemed to have been gently and impossibly stopped by an invisible cushion of some sort—both soft and firm, and infinitely comfortable, and holding me aloft without effort. Was this death? Was this an after-life wherein I sweated and feared and listened to my pulse pounding in my veins?

I opened my eyes and saw white marble, a mere inch from my nose.

Behind me, an enraged Roumanian curse, and from the Lucy-demon's throat, a shrill, frightened cry. Then the night grew suddenly calm, and I felt within the great sense of peace that comes when the vampire has fled.

And as I stared, relieved, into the swirling marble, I felt and saw a change. The soft cushion of air surrounding me hardened, until I felt skin and sinew and bone supporting me. Slowly I came to realise that my chin was resting upon a hard, bony shoulder—and that not a tall one; and in the periphery of my vision, I saw black cloth, upon which lay hair of radiant white.

I began to weep. And by the time small, strong hands had set me upright on the ground, I was laughing and weeping together. I could not stand, but sank down upon the earth and looked up into eyes so depthless I could not have named their colour, for they contained them all— eyes infinitely young and infinitely ancient, infinitely severe and infinitely loving, infinitely sorrowful and infinitely amused.

"Arminius!" I cried, in reproach and joy. "Arminius, why did you not come sooner?"

❧14❧

The Diary of Abraham Van Helsing

29 SEPTEMBER, CONTINUED. He looked precisely the same as the last time I'd seen him, twenty-two years before: small and wiry, yet strong of shoulder and straight of spine beneath an unadorned black wool robe. Beneath a black wool cap reminiscent of those an Orthodox priest might wear, his hair fell in thick curls almost to his waist. Like his long mustache and beard, it was shining white—which made the glowing, child-soft skin of his face and ears seem even rosier by contrast. But priest he was not, nor even Christian; his face was that of a Hebrew mystic, an eagle's, with prominent, downward-curving nose and large, heavy-lidded eyes. A Jew, yes, by blood—but far from orthodox in his beliefs. Whether he even believed in God, I could not say, for during my education as vampire-slayer, he always explained things in the most pragmatic terms. Perhaps he, like his student, believed not in religious formulae or particular names or titles, but in those things which endured, those things which transcended religion and science and touched all men too deeply to deny: Love. Compassion. Kindness.

His hair and bearing were those of an ancient; his demeanour and movements were those of a robust youth. At my question, he squatted down to the level where I sat, that we might speak eye-to-eye, and loosely folded his arms atop his legs.

"Abraham, Abraham," said he, grinning to reveal intensely pink gums and white straight teeth even a young man might envy. There was no cunning or reproach in that smile, only the bright, hilarious joy of a lunatic, a simpleton, a mage. "If I did not come, it was because you did not need me. Now, I am here." And he spread his arms (amazingly, without his legs wavering an inch).

"Here" had changed dramatically in the instant he had appeared. I squinted at my surroundings to find myself and my mentor enveloped in a circle of gentle radiance that brightened the night. Beyond its circumference, John, Arthur, Quincey, all sat upon the ground—frozen and still as statues, their eyes open yet unseeing, unblinking, their chests moving not a whit. Yet safe and alive—this I knew instinctively, even though I could not resist looking beyond and around them for Vlad and the Lucy-vampire.

But the night was quiet and sweet, free from the taint of indigo; both monsters had vanished, and Arminius and I sat safe within the borders of a different reality. This filled my heart with hope. For though Arminius had taught me many things—how to protect myself from the vampire, how to weaken Vlad and myself gain power to defeat him—I had never seen him in the presence of any vampire, and thus had not known the extent of his abilities beyond what he had told me.

Clearly, he was powerful indeed, to have saved me and caused Vlad and Lucy to vanish. And for the first time in many terrible days, I began to think Vlad could be overcome after all.

He saw me staring at my three companions and said:

"Your friends are well, but they cannot see us. And if you wish, they will not remember."

I was too curious, too exhilarated, too desperate, to respond to his statement; instead, I asked a question of my own. "What has happened to Vlad? I had done as you said —had destroyed vampire after vampire these twenty-two years, in order to weaken him. And so he *did* weaken—but now he has regained his strength, and more. He would have killed me—*me,* whose death would have brought about his own, according to the covenant. What has happened to him . . . and to the covenant?"

"Ah," he said; the sound was in part a sigh. "The covenant . . ." Rather than look at me, he lowered his gaze to the ground, his lips still curved upward in a mysterious crescent, and began to inscribe with his finger strange legends in a patch of mud. "In order to answer your question, Abraham, I must first tell you a story."

"A story?"

"Of a manuscript—a very special manuscript which some claim Lucifer himself wrote. It was stolen from the Scholomance, the Devil's school for the mantic arts, by one of the *sholomonari,* the alchemists who studied there. Thus says the legend. Its purpose is reflected in its title: *To Him Who Would Become the Eater of Souls.*"

I shuddered, suddenly overwhelmed by the terrifying image from a dream: a great Darkness that engulfed me, devoured me. Clutching my upper arms, I demanded, "But is that not the Devil's domain? To consume souls?"

He looked up, still smiling faintly, his eyes undimmed by the darkness of which he spoke. "It is, if that is the name you wish to use for the entity. And to answer your next question—yes, the manuscript does give instructions as to how others might become as he."

"But it is insane—why would he want to share his power?"

At this, the faint grin became a full-fledged smile. "Who can say? In time, all things will become clear." He paused. "At some point after the theft, the manuscript was acquired by one of the wickedest and most power-hungry immortals: the Countess Elisabeth of Bathory. It has gone through many hands, in part because the manuscript itself cannot be protected by even the most powerful magic—"

I interrupted. "Why not?"

Patiently, he replied, "Because the truth cannot be hidden, Abraham. Not realising this, the countess attempted to hide it with a spell—which, because of her newfound strength, she assumed would be sufficient. And because she had destroyed its previous owner, no one knew it had come into her possession, and no one attempted to take it from her. But when she went to the Castle Dracula, Vlad discovered it and stole it from her very quickly.

"As to why he has become increasingly powerful, now that it is in his possession, I must explain the manuscript itself. It is a riddle of sorts, consisting of six lines, or clues. The first line appears once the manuscript falls into someone's possession. Other lines appear only after the owner has understood the first and followed its direction; and with each step, the owner's power and abilities increase.

"I have done some small bit of research and discovered the first line: *In the land beyond the forest, the quest for godhood begins. The lines are six; the keys are two.*"

"Keys?" I asked.

"This is something of a mystery still; Elisabeth had solved only the first line, and though Vlad has gone farther, he has yet to discover the first key. No immortal ever has—except, of course, for the Dark Lord Himself."

With fear in my heart, I asked, "How many lines has Vlad solved? Do you know what these say?"

He did. He seemed to look past me, and the ghost of a smile faded entirely, leaving him solemn for the first time since we had met. "The second: *Do not linger. Cross the deep waters to the great island in the northwest.* Immediately, he made plans to leave for England, at which time a third line appeared: *To the east of the metropolis lies the cross-roads.*"

"East of London," I murmured, calling to mind the myriad locations. "A crossroads . . . Is it the actual inter-section of two streets, or something else? And how *far* east? Just outside the city, or in Purfleet or Dartford, or Grays . . . or as far east as Southend-on-Sea or Sheerness?"

"That I cannot tell you," he said, with mild regret. "But I can say that after Vlad purchased properties sur-rounding the city, the fourth line appeared: *There lies bur-ied treasure, the first key.*"

Four lines solved; a shiver passed through me as I asked, "And has he discovered it?" And the fifth line, and the sixth . . .

He shook his head. "But it is only a matter of time. Once he obtains the first key, he has only to find the second, and put them both in such a way as to solve the riddle. And while Elisabeth was privy only to the first line, I suspect she has found or will find a way to discover all that Vlad has learned. Then she, too, will join the search for the first key; for she is as cruel and ambitious as he— perhaps more so. At the earliest opportunity, she will seize the manuscript."

"Why has she not done so already?" I asked. "If she had it, and knew the first line, then she must have retained some of her newfound powers—"

"No." He tilted his head, and looked at me with utter

understanding and compassion, as if he felt my sorrowful desperation as keenly as I. "When the manuscript is lost, the power is lost, only to be gained by the next owner. She is not strong enough to defeat him directly now—but if, through skill or cunning, she obtains it again, then *she* will be the powerful one, and he the weak. Believe me, Elisabeth is nearby, awaiting her chance—and that is something to be greatly feared, for she is one of the strongest and wickedest of all the *sholomonari*."

"And what of Zsuzsanna? Does she not know of the manuscript?"

His expression became curiously veiled. "She knows. She knows almost as much as Vlad, now; and she, too, seeks the first key."

"And if she—or Vlad, or Elisabeth—solves the sixth line, and the riddle of the first and second key . . ." I could not bring myself to finish the statement, for the thought was too terrible to give voice.

But Arminius did. ". . . she will become as the Dark Lord: omniscient and omnipresent, so powerful that she controls all evil upon the earth. And if Vlad succeeds, he will have no need of covenants to prolong his immortality —and therefore, no need of your soul to buy him another generation of life. He will be as a god, able to do whatever pleases him. But until he solves the mystery, he might lose the manuscript—just as Elisabeth lost it to him. Were that to occur, he would most assuredly depend upon the covenant, and your continued existence, so that he can corrupt you before your death, and thus buy himself life.

"What he did to you to-night, in choosing to kill you, was the most arrogant of errors. He is already coming to think of himself as an immortal, invincible . . . and that, I think, will lead to his failure."

He fell silent at last, and gazed calmly at me whilst I

considered his story. His last words gave me hope; but the entire tale had filled me with foreboding. My task was harder now than ever I had imagined during all those difficult years spent hunting down and destroying Vlad's evil spawn upon the European continent. For now I had not only to kill a powerful vampire and his mate, Zsuzsanna— I had to prevent them from becoming as gods. And not only them, but the fearsome Countess of Bathory, as well.

"Arminius," I said, "you have relayed to me a disturbing tale; my duty, it seems, has grown harder than ever I imagined. Will you stay with me, and help me? And not only me"—here I gestured at the three men sitting motionless outside our sphere—"but my friends, who also are sworn to destroy Vlad?"

Again, the idiot's smile beneath the sage's eyes. "I promise you, Abraham, that I will come when I am again needed. But not before. Remember: Your task is to redeem your family from its curse; and part of that job is the difficult journey itself."

"Can you at least honour one request?"

He lifted his eyebrows, so thin and translucent white that the bright pink of his baby-skin showed beneath the hairs.

I stood up and held his gaze, intent on convincing him of this one thing. "Will you keep Miss Lucy in her tomb until morning? Vlad can no longer be restrained by talismans, and has removed them that we might not destroy her."

He said nothing; only held me with that marvellous and knowing gaze, then rose in one graceful movement to stand beside me. As I looked into his eyes, the edges of his body seemed to grow indistinct, then fade away into shadows as the sphere of light containing us suddenly dimmed.

Paler and paler he grew, until at last I stood staring at the great iron door of the Westenra tomb.

. Beside me, the vile Lucy-creature hissed, spewing blood-flecked spittle, in the ellipse of light cast by my lantern. It sat on the ground where I had laid it an eternity— or only minutes—before. I sensed, rather than saw, my three friends standing behind me in a semicircle; John, I knew, was nearest, holding aloft his own silver crucifix to hold his undead beloved at bay.

Oddly, the sudden shift in time did not disorient me; perhaps the recollection of my tutelage under Arminius had prepared me, for it was a trick he had often used in those long-past days. I took it as silent confirmation that he would grant me my one wish, and began at once to remove chinks of Host-infused putty from the tomb door.

When I had pulled out a sufficient amount, I stepped aside and let the vampiress rush unhindered past me. Whilst the others gasped, she became two-dimensionally flat, then collapsed into a needle-thin line like a lady folding a fan. This moved through the air as an eel travels through water, though infinitely faster; in less than the blink of an eye, she had disappeared through a crack as thick as a piece of paper and no wider than my thumb.

Immediately I replaced the putty in the crevice, sealing her inside. And then I turned to my friends—all just as they had been before the Impaler's appearance, Arthur pale and trembling at the sight of his sweet Lucy so defiled, and Quincey tight-lipped and drawn, with his big freckled hand gripping Arthur's arm in support. Neither was in the least bit dishevelled, as if Vlad's attack had never happened, as if my work at the tomb door had never been interrupted.

As if Arminius had never appeared.

Nor was so much as a single one of John's hairs out of

place, and his expression was darkly grim and troubled, as befitted the situation. Yet when I glanced at him, he caught my gaze, so sharply and pointedly and with such poignant confusion that I knew he recollected at least some of what had passed.

But Arthur and Quincey clearly did not. So I nodded to my companions, took my lantern, and walked over to the child she had dropped beneath the yews. He was a little street urchin, his golden hair and thin face crusted with dirt—and his neck with blood. Fortunately, we had encountered Miss Lucy just as she was beginning to drink, and so he still had some colour on his sallow little face. He had fallen from trance into a sound sleep upon the dying grass—in such cold, poor thing. I took him into my arms and said to the others, who had followed:

"Let us leave him someplace warm for the police to find. He is not badly off, and by to-morrow night will be entirely well."

And so we went away. Arthur and Quincey were headed to the asylum with John, so I made the pretense of going to the hotel instead, for we had been keeping the lie that I was staying elsewhere. From there, I returned instead to Purfleet, and crept to my lonely cell under the guise of invisibility.

⁘ ⁘ ⁘

Dr. Seward's Diary

29 SEPTEMBER, MORNING. It is aggravating to have to keep writing this by hand, as it takes forever and makes me feel like Neddy Ludd; I had thought to keep a separate

cylinder with my "private" entries, but the chance is too great that I might make a mistake and let the wrong ears listen to information they ought not to know.

Still, I *must* unburden myself this morning, or go mad as poor Renfield. Too many revelations, too many heart-rending emotions. . . .

It was enough, last night, to see the dead woman that I loved turned into a slavering she-devil; that alone was more than any man could bear without going insane. And then, to see Vlad himself—far younger and stronger than described, ablaze with wicked glory—hurl my beloved professor to his death—

More than I could bear, more than I could bear. And yet I bore it.

But when I saw the angelic figure save him less than a split second before his demise, I told myself: *There it is, Jack; after all this time, you've finally achieved total lunacy. How convenient that home is already an asylum.* . . .

And I listened to them speak together like long-lost friends, or rather, long-lost teacher and student, with Van Helsing in *my* role, and the shining angel in his. Oh, it is one thing to read of the occult and toy with auras and discuss theories of vampires and other noncorporeal entities and how might one deal with one, but—

Well, it is another thing altogether to *see* such beings. And to then find time itself interrupted, and an event dispensed with. In this case, it was as though Vlad had never appeared, and I and the professor never been endangered; worse, when we had finished at the graveyard, I knew from Art and Quincey's expressions and speech that they had not seen the same impossible events as I. That was a dreadful instant, for I was convinced for the space of a few seconds that I *had* truly gone insane. Until, that is, I looked into the professor's eyes, and saw that *he* knew too.

So then, it really had happened. Fortunately, neither Quince nor Art was in the mood for idle chatter after such a horribly painful evening; after I had the maid set them up in guest quarters in the private part of the house, they both went directly to their rooms.

Though by then it was almost three o'clock in the morning, I knew sleep would be quite impossible until I had answers to some troubling questions. I had no way of knowing whether the professor had returned, but I was desperate; so after a bit, when I was sure that Art, Quince, and the maid had all settled into their beds, I crept back to the asylum and went directly to the professor's cell. I knocked softly, calling: "It's John. I must speak to you."

The door swung slowly open. I could see no one inside though the lamp was dimly lit, but a soft veil of blue wavered in the air just inside the threshold. Boldly, I entered and stepped through the cerulean glimmer to find the room just the same—except that now the professor was sitting cross-legged upon the floor in his stocking feet.

He had removed his spectacles and set them upon his lap, so that his dark blue eyes seemed somehow unclothed, and the greying red-gold hair was dishevelled, as if he had been worriedly running his fingers through it. At the sight of me he sighed, replaced the spectacles, and in a weary but kindly voice, said: "Hello, John. I suspected you might come."

I could not help being somewhat cool with him, for I felt at best very awkward, and at worst, very betrayed. "And do you also suspect what I am about to ask?"

He sighed again. As the air escaped his lungs, all his cheer, all his strength, all his bravery, seemed to leave with it, until I realised, to my discomfort and dismay, that I was looking upon a frail, heartbroken man with shadows beneath his myopic eyes. "I do not suspect; I know. And the answer to your question is yes, John."

"I am your son," I said, my tone flat with disbelief, as I thought: *Then he is mistaken; he has forgotten all about what he shouted to Vlad, and he thinks I have come to ask about something else.*

"You are my son," he said, with such quiet conviction, such tenderness, such heartfelt apology, that I believed him at once. Conflicting emotions assailed me: doubt, rage, love, relief. It seemed horribly, horribly wrong; it seemed horribly, horribly right.

At my distress, his expression grew concerned. "You did know, John, that you were adopted?"

"Yes," I said, my voice strained almost to breaking; to my embarrassment, I was wavering on the precipice of tears. "Yes, but that's not it. I want to know *why*—" And at that point, my voice *did* break; I could say no more.

"Why I have been your friend and teacher all these years and have not told you."

I nodded blindly, blinking back tears, as he motioned me to sit.

I sat upon the cold floor. And he began to tell me a story which began long ago, when a prince named Vlad, who came to be known much later as the Impaler (Tsepesh) or the son of the Dragon (Dracula), made a bargain with the Dark Lord. Every generation that his family continued, he would offer up the soul of the eldest surviving son in exchange for continued immortality. But before that soul was offered, its owner had to have been *willingly* corrupted. If the sacrificial lamb died a good, honest man, then Vlad himself would lose his immortality, age, and die.

"My father, Arkady, was the eldest son of his generation; he died uncorrupted, but in desperation, Vlad bit him, to trap his soul between heaven and earth. Then Arkady was destroyed . . . and Vlad grew weaker, and older—but for some reason, did not die."

I stared at him as a revelatory thunderbolt struck; I knew the professor had only one sibling, a brother who had long ago died. "Then *you*—"

"I am Dracula's heir," he said bitterly. "And the eldest surviving son of my generation. You heard, I think, Arminius speak of the manuscript?"

I nodded, once again dumbstruck.

He looked away. "Only because of it did Vlad dare threaten me. John," he said, turning back to me abruptly and seizing my arms in desperation. "I swear by everything good that I would never have come here had I known of Vlad's increased powers. He was weak, failing; *I* was far more powerful than he, and believed my mission would be accomplished months before now. I would never have endangered you so . . ."

I signalled my acceptance by clasping his arms in return, but my mind had moved ahead, and was struggling to understand my own past, and my own destiny. "I—I am your eldest son, am I not? You had a little boy, who died. . . ."

He stared down at the floor and, for the first time since I have known him, spoke in a voice thick with tears. "A little boy, whom I killed," he said, and a spasm of such intense and violent grief crossed his face that I looked away. "My Jan. My little Jan . . ." And he broke into such raw, wrenching sobs that I could do nothing but stare down at my lap and watch my own tears spill.

After a time, we both collected ourselves, and he continued hoarsely, "Zsuzsanna—Vlad's niece and vampire mate—bit him, turned him into a tiny monster. I had no choice but to free him."

"So when you had another son, you sent him away," I said. "Far away, and told no one who he was."

"To protect him. But see, John"—and he spread his hands in despair—"see what has become of all my efforts to spare you the grief I have known. As the Buddhists say, it is your karma to suffer at Vlad's hands; without the vampire even knowing of your existence, he sought out and murdered your lady love."

"But your . . . friend, Arminius, is here to help."

"Yes." He gave a glum nod. "He is here to help. And he will help us, I think, make sure Miss Lucy is freed from the curse. But he comes when he lists, and I cannot predict when help will come again."

"Let us not worry any further until to-morrow's work is done." I pushed myself to my feet, and helped him up. By then I felt nothing for him but compassion and gratitude, for I saw what a dreadful burden he has carried all his life, and carries now; I wanted nothing more at that moment than to ease it for him. I put my arms round him and said, "You know, I trust, that I have always looked upon you as a father; and now, my affection for you is doubly justified. I realise that all you have done, you have done out of love."

He was too choked to speak with words, and so returned the embrace with a squeeze. We parted in silence, with tears in our eyes, and even deeper grief in our hearts.

For a long time, as I lay in bed, sleep would not come; and in the midst of my restless turning, the bittersweet thought seized me: *Dear God! That poor mad woman is my* mother!

I woke to the sunlight this morning a different man; more troubled, yes, but even more resolved to rid the world of the evil that is my heritage. We are off to Lucy's tomb at mid-day, and so my first effort is almost begun.

❖ ❖ ❖

The Diary of
Abraham Van Helsing

29 SEPTEMBER, NIGHT. It is done, thank God; dear Miss Lucy is at peace. John was right to make me let the three men who so loved Miss Lucy be present, and Arthur strike the blow that freed her. He did so with a resolve and courage—despite the gushing blood and shrieking of the vile creature in the coffin—that made us all proud, and gave me hope for the coming battle. I can see they are all the better for having aided me, and surely they are worthy. Our brave little group is expanding; before John took me to the station, he received a telegram from Madam Mina saying that she would arrive shortly to stay at the asylum, and that her husband would follow the next day.

I only pray Arminius does not desert us again.

I write this on the train. I told the others that I was bound for Amsterdam, and for once, I truly am. Arminius' assistance notwithstanding, I know the most dangerous task is to come; so I go to spend a few hours at Mama's bedside, lest she survive me.

❈15❈

The Diary of
Abraham Van Helsing

1 OCTOBER. Returned from Amsterdam yesterday, late afternoon, to find both the Harkers, and Arthur and Quincey, moved in. It makes little sense to continue the charade that I am staying at a hotel, so I declared that I was moving in as well (but when I sleep, Jonathan and the others will be hard-pressed to find me). Everyone, it seems, has fallen quite in love with Madam Mina—including, I confess, myself. She has taken on the role of lady of the house, bringing us cups of tea and seeing to our comfort; this is all our fault, of course, because we have all lived as bachelors so long that such behaviour is irresistibly endearing. It makes John's gloomy house, filled at times with the groans and shrieks of his patients' mental anguish, seem like a cheerful home—and we the family.

As for Amsterdam: Poor Mama was no longer lucid, and barely able to sit up to eat. Most of the time she merely lies with eyes closed, and rarely converses, according to Frau Koehler. But she had been well cared for, as she had been freshly bathed, and her bedsores lovingly cleaned and salved. The good Frau has done the impossible in preventing their spread. I thanked her most sincerely for her marvellous care—thanked her as though I might never see her again, and I think she somehow sensed it, for her eyes filled with tears. She has clearly come to love Mama, and I think it will grieve her greatly when her patient finally dies.

As I was leaving, Frau Koehler showed to me the accumulated mail, including a package which had arrived that very day from Buda-Pesth from an "A. Vámbéry." I could not imagine what it might contain, and so I took it to my study and opened it in private.

The contents were wrapped within several layers of black silk; this both intrigued and troubled me, for I knew that only an educated occultist would take such particular care in order to prevent a magical charge from escaping the contents. Could this have been a trick of Vlad's—to expose me to some noxious spell? I decided not, for despite the protective layers, I felt a strong sense that the contents were intended not to harm, but to help.

And indeed they were: The instant I unfolded the last layer of silk, a burst of power from the contents filled the room with such pure white radiance that I actually stood and breathed deeply, feeling as though the very act cleansed lungs, body, soul.

The *A.* stood for "Arminius," I decided, and though he had not appeared personally, he had again provided me with help. For within lay some twenty small silver crucifixes, and an equal number of sacred wafers wrapped within a thick padding of tissue. The heavy sorrow of seeing Mama so incapacitated lifted a bit, and indeed, as I took within my hand one of the crosses and felt its power surge tingling down my arm, I felt honest joy. Arminius must have personally charged each one, for these, I knew, would be sufficient to protect my friends from harm, and to keep the Impaler at bay.

I took them with me to England, and arrived in London much more confident than I had been in many months. On the way to Purfleet in the carriage, I gave John three of the talismans: one to wear always upon his person, one to put over his bedroom window, and one over the window in Renfield's room. It was a deep relief to be able to provide protection for my friends.

That evening, the six of us met in John's study and I told the others what I wished them to know about the vampire, bearing in mind that Jonathan's loyalties were questionable. However, I am coming to think less and less that he is under Vlad's control, for he relayed the outcome of his "research": He had tracked the fifty boxes of earth spoken of in his Transylvania diary right here to Purfleet— and the estate *next door,* Carfax!

The truth is sometimes too strange to believe; but when I learned of Vlad's proximity, I was gladder than ever to have Arminius' talismans in hand. Without explaining their origin or speaking of their special charge, I gave two each of the little crucifixes to Arthur and Quincey, bidding the men to hang one over their bedroom windows and wear one. I tried to do the same with the Harkers—one for the window, two for each person—but they both demurred, revealing that they were already wearing crosses round their necks. Still, I managed to press one upon them for the window, and noted with interest that Harker waited for his wife to pick it up. (Was it a vampire's influence, or merely chance?) The act did me a world of good, knowing that all would be protected—especially now that we knew Dracula was so close at hand.

By the end of our meeting, it was decided that we would rise in the wee hours next morning, and go at once to Carfax to inspect the boxes whilst Dracula was, hope-fully, still prowling in the night. However, all the men were of one mind regarding Madam Mina: after Lucy's recent death, none of them could bear the thought of her endangerment, and so pressed her to remain at the house, where she would be unquestionably safe, for the front and rear doors and every window of every occupied room would be sealed with a talisman. So before we discussed our plan of attack, we dismissed her, on the grounds that we were protecting her and the less she knew, the safer she would be. This she reluctantly agreed to, especially since her husband was quite adamant, though I was of two minds about it. I did not wish to see her endangered, but also was sorry to lose one of our best minds; frankly, of all of us, Madam Mina is made of the strongest mettle.

And, as John said in his angry grief, what good had ignorance done poor Miss Lucy?

Nonetheless, Madam Mina left before we made our plans for Carfax; with her gone, we agreed to leave at four the next morning. When our gathering dispersed, I went off with John for a private conversation, for during our discussion I had noticed his especial excitement in mid-meeting, sometime after Jonathan revealed the information about Carfax.

So it was that we took our leave of the others and stole to my cell, where we could be assured of remaining unseen and unheard.

The moment I had stepped inside and closed the door, John, who had entered before me, exclaimed, "Carfax! Don't you see, Professor? It's the crossroads!"

"What?" I neared him, frowning with curiosity.

"*Quatre face,*" he said, and when I continued to look at him askance, added, "Ah, I suppose you do not speak much French. *Quatre face,* the Old French for 'crossroads.' That's where the name 'Carfax' comes from!"

We stared at each other as the revelation overtook me; the smile which gradually spread over my face was mirrored in John's own. "The crossroads," I said softly, "where buried treasure lies. The first key!"

He joined with me on the last three words, and we laughed with delight—gently, though, and not overlong, for Dracula had been residing there some time. What if he had already found it?

John and I agreed at once that we would both look carefully for signs whether this had happened—and in case it had not, for places where the first key might be buried. Thus we went early to bed, for I was quite exhausted (not having had a sound sleep in the past two days, as I was either in a boat, train, or carriage).

So I slept deeply but woke intensely alert around three; I dressed and made my way to John's office. He, too, rose early and met me there. By three forty-five, both Quincey and Arthur had joined us, so we waited for Harker.

Before he arrived, the attendant rushed in to tell John that Renfield was pleading to see him. I frowned, thinking that this clearly was the result of Dracula interfering with our plans, and John caught my gaze and began to tell the young man that Renfield should have to wait. But the attendant persisted: "He is more desperate than I have ever seen him, sir, and if you do not come, he will throw one of his violent fits."

So John went; and I and Quincey and Arthur joined him. To everyone's surprise, Mr. Renfield seemed not only sane but positively elegant, making a very persuasive case that he had come to his senses at last, and begged to be let go. And he honestly seemed sane to us all, and most sincere—but John, who has dealt long with madmen, decided to observe him a period longer; and I, of course, trusted him not at all, and attributed his desperation to Dracula's influence . . . and the fact that the stronger talisman was indeed prevailing. Why should we free him that he might be used against us?

We left, whereupon most of Mr. Renfield's newfound composure deserted him, and he began to beg piteously for release.

By five o'clock we were at the door of the old Carfax estate, each of us with a small electric lamp affixed to his breast, and sporting one of Arminius' crucifixes—except for Mr. Harker, who wore his own. And all of us—except for Harker, whom we were all reluctant to trust—bore in our pockets pieces of Arminius' sacred Host in order to make the boxes uninhabitable to our foe. (In this way, even if Dracula were privy to Jonathan's thoughts, he would not be warned in advance of our real intention.) In addition, Arthur wore a silver whistle about his neck to call on canine assistance, if need be, for none of us doubted the old building was crawling with rats.

John utilised his surgical skill and an old skeleton key to get us in the front entry, and we moved quickly inside, and soon discovered a table in the hallway containing a ring of keys. These I gave to Jonathan, and bade him lead us to the chapel, as he was familiar enough with it to find the way. In my life, I have never seen so much dust collected in one place; in fact, the floor was buried under a carpet of dust and dirt some several inches thick, so that I could not tell whether I was walking on earth or stone or wood. Despite our desire to be as quiet as possible, lest the Impaler had abandoned his hunting early, both Arthur and John burst into a paroxysm of coughing at the throat-tickling clouds stirred up by our footsteps. The walls, too, were covered with a grey film and laced with thick, ancient spiderwebs, many of which hung low and swayed languidly in our wake, broken by the weight of the dust collected thereon.

I felt secure the Impaler had gone, for his aura had become so intense and large of late that I would have sensed it very near the entry. This notion was reinforced when we arrived at the arching wooden door to the chapel. After some false starts, Jonathan found the right key and unlocked the door.

When it swung open, the vile stench of the vampire's lair wafted out. I was inured to it after so many years, and proceeded directly in, but the others behind me had not expected it, and so were overwhelmed. Nevertheless, they forced themselves to follow.

Within was a pathetic ruin of what had once been a vast, high-ceilinged place of family worship: a few rotting timbers left of what had once been pews and an altar, and, on the filthy wall beneath a veil of spiderwebs, the outline of what had once been a large cross. Perhaps it had been a beautiful place, for there were two large arching windows —perhaps of stained glass, but long ago covered, as always, with the thick film of dust.

The room spoke strongly of gloom, decay, impermanence. This in itself was discouraging enough to see—but far worse was the realisation, after some silent counting, that the wooden boxes set out in careful rows were not fifty in number, but twenty-nine.

Twenty-one missing! I sidled over to John, and whispered for him to quickly tell Quincey and Arthur *not* to seal the boxes off with the Host. Doing so would only alert the vampire to our plan, so that he might more cleverly hide the remaining boxes. John managed to tell the other two men whilst Harker was distracted counting and look-

ing about for some other place the crates might be hidden.
I then instructed all the others to sift through the dirt and
dust and come up with any clue that might lead us to
where the other boxes had been moved; of course, John
knew well that he was meant to search for traces of the
manuscript or first key.

As we all searched, I sensed an abrupt change in the
room—a glimmering hint of indigo which disturbed me
. . . and yet did not. At that same instant, Arthur and
Jonathan both reacted to something in the shadows. "I
thought I saw a face," Arthur said apologetically.

I said nothing, but crouched down to open boxes and
sift through dust and cobwebs for any clue as to the manuscript or key. As I was doing so, one of the men moved
over and stood beside me, waiting to confer about something—or so I thought, for in my peripheral vision appeared a pair of trouser legs and boots.

I glanced up, mouth open to ask, *Yes?* But the question
died upon my lips as my eyes focussed upon a tall man
dressed in black, with flowing silver-and-jet hair and mustache; a man—nay, a vampire—whose skin gleamed immortal, mother-of-pearl white.

❖❖   ❖❖   ❖❖

Vlad, I thought, staring up at the intruder, but said
nothing—surprise had taken my voice. Disappointment
washed over me like the bitterest sea; so even Arminius'
help had come to naught. If his talismans could not even
discourage the vampire in his lair, then none of us were
safe, and poor Madam Mina, left alone in the asylum . . .

But as I stared, my dismay began to ease. For the eyes
were not the deep evergreen of the Impaler's, but hazel,
and soft; and the nose not so sharp, nor the lips so cruel.

Indeed, the face bore no wickedness nor wanton sensuality, but gentleness mixed with sorrowful joy.

"Dear God," I whispered, unaware that I'd had any intention of speaking; the words seemed to spill from me without the intervention of brain or teeth or tongue or lips. "Dearest God . . ."

I looked about me to see the others busily at work, quite unaware of the immortal standing near them. The vampire was invisible, but I was not; when he turned and motioned me to follow round a corner, I did so, doing my best to seem as if I had just thought of a new place to search.

Once we were both out of sight, he opened his arms to me, and we two embraced.

"Bram. You have made me proud," he whispered into my ear. "Very proud. . . ."

"Arkady," I breathed, and drew back to better look at him. "Father. . . . How can this be? Twenty years ago, I left you dead in Castle Dracula, a stake piercing your heart."

He patted his now-whole chest and smiled. "I do not quite understand it myself, but somehow I was resuscitated —by whom, I do not know. Perhaps it was possible because I was never decapitated." His smile faded and he looked intensely into my eyes. "I would speak more of it, but we have little time before the sun rises, Bram. And there is something that must be found, and quickly, else Vlad will grow so powerful that no one, not even the Devil Himself, will be able to stop him."

"Yes, I know—the manuscript."

He was taken rather aback. "Who told you of it?"

"Arminius."

A ghost of the smile returned. "I am glad, then, that he still helps you." And again more seriously: "Vlad has not yet found the first key—of that I am sure. If he does, he will gain even more strength than he has now. It is here, somewhere; I search for it when I am able, but I am no match for him these days. Hardly, probably, a match even for you now."

I smiled as I shook my head.

"Now I shall return to invisibility, and join your search. But we must work quickly, for there is not much time left before he returns." He stepped away from me, and began to fade—but ere his disappearance was complete, he paused, and with a wistful expression asked:

"Is Mary still alive?"

I am not a man given to tears; but I have shed many of late. And at the question, my eyes filled with them again. "She is safe, and in Amsterdam."

At my reaction, his expression became one of anguished concern. "But she is not well?"

"She is dying."

"Ah," he groaned, coming to full visibility, and turned away. "Were it not for Vlad, I would see her one last time. . . ." He gathered himself again, then asked, "And your little boy, Jan—I know it is a difficult thing, but did you—"

"I killed him," I replied bitterly. "And, yes, Gerda is still quite mad from it all."

"He rests," Arkady said, and wound a cold arm about me. "He rests sweetly and at peace, because of you. Soon Gerda will have respite from her sorrow; the time will come. You must believe. . . ."

And he put his face against my neck and wept cold, cold tears. John would have been terror-struck, I know, to have seen me permit a vampire such access to veins; but with Arkady, I had no fear. My one concern was not to yield to my grief—not here, in front of the others; not here, when there was work to be done.

Soon he straightened, and said, sighing, "Always sorrow with us Tsepesh. Always sorrow. . . . I had wanted so to spare you the pain Vlad can inflict. . . ."

"Just as I wanted to spare *him*," I said, pointing at John, who had moved to our periphery. He was working with his back to us, but even so, Arkady studied him with sad fondness.

"Another son," he marveled; it was not quite a question.

"Your grandson," I confirmed.

He looked back at me. "Then we *must* find a way to spare him, Bram. Your life and mine destroyed, and the lives of those we love. . . . That is enough."

And as I gazed back at him, he took on a gossamer appearance; before he had completely faded, I whispered, "Come to me again. The asylum on the very next property. . . ."

As I composed myself and returned to the others, I heard his voice whisper in my ear: *I have left them with a little distraction. . . .*

Indeed he had. I found myself ankle-deep in dust and squirming rats; in fact, the boxes and floor and walls were covered in the black crawling creatures, and their tiny eyes reflected the glow from our little lamps with an eerie phosphorescence. Almost immediately, Arthur blew his whistle; soon three terriers appeared, and after some reluctance (no doubt they sensed Arkady's presence), the dogs grew bold and dispatched the writhing lot.

By then sunlight was approaching, and it seemed that we had done as much as possible for the time. We left relieved that none of us were harmed, but quite concerned about the missing boxes. Any delay is to be feared, but at least Harker is out tracking down the other boxes.

❖ ❖ ❖

3 OCTOBER. The worst of all days since we lost poor Lucy.

Until last night, all had been going well, and I dared hope. I am glad we permitted Harker to join our party, as he has been an invaluable source of information as to where Vlad moved the boxes. The "count," it seems, has acquired other properties in east and south London—in New Town, where Whitechapel Road becomes Mile End; and Jamaica Lane, Bermondsey. He has also purchased a house in the city's very heart, at Piccadilly. To-day we shall go there, and search for titles to other properties, and keys to them. And perhaps, Fate willing, we shall come across a very different "key."

By yesterday, Jonathan had completed his research, and we were in possession of the necessary addresses; Arthur and Quincey spent the day rounding up horses so that we could all move quickly from destination to destination. *To-morrow,* I told myself, *the vampire will be ours!* I was filled again with optimism: but alas! In my foolish desire to protect Madam Mina from harm, and from knowledge of the evil, I have spent little time with her—and so did not see the obvious.

In the predawn hours, John came running to my cell, so distraught that I immediately emerged from my shelter to see what had so frightened him.

"Professor!" he shouted, without any concern that someone might overhear and learn my actual location in the house. "Renfield is dying. . . ."

Bag in hand, I ran back with him to see whether I could be of any medical help. The door to Renfield's cell was wide open, and the attendant squatted beside him with an expression of anguished helplessness.

The first glance proved that John had not overstated the situation in the least, for the poor man lay on his side, with his face turned upward, and his head and shoulders surrounded by an ever-enlarging dark halo of blood. Examination revealed a broken back and fractured skull, with pieces of bone pushed down into the brain; he would die soon if no action were taken to relieve the pressure of blood pooling inside the cranium.

Instinctively, I looked up from where I knelt beside the dying man, and squinted at the barred window, where only recently John had put one of Arminius' crosses.

Gone. In a terse voice I demanded of the attendant: "The crucifix above the window—where is it?"

He must have thought me mad or heartless, or both, to ask such an apparently unrelated question, with poor Renfield suffering at my knees. Sheepishly, the burly young man handed it to John, saying: "I removed it because this evening he just went wild trying to jump up and grab it; I was afraid he'd hurt himself, so I went in and took it down. He tried to snatch it from me, and begged me for it, but as it was sharp—"

"That's enough," John said, quite angrily; I suppose the attendant thought we suspected him of wanting to steal it, and were more concerned about Seward's property than our suffering patient, for he drew back with a hurt expression.

"Send him away," I ordered; and at the attendant's scandalised glance at me, then at John, explained: "We shall have to drill a hole in his skull to relieve the pressure. If you wish to stay—"

But he was already out the door, closing it behind him. To John I said, as I took instruments from my bag,

"Trephination is indicated. I do not think we will save him, but at best, he can spend his last moments conscious and more comfortable."

As I spoke, a soft knock came at the door, and both Arthur and Quincey peered inside. John gave them entrance; no explanation beyond the pool of blood and our horribly injured patient was required.

They stood by in silent dismay whilst I performed the operation, drilling just above the patient's ear. We were, for the moment, successful; after a few moments, the pressure was relieved. Renfield opened his eyes, and quite lucidly asked that the strait-jacket be removed. There was little point in obliging him, however, as movement would only increase his pain and speed up his demise; though death was not far off, I sensed he wished to speak, and "confess his sins," as it were. I was not reluctant to hear them, as the unsecured window spoke of danger for us all.

He spoke rationally, even kindly, in a way that evoked my pity—but never have I heard words that so sickened my heart. Our Renfield had indeed been under the vampire's sway, and quite adoring of his "Lord and Master"; but he had also been quite taken with Madam Mina, who had twice visited him out of kindness—the second time, that very afternoon. She had grown too pale to suit him, he said; "and it made me mad to know that He had been taking the life out of her."

Horrible moment! None of us could repress a shudder as he said it.

And Dracula, smelling of Mina, had come to him only moments earlier that night, entering easily once the talisman had been removed. And this man—this poor deranged lunatic—took the vampire in his hands and fought, fought to protect Madam Mina the only way he knew now.

When he had finished speaking and sighed as he lapsed again into unconsciousness, the air was electric: we four men said not a word, but left the valiant madman where he lay dying, and ran to our rooms to collect our talismans. Within seconds we had all arrived at the door to the Harkers' room—locked from within.

All together, we threw ourselves against it, and came crashing through. I fell forward, and the others surged past me, then abruptly stopped. Falling, I had the sense that I was passing through a cloud of glittering indigo—strong and cold, though not so strong as when I had last seen the vampire, and touched within by a hint of radiant white and the merest gleam of gold. Yet it was not Vlad—no, it was not Vlad who brushed by me, but something else entirely evil, and entirely feminine.

It passed, and quickly; the door banged shut behind me as it went. And as I struggled to my hands and knees (oh, and had I been standing, I would have dropped to them!), I saw:

Harker, snoring on the bed close to the window, and on the mattress' outer edge his wife—her face pressed fast against the bared chest of the Impaler, whose eyes were closed in deepest ecstasy. She turned her head, gagging, revealing in the moonlight mouth and cheeks dark and dripping with vampiric blood. The sight pierced like a jagged blade: this was the cruelest version of the blood ritual, a sanguinary exchange which tied victim most thoroughly to predator. If he had also drunk from her, then she was his.

But in the midst of my horror, the thought seized me: *He did not hear us come. He did not hear us come. He has changed. . . .*

I scrambled to my feet as the vampire at last became aware of his enemies' presence; with one swift, powerful move, he thrust his victim back upon the bed and sprang towards us. By then I had raised high the envelope which contained the sacred Host, and felt a surge like lightning travel from heart to fingers. Even without the infusion of Arminius' strength, never had I been more determined, more focussed, more confident, in my life; I think I could have driven him away by my will alone.

At the sight of the envelope he cowered—cowered in abject agony, as though the power emanating from it were searing his skin!—and I collected myself enough to find my second sight, whereby I saw his aura: shrunken, depleted, dimmed.

These both seemed even to him a revelation, for an expression of disbelieving and hellish rage contorted his features and reddened his green eyes to flame. He was confused; he had been so swept away by his deed that he was surprised by this sudden lapse! Had it only recently happened?

Whilst Jonathan still snored, I moved between the Harkers and the monster, advancing steadily with the Host aloft until Vlad gathered his wits and transformed himself to dark mist. Thus he moved past four armed guardians, and disappeared beneath the door—for the little silver cross above the window cast a barrier he could not cross.

At once, Madam Mina drew a rasping breath and let go a scream that pierced the very veil of Heaven.

Words cannot express the horror that followed, when poor Harker woke and saw the blood smeared upon her face and gown, and realised what had happened; we scarce could restrain him from grabbing his knife—the broad, curving blade known in India as the kukri—and pursuing the vampire on foot. As for brave Madam Mina, she was undone—not by fear for herself, but that she might be used to harm those she loved. For Vlad, in his arrogance, had tormented her cruelly, saying that she was now his to command, and that the time would come when she would become his vampire companion and helper—and infect each of the five men who were fighting now against him.

Gently I calmed her, and coaxed her to tell all that had happened, whilst John lit the lamp. Even with its light, I could not judge whether she had been freshly bitten and the rite completed, for she leaned against her husband's breast so that her long dark hair fell forward, veiling face and neck.

When she was sufficiently composed, she revealed the worst, in a brave voice that faltered rarely: the vampire had bitten her and she had been forced to swallow some of his blood. The exchange was complete, and our efforts to protect Madam Mina had resulted in her being lost to us.

Thank God Vlad is weaker! Even so, we are bound more than ever to destroy him, before he can fulfill his promise to poor Madam Mina.

And if he is weaker—as John and I discussed privately —it can mean only one thing: that another immortal has stolen the manuscript from him. But who?

By the time Madam Mina had finished her terrible story, the dawn was breaking. We all agreed to dress and meet shortly afterwards, to discuss what was to be done.

First, of course, John and I went again to check on Renfield—dead, poor fellow. Lunatic or no, he died bravely and for Madam Mina's sake, and for that, I shall always honour his memory. I pressed the talisman from his window into his cold hand, and said a silent prayer for the dead.

Once we had all dressed and assembled, our plan became clear: We will go to each of the four locations— Carfax, where twenty-nine boxes reside; Mile End and Bermondsey, which each hold six; and Piccadilly, where nine remain. These we will seal off with the Host, and so force a confrontation. I am hopeful of victory—but even if the Impaler succumbs to us, we must then face an even more powerful foe. . . .

❧16❧

The Diary of
Abraham Van Helsing

3 OCTOBER, NIGHT. To continue with to-day's adventure: We had gone at six-thirty this morning to meet for breakfast, since it was agreed that all needed to take in substantial nourishment for the day's events. So we trooped into the dining-room and breakfasted on scones and bangers and tea. Though everyone felt exhausted and beaten, we worked hard to maintain a front of good cheer; Mina was as bright and smiling as ever, and Arthur and Quincey joked with her quite a bit and made her laugh. I drank coffee, like a good Dutchman, and smiled as best I could as I sipped from my cup, watching them. Jonathan clearly was having the most difficulty. From time to time, as he turned to gaze upon his charming wife, his eyes filled with tears; and he would look away swiftly, lest she see his worry and lose heart herself.

In the midst of all, while everyone else was distracted by witty conversation, the doorbell chimed. A moment later, the housekeeper sidled up to me and said softly, "Dr. Van Helsing? There's a lady at the door who wishes to speak with you."

This quiet announcement left me—and John, who sat beside me—stunned. We shared a dark glance. Who else could know that I was here? I fingered the talisman in my pocket as I rose, wondering whether this was some trick of Vlad's. . . . Or had Frau Koehler taken it upon herself to announce Mama's death in person, rather than send a telegram?

I left, and John silently followed; the others were talking away, Mina laughing with false gaiety at something Quincey had said.

By the time I reached the foyer, however, John had moved in front of me, stride-for-stride with the housekeeper, who reassured him: "They're waiting outside, Doctor; I know you've asked me not to let anyone inside the house without your approval. . . ."

She moved off as John cracked open the door a mere finger's breadth. From where I stood, I could not see past him, but his profile was easily visible; the movement of his eyes revealed that there was one person standing upon the porch, and one standing slightly farther back. Apparently, he did not know them, for he demanded sternly, "I'm Dr. Seward. May I help you?"

I heard a voice first, one distantly, oddly familiar— that of a lady, with a vaguely Slavic accent, but excellent command of English:

"I pray you can, Doctor; but first, let me say that it is more of a pleasure than you know for me to see you. I have heard of you from . . . roundabout sources."

John lifted his head in puzzled surprise, and his eyes narrowed in that peculiar way which indicates that he is uncertain about whether to trust what he has seen.

The lady continued, in a voice that now was maddeningly familiar, but somehow changed so that I could not place it. "I wish to speak to Abraham Van Helsing, and as quickly as possible. Tell him I have information which can aid him in his . . . search."

At this, I pushed my way beside John, able to resist no longer. "I am Abraham Van Helsing."

In the doorway stood a woman—not beautiful, but handsome in a severe way, and pale, with strong, sharp chin and nose, and high, sculpted cheeks. Her silver-streaked raven hair was pulled tightly into a thick coil at the base of her neck, without thought for fashion or flattery. Likewise, she was dressed in a plain black gown—against which a thin, tall white dog pressed—and veil, which she had drawn back to speak. Beneath heavy coal-coloured brows, her brown eyes were somber, subdued, and when she saw me, they brightened slightly; but she did not smile.

Some several feet behind her stood a man, also dressed in mourning. My peripheral vision detected his presence, but I could not take my gaze from the woman's face, for I knew her—and yet I did not.

Her aura was not strong, merely adequate; most curiously, while it came close to the indigo shade of the vampire (though not so much black as a deep, deep blue), it was sprinkled with the gold of spiritual advancement. I could think only of a dark blue sky littered with stars.

If John had seen this, he had good reason to be confused.

"Bram," she said kindly, "who was born my nephew, Stefan George Tsepesh. It is I, Zsuzsanna Tsepesh. I have come to ask your forgiveness, and offer my help."

For some seconds I could not speak—could only stare at her with lips parted in amazement. For this lady *was* Zsuzsanna, the destroyer of my little Jan, tormentor of my poor Gerda . . . but Zsuzsanna without any trace of vampiric glamour, Zsuzsanna without any effort to mesmerise. I hesitated on the threshold; her sincerity seemed genuine, but to invite her into the house could mean disaster for all . . . especially if *she* had stolen the manuscript.

"Indeed, you need my forgiveness," I said bitterly. "But I am not sure I can give it. Because of you, my little son is dead, and my wife irretrievably mad." The memory evoked hatred within me, and a desire to be cruel; I lifted the talisman from my pocket and held it at chest level.

Her eyes narrowed with pain, and she stiffened, but made no movement to run away or strike out against me; instead, she held her ground. I knew not what to make of it all, for the more I looked upon her, the more grief and anger overwhelmed me. I wished only to slam the door and forget her face as quickly as I could—and made a move to do just that. But ere I succeeded, the man behind her called out: "Bram! Wait!"

And Arkady mounted the stairs and moved beside her; a single sunlit tear spilled onto her cheek as he put a comforting arm about her shoulder. "My son," he said gently, "with your weapons"—he nodded at the cross in my hand —"you have us both at a considerable disadvantage. I would never endanger you, and I ask you now: Will you hear her out?"

In reply, I glanced pointedly at John. He stared at the two with a profoundly perplexed expression, then back at me, and asked: "He is really your father?"

"He is," I replied, and Arkady smiled at his grandson, saying:

"And you are John. I saw you last night at Carfax; your father pointed you out to me. My name is Arkady; but, please, call me whatever you wish."

The colour drained from John's face, and his expression grew slack; the strangeness of it all, coupled with last night's terrible events, left him utterly dazed. He had come to see the vampire as our deadliest foe—and now we were contemplating welcoming two into the house. But he looked askance again at me—and, seeing affirmation, opened wide the door and said:

"Please. Come in."

•┼• •┼• •┼•

They could not, of course, pass over the threshold until John had removed the crucifix that hung above it. (The dog, perhaps, could have, but stayed close to Zsuzsanna's side and would not leave her.) Once they had passed, he immediately replaced the talisman. This caused them some unease, but they reassured us that what they had to say was important enough to merit temporary discomfort.

I led them into John's office, so that the others would not hear, and bade them all sit. They did, and after a reassuring glance from Arkady, Zsuzsanna said, her voice wavering:

"First and foremost, please know that I honestly regret all the harm I have caused you, your wife, and your first son. Will you forgive me?"

I nodded solemnly, for I was too pained to reply; in fact, merely to indicate assent was a difficult enough act of will, for my feelings were those of hatred and fury. But I swallowed them—a bitter-enough pill—and watched relief spread over her features.

"Thank you," she sighed, then gathered herself. "There are many things I must tell you before you continue in your efforts against Vlad. The first—"

"Excuse me," I interrupted, perhaps a bit too harshly, "but *you* must first answer a question for *me* before you continue. Why this abrupt change of loyalties? When last I saw you, you swore to kill me."

Zsuzsanna laughed—not an altogether happy sound, but one which caused the dog, who lay at her feet, to glance up at his mistress. She leaned forward to stroke his head with distracted affection as she replied:

"It has not been as abrupt as it might appear. Remember, Bram, that I have spent five decades with Vlad and, as time passes, have come more and more to see that he has misled me. He is not the honourable misunderstood hero he initially portrayed himself to be; he is a cold, vile creature, completely incapable of any kind or affectionate impulse. As he was in life, so he is in undeath. And I have grown to hate him"—she lowered her face—"and myself. I was at Carfax, too, last night—where I came upon Kasha." She glanced affectionately at Arkady. "I watched your encounter—how you both mourned Jan, and Gerda, and Mary"—again she bowed her head, and rapidly blinked to stave off tears—"and I knew that *I* had been a source of sorrow to all five of you."

I signalled the dog, which rose and came shyly over, head down, tail tentatively wagging. I stroked its head and ears, and gazed deep into its sensitive dark eyes; it was a common, mortal dog, nothing more—and *that* impressed me more greatly than the speech she had made. Dogs are noble souls and instinctively fear evil and the vampire; yet this one doted on his mistress, and she on him.

"Very well. That shall be sufficient—for the time. Go on." The dog settled comfortably upon my feet, and I was forced to continue stroking it or suffer repeated wet, cold nudges.

Her head lifted, and an impish glint came into her eye as she saw the dog lying upon my feet. "Friend likes you. He loves me dearly, but is always so relieved to find a nice, warm mortal." And then the sprite vanished, and her expression grew somber once again as she said:

"There is another immortal involved here, a woman, Countess Elisabeth of Bathory—who, during her life, brutally tortured more than six hundred fifty young women to death, then bathed in their blood. Have you heard of her?"

"I have."

"She is a vampire—and yet not, for she eschews sharp teeth and prefers to inflict the wounds on her victims with torture devices before drinking and bathing in the blood. She has always been a more powerful magician than Vlad, and more of a scientist; her pact with the Dark Lord is free from the superstitious trappings that mark Vlad's. She can move about during the day or night, sleeps when she pleases in a bed, and does not fear religious symbols—only those powerfully charged as talismans, such as yours." She nodded at my pocket, wherein I had replaced the crucifix; then she drew a deep breath. "I know, because I was her companion for some time. And I can say without reservation that, given a choice between Vlad and Elisabeth, I should fear Elisabeth more."

On instinct, I asked, "Was it Elisabeth who stole the manuscript from Vlad last night?"

"It was," Arkady volunteered, before his sister could reply. "When he was . . . quite distracted. Feeding, and doing the blood ritual with"—his expression grew mildly surprised—"someone *here*, wasn't it, Zsuzsa?"

She nodded, but was too intent on her mission to react. "Elisabeth's abilities are increasing rapidly; soon she will be as strong as Vlad was, as she comes to understand the riddle more and more. We have much to fear if she finds the first key, which will lead to the appearance of the fifth line."

At this John seemed to come out of his daze enough to speak. "She may already have found it."

"No," Zsuzsanna said, leaning towards him—then recoiling a bit, which told me that John had taken my instruction to heart, and still wore Arminius' crucifix on his person. "She has not. I know it."

"How?" My son's expression was that of the sceptical scientist, a trait I had encouraged.

"Jonathan Harker," she replied, and both John and I immediately sat forward. "When he was at Castle Dracula, I bit him. And Elisabeth drank his blood, which put him under her control, as well. One of her tricks is that she can heal wounds, so I left no mark upon him. He is both my agent . . . and hers. This causes some difficulty now, for we can sense each other's thoughts to some extent. As she is the more powerful, I dare only read him briefly, at odd hours. That is one of the things I wanted to warn you of; tell Harker nothing that you do not wish Elisabeth to know!"

She paused, then continued, "I regret it did not occur to me earlier to use Harker until I became suspicious of Elisabeth, and left her; it was then I discovered that"—she lowered her gaze, embarrassed—"that she was kind to me and pretended to love me in order that I might love her; for the terms of her covenant were that she should win a lover, and keep that love constant for six months . . . at which point, her victim would become the property of the Dark Lord. I believe that *I* was the incentive for her coming to Castle Dracula."

An awkward silence fell over us all. John and I both blushed, and lowered our gazes; Arkady again put a protective, reassuring arm around his sister's shoulders.

It was John who spoke up first. He tilted his face, intrigued; I could see that he had begun to trust her (a good sign, for I am coming to think he will soon become more adept at reading persons and auras than I). "Tell me . . . what is Harker doing now?"

The muscles in her face relaxed slightly, and her dark eyes took on a distant look—for an instant, no more. She shifted and said matter-of-factly, "Chewing a sausage, though he is too heartbroken to taste it. What has happened to his wife?" And as the realisation struck home, she lifted a gloved hand to her lips. "Oh! I am so sorry. . . ."

Again, there was a strained lapse in the conversation; this time, Zsuzsanna reinitiated it herself by rising. "That is all I have come to tell you: that, and that we must all try again to find the first key before Elisabeth or Vlad does. We shall give aid and information to you whenever we can."

The rest of us rose, as gentlemen will. "Now *I* must tell you one last thing," I said, quite solemn myself. "For I want no deception, no secrets, between us. I am bound to destroy Vlad . . . and *all* vampires. If you help me, Zsuzsanna, do so with the realisation that, if we succeed, I will not permit you or my father to live."

She reached out to take Arkady's hand, and a look of understanding passed between them. "I know. I'm prepared for that now."

Arkady looked back at us both and said, "We will be at Carfax this morning—if Elisabeth permits."

"As will we," I said. "We go ostensibly to seal off Vlad's boxes; but John and I will be looking for the manuscript and key. The others know nothing of either; we thought it safest, as we suspected Harker was somehow . . . vampirically connected."

Arkady nodded. "Then we will stay out of sight, and not interrupt you except in an emergency."

So the two visitors turned to leave—Zsuzsanna hesitating at first, for I think she wished to embrace me, or to say something more to convince me of her heartfelt regret. I wanted nothing of it, for the deep pain she had inflicted on me and my family could not be erased by a mere confession. Thus I turned away from her, and she sighed reluctantly and began to leave.

But as John put his hand upon the door to open it for her, I called out:

"Why?"

The two men frowned back at me in puzzlement, unsure of both my question's meaning and target; but Zsuzsanna understood.

"Why?" I asked again. "The full truth." She looked over her shoulder at me, and on her lips played a bitter smile.

"Because I grew bored, Abraham. In half a century of undeath, I have achieved the heights of pleasure and the depths of depravity; I have known unlimited wealth, unlimited beauty, unlimited power over men. I collected about me all the exquisite things of the world: jewels, clothing, creatures. But the loveliness I sought could not mask the ugliness of what I had become, nor hide the fact that my existence had become a weary attempt to repeat pleasure after pleasure throughout eternity. Nor could it ever win me a moment's honest affection from another." And here she again took her brother's hand and squeezed it; and he smiled, eyes bright, down at her.

Gazing up at him, she said softly, "Without death or compassion, life has no meaning. And so I have returned to the only one who truly loves me. For his sake, I would sacrifice all. What else was left to me? Should I become like Vlad and Elisabeth—bored predators who have staked their continued immortality on games, with mortal pawns?" She faced me, eyes flashing. "Ask your father, Bram—ask Kasha how Vlad toyed with him, slowly trapping him in a web where he could do naught but be accomplice to the cruelest murders! It was the only way Vlad kept the centuries exciting: every twenty years, another eldest son, another gradual conquest, thrilling only because his undeath depended on it."

Her voice rang with a passion and fire I had seen twenty years ago, in the vampiress—now I know it belonged to the woman herself. "I will not become as he! I will not fear Death so much that I care not what suffering I inflict! I have inflicted enough anyway—and if I can make some small amends, I will."

❖ ❖ ❖

So she and Arkady left to precede us to our destination. John and I returned to the others, and, with Jonathan, Quincey, and Arthur—and several of the consecrated Hosts—went to Carfax. By then, it was half past seven in the morning, and though morning made the old house seem somewhat less gloomy than the night before, it accentuated more than ever the dismal degree of filth. Certainly the chapel seemed less daunting; pale shafts of sunlight streamed through the dust-covered eastern windows, dappling the wall where the cross had once hung.

At once I produced wrench and turnscrew, and, with these in hand, proceeded to unscrew the lid from the first of the heavy boxes. The others assisted me by lifting away the lid, and setting inside a piece of the Host. So we went one by one, treating each box the same—difficult work, and at one point I gave the turnscrew to John and asked him to continue, as my back had grown tired of bending and I wished to stretch it. It was the truth, though in part, I also wanted to surreptitiously wander a bit in search of the first key.

Before starting, however, I wandered over to the wall and stretched a bit in the sunlight—for the day was chill and the old house cold as the tomb it was, so any bit of warmth was welcome. As I stood there, one hand pressed to the filthy wall for balance, a flash of dark, dark blue appeared in front of my eyes; I blinked, and when I looked again, there stood Zsuzsanna.

Invisible and silent, I hoped, for her agitation was exceptional; she was near to wringing her hands as she cried, "See there! The wall! He has taken it!"

She pointed, and I followed the direction with my gaze. To my left, slightly above my head, a shaft of pale daylight painted the wall—at the very centre of the now-departed cross. The dust and spiderwebs there had been brushed away to reveal a hole in the rotting wood, wherein had been placed a small wooden box. The box's lid had been sprung open, so that if one stood perpendicular to the wall, careful examination would show the lid protruding.

I reached up casually and felt its inside with my fingers: emptiness, and polished wood. An effort to pull the box free failed. "And how do you know it was Vlad," I breathed, turning my face to the wall, "and not Elisabeth?"

She glanced at Harker, who, along with Quincey, was lifting the heavy lid of the third box so Arthur could set inside another piece of sacred wafer. "It cannot have been she. I do not know where she is, but she is still frustrated, and now bitterly angry. I think she made this same discovery this morning—which means that Vlad must have found the key sometime last night."

"And read the fifth line?" I asked grimly.

"I don't know. I must hurry—Arkady has gone to try to follow him, and I must join him!"

Before I could say another word, she had vanished; and so I rejoined the men and helped them finish their task.

It was long, hard work, and mid-day had arrived before we were finished. The others seemed cheered by our early success, whilst I struggled to hide my own disappointment; John alone noticed. As we could spare no delay, we proceeded almost immediately to the station and took the train into London.

We located the old mansion at 347 Piccadilly quite easily, though the bustling neighbourhood in which it was located and the bright light of day precluded our breaking house as we had at Carfax. Arthur came up with the excellent notion of pretending to be the owner of the property, and hiring a locksmith to open the front entry. This he did most successfully, feigning such casual ease and confidence as he watched the hired man do his job that a patrolling policeman took no notice of them.

After some wry comments from Quincey as to Lord Godalming's native talent for crime, we entered the house. Making a thorough examination of the property, we found Dracula's effects upon the dining-room table: a bundle of deeds (thank God, only to the four properties) and another ring heavy with keys.

But within the same room were the boxes: not nine, but only eight in number! Nevertheless, with the aid of turnscrew and wrench, we opened each one and sealed it with the Host. Then the tools were turned over to Arthur and Quincey, along with the ring of keys; off they went to Bermondsey and Mile End, whilst Harker, Seward, and I remained at Piccadilly, to lie in wait for the "count," should he come.

Come he did—after a wait of many hours, and just after Quincey and Arthur returned with the report that they had successfully sealed off six boxes at Bermondsey and six at Mile End; but *one* box remained unaccounted for!

It was just after that frustrating revelation that we

heard the key turn in the lock, followed by footsteps—
sounds that put us all on alert, but also filled me with
bittersweet gladness, for they signalled Vlad's return to
limited powers in daylight. He could move only in human
guise now, until the setting of the sun—all the better for
us!

Even so, he proved a fearsome foe, and sprang through
the dining-room door with feline grace and cunning.
Harker wielded his great kukri knife and slashed out, eyes
blazing like those of an avenging angel. Had he been an
inch closer, he would have won the day, for the tip came
perilous close to the vampire's cold heart. As it was, the
huge blade sliced through the breast of his coat, and out
spilled a cascade of gold coins and banknotes.

With speed and skill, the vampire ducked beneath
Jonathan's arm to scoop up what coins and notes he could,
and with them ran off, so swiftly that none could catch
him.

Harker was undone by his failure, for he had sworn to
free his darling from the curse by nightfall; we comforted
him as best we could. But secretly, I felt encouraged by
that afternoon's encounter: Vlad's hair had been streaked
with silver, his face lined with the first traces of age. He is
growing steadily weaker, key or no! And soon we will obtain it from him. . . .

If Elisabeth does not reach him first.

∗⊦∗   ∗⊦∗   ∗⊦∗

4 OCTOBER. In the hour before dawn, John came to
wake me. He and the other men had been taking turns
spending the night outside the Harkers' room—in part to
make Madam Mina feel protected, and in part, I think, to
protect *me* from Jonathan. At any rate, Jonathan had come
rushing out of the room to wake John, as Madam Mina

had asked me to come hypnotise her at once, before the sun rose.

I wasted no time, but pulled on my dressing-robe and followed John. By then, both Arthur and Quincey (who, I suspect, were too restless to sleep) had risen and the whole lot of us made our way to the Harkers' bedchamber.

The gaslight was burning bright, and Madam Mina was sitting upon a love seat in her dressing-gown, her long dark hair falling in waves upon her shoulders. Jonathan sat beside her, holding her hand in both of his with a solicitous air; his demeanour, too, was cheerful and excited, but his eyes were anxious. At the sight of me she smiled, looking more her old self than she had in many a day; but the smile faded almost at once as she said, with an air both businesslike and excited:

"You must hypnotise me at once, Doctor! Don't ask me how, but I *know* that I am privy to information about Vlad which can help us—"

Before she finished speaking, I lifted a hand, and bade her fix her gaze upon it—more for the sake of the others watching than Madam Mina. I moved my hand this way and that, for show, but in the end, it was a mere glance into her eyes that closed them and sent her deep into trance.

"Where are you?" I asked.

A crease appeared in her smooth forehead, and her head moved languidly from side to side as if she were shaking it in refusal. "I don't know. . . . It's dark, very dark, and still as death. . . ."

"What do you hear?"

Here she tilted her head, as though listening. "The lapping of waves . . . footsteps overhead, and men talking. The creaking of a chain, and the tinkling of metal. . . ."

A ship, I realised, and shared a triumphant glance with my three friends. Fear of Elisabeth, perhaps—or even, dare we think, fear of *us* and our determination, now that he was weaker—had driven him from the country!

Inspiration filled me. Leaving Madam Mina entranced, sitting quietly, I turned at once to Jonathan—and, without hesitating, put him at once into a deep trance, then signalled John to step forward and put his hands over his ears, lest Elisabeth should be made privy to any more of the information we were seeking. Quincey and Arthur looked a bit scandalised at first, but relaxed as they realised the necessity for it; in fact, both offered up handkerchiefs to John, which he wadded up and pressed against Harker's ears, to better muffle Mina's murmured replies.

That done, I turned back to my first patient and commanded, "Tell me your thoughts."

"To the first return," she intoned, "and the castle deep within the forest."

Arthur dashed about the room, found a piece of paper, and scribbled it down.

"Where is the key?" I continued.

"The first? Lying cold against my heart. The second, at my home—though where, I cannot say."

She fell silent then, and would say no more; I motioned for Quincey to lift the blind, which revealed the first pinkish light of dawn.

Immediately I turned towards Jonathan; John at once released his hands so that I could ask the entranced man:

"Where are you?"

"I follow."

"Whom do you follow? Van Helsing or Vlad?"

At that, he turned his face stubbornly away, like a spoiled child who refuses his supper; I tried a different approach.

"What do you see? What do you hear?"

A grimace of the most vicious exasperation came over him. With eyelids still lowered, but aflutter, he growled in a low but distinctively feminine voice, "Look here, Van Helsing! You are a stupid bastard, indeed, to tangle with me. I'll see you dead—if not with these hands, then a pair of others!"

At once he leapt up from the chair and ran to the bed. From beneath the mattress, he pulled the fearsome kukri knife and ran towards me with it.

I knew now, without doubt, that Arminius' talisman would keep him at bay—but my confidence in it was not total. While it might hold Harker's person an arm's length from my own, the kukri knife could reach much farther—and it was no respecter of talismans or magical charges. Only the presence of John, Arthur, and Quincey saved me, for they rushed him from the back and sides, and caught the arm hoisting the knife. It took the bone-crushing grip of three strong men upon his wrist before he let go the weapon with a howl; Seward, much accustomed to dealing with violent outbursts, soon had him back in his chair and pinned fast.

Of a sudden, he relaxed completely, sagging. I released him from the trance quickly, then watched as John slowly, carefully, eased his grip.

Jonathan opened his eyes and blinked in confusion for some seconds; then looked over at his hypnotised wife with avid interest and concern, as if nothing out of the ordinary had happened.

I picked up the cue and brought Mina out of her trance, as well; she was bright and cheerful, but completely unaware of what she had said or what else had transpired. So we left the Harkers, and told them both to rest well, and not hurry to breakfast. They both were clearly exhausted, and took our advice gratefully.

⁘ ⁘ ⁘

Whilst the Harkers were sleeping, the rest of us discussed the situation. Dracula was on a sailing ship weighing anchor somewhere in the Port of London—this we all agreed was a logical assumption, given Madam Mina's report. But whither was it bound?

There were hundreds of ships weighing anchor in London on any given day, and at first glance the task seemed hopeless. But Arthur pulled the scrap of paper from his pocket and read it to us:

"To the first return, and the castle deep within the forest."

"The 'castle deep within the forest' sounds like Castle Dracula to me," John said. "After all, didn't Mina say that the second key was at 'home'?"

The other two men nodded agreement, and Quincey said, "It has to be. What else can you make of 'to the first return' except 'return to the first line'? And the first line talks about Transylvania."

So it was agreed: We would try to discover which ships had set sail yesterday for the Black Sea, the most logical route and the way by which the Impaler had first come. Madam Mina's description of the sounds indicated a sailing ship—too small to be listed in the *Times*. Fortunately, Arthur knew that at Lloyd's we would find a listing of *all* ships that had set sail.

We went there at once—without disturbing the Harkers, especially as we wished to avoid any further encounters with Jonathan. There we learned that only one ship had set sail for the Black Sea on 3 October—the *Czarina Catherine*, bound for the port of Varna.

She had sailed from Doolittle's Wharf, our next destination, where we learned from the manager that a tall, very strange pale man had come at five o'clock yesterday afternoon, and insisted that a box be loaded onto the ship.

There can be no doubt: He is headed for home!

❧ 17 ❧

The Diary of
Abraham Van Helsing

15 OCTOBER, NIGHT. Left London the morning of 12 October and arrived via the *Orient Express* in Varna this afternoon, after travelling day and night. Madam Mina continues to give the same report at every sunrise: waves lapping, darkness.

After much debate, we decided to let Jonathan come with us. It would have been cruel not to permit him to come, since we were taking his wife (who has been of great use thus far). We remain ever-vigilant around him, and wear our talismans at all times, as my death would be most convenient for Elisabeth. It would cause Vlad's immediate destruction, and she would have no more worry from us; she could merely meet the ship when it docks, and retrieve the first key from Vlad's pitiful remains.

According to Zsuzsanna, the fact that Elisabeth is nearby awaiting an opportunity to attack, means that she has not seen the fifth line; she needs the first key in order to read it! Apparently, after Vlad discovered the first key and read the fifth line, it disappeared when Elisabeth stole the manuscript. This is good news, for it means she will not rush to Vlad's castle ahead of him (and us). No, she follows *us* (or rather, Harker) because we follow Vlad. But her proximity is not the best news for me; only Arminius' talisman upon my person—even when I bathe—protects me. (Thank God, it is still strong enough to repel her!) Another hopeful piece of news: Zsuzsanna says that when she travelled with Elisabeth to London, she noticed that, despite her abilities to move about freely during the day, she was still limited by the slack of the tide. Knowing this —and knowing that when Vlad was at his most powerful, he, too, was still restricted by flowing water (evidenced by his decision to come to London by boat, and, Zsuzsanna says, the route he chose as bat when she followed him one night to Hillingham)—we can posit that Elisabeth is still so restricted.

I have finally pressed one of Arminius' crucifixes upon Madam Mina; I explained that it was a "specially blessed" piece designed to ward off the vampire, and would protect her more securely than her own little golden cross. She now wears both; I suspect it has had more than a little effect upon her and Jonathan's private life. . . .

As for Zsuzsanna and Arkady, they have secretly accompanied us the entire way, and serve as our "spies." They will be of much use to us if and when we find it necessary to continue on to the castle. However, before we departed for Varna, Zsuzsanna announced that she had broken off all psychical contact with Harker—this so Elisabeth has no means of learning what our little band is up to. With that assurance, we have taken her into our confidence regarding the fifth line, and our plan for dispatching Vlad and obtaining guardianship of the first key.

I still find it difficult to trust her; were it not for Arkady, I do not think I would even deal with her. So she has come to her senses and is filled with regret—am *I* to pity *her*? She has cost me my wife and son. I do my best to be civil to her, for my father's sake. Beyond that, I owe her nothing.

Arthur continues to put his lordly title to good use on our behalf. He has convinced the shipper of Vlad's box that it contains something stolen from His Lordship's friend; we now have surreptitious permission from them to board the ship when it docks and open the chest—at our own risk.

❖ ❖ ❖

29 OCTOBER, NIGHT. After an agony of waiting—day after day of sitting, reading, contemplating, conversing, all of us now obsessed with putting an end to this affair— Arthur received a telegram from Lloyd's yesterday, saying that the *Czarina* had entered Galatz at one o'clock, 28 October.

Galatz—more than one hundred fifty miles to the north! We had languished in Varna thirteen days, waiting restlessly, while the Impaler laughed at us all!

Somehow, Madam Mina's thoughts revealed to Dracula our presence in Varna; now he has cut her off from his own plans. Zsuzsanna advises me that Vlad cannot do so without also losing access to Madam Mina's thoughts as well (just as she, Zsuzsanna, no longer has access to Jonathan Harker's thoughts), and Arkady confirms this. For the time, we are free to use Mina's great intelligence to assist us without revealing to Vlad our strategy.

I write this on the train to Galatz.

❖ ❖ ❖

30 OCTOBER. To-day we set foot upon the *Czarina Catherine* at last. As feared, we had come too late; the box

had already been taken, but we managed to speak with the captain, an amicable and forthcoming Scotsman. The box, he said, had caused such consternation among his Roumanian crew that it would have been thrown overboard were it not for his intervention. He cheerfully produced the receipt, which showed that it had been recovered by an Immanuel Hildesheim, Burgen-strasse 16.

Blessedly, Hildesheim was in his office and, after a bit of *baksheesh,* directed us to a Petrof Skinsky, a businessman involved in shipping from upriver to the port. Hildesheim had turned the box over to Skinsky—who, unfortunately, we could not find at his address. As we were leaving, however, one of his neighbours came running out of a house, crying that Skinsky had been found murdered, with his throat torn out.

When we returned home this evening, discouraged, Madam Mina looked over our notes, and in her logical, precise manner wrote down a series of deductions concerning Vlad's whereabouts. She then read them to us, and I summarise them here:

Since Vlad had chosen Skinsky as agent, it only makes sense that he arranged to have the box shipped upriver, such being Skinsky's primary business.

Now, the Danube meets two rivers leading to Transylvania, the Pruth and the Sereth; of these, only the Sereth flows into the Bistritsa River—which runs near the Borgo Pass!

Here is our plan: Arthur will obtain a steam launch, and he and Jonathan will follow the vampire by boat. (In secrecy, we agreed that Harker would not travel with me, as I would be too imperiled; Lord Godalming is less at risk, and knows to take precautions around him. At any rate, he will also have Arkady's invisible presence to protect him.) Quincey and John will pursue on horseback along the riverbank, in case Vlad makes a sudden decision to come ashore, whilst Madam Mina and I take the train to Veresti, and from there travel by land directly to the castle.

Our hope is that Elisabeth will not follow myself and Mina to the castle (nor Zsuzsanna, who will guide us through the forest, and knows Vlad's lair best of all). As long as Elisabeth does not possess the first key, and thus no knowledge of the fifth line, she will stay close to Vlad, with the intent of destroying him and obtaining the second key.

Once we dispatch the Impaler, however, the question arises: How shall we then destroy *her*, who is so powerful?

Arminius, be not far!

❧ 18 ❧

Dr. Seward's Diary

5 NOVEMBER. Six days riding, in falling snow and bitter cold—and always with a faint sense that behind us, just beyond my peripheral eyesight, follows a great darkness, that darkly glittering indigo that I have come to dread. Quince knows it, too, for late last night when we made camp and were sitting round the fire, he said softly: "Can you feel it, Jack?"

I nodded, and as quietly as I could said, "Elisabeth."

At this he gave silent assent, and we have spoken no more of it. It means the professor's assumption is right; she is not so powerful yet that she can travel upon the river, and board Dracula's boat whenever she lists. I am glad she chose to follow us, and not the professor. That was my greatest concern, that she would pursue and kill him, then board the ship and remove the key from a box filled with Vlad's rotting remains. Perhaps she fears that we would obtain the key before her, and with our talismans keep her at bay forever.

She is wise to do so.

Just after dawn now—a grey sky, lightly falling snow. I woke to Quince's hand upon my shoulder, and the distant sight of the *tsigani*'s big leiter-wagon, flanked by a small army of gypsies, hurrying away from the shore. Quince has the horses ready now: we follow!

+‡+ ‡+ +‡+

The Diary of
Abraham Van Helsing

5 NOVEMBER, MORNING. In Veresti, I procured a carriage and a fine team of horses, and enough provisions to last us a minimum of ten days. With our blankets and fur wraps, Madam Mina and I were quite comfortable, and took turns driving whilst the other slept; I sensed Zsuzsanna following at a respectable distance, lest she frighten the horses. Travelling day and night with a few stops to refresh the animals, we reached the Borgo Pass by dawn, 3 November.

By that time, Madam Mina was becoming more vampiric, sleeping during the day and becoming lively at night, and giving up altogether her little diary.

By yesterday, we had reached the perimeters of Vlad's castle—though we camped a slight distance away. I would not take Madam Mina inside, for the closer she drew to it, the more she fell under its spell; thus, whilst she rested, I inscribed round her a magical circle, and sealed it with the Host. This she could not cross, even when I asked her to do so, so I was satisfied as to her safety therein.

Last night it was that three vampire children—two boys, and a little girl—appeared to us; I remembered Jonathan's diary, and knew they must be the vile progeny of Zsuzsanna and Elisabeth. (No sign of Zsuzsanna at the time; perhaps she became distraught at the sight of them, or perhaps she was, in response to desperate need, out hunting for more sustenance.) Outside the circle, in the fire's orange glow, they took form—beautiful, sweet, alluring, and possessed of a grotesque innocence. Madam Mina and I were safely ensconced within our circle, and there we remained. I could not bear to look at them, thinking of my little Jan; I looked instead at Mina's face, and was deeply relieved to find there horror and disgust.

At dawn to-day, I rose, leaving Madam Mina trapped and protected within the circle, and headed for the castle. (Where Zsuzsanna was, she had not said, though we had agreed that she would serve as scout, to alert us when Dracula and Elisabeth approached. The cold morning air was peculiarly electric; this was the day, I knew. This was the day. . . .)

It was a sad, sad duty that lay before me, in the Impaler's lair; I had been inside this castle two decades earlier—once, in a failed and tragic attempt to rescue my adoptive brother; another time, to murder the foul creature that my poor little Jan had become. Each dark stone, each decay-scented room, was laden with anguished memories.

Even so, I had learned many years before, when Arminius taught me the painful art of vampire-hunting, to harden my heart against emotion and approach the task with the coolest of heads. This I did when I found the lair of the three children—two of them nestled together, sweetly asleep in the same overlarge coffin. No pity did I have; not until I had wielded stake and knife, and saw their immortal, gleaming bodies pass into merely mortal remains. Only then did I weep for them and their mothers and fathers.

And when I had mourned them, and whispered over

their resting-places a prayer for the dead as I placed in each coffin a piece of the Host, I called to mind the fifth line:

To the first return, and the castle deep within the forest.

Here I was, within the castle, but where should I begin to look for the second key? I wandered a time through each room—Vlad's vast throne room, with its Theatre of Death, and the inner keep wherein rested his great, lordly coffin. This I sealed with a portion of the Host. And again I roamed, examining each item in each room, looking for clues, for places where something may have been buried. I spared no one place, not even the dreadful catacombs of earth deep beneath the castle—more horrible to me even than the Theatre of Death, for more had met death down in that evil cellar, and more had suffered there a long imprisonment. And so many hundreds—perhaps thousands—are buried there that I could hear their bones still crying out in agony.

It was late afternoon when I emerged empty-handed and perplexed, and as I headed down the slope towards our little encampment, Zsuzsanna appeared before me, so abruptly that it gave me a start.

Her dark eyes were ablaze, her pale skin aglow—not with any magical glamour, but with pure anticipation.

"They come," she said. "They come, and Elisabeth follows!"

Thoughtlessly, I reached out and grasped her arms—dropping my hands only when she recoiled and winced in pain. "Dracula comes?"

"The *tsigani* bring his box in their great wagon—many of them, surrounding it and bearing arms."

"And of our party?"

"All of them! They follow on horseback . . . and

Elisabeth follows *them*." Just as suddenly, she disappeared.

I ran swiftly down to where Madam Mina stood inside the circle, waving her arms at me with unabashedly joyous excitement. "Doctor!" she cried. "Dr. Van Helsing! We must hurry." And she pointed to the east. "My husband is coming!"

Her words evoked within me similar excitement—and also a certain unease, for she was mentally linked not to Jonathan, but Vlad; to which was she referring? But her joy was so innocent, and her eyes so pure—like those of our Madam Mina of old—that I smiled, and re-collected the pieces of Host from the snow, freeing her.

So we struggled together down the steep slope that faced the east, I carrying furs and rugs and provisions, until the castle stood high above us against the clouded sky. I found a hollow worn within a great rock nestled into the mountainside; this I lined with furs and enclosed within a circle, again sealed with the Host, and settled Madam Mina comfortably inside.

Beneath us wound the roadway leading upward to the castle. From my pocket, I produced a pair of field-glasses; though a hard wind had suddenly picked up, and the light, constant snow began to swirl, I made out the dark figures of the *tsigani* riding alongside the leiter-wagon—at such a furious pace that the wagon swerved dangerously from side to side, coming very close to knocking some of the accompanying horsemen from the roadway.

Suddenly, from the north, I saw two dark figures on horseback rapidly approaching the gypsies . . . and, with a cry of gladness, recognised Quincey Morris' great Stetson —white, but not so white as the swirling snow. "Thank God!" I cried, relieved that they and not Jonathan Harker would be first to approach the wagon, and lowered the field-glasses to pass them to my excited companion. "Madam Mina, look!"

⊷ ⊷ ⊷

Zsuzsanna Tsepesh's Diary

5 NOVEMBER. I left Bram and Mrs. Harker upon the hillside, and swept down to where the fierce *tsigani* rode beside the great wooden chest. I knew I must stop them, and quickly, before Elisabeth arrived, for I could sense her nearing, waiting for the perfect moment to lay claim to the key. Thus I flew down to the roadway, perfectly invisible, and hovered between the two horses pulling the wagon. Gently, I set my palms upon their muzzles.

The effect was immediate: The poor frightened creatures reared at once, causing the wagon to rock crazily to one side and very nearly overturn. The driver swore, and the gypsy army reined in their mounts, who also shied at my unseen presence.

At that same instant came the thunder of approaching hooves, and a calm, steely voice shouting: "Halt!" I smiled, for the voice belonged to Quincey Morris; and he and John Seward came racing up like apocalyptic horsemen bent on godly vengeance. Once they had the key, their talismans would protect them from Elisabeth, and we would all escape and formulate a plan against her; I was overwhelmed with joy, for we were so close, so close to the first victory. . . .

Yet at once those clattering hooves were answered by others, as from the opposite side came Harker and Lord Godalming. Godalming struggled valiantly to overtake his companion; I could see the anguished grimace on His Lordship's face as he flogged his steed to go faster, faster. But Jonathan rode with a deadly fury straight from the maw of Hell, at a speed born of immortal desperation.

"Halt!" cried he, with such fervent passion that even the *tsigani* looked upon him with fear. Now the gypsies were trapped between our men upon the narrow passage; and to translate their intent, Seward, Godalming, and Morris raised their Winchester rifles. (Only I noticed that Godalming's rifle was placed so that, with a very slight movement, he could quickly have Harker within his sights.)

And on the cliff above, Van Helsing stood, pointing his own rifle down at the colourful army below. Even so, the gypsies drew their knives; and their leader pointed up at the reddening sun, which now kissed the tops of the mountains. Again, I stroked the horses' muzzles in order to create a helpful distraction; again, they reared.

But only one of our party took advantage of it. In a wink, Harker let go his rifle so that it hung from its strap, unsheathed his kukri, and, with inhuman daring, slashed through the wall of armed men guarding the wagon. From the opposite side, Morris did the same with his Bowie knife in an effort to reach the chest—but alas! Jonathan reached it first and, with vampiric strength, lifted the box and flung it down to the ground.

He leapt down and began to pry off the lid with his knife; Morris, who had come thus far with only a few shallow wounds upon his arms and face, jumped down as well and attacked the chest's other end with his Bowie. By this time, I saw that Van Helsing's aim had shifted, and Godalming's, too, in case Jonathan were to seize the key.

Soon, the lid of the box was pulled off, and there lay Vlad, helpless and exposed, eyes red with rage and the light of the sinking sun. That rage turned to triumph as the sun slipped down past the horizon. . . .

But his triumph lasted less than a second. Harker's curving knife tore through the Impaler's throat, while at the same instant, Morris' weapon plunged deep into the vampire's heart.

The frightened *tsigani* turned their horses and raced away, abandoning the wagon. I remained and watched with bitter joy as the body dissolved at once into dust: mere dust, lifted by the swirling wind to expose beneath a small golden key.

It lay closest to Morris, who swooped down for it; at once, Harker moved forward and embraced him, as if in celebration. But as he pulled back, I saw the bright flash of the kukri knife—bloodied, as he drew it from Morris' chest.

The wounded man groaned, and fell forward, half into the coffin. Callously, Harker thrust an arm beneath him, groping for the key; fearful of further harming Morris if they fired upon his attacker, the other two men instead dashed up behind the pair. Gentle Seward, whom I had judged incapable of the slightest violence, lifted the butt of his rifle and brought it down with force upon Harker's skull. He then bent down to retrieve the key—but I was faster and, in a swift move, seized the shining object and at once sped towards the castle.

At once the sky deepened—not with night, but a burst of glittering indigo which reflected darkly off the fallen snow. Elisabeth had appeared, I knew, but I dared not look behind me. So long as the others did not yet possess the golden key, she would be too much involved in the search to do them harm.

I hurtled with the key towards the castle, with no plan other than instinct, no desire but to protect the others. In my heart, I knew I had to find the second key, and somehow hide it from Elisabeth . . . but what my heart desired, my brain could find no way to produce.

Even so, I flew up the mountain towards the castle, key gripped tightly in my hand. All had grown silent as the men tended to Quincey; I heard nothing save utter stillness, and one sound that pursued me, echoing off the mountains:

Elisabeth laughing.

Elisabeth laughing. . . .

+I+ +I+ +I+

The Diary of
Abraham Van Helsing

5 NOVEMBER, CONTINUED. In horror, Madam Mina and I watched as Jonathan brutally stabbed Quincey; her horror continued as John came forward and struck her husband a solid blow upon the head with his rifle, but in truth, I felt only relief. As she wept silently into her hands, I gently took the field-glasses from her, and again watched.

Yet my hopeful emotion changed again to fear as John and Arthur searched futilely within the earth-box for the missing key. Had Elisabeth somehow stolen it—or Arkady, or Zsuzsanna? Or had it never been within the box at all?

As Seward and Arthur gave up the search and knelt to attend their mortally wounded friend, the snow about them glittered indigo, with such intensity that I knew it could only herald Elisabeth's arrival.

So it did. She appeared in radiant glory, brighter than the full moon and infinitely more compelling, and with the merest sweep of her hand, John and Arthur fell mute against the snow. The unconscious Harker evoked from her a shrug of disgust, but when she peered into the empty coffin, she bared her teeth in feral anger; and then she gazed up in the direction of the castle and began to laugh.

"Zsuzsanna!" she called, with malicious gaiety. "My foolish love! The mortals can protect themselves from me —for the moment—with their silly charms. But you, my darling, cannot. Certainly the key cannot protect you— you have seen the good it has done Vlad!"

Abruptly, she disappeared, and John and Arthur raised themselves slowly to their knees. I handed Madam Mina, who was still distraught, the field-glasses, and, taking her arms reassuringly, said:

"Dear Madam Mina, do not be sorrowful. You are free from the vampire's taint—and soon your husband shall be too. Remain here in the circle, which shall protect you from all harm, and should Jonathan approach, do not heed him, but stay within!"

And I ran upward towards the castle. What I could accomplish there, I did not know; but Elisabeth knew Zsuzsanna had gone there with the first key, and thus I was bound to follow. Yet the deepest panic I have ever known gripped heart and lungs, so that I struggled to draw in air. I had to find the first key somehow, and prevent Elisabeth from finding the second—but how?

Over the castle above, a great looming shadow gathered—a darkness blacker than the depths of night, a sign of the Dark One's impending arrival. Beneath my coat, my skin prickled; this was the image I had been warned of in my dream, the dream where I had been utterly, irrevocably engulfed, devoured by that darkness.

On the way up the hillside, I prayed fervently with each ragged breath:

"Arminius, help us! Arminius, *help* us. . . ."

⋅✛⋅   ⋅✛⋅   ⋅✛⋅

Zsuzsanna Tsepesh's Diary

5 OCTOBER, CONTINUED. Key in hand, I entered the castle in desperate flight—though where I would find refuge, I knew not. So I raced wildly from place to place, searching; searching, without knowing what it was I sought. To Vlad's throne room first, then to the room Dunya and I had shared, and the chambers I had enjoyed with Elisabeth. . . .

At last I went to the chapel, thinking of Carfax and the "crossroads," perhaps, and that there I might find the second key, and deliver both treasures to Van Helsing's hands. Yet as I wavered there, standing amid broken coffins and ruined earth, my eyes were pained by a dazzling, overwhelming radiance—a brightness that was nonetheless dark.

I recoiled, but too late; Elisabeth stood beside me, more preternaturally beautiful than I had ever seen her—and crueler. Her lips were fixed in a sneer, and her eyes—the coldness, the emptiness, the *hatred* in them, I shall never forget! I felt I looked upon an exquisite jewelled viper, poised to strike.

She gripped my wrist, so hard that the bone snapped at once, and I cried out in pain; at this, her smile widened. "Of the two of us," she said, "I would say time has treated me more kindly; you are looking less than lovely, my dear."

"I have better use for my power," I retorted, then

cried out again as she twisted my hand *completely round,* and pulled back each finger one by one; grinning, she took from me the key.

A sudden brilliance shone from her bosom; she dropped the key within, then pulled forth from the same spot the gleaming white parchment. As she unfurled it, beneath the golden text another line of shining letters appeared:

In the keep amidst the bones lies the woman with the golden heart; the second key.

"The bones!" she demanded, shaking my arm with near-godlike strength. "Where is the keep? Speak, my darling! You know this place better than I!"

I was powerless in her presence, and ashamed of my helplessness; when she sank her dull teeth into my shoulder and tore away fabric and flesh, I could not hold back a shriek. *God,* I prayed silently, *or Dark One, I care not which! Do as you will—inflict on me the worst torment for all eternity, only let me stop her. . . .*

"The keep!" she shouted again, then fell silent; a look of inspiration eased the viciousness of her expression. "Yes—the place with the bones, where you took me to see Arkady . . . Take me there at once!"

"I will lead you," I said, "if you answer but one question for me. Who raised him?"

Her eyes narrowed. "So you have encountered him, I take it. . . . Bah! He was a waste, a total waste of effort. You *lied*—you said he was intent on destroying Vlad. What good has he done me?"

"At the cost of Dunya," I remarked bitterly. "You killed her to raise him. . . ."

She did not deny it, but cuffed me roughly, saying, "Lead! Take me now—and know that you'll pay for this insolence later. For when I become as powerful as the Dark

Lord to-night, I shall treat you to the cage and the Maiden for all eternity! And you, my darling, shall be the first to witness my transformation, and my vengeance; this you have earned by your betrayal."

I knew not what else to do. So I led her back up to the castle's main entryway, for it was only by going up that we could make our way farther down to her destination. And as we passed there, she paused as the great front door flew open, and smiled at the sight of Bram, gasping, wild-eyed, upon the threshold.

"Dr. Van Helsing," she said, with mock sweetness. "How kind of you to visit us. I'm afraid I'm distracted at the moment with one of your relatives; but fear not! I shall return to you—whether you flee by boat or train or carriage, it matters not. I will find you, and see you and yours to a disagreeable end."

And she flicked her hand at him, as a cold lady might motion a servant away; at once he fell back, mute.

Bram, I told him silently, *take the others and flee. You* must *find Arminius. . . .*

I left him there and led her deep into the castle's belly, to the dank cellar dug from earth, now thoroughly laced with the bones of the many who had died here in torment.

"The woman," Elisabeth said, her voice muted with anticipation. "Where would be the woman with the golden heart?"

I honestly knew not. "These are mostly men," I said, gesturing down at the bone-strewn earth, "but a few are women. I cannot imagine where—"

My words were swallowed up by a mighty wind, which lifted up the packed ground and began to rotate it, until the room was filled with stinging, swirling sand. I covered my face until it had settled, then lowered my hands to see that my feet were resting upon an uneven platform of stacked skeletons, all so old that the bones had come apart and lay scattered in disarray. Thousands and thousands of skeletons, so many that I realised they, and not the earth, comprised the castle's foundation.

Only one small spot stood out amidst the ghoulish tangle of yellowed ivory: the corner where Arkady's cata-falque stood, from which Dunya's dust and coffin had now been swept away. The stone catafalque remained, but be-neath it—centuries beneath, surrounded by legs and arms and hands of bone, and fleshless fingers that clawed its polished surface—was a casket of shining steel.

Still clutching my arm, Elisabeth dragged me to it— then slowly released me with a sly smile, for she knew I would not, could not, run from her now. With one hand clutching the manuscript, she used her other to push the solid stone catafalque aside, as easily as a mortal woman might push away a chair.

The stone toppled onto more bones, crushing them as it fell onto its side. We both bent over the coffin to read the etching there, in archaic Roumanian:

ANA, BELOVED CONSORT OF VLAD III

With a hiss of triumph, Elisabeth pulled away the lid and threw it aside; it clanged upon the stone, cracking it.

Within lay a small, fragile skeleton, the jawbone dis-integrated so that the skull had fallen forward onto the neck bones and lay perpendicular to the ribs. Beneath the head was a long strip of black, liquefying hair; beneath the crossed arms was a tattered shred of yellowed silk.

And to the left of her breastbone rested a heart-shaped locket of beaten gold, slightly larger than the real lady's heart could ever have been. In the centre was a small key-hole, and above the keyhole, inscribed in Latin, were the words:

ETERNAL GODHOOD

Elisabeth at once snatched it up; and, with a hand that trembled, withdrew the small golden key from her bosom and slipped it into the lock.

It fit smoothly, with a click. And as she drew it slowly open, she looked up at me with a dark, dark smile.

◆◆◆   ◆◆◆   ◆◆◆

The Diary of Abraham Van Helsing

5 NOVEMBER, CONTINUED. As I staggered gasping into the castle, still overwhelmed by the sense of the Dark One's proximity, I chanced to meet Zsuzsanna—cruelly trapped in the Countess of Bathory's powerful grip. The sight filled me with even greater despair; Elisabeth had in her possession the first key! Yet she had not discovered the second, and solved the mystery, for she appeared no more powerful than she had out in the snow. But how was I to stop her?

Zsuzsanna's expression was calm, fearless; she said not a word as Elisabeth mocked me, threatened me, struck me down as she had the others with the merest gesture. But before the countess dragged her captive away, promising to return to me later, Zsuzsanna caught my gaze.

And her silent words filled my head: *Bram, take the others and flee. Find Arminius. . . .*

She was bound, we both knew, to the most unpleasant of dooms, yet seemed utterly resigned to her fate, as if it were her just due, and showed me naught but concern. And in that instant, I forgave her all.

Arminius! Damned Arminius! Once they had disappeared, I rose to my knees and sobbed, shaking my fist at the empty air, demanding that my protector appear and give us aid.

From somewhere beneath me, in the castle's very bowels, I heard Zsuzsanna's muffled shriek, and rose in anger. I would not sit by. I had seen the direction they had gone, and followed until I found a trapdoor that clearly led below. Yet it was stuck fast; I could not open it, could not enter, could do nothing but moan in helpless frustration. In moments, perhaps sooner, Elisabeth would emerge again, and no talisman in all the world would stop her.

So I sat upon the floor, head in hands, and, agnostic that I am, prayed to God.

And in my head, a voice spoke again—the blessed voice of Arminius.

Abraham, my son. We are close to defeat. Only one thing can stop her: to forge your own pact with the Dark Lord, and purchase our victory.

"No!" I pressed my hands against my skull, to blot the vile words out. "No!"

Again I prayed to God, and again God was silent; but Arminius spoke. *God cannot help you now. Only the Dark Lord can.*

The floor rumbled as with an earthquake, and from beneath came the howl of a mighty storm. I tried to stand, to gain my footing, but lost my balance, and fell to one knee. In my mind's eye, I saw the great looming darkness of my dream, and saw myself devoured by it. . . .

And then, stillness. Stillness so profound that I was filled with a different terror, waiting for the sound of Elisabeth's voice beside me.

"Dark Lord!" I cried out. "Hear me! I, Abraham Van Helsing, will make a pact with you!"

Scarcely were the words uttered before the terrible darkness *did* appear, the great advancing shadow of my dream, and began to swirl: deeper than indigo, deeper than black; deeper than night or death or eternity.

Yet it was an entity, a being. As it approached, I felt its intelligence, and rose upon my two feet to greet it as a man. I mastered my fear; I hid my trembling. And called out sternly: "I will make a pact. My life in exchange for Elisabeth's destruction."

From the centre of the swirling darkness came a small, gentle voice. *The Dark Lord does not exchange life for life. Speak to me of souls. Speak to me of forever.*

"My soul," I cried, "in exchange for Elisabeth's destruction!"

I offer only immortality: the vampire's curse. What shall you offer me in exchange?

"I will not become a vampire! I will not prey on living or dead! Why can you not take me as I am?"

The darkness began to fade, to recede, to withdraw from me; down below, I heard a woman's horrified scream. For a terrible instant, I believed I was too late—that Elisabeth had become the Dark Lord's equal.

"Very well," I whispered bitterly. "I shall be a vampire —but one far stronger than Elisabeth, able to overpower her—in exchange for my soul. In exchange for any suffering in all the world, if you make me able to defeat her."

At once, a sense of infinite calm and acceptance flooded through me, and when the darkness flowed over me like the deepest ocean waters, I felt no fear. As it engulfed me at last, I whispered, "If I am to be yours, show me your face."

Within its centre, a small dot of golden light appeared,

then began to grow—brighter and brighter, wider and wider, until its radiance cast off all darkness. Blinded, I closed my eyes.

And when I opened them again, I saw before me my beloved mentor, Arminius.

"We meet again, Abraham," said he, smiling. "As I told you so long ago: there are many types of vampires . . . and of them, I am chief."

※   ※   ※

Zsuzsanna Tsepesh's Diary

5 NOVEMBER, CONTINUED. I watched Elisabeth's face as she examined the contents of the locket—watched it carefully for the change that would herald my destruction.

Her expression grew intent, then puzzled; then frustrated, as she muttered, "There must be more!" She held it up, and turned it round in her hands to examine it more closely, as if searching for a hidden spring; then once again produced the manuscript and read it carefully, then waited a bit, as if hoping another line would appear.

Finally, with a cry of raw anger, she hurled the locket, with key still attached, down into the piles of bones near my feet. I bent down and struggled to reach for them, but could not; the key had fallen deep into the layer of bones, and the locket lay facedown just beyond my reach, so that I could not even turn it over to see its contents.

Above us, a sudden darkness veiled the vault—a *moving* darkness, like the most furiously roiling thunderstorm. It dropped lower and lower until it stood like a pillar before Elisabeth, coagulating until it was so dense I felt I could touch it as I would a being.

With a snarl, Elisabeth threw herself to the skeletal ground, scrabbling so desperately to reach the fallen items that she ignored the manuscript, which fluttered down beside her.

"You have no right!" she screamed at the darkness. "This moment is *mine*, these trinkets are *mine*, and if you take them from me . . ." She hesitated in her sputtering rage, apparently realising that there was no way whatsoever to threaten this entity. With a fiendish howl, she turned as if to flee.

But she could not. For beside her stood Bram, glowing with an internal light far brighter than hers. She moved to pass him, and discovered herself entrapped between the darkness and his light.

I turned back in amazement towards the pillar—and saw in its stead a radiantly beautiful child. In his dimpled hands were the manuscript and the fallen locket, and he offered them both to me.

I took them both reverently, set down the gleaming parchment, and ran my fingers over the locket's outer message: ETERNAL GODHOOD. Then, like a book, I opened the heart—opened it as I did my own—and on the inner leaves read:

ETERNAL LOVE
ETERNAL SACRIFICE

I began to weep, for I remembered most poignantly the suffering of my ancestors, my mother and father, my dear brothers, my nephew and his little son and wife, and that of all my victims and their families. I wept, and knew most intimately the cost of fear and greed.

"Zsuzsanna," the child asked sweetly. "Do you understand, and accept?"

I nodded, too stricken to speak; and the child held out his hands to me, and helped me rise.

"A kiss, then," said he. "Only a kiss. . . ."

As I stooped to oblige, he sternly shook his head. I felt his hands grow and change within my own, and his stature increase; his golden locks turned white and grew decades in length.

"Arminius," I whispered, to which he replied, smiling: "You shall not bow to me."

And we fell into each other's arms, and embraced.

❧19❧

Dr. Seward's Diary

7 NOVEMBER. Headed for Paris on the train this morning. Art and I talked a good length about Quincey's funeral arrangements, as his body travels with us. It seems there is no family in America, and so Art is determined to have Quince buried on his family estate. There is a very large tree there, with a lovely view, and Art says it will suit Quince just fine.

Mina also was up early, and came into the compartment whilst we were talking. She is the bravest of souls, that lady. I told her outright that Art and I had decided on a story about Quince's death: that one of the gypsies had inflicted the mortal wound. Poor Harker is back to his pleasant self now and overcome with joy to see his wife freed from the vampire's curse. But he has no recollection whatsoever of the events that occurred after we stopped the leiter-wagon.

She agreed at once that this should be the same story told by all, and I assured her I would write the professor and let him know. Very bluntly, she said, even though tears shone in her eyes, "It would break Jonathan's heart to think that he had killed your noble friend, and he would turn himself in to the authorities at once; and that would break *my* heart. I think you do Quincey justice as well, for I know he would insist upon the very same thing."

And she is right. As he was dying, Quince begged us that, if we survived and Harker came through unscathed, we should never bring him to justice—for it was Elisabeth, not Jonathan, who was his murderer. I close my eyes now and can just see him smiling down upon the Harkers, and us all, for keeping our promise.

The professor (I cannot remember to call him "Father," and certainly the word *professor* has for me come to be a term of endearment) has returned to Amsterdam. I would have gone with him had it not been for poor Quince; as it is, I will travel there after this funeral to attend another one very soon.

It is strange to see him so transformed.

⊹⊹⊹   ⊹⊹⊹   ⊹⊹⊹

The Diary of
Abraham Van Helsing

7 NOVEMBER. When I arrived home with my visitors, Frau Koehler hurried down the staircase at the sound of my footfall and at once burst into tears when she saw it was me.

"Thank God! Oh, Doctor, thank God! She is dying . . . it could be any moment now, and for days I have not been able to reach you! I sent telegram after telegram to Purfleet, but always, no reply!"

I put my arm round her and kissed her on the forehead to comfort her, then explained I had brought with me Mary's sister-in-law, Zsuzsanna, and her brother.

"Ah yes," she said, voice trembling. "I met the young lady before."

At this, I shot Zsuzsanna a telling glance, but at the news of Mary's impending death, her eyes showed naught but concern. I whispered into the good Frau's ear my request for some time for us alone with Mama, then motioned for Zsuzsanna and Arkady to join me.

I was used to the sight of the last stages of death, and could face it with composure—but not so with one I so dearly loved, whose former beauty and grace I knew well. Mama lay curled upon the bed like an unborn child, blind, mute, deaf, unaware of our presence. Yet even in her unconsciousness, her face was cruelly twisted with pain.

Arkady at once rushed to her side, knelt upon the floor, and gently lifted her hand to his lips; and there he kept it whilst Zsuzsanna and I wiped away our tears and set to the work at hand. Zsuzsanna moved first, her silent gaze speaking of her need to do so, for it was she who had caused Mary some pain, and she who therefore had the right to remove it.

She bent low, and gently turned Mama's contorted face towards her radiant one; and when she pressed her lips against Mama's chapped, gaping ones, I saw her shudder, then bear up stoically against the agony.

I watched her drink deep and lovingly of pain. And when Mama's brow yielded its last furrow, I drew Zsuzsanna aside, and bent down for my own kiss.

Eternal love; eternal sacrifice. Only through these two could Elisabeth's goal of omnipotent immortality be achieved. The truth cannot be hidden; but fear and hate obscure it. One might say that Arminius was cruel to offer immortality to all who wished it, even the most wicked.

Yet how else could those who most needed it be redeemed, save through centuries of opportunity, of contemplation, of boredom, which can only lead to one inevitable conclusion?

The Dark Lord is also the Lord of Light.

For Vlad, there is no more hope; as to Elisabeth, we have given her the gift of solitude and time. She is trapped forever within the catacombs where she came so close to understanding, with the golden locket and its message that so puzzles her. The entrance to that subterranean tomb we have rendered invisible, so that none can find it.

As I kissed Mama, I shuddered beneath the first round of agony—Zsuzsanna had drawn away all physical pain, and now bore it, and her own grief, in silence. But this was suffering of a different sort I encountered; emotional hurt, perhaps of all anguish, the most difficult to bear.

Still, I bore it, and gladly. "There are many different types of vampires," Arminius had said, and I remembered also what that wise alchemist had told me during my first tutelage: that he was a vampire, of the psychical kind.

It was at first a pleasurable process for me, for I saw the faceted jewel-like intricacies of each shining soul, the incredible infinite wealth of knowledge stored in each memory. But over time, the very beauty of what I stole began to haunt me; and the treasure I accumulated preyed upon my conscience until I could bear the guilt no more.

"And what did you do?" I had asked him.

I repented. I made amends.

Just as Zsuzsanna and I both have; taking on the suffering of others willingly—as our food, our nourishment—instead of their life's blood. We require their pain to survive—but if we wish to end our sacrificial existence, we need merely starve.

I shall live forever, long past the time it takes to redeem the collective suffering of my ancestors.

And when my dying mother's pain had eased, I rose, and smiled tearfully as she opened her pale blue eyes. "Bram," she whispered—and *knew* me, and when Arkady rose beside her in excitement, her eyes widened, with such joy and happiness it broke my heart. She took his cold hand, pressed it to her lips, and sighed, "Am I in Heaven? Or has God heard my prayer?"

I glanced at Zsuzsanna, and she followed me out into the hall, softly closing the door behind her. There we stood until Arkady, tears shining upon his cheeks and falling into the curve of his smiling lips, said:

"It is over. She has died in peace, in my arms."

We found her, too, smiling faintly where she lay, in peaceful, untainted death, and Zsuzsanna and I both laid a final kiss upon her smooth brow.

When we left the room, my father took my hand and said, "I am prepared."

The look of sad and happy acceptance in his eyes wrenched my heart, but this was a pure and blessed grief, with joy amid the pain. We walked arm in arm down to my medical office, which had stood so long unused, and he lay down upon the surgical table and bared his neck to me.

But first, I bent down and pressed my lips to his, and took from him all the accumulated sorrows of his life and undeath, which were many. At the end, he smiled up at me, eyes shining, and I gave him peace.

A blessing upon my family, and yours; may God grant us all such peace. Amen.